WHAT READERS ARE SAYING ABOUT
THE LIES WE TELL

'I was **hooked**. I couldn't put it down – so many twists
keeping me on the edge of my seat'
★★★★★

'This is a **total page-turner!**'
★★★★★

'**LOVE** this book. **Completely brilliant**. Jane Corry,
you have done it again'
★★★★★

'Such a **thought-provoking** book, I can't wait to
read more by Jane!'
★★★★★

'Another **absolute cracker** from Jane Corry!'
★★★★★

'It is a long time since I have given 5 stars to a book . . . but
this pushed all the buttons!'
★★★★★

'**Completely engrossing**'
★★★★★

'I haven't read a book this good in a very long time . . . and no,
I really couldn't put it down!'
★★★★★

'**Wow**, what an **epic** novel about families, lies and
misunderstandings'
★★★★★

'This is Jane Corry at her **twis**
★★★★

D0452524

ABOUT THE AUTHOR

Jane Corry is a former magazine journalist who spent three years working as the writer-in-residence of a high security prison for men. This often hair-raising experience helped inspire her *Sunday Times*-bestselling psychological thrillers, *My Husband's Wife*, *Blood Sisters*, *The Dead Ex*, *I Looked Away* and *I Made A Mistake*, which have been published in more than 35 countries and sold over a million copies. Jane was a tutor in creative writing at Oxford University; an RLF Fellow at Exeter University; and is a regular contributor to the *Daily Telegraph* and *My Weekly* magazine.

The Lies We Tell

JANE CORRY

PENGUIN BOOKS

PENGUIN BOOKS

UK | USA | Canada | Ireland | Australia
India | New Zealand | South Africa

Penguin Books is part of the Penguin Random House group of companies
whose addresses can be found at global.penguinrandomhouse.com.

First published 2021
002

Copyright © Jane Corry, 2021

The moral right of the author has been asserted

Set in 12.5/14.75 pt Garamond MT Std
Typeset by Jouve (UK), Milton Keynes
Printed and bound in Great Britain by Clays Ltd, Elcograf S.p.A.

The authorized representative in the EEA is Penguin Random House Ireland,
Morrison Chambers, 32 Nassau Street, Dublin D02 YH68

A CIP catalogue record for this book is available from the British Library

ISBN: 978-0-241-98900-5

www.greenpenguin.co.uk

MIX
Paper from
responsible sources
FSC
www.fsc.org   FSC® C018179

Penguin Random House is committed to a
sustainable future for our business, our readers
and our planet. This book is made from Forest
Stewardship Council® certified paper.

To my family, in particular my father, Michael Thomas, who encouraged my love of reading and whose motto during my childhood years was 'Just do your best'.

Rain.
The kind that makes your hair stick to your head.
Boredom.
The sort where you want to MAKE something happen.
Other people laughing.
The kind where you want to join in.
To be liked.
Whatever it takes.

Sarah

Freddie should be back by now.

'Midnight and not a second later,' I'd said. Or, rather, pleaded.

That's what we'd agreed after a terse negotiation before our son had stormed out in those deliberately ripped denim jeans, scruffy trainers and a flimsy white T-shirt on which he'd written I HATE THE WORLD in red felt-tip. No jacket, even though it was March.

Why on earth don't teenagers feel the cold?

I'd dozed off earlier, despite intending to stay awake, my ears tuned to the sound of our only child tiptoeing or thudding up the stairs, depending on the state of his almost sixteen-year-old hormones.

But the neon numbers from my alarm clock on the bedside table now tell me it's 2.53 a.m. A sharp stab of fear pierces the pit of my stomach. Where is he? And why hasn't he texted? I send an *Are U OK?* Of course, there's no answer.

Searching for my slippers in the dark, I edge around the packing boxes marked *Main Bedroom* and pad across to the wooden sash window. I'm going to miss this old house, despite everything. Outside, in our quiet north London street, the lampposts are spilling their orange light onto the water-filled potholes that the council has promised to repair 'shortly'. It's been the wettest spring for five years, according to the radio. No one is in sight. Not even a car driving past.

I crawl back under the duvet, wondering what to do. Freddie's never been this late before. I don't want to wake Tom, but suppose something's happened? I lean over my husband. His back is to me and his shoulders are rising and falling in a steady, solid sleep that matches his character to a T. He's wearing pyjamas, of course, as he always has since I've known him. This pair has blue and white stripes. There's a faint whiff of last night's sex from the sheets; the kind of urgent coupling we have once in a blue moon, as if to prove to ourselves that we're still OK together.

We might be if it wasn't for Freddie.

Guiltily, I drive the thought out of my mind. No. I won't wake him. It will only cause another argument. Besides, the removal men will be here in the morning to finish off and take us away. It's our clean start. I don't want to mess things up.

I try to read for a bit with my torch. Ours is the last room in the house that isn't fully packed up. I was at it until late and gave in only out of sheer exhaustion, telling myself I'd get up early to finish it off instead. Besides, it helps to have some normality. I hate that unsettled feeling when a house is not a home because it's half-empty or in transit. I'd had enough of carting my belongings from one place to another in my early years but this time, I tell myself, it will be worth it.

It has to be. If this doesn't work, I don't know what will.

On my bedside table, next to the clock, there's an untidy pile of novels, magazines, art books and a poetry anthology (*Other Men's Flowers*), which usually soothes me. On his side, Tom simply has a book of advanced cryptic crosswords. Inside is an inscription: *To Dad. Happy Christmas. Love Freddie.* I had to forge the handwriting because our son 'couldn't be arsed' to do it. I'd even had to buy the wretched book.

I'm trying not to look at the time because, if I don't, Freddie will just come back and I will have worried for nothing. But I can't help it.

3.07 a.m.

The last two digits make it feel much worse because we're now into the next hour. The print on the page I am trying to read has become blurred by anxiety.

Suddenly I feel cross that my husband is sleeping soundly while I'm the one who's panicking. Then again, hasn't it always been like this? He's the sensible pragmatic half of our marriage. Me? I'm the one whose imagination plays havoc with my mind.

Not surprising, really, given my past.

'Tom,' I say, prodding him. 'Freddie still isn't back.'

He wakes immediately. My husband is the type who will swing his legs over the side the second the alarm shrills for work. He'll be instantly alert, as if someone has flicked an on/off button inside him. I take longer to greet the world in the morning, preferably with my hands cupped around a mug of hot sweet tea. Not sugar. Always honey. During the last few years I've become more careful about what I consume. Maybe it's a sign of middle age.

'What time is it?' he says.

'Gone three o'clock.' My voice comes out in a panicky squeak. 'He promised to be back by midnight.'

'Hah! That boy never keeps his promises.'

'That boy,' I say tightly, moving to the far edge of the bed, 'is our son. He has a name.'

There's a snort in the darkness. Anger, too. 'Well he doesn't reply to it, does he? He doesn't reply to anything. Honestly, Sarah. You let Freddie get away with murder. How's he ever going to learn if you don't set boundaries?'

Me! Why is it always my fault? Besides, Freddie loves me. All teenagers test their parents, don't they? It's part of finding their independence.

I prop up both of my pillows and lean back, all thoughts of sleep over. 'I do. But if we're too strict with him, we could alienate him and then he might end up like . . .'

I pause. A heavy air hangs between us. We both know what the other is thinking.

'If we're too strict with him,' I repeat, 'he might rebel.'

Tom's tone is a mixture of condescension and ridicule. 'Isn't that what he's doing now? You agreed on a curfew. And he's broken his promise. Like he always does.'

'I know. But it's not easy being a teenager. You must remember that.'

'I do, but I didn't act like he does.' *Or like you did.*

My husband doesn't actually say the last sentence. He doesn't have to. The implication is there, loud and clear. 'Well, we're awake now,' he continues. 'I might as well ring him.'

Ring? Freddie gets upset when I do that. 'It's embarrassing if I'm out with friends,' he scolds. 'Just text, Mum.' But I've already done that and he hasn't replied.

I shield my eyes as Tom switches on his bedside light.

I look at my husband as if he is someone I do not know; this tall owlish man with sandy hair and a naturally pale complexion searching for his round-rimmed steel-framed glasses and mobile phone next to the cryptic crossword book. Not for the first time I think how he has aged in the last few years. As it is, our delayed start means that on average we're older than many of the other couples at parents' evenings. Tom especially. Would he have been more understanding of Freddie if he'd been younger?

Tom makes a frustrated sound. 'It's going through to voicemail. Who's he with, anyway?'

I glance at my phone in case Freddie's texted me back in the short interval since I last looked. He hasn't.

'A friend.'

'But who?'

'I don't know,' I admit, twisting my fingers. 'He wouldn't tell me.'

'You should have made him. Or got this friend's number at the very least.'

'He wouldn't give it to me.' My statement comes out almost as a cry. It's true. Freddie tells me very little about his personal life now. He hasn't brought anyone back to the house since the night of the party. It's not like when he was little and I was the centre of his world. He's nearly grown up now. Fifteen and three-quarters. Almost a man. Embarrassing your teenager is one of the worst crimes a mother can commit. I didn't want to push him away.

'But what if you don't come home?' I'd said, remembering the last time when he'd stayed over with one of these so-called 'mates' and hadn't told me. I'd woken in a panic the next morning and was on the point of ringing

999 when he'd turned up on the doorstep. They'd been listening to music and had 'fallen asleep'.

'I *will*,' he'd retorted. 'I've only got one more night left here. You're the ones making me leave. At least let me have some fun for once. Stop worrying.'

But I've got cause to now. Is he with the same unknown 'mate' as before? Or is he lying in a ditch?

'I'm going back to sleep,' says Tom. 'I've got three hours and fifty minutes until I have to get up for work.'

That's right. Even though we're moving house, Tom is going off to work as usual. And then he's out for the count, breathing steadily again. Just like that.

I slump back on my pillows, my eyes half-closed, wondering how long I should give Freddie before calling the police. What would they do if I did? There are probably hundreds of teenagers out there in our leafy part of north London who are late home. Most will get back safely. But what if our boy is one of the unlucky ones? Supposing I wake up to the radio, informing me that yet another teenager has been stabbed to death? There'd been one on the front page of our local paper only last week. He'd had a mournful look about him, as if he knew he was going to die, reminding me of that poem by Yeats about an Irish airman foreseeing his death. The grainy photograph showed strangely thick eyebrows that appeared to be reaching out for the adulthood he was never going to meet.

There's the sound of barking downstairs. Jasper, our chocolate Labrador. I leap out of bed, grab my dressing gown and fly down the stairs. Someone is banging on the door. Is it the police? There's been an accident. Freddie has been run over. He's taken drugs.

I open the door, trembling. It's him! Despite his appearance, my heart soars with relief. Our son is soaking wet. His face is down, the black curls on the left of his head plastered flat from the rain. The other side is shaved short – something he did himself the other week. He's wearing a denim jacket I haven't seen before. 'Sorry,' he says, pushing past. 'I lost my key.'

Again? That's the third time this year. I'll have to tell the new owners, although they'll probably want to get the locks changed anyway. What's Tom going to say? I decide not to tell him yet. The important thing is that our boy is home in one piece.

Relief turns to anger. 'You promised to be back on time –' I begin.

'I said I'm sorry, didn't I?'

'You stink of beer. How much have you had?'

'Not much.'

'Four pints?' I press.

'Please, Mum. Leave it.'

'No spirits?'

'I said leave it, will you?'

Something's wrong. Instead of the usual defiant adolescent scowl, Freddie looks vulnerable. Knocked down. His deep brown eyes, a mirror reflection of mine, are reddened. He's been crying. He hasn't cried for years. Not even after the party.

'What's happened?' I say, but he's already on his way upstairs.

I follow him up, but by now he's in his room, the door fastened from inside with the bolt that he insisted on fitting last year. 'Please let me in, love,' I plead.

'Go away, Mum. I'm fine.'

'Where did the jacket come from?' I ask.

'Someone lent it to me. It's not *nicked*, if that's what you mean.'

There'd been an incident last year when Freddie had returned with a plastic security tag on a pair of jeans, still bearing the price label. He'd argued that the staff must have forgotten to remove it. 'So why didn't it set off the alarm, then?' I'd demanded. This led to a furious argument, during which he accused me of not believing him. I'd marched him back to the shop, where it transpired that he had indeed bought the jeans and that they really had forgotten to remove the tag. Apparently, the alarm system hadn't been working that day.

I wait for a while, begging him to talk to me, but he doesn't make a sound.

In the end I go downstairs to turn off the lights and then slide into bed next to Tom.

'Freddie back?' he murmurs.

'Yes.'

He turns over, away from me. 'That's all right then.'

But it's not. My mother's instinct tells me that something *isn't* right. I just don't know what.

'I'll talk to him in the morning,' adds my husband. Within seconds, he is snoring again.

I wait to make sure he's asleep. Then I get out of bed and tiptoe towards Freddie's bedroom. The door is open. He's not there. My stomach freefalls with panic, but then I see the light coming from the bathroom. He's sitting on the edge of the bath, still wearing the soaking wet jacket. It's hanging open and I can see that his T-shirt is now red instead of white. For a terrible second I think it's blood, but then I realize the red ink of his handwritten I HATE THE WORLD slogan has run from the rain.

Tears are streaming down his face. He is shaking in huge convulsions. Drawing breath noisily with rasping sounds. I've never seen him like this.

'Freddie,' I whisper, moving forward and cradling him in my arms. I wait for him to shake me off but he doesn't. 'What's wrong?'

No answer. He continues to sob. I hold his face between my hands; I want to look into my son's eyes. 'What is wrong?' I repeat.

Again, I expect him to push me away. Tell me with his usual adolescent disdain that it's none of my business. But instead he crumples. 'Mum,' he chokes. 'I've killed someone.'

'You've what?' I whisper, a chill running down me. A young woman's face flashes before me.

No! Help me!

His eyes are scared. Like they were as a child when he first got detention and we had to go into school to sort it out for him. But this is worse. This isn't possible.

'I've killed someone,' he repeats.

No! Emily!

I'm so shocked that I can't speak. My thoughts are scrambling around in a hazy fog.

He can't have. Not my sweet, gentle boy whom I'd tried so hard to conceive. Yes, of course he's going through a difficult stage. Most teenagers do. But not murder. Not the cold wilful snatching of life from another. That's not my Freddie.

Then he looks up. Beyond my shoulder. He's seen something. I turn. It's Tom.

'Killed someone?' repeats my husband. His eyes are glittering with anger. Horror. Disgust. Then he pushes past me and grabs Freddie's wet jacket by the neck, trying to lift him off the ground. 'What the fuck do you mean?'

'Don't hurt him!' I shout.

'Then he'd better bloody tell me what's going on,' says Tom.

'I can't say,' sobs Freddie.

'Yes you can,' roars Tom, pushing Freddie away. My husband has always been the stricter parent but I've never seen him like this before. His fists are raised. His neck strained. Instinctively I move to stand between them.

Freddie's face is creased. With anger or pain? It's hard to know. 'I said I can't say, didn't I?' he yells.

'But you've got to,' I cry. 'This doesn't make sense.'

'That's because he's lying. Don't you see that, Sarah?'

'Are you, Freddie?' I plead. 'Simply tell us the truth. We'll help you through this.'

Freddie throws me a look. His now stony features are wracked with agony. And also hate. 'We?' he repeats. 'I don't think Dad will help me through this.'

Tom's face is like flint. 'I'm not helping anyone who has broken the law.'

'Not even your own son?' asks Freddie.

I look at the two men in my life, glancing from one to the other. None of this feels real. It's as if I am watching a movie.

'Not even my own son,' repeats my husband. 'If you won't tell me exactly what you did, then I'll hand you in.'

Tom moves to the door. 'Where are you going?' I ask, already knowing the answer.

'Where do you think? To ring the police.'

Freddie starts to howl like an animal. Downstairs, Jasper howls too, as if echoing sympathy.

The police? My heart, which has been beating against my ribcage, now gets louder and stronger, as if there's a whole cage of butterflies with iron wings inside, battering to be allowed out.

Help me!

'No,' I shout, grabbing Tom's pyjama sleeve. 'Not yet.'

My husband stares at me. It's as though he too is wondering who I am, just as I'd thought about him earlier.

'Sarah,' he says slowly, addressing me like a child who needs something simple to be explained. 'Don't you see? It's the only thing to do.'

But it isn't.

I won't allow it.

It can't happen all over again.

Not to my boy. My precious only son. I'd do anything to save him. And I mean anything.

Sarah: Truro Crown Court

'All rise,' says the court clerk.

We stand uncertainly. Unsure of what is going to happen. Awed by this massive room with its big-screen monitors on the walls, tiers of wide desks piled with papers, grim-faced men and women in wigs; and the jury, shuffling with a mixture of awkwardness and self-importance. They will be responsible for deciding the future of not just the defendant but everyone else connected with him too.

Like me. A mother. A mother who loves her son. A woman without a husband.

I didn't expect a courtroom to be like this. It's too modern. The ones I've seen on television are old, with wood-panelled walls, a stern-looking male judge and a terrified defendant cowering on an open stand.

But this is more like a smart boardroom. The judge is a woman, middle-aged. She's wearing rose lipstick and a purple robe with a red sash, but this does little to soften the severity of her grey-white wig.

Yet the only figure I'm interested in is the young man with scared eyes, caged behind a glass-fronted screen, staring around him in what appears to be a complete daze.

The maternal side of me is tempted to comfort him. Put my arms around that slightly crumpled suit jacket. Tell him that, of course, I believe him. But there's another part that makes me feel sick with revulsion.

As the prosecution barrister begins to outline the case in his opening speech, my eyes begin to close with the weight of it all. My mind drifts back.

Not to that night when Freddie came home so late in the rain, wearing someone else's jacket. Beyond that. To the day I met his father. When it all began.

At least, that's the way I see it. Tom might view it differently. And so might you.

PART ONE
Tom and Sarah

I

Tom

Vegetarian risotto. That was the first meal Sarah cooked for me. I hate rice, because they virtually force-fed us with it at school. This was particularly the case during the holidays, when I would continue to board because my father worked away. At the time, I'd accepted this without question. The working abroad bit, that is. Not the rest of it.

'Did you know that rice is the staple food of more than half of the world's population?' I'd asked Sarah on that first evening. I was aware as I spoke that I was taking off my glasses and wiping them carefully before I replaced them. I did this when I felt nervous.

Sarah looked down at the plate on her lap as if I'd just criticized her cooking. Then she looked up at me again, with an almost childish expression that made me wonder how old she was. I'd learned, through past experience, that it was difficult to guess a woman's age and that the wrong digit could cause great offence. One had to exercise extreme caution.

'Really? I hope you like it,' she said, with those extraordinarily thick pink-and-blue plaits swinging at the side of her face, and her wide blue-and-white spotted skirt. A curious combination with her heavy-looking brown laced up Doc Martens, as I believe they were called – though that was the fashion in the nineties. The latter were lying on the floor next to her after she'd casually kicked them off.

It was all I could do not to position them neatly.

Instead, I forced myself to swallow the congealed lumps of rice. 'Delicious,' I replied, though I hate lying. If you were caught out at school telling a fib, you got thrashed on the platform at assembly by the headmaster. '*Wilkins! Up here. Now.*' It was a Catholic school, after all – lies meant you went to hell.

Or maybe my aversion to lies came from my father's clumsy half-truths about how long he'd been seeing my future stepmother after – or before – my mother's death when I was eight.

We were sitting cross-legged opposite each other on beanbags close to the two-bar electric fire in Sarah's bed-sit. I'd never experienced a beanbag before in my life and was, to be honest, finding it hard to keep my balance.

Coordination had never been my speciality. Nor sport, as my short-tempered games master had made clear. My amblyopic left eye – most people called it a 'lazy eye' – made it hard to see the ball clearly. I hated every second of PE. In fact, the only decent thing that had come out of that school was my friend Hugo. The one person who understood.

'Where are you from?' I asked after forcing down another mouthful of risotto.

Sarah gave me another of her lovely smiles. It lit up her face and, for some reason, made it impossible for me to look away. I was not usually given to such thoughts, but there was no other way of putting it. Her eyebrows, I noticed, were quite thick and might, on another woman, have seemed obtrusive. But hers framed those beautiful brown eyes in such a way that the two appeared to combine as neatly as any mathematical equation.

'I come from a pretty ordinary background, to be honest,' she said, putting her head on one side as she spoke. Her neck, I observed, was very long and thin.

'Five of us, there were,' she continued. 'Two sisters and two brothers, although we're scattered all over the place now. We grew up on a council estate in Kent and went to the local comprehensive. But we were happy and loved then. It's all you need in life, really.'

Despite the council estate and comprehensive school, neither of which I had ever experienced, I couldn't help envying her. But I also observed her use of the conditional 'then' after 'we were happy and loved'.

Later, when I finally told her about what happened at school, she was shocked. 'When I have children,' she said, those big eyebrows knitting together, 'I'd never dream of sending them away. And I'd kill anyone who laid a hand on them.'

To look at her slender figure, you wouldn't think Sarah was capable of harming a fly. But by then I was already beginning to suspect that there was a certain steeliness on the inside. She was different from any other woman I'd come across.

For a start, she had a small silver stud in her right nostril. She also held her cutlery between her thumb and forefinger instead of having the latter on top of the knife and fork as I had been taught. But I was mesmerized by this woman. She saw the world in an entirely different way from anyone else I knew. She noticed things such as a blackbird singing or the colour of a sky that looked grey to me but was, as she explained, a mixture of green and mauve and pink. Then there was the physical side. (I feel almost embarrassed to say this.) In my view, sex was, rather like money, something that wasn't discussed in polite company. But I couldn't stop staring at that smooth, flawless skin and those amazing cheekbones that were so reminiscent of my mother's bone structure. 'Your skin looks like velvet,' I still remember telling her. Part of me – a side I didn't know I even had – wanted to run my finger over Sarah's face to see if it felt the same.

My father had died the month before I met Sarah. But I knew what he'd say if he'd had a chance to meet her: 'Not exactly one of us, is she?'

At the time, it was partly *because* Sarah came from a different background that I'd fallen for her. What had my traditional upbringing given me? Nothing but pain.

All I'd wanted was to be loved and to have a proper family. A wife and children. I'd tried the traditional route with Arabella. That hadn't worked. So maybe this was my chance to be with someone who was unlike anyone I'd met before.

Sarah and I met one cool spring evening at a drawing class 'for beginners and improvers'. I was in the first category. Hugo thought this was a huge joke when I signed up for it.

'Drawing? *You?*' he guffawed. 'You haven't got an artistic bone in your body, Wilkins.'

Every now and then he called me by my surname, as we had at school. I chose not to do the same to him. It was not a time I wanted to recall.

'You'd be better off sticking to figures, if you ask me,' he added.

He had a point. Numbers weren't just safe, they were also lucrative in my profession. But they hadn't got me a wife. I was thirty-five. Hugo, a banker, and his wife Olivia had two children to whom I was godfather. Although I wasn't particularly paternal I was beginning to feel fed up with comments like 'Still not settled down yet?' or 'If you're not careful, you'll end up a confirmed bachelor with a penchant for checking sell-by dates.' If I'd been a young man nowadays, I wouldn't have worried so much about my bachelor status. But back in the nineties, it was more common to marry young.

As I said, I'd thought Arabella might be the one. Arabella, who worked at a prestigious auction house as a personal assistant and trailed around after me in a waft of Chanel and pearls, suggesting that she'd say 'yes' at the drop of the hat that her mother, on more than one occasion, made it very clear that she'd like to buy.

Of course, I was flattered. No one else had ever been remotely interested in me. I could still hear the taunts at school: '*Can't you see straight, Wilkins?*' Later, when we'd had sixth-form dances, I was turned down by every girl I'd summoned up the courage to approach.

So when I met Arabella – through her brother, who had been at university with me – and she agreed to go out, I couldn't believe my luck. We dated for nearly four years.

Yet, I still had my doubts. How did you know if someone was the right person to marry, especially if, like me, you weren't very familiar with the 'fairer sex'? But when I'd decided that I might as well propose, she dropped me. On my phone's answering machine.

'*I'm sorry, Tom. I don't think we're suited.*'

Fired by what I thought was passion, I immediately marched around to her Pimlico flat in high dudgeon. 'What do you mean, not suited?' I said.

She'd had the decency to look embarrassed. 'Don't take this the wrong way, Tom, but you're too predictable. You have this routine, which no one is allowed to alter. It's like you are still at school. You're too staid to take a chance on life. I want *more* than that.'

It turned out that Arabella had met a surfer during a girls' holiday in Cornwall. A rich surfer, of course, who also owned his own beachside hotel. And off she went. The marriage announcement appeared in *The Times* a few months later.

Suddenly Arabella seemed to be the perfect woman whom I'd stupidly allowed to get away. My previous 'take it or leave it' attitude to marriage now felt short-sighted. I'd never had a proper family to speak of. Supposing I carried on through life that way? What if I ended up on my own – a crusty single chap who was only interested in figures and routine? The sort who had an obituary in the *Daily Telegraph* that ended 'He died unmarried', leaving readers to draw their own conclusions.

Arabella's rejection was still stinging when I went for a walk after finishing work early for a change and saw a poster advertising a drawing class at my local arts centre in Hackney, where I'd cannily bought a three-bedroom terraced house before the area became gentrified. The class was that night. It was about to start. It was completely unlike anything I'd ever done. *Too staid to take a chance on life.*

I would prove Arabella wrong. And Hugo.

'Third room on the left,' said the girl at the desk. 'You haven't much time so pay when you leave.'

I took my place at a table lined with newspapers. I noticed Sarah immediately. It was hard not to. Not only because she was the tutor but because her bright red lipstick, wide swirly spotted skirt and those pink-and-blue streaks in her dark plaited hair made her look as though she was on her way to a fancy-dress party. But what made her really stand out was that smile. It was one of those broad sunny beams that might have made anyone else look like a clown. But on her, it was amazing.

Maybe it's because I don't know that many smiley people. The nearest that my colleagues get to it at work is if a satisfied smirk creeps across their faces when they are pleased with their figures. Perhaps I'm the same. But Sarah's smile lit me up inside. It made me feel warm and comfortable and happy and hopeful all at the same time. I couldn't remember feeling like that since my mother had been alive. She'd had a smile just like that.

Then my attention was drawn to an old woman who came out from behind a screen with a sheet around her. Was this some sort of Roman theme? To my astonishment and horror, she let it drop to the ground, revealing rolls of flab and drooping breasts with awful wrinkles. I had to look away.

Everyone else immediately got stuck in with the charcoal stick we'd been given next to our sheet of A4, but I didn't know where to start! The left nipple? The leg? I was totally out of my depth. So I helped myself to a ruler from the 'art box' which was being passed around and started to measure.

Wasn't the poor woman cold? And what if she was hungry or needed to go to the lavatory? What on earth was she thinking of as she kept that pose, sitting on a chair and staring out into space?

'I couldn't help noticing you seemed a bit surprised by our subject matter,' Sarah said over my shoulder some twenty minutes later when she finally got round to me.

I tried to sound casual. 'Actually, I thought this was a still-life class. You know. Flowers and fruit. That sort of thing.'

She laughed but it wasn't an unkind, scornful sound. More like a merry tinkle. 'You'd be surprised how many others make the same mistake.' That made me feel a bit better. Then her voice grew more serious. 'The human body is a work of art, though, isn't it?'

'It's also a numerical puzzle,' I retorted. We both looked down at the angular shapes on my paper that I'd carefully drawn to represent the different areas of the old woman's body.

'Leonardo da Vinci and Picasso thought so,' she said, as if I was one of the trainees at work who had made a small mistake and needed to be encouraged. 'But in my mind, the beauty of a nude is that it appears the model has nothing to hide. He or she is stripped bare. At least on the outside. This forces the artist to look under the skin to find the soul. That's what makes a portrait really work.'

I'd never thought of it that way. 'But how do I do that?' I asked.

'Allow your instinct to take over.'

Instinct?

'I don't know how,' I mumbled. It was a mistake coming here. I could see that now.

'Mind if I help a bit?'

Her hand closed over mine, guiding the charcoal stick. At precisely the same second, a flash of lightning went through me. It was as if she had actually given me an electric shock. I couldn't understand it. This woman simply wasn't my type. And yet . . .

'See?' she said. 'All you needed was to make a slight curve here and then do this . . .'

'You make it sound so easy,' I said, trying not to look at that beautiful swan-like neck, even though it was rather spoiled by a cheap-looking pendant that she kept touching as she talked.

My teacher stood back as if appraising me. I felt slightly uncomfortable. 'Everyone's got their own strengths. What do you do?'

'I'm an actuary.'

Sarah put her head to one side, questioningly. She had, I noticed, one of those smooth high foreheads that made her look quite regal. 'What's that?'

I'd been asked this so many times by people outside the field that I had my answer off pat. 'Basically, I'm a mathematician who measures the probability and risk of future events in order to predict their financial impact on a business and their clients.'

She burst out laughing. 'Come again?'

I felt rather offended by the mirth. 'It's actually very useful. For instance, I can help clients work out how long they have to live so they can get the right life insurance.'

'I've never met anyone who did that before. So how long have *you* got left to live, then?'

No one had ever asked me that question. 'I don't know.'

'If it was me, I wouldn't *want* to know,' she said lightly. 'I believe in living life for the moment. That's far more important than money.'

Then she suddenly seemed to realize that her hand was still on mine and took it away. I felt cold. Empty. I couldn't even reply by pointing out that insurance was one of those essentials in life that people ignored to their cost. By then, Sarah had already moved on to the next student, bending over him and making suggestions in a positive manner. I felt a ridiculous flash of jealousy.

'Time for a break now,' she called out sometime later. 'Maude, do help yourself to tea, won't you? Are you all right to start again in about ten minutes?'

I was struck by Sarah's concern. The old woman stood up and covered herself in the wrap next to her chair before waddling off to the kettle. It was impossible not to look with a sort of horrified fascination. How much did she get paid? Surely there must be easier ways of making money.

For the next hour I kept glancing across at Sarah, absorbing her. Watching her helping the others. Observing her kindness. Encouraging everyone with a positive phrase – 'I like the way you've got that shadow'. A touch of advice – 'If I were you, I'd add a little mauve shading here'. There was softness there, yet also resilience. Something that said 'I can stand up for myself'.

But most of all, it was her physical presence: those childish plaits, the slim bare arms, the beautiful brown eyes. It might sound like a cliché, but Sarah felt like a drug (not that I've ever taken any), making me more addicted the longer the hands on the wall clock continued to turn.

At the end of the class, by which time I'd made a total hash of my sketch, I went up to her. 'I'm sorry,' I said. 'I don't think life drawing is for me.'

She gave me the sweetest understanding look that, once more, reminded me of my mother. 'You don't want to give it another go?'

'Not really.'

I could hardly add that I was revolted by the model's saggy breasts and that I did not like the mess the charcoal had left on my hands.

'We'll be sad to lose you.'

Then I heard the words coming out of my mouth before I could take them back. 'Actually,' I said. 'Would you have dinner with me?'

I waited for her to tell me to get lost. No girl would go out with a man she'd only just met and had merely exchanged a few words with, would she? Not a nice girl, anyway.

Or was that the point? Maybe I'd asked Sarah out because we were poles apart. To prove that I wasn't the boring fuddy-duddy that Arabella had scorned.

'All right,' she said casually.

Had I heard her correctly?

'But I'd rather you came back to my place than go out,' she continued. 'I've got some spare food and it seems a waste not to have it. I hate waste, don't you? Especially when so many people in the world are starving.'

I didn't mean tonight, I almost said. I meant sometime. Next week perhaps. This week at a push. Or maybe never, to be honest, because I was banking on her turning me down. But this unusual girl had said yes. And what's more, she meant now.

'Your place?' I said, trying to sound confident. 'Sure.'

'Great!' said Sarah. There was that sunny smile again that made me feel oddly light inside. 'I don't live far. It's only a forty-minute walk. By the way, you do like vegetarian risotto, don't you?'

I swallowed hard. How could I possibly tell her that the very thought of rice made me feel physically sick? Not 'simply' because of the taste from my schooldays but also because of what had come after.

2

Sarah

Tom really wasn't my type. If it hadn't been the anniversary, I wouldn't even have said yes to a date. But I couldn't – wouldn't – allow myself to be on my own that night. The pain was still there every minute of every day. Anniversaries shouldn't make a difference. Yet they do, don't you think? So I was grateful – no, desperate – for company. In fact, I still remember the evening as clearly as if it's playing out in front of me on the cinema screen right now.

'What's that smell?' Tom said after I found myself suggesting he came back to my place instead of some fancy restaurant. I knew it would be fancy because this guy was clearly posh, with that accent of his and those stiff smart clothes. But the thought of people around us, all jabbering away about trivial stuff, freaked me out. Especially today of all days.

Also, I genuinely *was* worried about wasting the risotto. I couldn't bear throwing away food. Still can't. I've been hungry too many times.

'The smell?' I said, repeating Tom's question. 'It's incense.'

I watched him taking in the mess. If I'd known I was bringing someone home, I'd have tidied up a bit first. There were clothes drying on the backs of chairs and sketches everywhere, as well as dirty plates still in the sink. I should also have opened the windows before going out to get rid of the weed smell.

Now we were alone, away from the class, I had a chance to observe my guest in more detail. I took in his rangy height and bone structure in the way that I might if I was drawing him naked. You might not be aware of this but most artists do the same when meeting someone for the first time.

Tom Wilkins wasn't my usual type. He had short fair hair, for a start, with skin that looked baby smooth and very clean. I suspected he was clean in the other sense too, although you couldn't always tell. He had a habit of twisting his hands nervously. I found that rather sweet. He'd already told me on the walk back that he didn't drink alcohol and that he was 'keen on' Mozart. I knew the name, of course, but I'd never listened to the guy's music.

'I like Pearl Jam,' I told him.

'Are we talking food now?'

'Very funny.'

He frowned. 'Why?'

Then I realized he was serious. 'Pearl Jam is the name of a band.' I burst out laughing. 'Where have you been?'

'Let's see,' he said, counting on his fingers, 'I grew up in London. Then boarding school in Somerset. University at Reading and now back in London again.'

'I wasn't asking for your life story. I was making a joke about you not knowing Pearl Jam.'

'Really?' he asked, frowning.

Was this guy for real? Yet my instinct told me that the tall, gawky-looking man with a very slow, deliberate way of speaking, meant every word. This Tom was a straight talker. He took everything I said at face value. It was surprisingly refreshing.

He was also funny, like he didn't mind taking the mickey out of himself. 'See this,' he said, pointing to his left eye, which had a slight droop. We were sitting opposite each other on beanbags to eat the risotto, which I'd already warmed through twice this week. He seemed appreciative, though, wolfing it down so fast that each forkful could hardly have been in his mouth for a second. I felt rather embarrassed that I couldn't offer him more.

'They called it a lazy eye when I was a child,' he continued with a slightly bashful look. 'But I've never been lazy. Instead I was academically conscientious to a fault. Always have been.'

I wasn't that bothered by his eye, although it was clear that he wanted to bring it out into the open. I admired that.

'The medical name is amblyopia,' he added, 'and it affects two to three per cent of children. It can be treated if it's caught early enough. But Matron dismissed it.'

'Matron? Were you in hospital?'

'No. She was in charge of what we called pastoral care at school.'

Then he made a 'huh' sound as if there wasn't much care at all.

My mother had cared for me. 'Smile, Sarah,' she was always saying when she took photographs. 'Show me your beautiful smile.' Back then, our lives had seemed idyllic. But I'd known nothing better. At least Tom didn't ask me too much about my past. Instead he'd accepted all that stuff about growing up in a big happy family. If he'd known the truth, there would never have been a second date.

'What made you specialize in life drawing?' he asked.

I shrugged. 'Someone asked me to pose when I was at art school and I got interested.'

'Weren't you embarrassed, taking off your . . .' he said. Then he stopped as if too ashamed to finish the sentence.

'My clothes? No. Why should I be? The body is a beautiful design. It's made to be shown off.'

'But why do people model?' He frowned as if he was a small child who needed something explaining. 'I mean, it can't pay very much.'

'You might not think so, but Maude says that every little helps. She also likes the company.'

He was silent for a bit after that, as if chewing this over.

'I was wondering if I could . . .' he started to say when we'd finished eating. Then he stopped.

'Yes?' I asked, leaning forward in encouragement. Wasn't that why I had brought him back here? I needed someone or something to block out the memories in my head. Sleeping tablets didn't work. Drink made me morose. Instead, I tried to hide all the turmoil inside by smiling a lot. It helped me kid myself that everything was great. That I was one of those happy-go-lucky people who sailed through life without any hitches.

'I was wondering if I could wash up for you.'

Was that really what he'd meant to say? Or had he been about to suggest sex and lost his bottle halfway through the sentence? 'Oh! No, don't worry.' I shrugged. 'I'll do it later.'

He frowned. 'Did you know that bacteria can double in number in twenty minutes if food is left on plates?'

'Are you kidding?'

'No. It's true.'

This man was like some walking fussy encyclopaedia. He was beginning to do my head in. But I couldn't be alone that night. I couldn't. So I waved towards the sink that was already full of cereal bowls and grimy mugs that doubled up as paint pots. 'Be my guest.'

'I already am your guest,' he said seriously. 'Tell me where you keep the washing-up liquid.'

'Actually, I've run out.'

I didn't add that I usually simply slosh plates and mugs under the tap even if the water is cold because I didn't have any money for the meter.

'Then I'll go and buy some. Where's the nearest shop?'

That was it. I couldn't bear much more. All I wanted was sex.

I went up to him, stood on my tiptoes to cradle my arms around his neck and pulled his face down gently towards me. 'Kiss me,' I pleaded. 'Please.'

He looked as though I'd suggested marriage. 'Are you sure? We don't really know each other.'

That's exactly the point, I wanted to scream. It was distraction I needed, not commitment.

'I've never met anyone like you, Tom,' I said. This was true enough.

'That's because –'

I silenced whatever was coming next by taking the initiative myself. His lips were warm. I half-expected him to push me away but he didn't. Instead, his tongue was more experienced than I'd anticipated. Only one person had ever kissed me like this before. Long, deep kisses that penetrated right inside me and went on for ever. He cupped my head between his hands. It made me feel wanted. Special.

Tom Wilkins was not my sort! No way. But something in his kiss changed all that. My body was on fire. And so was my head.

He bent down for more. It was as if our lips were magnetically joined.

'I'm going to leave now,' he said eventually. The panic swept back in.

'You don't want to stay over?'

'Yes, Sarah. Of course I do. But not until we know each other better.'

'Please stay.' I couldn't keep the sob of hysteria out of my voice. 'I don't want to be alone.'

He hesitated. I sensed I'd struck a nerve.

'Only if I sleep on the floor,' he said slowly.

'Don't be daft. We're grown adults.'

'Exactly. Sex isn't a piece of confectionery you can just sample for free. It's something that needs to be earned with love.'

I felt patronized. 'Go,' I almost said. Then he cupped my face with his hands again. 'I'll stay. But there's something we need to get straight. The so-called incense. I'm not that stupid, Sarah. If we want to see each other again, you've got to stop smoking marijuana.'

I could have told him that it wasn't me. That a neighbour had come in earlier to warn me about another break-in and had lit up a spliff while he was here. But I had a feeling that Tom wouldn't believe me. The irony is that it would have been one of the few truths I'd told him that night.

Anyway, I argued to myself, there was a certain balance about 'confessing' to something I didn't do and keeping quiet about the terrible thing I *did* do. Exactly ten years ago to this day.

'OK,' I heard myself say.

'Do you do anything stronger?' he asked.

'Of course not.'

He seemed to believe me.

'What's your lucky number?' I asked him suddenly.

'Lucky number?' He looked puzzled. 'How can a number be lucky?'

'But everyone has one! Mine's two.'

I didn't add that this was because it had been Mum's lucky number. She used to say it was because there were only the two of us. Her and me.

'Please. Pick one,' I urged.

He shook his head but he was laughing. 'All right. Two.'

'That's the right answer!' I said. My heart was singing. It was a sign. It had to be.

That night I had the usual nightmares. Doors slamming. People shouting. Unable to breathe . . .

But instead of waking up in a cold sweat, I was vaguely aware of someone telling me that it was 'all right'.

In the morning, when I woke, Tom had gone.

In his place, was a bottle of green washing-up liquid with a note. His writing was a series of very clear capital letters, each one the same size.

I DIDN'T WANT TO WAKE YOU TO GET YOUR
MOBILE NUMBER, BUT I'LL SEE YOU AT CLASS
NEXT WEEK. THANKS FOR DINNER. I HOPE YOU
WILL ALLOW ME TO TREAT YOU NEXT TIME.

And even though Tom Wilkins was the complete
opposite to me, in more ways than he could ever know, I
just couldn't wait.

The rain has stopped now.
  It's a black night.
  No stars.
  That's good.
  Makes it less easy to be spotted.
  Keep your head down, I tell myself.
  Walk quickly.
  Don't be late.

3

Tom

Figures – which had always been the only constant in my life became my torment in the week after that vegetarian risotto. They counted themselves down in my head.

Six days and twelve hours until I see Sarah-with-the-sunny-smile again.

Six days and five hours.

Facts – which had always been my friend – made my head spin.

She's not your type.

You have nothing in common.

I want to sleep with her.

Her smile lights me up inside.

She smokes marijuana.

I'd been anti-drugs since school. Ever since then, I'd vowed to do the right thing. This self-imposed rule applied not merely to taking substances but to life generally. I had to be in control of myself. Otherwise I might make another terrible mistake.

So what was I doing with a woman like Sarah Vincent?

'You've got it bad, Wilkins,' said Hugo when I told him. He was my best friend. Or to put it more accurately, my only friend. Our friendship had started at the age of eight when he'd been the sole pupil at school not to tease me about my eye. And then, of course, there was the other thing. The thing we never talked about.

Hugo and Olivia had asked me round for supper but my youngest godchild was still awake and the meal wasn't ready. This was irritating, as I was hungry. I'd been brought up to believe that punctuality was synonymous with courtesy.

'Why wait?' he continued. 'You know where she lives. Just surprise her with a bunch of flowers.'

'I told you,' I pointed out. 'My note said I'd see her at the next class.'

'You can change your mind,' said Olivia, coming downstairs with the baby in her arms. I couldn't help thinking that it should have been asleep by now.

'No I can't,' I said, embarrassed that she'd overheard our conversation. 'It's in my diary.'

'Diaries can be altered, Tom,' they both said. I'd noticed this about married couples. From the minute they get those rings on their fingers, they start to talk as if they are one person.

Three days and two hours.

One day and seven hours.

Eight hours.

One hour.

I'd taken the precaution of bringing a freshly ironed pair of jeans and a new turtle-neck brown jumper so I could change in the office before the art class. Last time, I'd been the only person there in a suit. The other students had been in sloppy denim boiler outfits that looked as though they hadn't been washed for some time. The 'grunge look', I believe it was called.

'You look nice,' said one of the trainees as she stepped into the lift on my way out of the office.

Nice? I'd never cared for that adjective. It could mean exactly the opposite of what it was meant to.

Words like that could be misleading. It was something we'd talked about at the meeting last week. The one I went to every Wednesday evening without fail.

I counted my steps as I walked to the arts centre. *Eleven, twelve, thirteen*. It was a trick I'd learned at school when waiting for something I either wanted very much or was scared of.

LIFE DRAWING CLASS CANCELLED DUE TO ILLNESS

I stared at the notice on the door. I had arranged to see Sarah here. But now it appeared I couldn't. The thought of not seeing her was like a punch in my stomach.

Then I reread the notice. The phrase was decidedly unclear. Did it mean that other students had fallen ill, thereby precipitating a low attendance rate? Or was Sarah herself unwell?

I spoke to the girl at the desk.

'There's a nasty flu virus doing the rounds,' she informed me. 'Sarah came in earlier looking terrible but had to leave. She's gone home.'

Usually I avoided viruses. You have a high chance of catching them simply by getting on the Tube. But somehow common sense didn't seem as important as it usually did. Action was needed, I told myself. Lemons. Honey.

I remembered exactly where Sarah lived, in what used to be a block of council flats. They were now, she'd explained on my previous visit, rented to private tenants. Hers wasn't really hers at all. It belonged to a friend who had gone to run a yoga retreat in India. She'd said all this as though it was quite normal.

The front door to the block was open. That didn't seem very secure. I made my way down the narrow corridor to her flat. There was a bike propped up outside the door with flowers wrapped around the basket. There was no proper knocker or, indeed, a bell. So I used my bare knuckle.

'Yes,' called out a faint voice.

I'd wanted Sarah to be in so much that I'd expected her not to be. My chest thudded as I heard footsteps on the bare floorboards on the other side. Then the door opened. A different Sarah looked up at me. Her hair was loose around her shoulders. She didn't have any make-up on. Not even the red lipstick. The room was dark but nevertheless I could see she was wearing a scruffy black baggy tracksuit and jumper with that cheap-looking pendant round her neck.

Yet she still looked beautiful.

'Don't come near me,' she coughed. 'I've got the lurgy.'

It was a sign of my condition that I stood firm. 'I'm here now, so any germs that you are carrying will already have entered my system,' I pointed out.

She looked uncertain.

'I've got honey and lemon,' I said quickly. 'Let me make you a drink.'

'You can't boil a kettle. There's no electricity.'

'That's terrible. Have you rung the power company?'

'They've cut it off because I couldn't pay,' she said. 'And I can't boil it on the cooker because I've run out of money for the gas meter.'

No wonder it felt freezing inside the flat. I could, of course, have lent her money for the meter, but that wouldn't solve the electricity problem.

'Come back with me,' I said firmly, surprising myself. 'This place isn't right. It's not even secure. Anyone can walk into the block.'

She put a hand on the doorframe as if attempting to steady herself. 'I don't feel well enough to go anywhere.'

I'd learned to concentrate on the practical element of a situation first and then sort out the emotional later on. 'You can't stay here in the cold or you will get worse. I'll get a taxi. Please wait there. I'll be back in a minute.'

I expected her to say that she couldn't possibly impose and that she didn't know me well enough to come back to my place. But instead a look of gratitude spread over her face. 'Thank you,' she said, smiling. 'You're my knight in shining armour.'

I was surprised to discover how good that made me feel.

Sarah's eyes visibly widened as she took in the 1950s three-bedroom semi-detached house and neat front garden with the box hedge that I clipped every Sunday. I had been lucky to buy it through a bank repossession. The estate agent had described Hackney as an 'up-and-coming' area and he was right. The property's value had already risen by seventeen per cent. 'It's lovely,' she said.

Lovely? I'd never thought of it in those terms.

'Thank you,' I said, giving the driver the exact fare, which I'd got ready as we arrived. 'I'm very pleased with it.'

Sarah began coughing again, so I supported her as we walked up the three steps to the front door.

As soon as we entered the house, I turned up the central-heating thermostat to twenty-three degrees, three higher than my usual setting. The black-and-white chequered tiles of the hall floor stretched out before us. Some had been cracked when I'd moved in but I'd soon had them replaced. I've never liked imperfection. It's another reason why my eye bothers me so much.

'Wow,' said Sarah, staring around in a manner that, in normal circumstances, I would have considered impertinent. 'This is a flipping palace!'

Then she gave me the sort of intense look that I might give a junior at work when appraising them during their biannual review. 'It *is* yours, isn't it? You're not having me on.'

I wasn't quite sure how to take this. 'I have a mortgage,' I said. I could have added that I should be able to pay it off in twenty years and one month precisely if my earning abilities increased as I had forecast. I was actually rather proud of this.

'Now,' I added, 'let's get you into bed, shall we?'

She began to giggle. Then cough. Then giggle again. 'I thought you didn't do that sort of thing until you knew someone better.'

'I didn't mean it like that,' I said quickly. 'I want to look after you.'

Sarah was leaning against me now as if she might slump onto the tiles any minute. I picked her up. She was heavier than she looked. I carried her up the first flight of stairs and placed her gently on my bed, which I'd made, as I always did, before leaving for work. The two other bedrooms were empty. There didn't seem any point in furnishing them because I never had guests.

'Do you want to change into something?' I asked. 'You could wear one of my shirts to sleep in.' Then I blushed. 'I'll go out of the room while you do so.'

'You're a good man, Tom,' she said, looking up at me with those big brown eyes. Her smile, although not being quite as broad as before, was still there.

Good man? If only she knew.

'That was quick,' quipped Hugo, when I told him about Sarah staying with me. It was Sunday morning and we were playing tennis in one of the club's indoor courts. I booked it once a week throughout the year. Outdoor courts were not reliable with the weather. I'm afraid to say that Hugo hadn't always been reliable either since becoming a father. If Olivia had had a bad night with the children, he would allow her to lie in while he took over. He'd cancelled our tennis appointments fifteen times this year already.

'She needed someone to help her,' I added, tossing the ball high in the air.

'Of course she did! What's the sex like? No. Don't tell me. I can tell. Your face reminds me of mine when I had a fling with this hippy girl in California during my gap year. Remember me telling you?'

'Yes. Several times.'

'It was bloody amazing,' he continued, as if I hadn't spoken. 'She did things I hadn't dreamed of.'

'It's not like that,' I cut in. 'I've told you. She's got flu. I'm looking after her while she's ill.'

He stepped back further to serve. 'You'll catch it, then. Don't come round for a while, will you? The children might get it. Then we won't have any sleep.' The ball whizzed past me. 'Game to me, mate.'

After that, I didn't contact Hugo for a bit. Instead, I concentrated on work and looking after Sarah. Her flu was nasty. She had to cancel the next two weeks' worth of classes as well as the others that she ran locally to 'get by'.

'I don't get paid when I don't work,' she said as she tried to get up for the third time.

'It doesn't matter. I said I'd look after you.'

'But you hardly know me.'

'I feel as if I do.' The words came out of my mouth without me thinking. They took me completely by surprise.

'I know what you mean,' she said softly.

A strange glow began to spread through me. Almost as if I had put on a warm jumper.

As the days went by, I began to act like a different person. This was both unsettling and also strangely pleasurable. I even went into a women's shop and bought underwear and a couple of nightdresses, albeit with the help of an assistant.

'It's very kind of you, but I don't usually wear anything in bed,' said Sarah when I brought them back.

I had suspected as much, but I wanted to show respect. The truth was that, despite Hugo's presumption, we hadn't had sex. Of course, I wanted to. My body burned with desire. It was the only way I could put it. I couldn't forget the electric shock that had gone through me when she'd first put her hand on mine. I'd never felt anything like it before.

But at the same time, I didn't want Sarah thinking I'd brought her back to take advantage of her. This was why

I had been sleeping on the sofa downstairs. Besides, she was ill.

Thankfully, a few days later, she got better. 'I feel all right today,' she said when I came in with a cup of tea. Sarah was propping herself up on one elbow. Her beautiful black glossy hair with those pink and blue streaks was hanging loose on her shoulders, and despite that earlier assertion that she slept naked, she was wearing one of the nightdresses I had bought: the pale blue one with the 'sweetheart neckline', as the assistant had described it. I wondered if she was doing that to please me. Her brown eyes were no longer bright with fever. And, most important, her wonderful smile had returned.

'I'll probably be able to go back now,' she said, dipping her head to one side in that way of hers. She reminded me of a picture of a woman in a Pre-Raphaelite exhibition that Arabella had dragged me to at the Royal Academy. 'Thanks so much for looking after me.'

I'd been dreading this.

'I don't want you to leave,' I said.

'Nor do I.' She got up and went to the window, pulling up the sash to let in air. 'The roses are out in the square.'

'Really?'

'Yes! Look.' Her voice rose in excitement. 'All kinds of colours! My favourites are those apricot ones. What are yours?'

I'd never thought about it. Instead of replying to her question, I cleared my throat, which felt inexplicably constricted. 'When I said "Really?" just then, I wasn't talking about the roses being out in the square. I was talking about not wanting you to leave.'

'Yes,' she said, turning round. 'So was I.'

I was so taken aback that I did not know what to say.

She went back to bed – my bed – and curled up like a kitten. 'You must be fed up with that sofa,' she said, smiling.

'It's pretty comfortable.' I didn't add that I'd spent a long time doing my research before settling on that particular design.

Then she held out her arms. 'I want you,' she said simply.

My brain hadn't prepared for this, right now, although I had, of course, imagined it so many times that I had stopped counting.

Then Sarah reached out her hand and took mine, guiding it towards her.

My first thought was that this was rather forward on her part. My second – which was more anxious – was that Sarah would not find me very interesting in bed. It was not as though I'd had much experience, apart from Arabella.

Yet Sarah didn't seem to mind as she slowly began to undress me, undoing each button of my shirt with a slow deliberation that almost felt teasing and then caressing me with gentle kisses that became more urgent as our bodies intertwined.

'That was great,' she said afterwards, as we lay back on the pillows. 'What about you?'

'Great too,' I said, embarrassed. Like I said before, I've always disliked talking about sex.

All I can say is that she seemed to like what I did. And that turned me on. It gave me confidence.

'I love your body,' she said, stroking me.

I found myself tracing the outline of her right breast with my forefinger. Then my finger touched on something round and hard underneath. 'It's a mole,' she said. 'When I had it checked out, the consultant told me it was sometimes known as a third nipple. Apparently it was seen as a sign of witchcraft in medieval times. Just imagine. I could have been burned at the stake!' She laughed.

That was the thing about Sarah. You never knew what she was going to do or say.

Was this – could it really be – love? Was this what the songs meant about 'sickness' and 'not being able to do anything about it'? Like my father, I always needed to be in control. (This isn't a characteristic I'm proud of but it's a fact. It helps me to feel safe.) And yet I couldn't imagine life without Sarah, even though we'd only recently met.

I never went to another of her art classes, because I couldn't bear to see the woman I loved bending over another man to give him advice. Instead, I had dinner ready for her when she came home. Never rice-related, obviously.

'This is nice,' she always said. Yet she never ate very much. 'Our meals were a bit hit and miss when I was a child,' she said. 'So I don't have a big appetite.' Then she pushed her plate towards me. 'You finish mine. Remember how I hate waste? I have nightmares sometimes about starving.'

I reached out across the mahogany dining-room table that I'd bought from a local antique shop when I first moved in. 'You don't have to worry about anything now I'm here.'

Her smile dipped. 'But I can't stay here for ever, can I?'

'Well, not for ever, obviously. None of us can. But you can stay for as long as you like.'

'Really?'

'I wouldn't say it if I didn't mean it. Besides, isn't your friend back from India now?' She'd mentioned this the other night, and that she'd need to find somewhere to live. I'd wanted to ask her to stay then and there, but I'd been too shy.

Her eyes were shining. 'Let's celebrate! We could go ice skating.'

'Ice skating? Why?'

'Because it's fun! I'll teach you.'

I'd grown up with the idea that 'fun' was self-indulgent. 'The only way to succeed in life,' my father used to say, 'is to work hard.'

Besides, how could I skate with coordination like mine?

'Please try,' she said with that smile.

I couldn't disappoint her. Later that week, we went to Queens in Bayswater. It was very cold and full of extremely competent people.

'I'm afraid I'm not very good at this,' I said, after falling over twenty-seven times in half an hour.

She helped me to my feet. 'At least you gave it a go. I'm proud of you.'

'Really?'

'Yes.' She pulled me to her and buried her face in my chest. I put my arms around her, breathing her in. Who *was* this woman?

After lunch, we went for a walk along the Thames. 'One day,' she said dreamily, looking at the barges, 'I'd like to get into one of those and sail away. Wouldn't you?'

'No,' I said firmly. 'I'm happier in places I know.'

Our politics were different too.

'What do you think of the Republicans?' asked Sarah when she saw me reading the *Financial Times* over breakfast one weekend. Bill Clinton was now in office.

'I think they've got a lot going for them,' I said.

We had our first argument over that one. 'Let's agree to disagree,' Sarah said afterwards.

And to my surprise, this worked. Rows with Arabella had always seemed threatening. But Sarah believed that 'arguments can be healthy because they open our eyes to the other person's point of view'.

We began to take it in turns to choose days out at weekends. Sarah loved art galleries, especially those exhibiting modern paintings, which looked to me as though they'd been made by children. I preferred the Natural History Museum, or the V&A with its clear labels. I also introduced her to opera.

Certainly, an outsider would never have put us together. She smoked – although never anything other than tobacco and never inside my house. She also drank and could get through half a bottle of white wine every evening without even being tipsy. She no longer wore the nightwear I had bought when she'd been ill. Instead, she went back to sleeping naked, apart from that old pendant.

'Don't you want to take it off at night?' I asked.

She clutched it with fear in her eyes as if I might try to snatch it. 'No. Never.'

I didn't ask why. It wasn't my business. Besides, if I started to ask her too many personal questions, she might do the same to me. 'I always have to work late on Wednesdays,' I said.

'That's fine,' she said. I told myself we were both allowed our secrets.

But then, one day, when I happened to be walking through a park near Sarah's old flat, I saw a notice attached to a railing with a rain-stained photograph. LOST. LADIES' BIKE. It was identical to the one I'd seen outside Sarah's front door when she'd been ill, which I'd presumed had belonged to her friend. I recognized it because of the plastic flowers on the basket. But the name to call on the notice wasn't her friend's. Lydia was her friend's name yet the bike belonged to someone called Anita.

'It can't be the same one,' Sarah said when I'd asked about it. 'There's loads that look like that.'

'But don't you want to check with Lydia just in case?'

'No, I know it's hers because I saw her with it the other day.'

'You didn't tell me that.'

Sarah looked at me with an odd expression. 'I can't tell you everything, Tom. What's the problem?'

I wasn't sure. I simply felt uneasy.

Then, the next day, Hugo rang me at work. I hadn't heard from him since that tennis game. Immediately, I knew something was wrong.

'Chapman's writing a memoir,' he said. 'It's being published next spring.'

I'd waited years to hear that name again. But now it had come, I couldn't believe it.

'It's bound to be reviewed,' added Hugo. 'Chapman's a big cheese now.'

I didn't need reminding.

'We don't know he'll mention us,' I said.

'Word is that he's going to do a full exposé.'

'Fuck!'

I hardly ever swore.

'What are we going to do?' I asked.

'I'm trying to work that one out.'

'Have you told Olivia?'

'Yes.' Hugo's voice sounded cracked. 'She was shocked but surprisingly supportive. Are you still seeing Sarah?'

'I am.'

'Well, if you plan to keep her, I'd tell her what happened before it comes out.'

A cold shiver passed through me. Just as I'd found someone I really loved – and who seemed to care for me – my past had returned to get me.

A car splashes me.
  I put my middle finger up.
  The brake lights go on.
  Shit.
  I've pissed off the driver.
  I take a sharp left.
  Down an alley.
  I look back.
  Nothing.
  I breathe again.
  And then I take a right.
  He's waiting for me.

4

Sarah

I felt shitty about the bike. You've got to believe me about that. The truth was that it was propped up against the railings at the arts centre without a lock. It was the day before I got really ill but I could feel I was going down with something. All I'd wanted to do was crawl into bed as quickly as possible, so on impulse, I got on it and cycled back. I'd return it tomorrow, I told myself. But I woke with a raging fever and to be honest, I forgot all about the bike until Tom mentioned it.

I couldn't tell him I'd borrowed it without the owner's permission. So I pretended it wasn't the same one. Still, it was small fry compared to the other stuff that Tom must never know about.

He wasn't like anyone else I'd ever met. I meant it when I said the sex was great. I didn't expect it to be. But it was fireworks. Not just Catherine wheels or sparklers. The whole bloody display! Shooting rockets that showered silver and gold raindrops.

I don't know why. I could tell he wasn't experienced. Perhaps that was it – I'd had too many men who knew exactly what they wanted. Tom, on the other hand, seemed to be in tune with what *I* wanted.

But the most important thing was that Tom was a

decent, honest man. One day we were walking down the street and he spotted a loose fiver on the pavement. If that had been me, I'd have thought it was my lucky day, but he walked straight into the newsagent and asked if anyone had lost some money. No one had reported it so he put it in the charity box on the counter instead.

'At some point in the future,' he said to me after he'd made love to me twice in six hours, 'I'd like a family of my own.'

I'd never met a man who'd said that after a few weeks of being with me. I was used to what they called 'baby daddies' in my old place. Men who got women pregnant but didn't want to support them or their children.

'How about you?' he asked.

'Sure. One day.'

I wasn't even thirty then, so I reckoned I still had plenty of time. Besides, the responsibility daunted me. But at the same time, I liked the idea of being part of a proper family.

But then Tom came home from work with one of those 'set' faces.

As I looked at that grim expression, I knew something was up. Maybe he was upset because I had all my art stuff spread out over the floor. If Tom had one fault, it was his over-fussiness.

'I've got something to tell you,' he said, taking off his glasses and wiping them before putting them back on.

I'd been waiting for this. He wanted me to leave. I'd have to find somewhere to live. Lydia, who'd lent me her flat for free while she was travelling, was back now so I couldn't go there. I didn't earn enough for rent. I'd have to sign on . . .

'Can't we eat first?' I suggested, playing for time. 'I've made cheese pasta. It's in the oven.'

'Please, Sarah. This is important.' He led me by the hand to the sofa. I'd never liked it. Leather was too cold. He sat at the far side, looking at me. Had he found out? No. He couldn't have. Could he?

'When I was at boarding school,' he said carefully, 'there was this boy who . . .'

He stopped. I hadn't expected this.

'Who what?' I said.

'Whom we bullied. When I say "we", I mean my friend Hugo and me.'

My skin prickled. I didn't do violence. And Tom wasn't the type. Or was he? They say it's always the quiet ones.

'Physically or mentally?' I asked with a quickening in my chest.

He looked away. 'A bit of both. We put his head down the loo and sent him to Coventry. You know – wouldn't talk to him.'

I got up from the sofa and sat on the floor. I felt more comfortable that way. It helped me think more clearly. 'Why?'

His eyes still weren't meeting mine. 'Because a group of the masters used to . . . to bully us,' he said in a rush. 'The boy we were nasty to was called Chapman. He wanted us to report the masters to the head, but Hugo and I thought he'd deny it and accuse us of lying, which would make it worse. So we pressurized him into agreeing to stay quiet. We were only ten . . .'

His voice came out as a choke.

I hadn't expected this. 'That's awful,' I whispered, getting to my feet. I wanted to ask him more and to hold him, but something stopped me.

He was looking at me now. His eyes red and scared. Outside, a siren screamed. You heard them a lot round here. They always made me nervous. It passed, but the noise carried on ringing in my head.

'Now he's pretty high-profile and is writing his memoir, which is being published next year,' continued Tom. 'I've heard he's including his time at school and that he's naming people. He'll probably mention me and Hugo being horrible to him. What will people think of me?'

'Look,' I said, 'if this does happen, you simply say you were only a kid.'

'I knew it was wrong.' His eyes were screwed up like they were in pain. 'I was too scared to do the right thing. I thought my father would tell me I was being weak. That big boys don't cry.'

'Really?'

'I knew you wouldn't understand. How could you?' His voice sounded angry. 'You grew up in a big happy family where things like this didn't happen.'

'That happy family of mine,' I blurted out. 'It's only true up to a point. I lived in a commune with my mother. I never knew my dad.'

'A commune?' Those sandy eyebrows frowned at me. I'd had all kinds of reactions to this in the past so I wasn't surprised. Some people are shocked. Some intrigued. A few envious.

'Actually, it was quite organized.' I couldn't help smiling

at the memories. 'We lived in vans on a farmer's land in Kent. He let us stay there for free while we worked his land. It was a beautiful place.'

I felt wistful for a moment. 'I had loads of friends; we were like brothers and sisters. We had chickens and dogs. In the evenings, we'd sit around and sing and play the guitar. I used to join in.' My voice softened as I recalled Mum's words in my head. *'You've got a voice like an angel, Sarah!'*

Then I felt a shiver going down my arms. I told myself not to say any more, but I just kept going. 'Then . . .'

This was the hard part. I'd never talked to anyone about this. Not even Emily. Yet if Tom and I were going to be serious, he had to know at least some of the truth.

'My mum died in a car accident when I was eight. One of her friends was babysitting me in our caravan when the police came to tell us.'

He looked shocked. 'That's awful.'

I nodded, rushing my words to get to the next bit before my courage left me. 'Social Services got called. In the end, my mum's sister took me on. She and her husband didn't have kids of their own and had no idea how to deal with me.'

All the old hurt was pouring out. I tried to stop it but Tom had such a kind 'I'm listening' expression that I couldn't stop. Besides, hadn't he told me about his own difficult time?

'They were strict and cruel. I had to eat at separate times from them because they said I chattered too much. My aunt destroyed the only photograph I had of Mum. She said it must have gone into the wash by mistake but I knew she'd done it on purpose because I always kept it under my pillow.'

'*You've drowned Mum! You've drowned her!*'

'*Don't be such a stupid girl. It was just a photograph.*'

It was so good to share this with the man I loved. My heart actually felt lighter.

Tom frowned. 'So why did you tell me a different story before?'

My relief turned to a cold feeling in my chest. Tears pricked my eyes.

'Because,' I said, still trying to smile, 'it was wishful thinking. The only way I could cope when I was growing up was to pretend that none of this was happening. I'd imagine that I had older brothers and sisters to protect and love me. On my way back from school, I'd fantasize that my mum was still alive. We'd be living in a proper house and she would be waiting for me . . .'

I touched my pendant in the way I always do when I'm upset. I used to imagine that my mother was sending down courage from wherever she was.

'Mum always used to wear this. She made it herself.'

'And that's why you don't take it off,' he said.

I nodded. But instead of stopping there, I found myself going on. 'The thing is . . . there's something else.'

I swallowed the lump in my throat. 'After school, I went to art college, but then everything went wrong in my second year.'

'In what way?' he asked quietly.

No, I realized. This was a huge mistake. I suddenly sensed he wouldn't be able to take what I'd been about to tell him. I couldn't risk losing Tom. I had to think quickly.

If you want to tell a story that sounds convincing, you have to mix the truth with a couple of lies. It was a lesson I'd learned over the years.

'Like I said,' I continued quickly, 'my uncle and aunt were strict. It made me rebel a bit when I got my freedom at college. I went out with friends late at night and didn't work hard enough. I flunked my exams so I didn't get my degree.'

Was it my imagination or did he look relieved? Perhaps he was expecting something far worse.

If so, he was dead right.

He stroked my hand in comfort. 'But you're a talented artist now.'

'Are you kidding?' I burst out. 'I can't sell my paintings. I just about survive with my teaching. If it hadn't been for you, when I was ill and couldn't earn, I don't know what I would have done. If you decide you don't want me living here any more, then . . .'

'Marry me,' he said, cupping his hands around my face and pulling me towards him.

What? Had I heard him right?

'But we've only known each other for three months.'

'I know. But I mean it. Please. I've never met anyone like you before, Sarah. I love you.'

The last bit came out like a groan. It took the wind out of me. This, I had not been expecting.

Then – maybe it was nerves – I began to giggle.

Instantly I realized I'd done the wrong thing. Tom's face looked like a deflated balloon.

'I'm sorry,' I said. 'I didn't mean to laugh. I do that sometimes when I don't know what else to do.'

He frowned. 'It's my fault. I've rushed you.'

'No,' I lied. 'It's all right. I'm flattered.'

Another siren went past.

'I'm not used to showing emotions like you.' He wiped his forehead with the back of his hand. 'I'm out of my depth here, Sarah.'

'I know you are, and I love you for it.'

'Love?' he repeated. 'You love me too?'

How could I take it back? Besides, perhaps I did love him. He was so good to me. So loving. So kind. And we both had things in our past we didn't want to talk about. But I hadn't told him half of mine.

'I do, but I'm sorry, Tom. I can't marry you.'

His face creased with disappointment. 'Why not?'

I couldn't explain. If I did, he'd be out of here. And I wanted this man to stay. I really did.

'Just trust me,' I said.

Tom

'All rise,' says the clerk, breaking into my thoughts.

There's a break in the proceedings.

The lawyers are flapping about like black crows, shuffling paperwork and whispering hurried comments to colleagues.

I look down on the jury as they file out. There are more women than men. Is that a good thing or not? Hard to tell.

Our lives are in their hands. As was another life all those years ago.

I wonder if Sarah is thinking the same. She is at the

other end of the public gallery from me. I look across at her. Her hair is different. Is she still the same person inside?

Are any of us?

I suspect not.

How can we be after what happened?

5

Tom

Ever since Hugo had told me about Chapman writing his memoirs, I'd been even more nervous than usual. I couldn't stop checking my phone in my top drawer.

Still nothing.

Then, three minutes before I was due to go into a management conference, I looked again.

Bad news about Chapman. Ring me.

I was tempted to go to the Gents but I couldn't make this call without total privacy. It could ruin my career.

'Tom,' called out my boss. 'We're going into the boardroom now.'

Only when the meeting ended, one hour and fifty-six minutes later, could I justifiably collect my mobile and the grated Cheddar cheese and thinly sliced cucumber sandwich I'd made before work. Then I headed for the park.

Hugo picked up immediately.

'What happened?' I asked.

His voice was quieter than usual. 'Chapman shot himself. He's dead.'

'What?'

My head spun. I felt dizzy with horror. Yet the terrible truth was that I felt a shameful sense of relief too.

'Did he . . . ?'

I couldn't finish my sentence. But Hugo knew exactly what I meant.

'Did he talk about us before he did it? I don't know. I've just heard a news flash. We're going to have to wait until the whole story comes out in the papers.'

In an instant I could see my whole life dissolving. Everyone would know. Work, Sarah, the Wednesday group . . .

'Did it in the weekend farmhouse, apparently, while his wife and kids were up in London,' continued Hugo. He sounded more detached now; as if distancing himself from his feelings. 'Shot himself in the head.'

A vision of a pale, lanky schoolboy with a terrified look on his face loomed into my head. I physically retched. A mother walking past with her child gave me a disgusted look.

'This was our fault,' I spluttered, mopping my mouth. 'If we had allowed him to tell someone . . .'

'Stop,' said Hugo firmly. 'You can't think like that. They'd have hushed him up. Maybe even expelled us all on some other pretext. Things were different in those days. You know that.'

He was right, but it didn't make me feel any better.

'Did you tell this Sarah girl of yours?' he asked.

'Most of it.'

'Not all?'

'No. She didn't ask.'

A dog was sniffing at my ankles now. Its owner was

walking towards me, presumably to put a lead on it. I stood up and moved away.

'You don't think Olivia will say anything to Sarah, do you?' I asked.

'How can she?' scoffed Hugo. 'We've never met her.'

'But when I introduce her to you, it might come up in conversation.'

'I doubt it. Besides, they're not likely to be bosom friends, are they?'

Secretly, I agreed, but his comment annoyed me. 'Why not?'

'They're two very different women.'

I felt a surge of irritation towards my old friend.

'Actually, I asked her to marry me,' I said boldly.

There was silence. 'Are you still there?' I asked.

'Yes.'

'She turned me down.'

'Just as well.'

'What do you mean?'

'Well, you hardly know each other, and even if you did, you're chalk and cheese!'

I felt defensive. 'Like you said you've never met her.'

'I've heard enough.'

'Difference can be a good thing.'

'Shared values and similar backgrounds are important when it comes to getting married,' said Hugo firmly. 'From what you've told me, she'll never understand you properly.'

Exactly what my father would have said if he were alive. But I had a feeling that my mother would have been more understanding. I suddenly realized my feet had carried me to Waterloo Bridge.

'You know what, Hugo, I am going to tell Sarah. I don't want any more secrets between us.'

'If you do, you'll be dropping me in it.'

'She'd never tell anyone.'

Hugo sounded panicky now. 'I hope you're right. And if you're determined to get married, get to know her properly, at least. You need to make sure she's not after you for your house and money . . . Tom? Are you there?'

I put the phone down. Hugo's warnings about Sarah hurt. He was wrong. Hadn't I always promised myself, after school, to do the right thing? I couldn't marry someone without being honest.

I found Sarah sitting on the floor of the kitchen, surrounded by canvases and paintbrushes. She liked to work that way and, even though part of me disliked the mess, another part admired her.

'I need to tell you something,' I said. 'Come and sit here.'

She walked towards me. 'What's wrong?'

I held her to me. This might, I realized with a pang, be the last time we would do this. I stroked her hair. She'd braided it since this morning with little pink and pale blue beads. 'I've got something to tell you.'

As I spoke, to my horror, I could feel tears running down my cheeks. '*Big boys don't cry.*' I could hear my father as though he was here.

'Tom!' Sarah was holding my face in her hands. I looked into her wide brown trusting eyes. 'What's happened?' she said softly. 'You're scaring me. Are you ill?'

'It's Chapman,' I sobbed.

'The boy from school?'

'He's killed himself.' I took a deep breath. 'He shot himself because we were being abused. Me and him and Hugo. It was one of the masters. He used to make us come to his room after dinner. None of us have ever really got over it.'

There. The words had fired out as if they were the bullet Chapman had pumped into his own head.

Never had I cried like this before. Not even when my mother had died.

'Hush,' Sarah was holding me in her arms, rocking me back and forth.

'You don't think badly of me?' I wept.

'Of course not. It wasn't your fault. None of it's your fault.'

My heart swelled. Hugo was wrong. This woman *did* understand me.

Neither of us felt like eating. Instead, we went to bed. Not to have sex but to hold each other while I continued to cry. It was as if all the old hurt was finally flooding out. In the morning, I woke up, forgetting what had happened for an instant. The window was slightly open. I could hear a bird singing over the morning traffic. And then I got that terrible jolt of panic as it came back to me. *Did it in the weekend farmhouse. Shot himself in the head.*

Sarah was leaning over me, her long dark hair swinging against her breasts. 'I've changed my mind.'

A jolt of fear passed through me. 'You're going to leave me?'

'No. I want to marry you after all.'

'Because of pity?'

'No. Because you're a good man, Tom. And I want to

spend the rest of my life with you.' Then she looked nervous. 'Unless, of course, you've changed your mind too.'

I wrapped my arms around her, breathing in this extraordinary woman. 'I haven't.'

I got out of bed and down on one knee, not even embarrassed that I only had my pyjama top on. 'Sarah. Will you do me the honour of being my wife?'

'Yes,' she said. 'I will.'

Then she lifted my face to hers with that wonderful sunny smile of hers. 'I want us to have loads and loads of kids. A football team, in fact! And you're going to make the best father in the world! I know it.'

I would. I really would. My heart lit up inside at the thought of teaching our children how to do sums, of taking them to cricket matches, of being there for them. I could see myself reading a story at night to them, holding hands with Sarah as we watched them receiving end-of-term prizes, just as I had done – but without anyone I loved in the audience.

Parenthood would give me a chance to start a new life. I wasn't going to mess it up like my father had.

I had to get it right.

After all, how hard could it be?

6

Sarah

It was time to make a new start. Become a different Sarah. Banish the past once and for all.

'I don't want a big wedding,' I said, when we began talking about the arrangements. 'I don't have anyone to invite.' I thought of how happy Mum would've been, even though I remember her saying that she didn't believe in marriage.

Was I imagining it or did I glimpse a look of relief on Tom's face?

'How about a registry office with only Hugo and Olivia. And the children as bridesmaids?' he suggested.

I hadn't been that keen on Hugo or his wife when they'd asked us round for a 'kitchen supper' shortly after Tom had proposed.

'Tom says you're an artist,' Olivia had gushed over the vegetable terrine, made especially for me because I didn't eat meat. (This was said in an almost disbelieving tone.) 'How *wonderful*.'

'I like it,' I'd said, wondering which knife and fork I was meant to use – there were three of each on either side of my mat. 'But it's the only thing I can do, so I wouldn't know any different.'

She'd given me a smug smile. 'I used to be in marketing but gave it up when I got pregnant. It didn't make sense financially for us to both work, with the cost of childcare. And besides, I wanted to give them all of my attention.'

Presumably this included Hugo, whom she fussed over like a baby, putting food in front of him and never once asking him to help out. He was exactly the kind of man I couldn't stand. But now I knew what he and Tom had been through, I understood their closeness.

Initially, I'd dismissed Olivia as the 'perfect' stay-at-home wife and mother with her impossibly stunning strawberry blonde hair and creamy peach complexion. But later on in the evening, when Hugo had been ranting on about the government, Olivia had rolled her eyes at me. Maybe there was more to this woman than I'd realized!

'What do you think?' Tom now said.

'Sorry?'

For a minute, I'd been back in Olivia's house wondering what Emily would have thought of her. Emily had always seen the best in everyone.

'I was suggesting a small wedding with only Hugo and Olivia, and the girls as bridesmaids,' he said slightly stiffly.

'Perfect,' I replied, getting up to put on Tom's shiny stainless-steel coffee percolator, which looked as though it cost more than an average month's wages.

'Let me do that,' he said quickly. I noticed that he didn't like me touching his things. Or maybe it was because I wasn't used to being looked after.

'But please tell them we don't want a wedding present.' I stood on tiptoes to put my arms around his neck. 'You're all I need,' I added. 'And if you want to do a pre-nup, that's fine by me too.'

Hugo had mentioned this at the kitchen supper, saying it in a joking fashion, though I could tell he was serious.

'Nonsense,' Tom said in that brisk tone of his. 'What is mine is yours.'

'Only if you're sure.'

'I am.' He took off his glasses and polished them. He often did that when he'd made a point and didn't want to discuss it any further. 'Now, where shall we go for our honeymoon?'

'Could we go to the Scilly Isles?' I asked. 'My mother used to talk about it. She took me there once when I was a child.'

I could almost hear her telling me now. 'We hitched our way with some friends to the coast to get a ferry,' Mum had said, smiling at the thought. 'You were only little.'

I didn't know what 'hitch' meant so she'd had to explain it to me. Only when I was older did it strike me that this might not have been a very sensible thing to do with a child in tow.

'That's really sweet,' he said, leaning across the table to kiss the tip of my nose. 'Just like you.'

Sweet? No one had ever called me that before.

The wedding didn't feel real. I wore a floaty cream dress I made myself from some pretty silk and lace I found in the market. All the way through the short ceremony I kept waiting for someone to come rushing in and tell Tom what I had done. But no one did. I knew he was on edge too, because there had apparently been a small piece in the business pages about Chapman's suicide. But it didn't mention any book he was writing. Nor did it name Tom or Hugo.

Little Clemmie and her sister Molly couldn't be bridesmaids after all. They both had tummy aches so Olivia's mother was looking after them. Even though I hadn't met them – they'd been asleep on my one and only visit – they sounded lovely. 'I hope they're all right,' I said to Tom anxiously. 'I had a burst appendix when I was twelve.'

I heard my aunt's voice in my head. *'I can't bother the doctor on a Saturday with a simple stomach ache. You'll have to wait until Monday.'*

By then it had been too late.

I shivered at the memory, pushing it out of my head. The bad days had gone now. This was my new life.

Tom gave me a beautiful necklace that had belonged to his mother as a wedding present.

'Real diamonds,' he told me.

Fucking hell! I thought, staring at it intently. I was trying not to swear out loud as Tom didn't like it. 'It's stunning,' I said. 'Really it is.' I touched my neck. 'But I've always worn my mother's pendant.'

His eyes looked like those of a little boy who'd been told he couldn't do something. 'I understand that,' he said, even though his face didn't look like it. 'But I thought you might like this for special occasions.'

'Of course. Thank you.' I put it on with the pendant. 'I think they go well together, don't you?'

Marriage, I told myself, had to be a compromise. I owed him that, after what I had done.

Afterwards, the four of us had lunch at a posh London hotel. I'd never been anywhere like it in my whole life. The waiters kept bowing every time they served us. I saw Hugo giving me a look as I sent a carrot shooting onto the floor, but I ignored him and watched Olivia so I'd know what to do. *I don't belong with these people*, I thought. *What am I doing here? Have I made a mistake after all?*

Then Tom and I drove to Penzance and got a ferry. Only then, when we stood at the side of the boat, did I start to feel better. 'It's too cold for me,' Tom said. 'Shall we go inside?'

'I need some air,' I said, putting my face up into the wind, gulping it in. 'Be down in a minute.'

He dropped a kiss on the top of my head. 'Whatever you want, Mrs Wilkins.'

Mrs Wilkins? The name, like the wedding, didn't feel real. But there was the ring on my left hand as proof. A simple gold band. Tom had wanted something more elaborate, but this was perfect.

Quite a lot of the ferry passengers were being sick. Not me. I stood and waited until I could see land. This must be Tresco, the island where we were going to stay! 'You didn't come down,' said Tom, coming up to find me.

'I wanted to watch the sea,' I said. 'Look at all those different colours!'

He squinted. 'It's just blue.'

'No it's not!' I laughed. 'There are all kinds of different blues and greens and purples.'

'If you say so.' He spoke in a jokey way, like he was humouring me.

When we got off at the small harbour, with lots of little boats bobbing around and fishermen mending their nets, a strange peace settled over me. The air was so fresh. It smelt pure, not like London. But most important of all, my mum had been here with me. Perhaps on this very spot! Maybe she'd held my hand as Tom was holding mine as we walked up from the water towards our hotel.

'They don't allow cars here,' he told me. 'That's why it's so clean and quiet.'

I felt a tingle of excitement as I took in the cosy-looking honeystone hotel. Like other children with few memories of their parents, I hung on to any tiny thread that I could recall, such as the smell of my mother's skin after dipping her finger into the jar of Nivea on her dressing table. How old had I been exactly when I'd come here? How did she afford a holiday?

There were some questions that could never be answered.

'Did you know,' I told Tom later in bed, staring out of the window at a little boat on the horizon, 'that when artists used to run out of canvases, they would often whitewash them and paint a new picture on top?'

'Really?' He had his eyes closed and looked as though he was about to fall asleep.

'Sometimes art historians can reveal the original picture underneath,' I added.

Tom was gently snoring now.

'People can be like that,' I whispered. 'They look like one picture to the naked eye but underneath, they are an entirely different picture altogether.'

Nothing.

'What would you do if I was like that?' I found myself saying.

No answer.

Just as well my new husband was asleep.

*

'We could hire bikes,' I suggested on the second day.

'Are you joking?' he asked. 'You know I'm hopeless at balancing.'

I was a bit disappointed but instead we walked everywhere. And on one evening we took a picnic up to an abandoned castle, where I painted the sea below. 'The sun looks like it's burning the sky,' I said to him, pointing at the apricot sunset.

'What an imaginative way of putting it,' he said.

'It's how I think,' I said, shrugging.

Apart from walking, we spent most of our time making love. Wild passionate love that left us exhausted, gasping on the bed. I never knew I could feel like this. Sex was no longer something you did to please someone or get something. It was clean. Honest. Pure. And it blanked out the black stuff in my head.

One day, while Tom was still dozing, I went out on my own to a pretty craft shop and bought something. I'd seen it in the window earlier and couldn't resist. I wouldn't tell anyone.

'I feel pregnant,' I said when we got on the ferry to go back.

'What?' asked Tom, with that funny, quizzical look on his face that I often noticed. 'It usually takes an average of six months for a couple to conceive.'

'When did you look that up?' I asked.

'I did a bit of research at work the other week.' He seemed slightly embarrassed. 'So let's not count our chickens before they hatch, shall we?' Then he gave a little shy laugh.

'Do you get it?' he asked. 'Chicks! Hatch!'

'The thing about facts,' I said, 'is that they don't take a mother's instinct into account.' Then I breathed in the fresh air, feeling as light and heady as if I was one of the waves, dancing below. 'I know I'm expecting.'

How lucky I am, I thought, watching my new husband swaying as he went inside the cabin. This was my chance to get life right. To put my past behind me. To finally have the secure family I'd always wanted.

Just as long as Tom didn't find out the truth.

7
Tom

A week after coming home from honeymoon, I surprised Sarah by having her painting framed and hung it in the drawing room. Or the lounge, as she called it.

'You're so talented,' I said.

She shrugged, her pigtails swinging. 'I prefer nudes.'

I looked at the cliff, where we'd had our picnic, dropping down to the flaming orange sea. 'This is less contentious than naked bodies, don't you think?'

'What do you mean?'

'Well, it's less likely to cause offence when we have people round for dinner.'

There were a couple of important colleagues at work whom I needed to invite over at some point. They'd asked me to theirs in the past but I'd managed to avoid returning the favour. Now I had a wife, I felt more enthusiastic, so long as Sarah didn't do anything odd, like suggesting we had dinner on our laps in front of the TV. You never knew quite what my wife was going to do next. At times this was refreshing, but it could also be potentially awkward.

'I prefer the human form,' she said firmly. 'It never ceases to amaze me that each one of us can be so different.'

The same thought had occurred to me, although I would never consider voicing it.

'I keep wondering what I'll look like when I'm pregnant,' she said, leaning her head on my shoulder. We were sitting on the sofa now, below her picture.

'Do you still think you might be, then?' I asked.

'Actually,' she said, sitting back and half-looking at me under those dark eyelashes. 'I did one of those home testing kits this morning.'

I didn't normally show my emotions, but I felt my heart racing inside my chest. 'Are you . . . ?'

She shook her head. 'It was negative. But the instructions said your period had to be overdue and mine wasn't. Still, it's been a bit iffy in the last year or so. Sometimes early and sometimes late.'

I didn't know that. Isn't this a fact she should have mentioned to me before? Or was that the sort of subject women kept to themselves?

The next day, it was time for me to go back to work. For the first time in my life, I didn't feel my usual enthusiasm.

'Don't bother about the housework,' I said. 'I'll do that when I'm back.'

'Mr Particular!' she said, nudging me. This wasn't the first time Sarah had called me that. I didn't care for the term. What was wrong with wanting things to be kept in the right place? This was another thing about Sarah that I was learning. I liked tea towels to be neatly folded in kitchen drawers but she would sling them over chairs or abandon them, scrunched up on one of the kitchen surfaces. She also chucked tea bags in the sink, which stained the white porcelain. And when she washed my shirts, she didn't shake them out properly before drying them.

'I suppose boarding school and all those years on your own made you independent,' she said with that light laugh of hers. 'No worries. It will give me more time to paint.'

But when I came back at the end of the day with a pretty blue and pink scarf that I had bought Sarah at Liberty's, I found her kneeling over a blank canvas on the kitchen floor. 'I can't do it any more,' she said with a wild look in her eyes. 'It's like I need that kick up the arse – the fear of not having any money for food or the meter – in order for the magic to happen.'

'Sarah, you really should . . .'

I was going to say 'mind your language', since 'arse' wasn't a word I cared for, but she misinterpreted my interruption.

'I know! I should be relieved that I don't have to worry about brown envelopes with DO NOT IGNORE on any more. And I am.'

'Don't I make you happy?' I asked.

'Of course you do.' She got up and put her arms around me. There was an odd smell about her.

'Have you been smoking?' I asked.

'No.' She pulled away. 'If you really want to know, I found myself going into a newsagent to buy a packet of fags but I stopped myself by digging my nails into my wrist.'

Really?

'I can smell tobacco,' I persisted.

'That's because it's on my shirt. I haven't got round to washing it since my last class. Some of the students smoke during the break.'

Then her expression changed. Instead of looking miserable like she had just now, her face had broken into one of those lovely smiles. 'That reminds me. I'm starting another course next week so I won't be around on Thursday evenings.'

I felt uneasy. And not only because she wouldn't be at home when I was back. Something didn't feel quite right. Then again, we were still getting to know each other, weren't we? It was what married life was all about.

That's when I remembered. 'I've bought you a present,' I said, taking out the scarf.

'A present? Why?'

'Because I felt like it.'

And there it was again. That wonderful smile. 'Oh, Tom, that's beautiful. What amazing colours. Such a pretty paisley design.'

I didn't know what that meant but didn't like to say. The important thing was that she had flung her arms around me. And everything felt right again.

A few weeks later, the arts centre closed because of a lack of funding. No more classes. I tried not to show my relief. 'Never mind,' I said. 'You'll want to stop when we have babies anyway.'

'But I'll miss my students!' There were tears glistening in her beautiful dark brown eyes. 'I love steering their hands and watching their faces light up when they make a line they didn't know they had in them.'

'Aren't I enough for you?' I asked, knowing as I spoke, that this sounded stupidly childish.

'Of course you are.'

She flicked back her hair and reached up to kiss my mouth. I was lost. It was incredible, the effect she had on me.

Then, a few weeks later, she rang me at work. I'd already asked her not to do this. It didn't look professional. I needed to set an example to my team. 'Are you all right?' I asked.

'Guess what?' Her voice was all bubbly. 'You're going to be a dad!'

As she spoke, I could see one of the senior partners coming towards me with his measured, purposeful walk.

'Very good,' I said politely.

'I thought you'd be over the moon!'

'I'm going into a meeting now.'

'So you can't talk?'

'Exactly.'

I put down the receiver just in time. 'Hope I wasn't interrupting something important, Tom?'

'Not at all,' I said.

Then he started telling me that the board was 'very impressed' by my performance and would like to consider me as a junior partner. But I couldn't concentrate. I was too excited by what Sarah had told me. I was also scared. Being a father was such a responsibility. What if I messed up, as mine had done? On our honeymoon, I'd told myself it couldn't be that difficult to be a decent parent. But now it was reality, I was beginning to have doubts.

On the way home I stopped off at the florist and asked for a 'mixed bunch', to be on the safe side. Arabella had once made a terrible fuss when I'd bought her chrysan-themums. 'Garage flowers,' she had called them.

I found Sarah in the kitchen.

'I'm sorry I couldn't talk earlier,' I said, carefully handing the bouquet with pink ribbon over to her. 'It was a difficult time when you called. Your news is amazing!'

'*Our* news,' she corrected me, taking off her apron. She was making some kind of stew-looking thing called tofu goulash.

'It *is* amazing, isn't it!' She took my hand and placed it against her stomach. I didn't dare move in case it disturbed anything inside her.

'Talk to it,' she said.

I laughed out loud. 'It's not a real person yet.'

'Rubbish! He or she can hear us, you know. The baby books say so. Are you listening, little one? We're going to love you for ever. Aren't we, Daddy?'

She gave me one of her wonderful smiles.

'Yes,' I said, suddenly feeling a great deal better. 'We are.'

It was three weeks later on a Saturday morning when Sarah woke me. The sun was beginning to stream through the curtains. There was, I noticed, an annoying little gap between the two pieces of material because Sarah had drawn them together the previous evening instead of me.

As I got out on my side, Sarah gave a groan. 'My stomach hurts,' she said.

'Try sitting up against the pillows,' I replied gently, heading towards the offending curtains.

There was a small gasp and then a cry behind me. I turned around. 'Look!' she cried, pointing to the sheets.

She was lying in a rapidly growing pool of blood.

My mind raced. I fought to keep it in check. Think. Be calm.

'It's all right,' I said.

'How do you know?'

I ignored the question.

'We'll ring 999,' I said instead.

Numbers. Practical steps. That was the thing. I felt on surer ground with those. It would be all right.

It had to be.

But now, if the jury on their benches knew the truth, they would surely be the first to disagree.

The driver's window is open.

'Get in,' he says.

'I've got to be back by midnight.'

'Just get in, will you?'

He's drumming his fingers on the wheel. There's a big silver ring on his right hand.

It looks like a skull.

I glance around.

The street is empty.

'Come on,' he says. 'I've got an idea. It'll be fun.'

8

Sarah

Our baby had gone.

When I woke up on the ward they'd told me I'd had a D&C. Apparently, this was a 'scrape' to clear out my womb 'so it's ready for next time'.

But what if there wasn't a next time? Was this somehow my fault.

How could I be pregnant one minute and not the next? When I had a shower, more blood ran down my legs. It made me weep even harder.

When we got home, Tom was so sweet, bringing me cups of tea in bed and stroking my back.

'Of course I'm coming with you,' he said, when I received a hospital letter telling me to attend a check-up a few weeks later. 'I've got a meeting then but I'll cancel it. You're far more important.'

To my dismay, we were directed to the antenatal clinic, where we had to wait in a room, surrounded by smug pregnant women protectively stroking their bumps and talking to others about 'how many weeks gone' they were.

'Mrs Wilkins?' called the nurse.

I still got a feeling of 'who?' when someone used my married name.

'Often,' said the nurse once we were in her office, 'a

spontaneous abortion is nature's way if something isn't right with the foetus.'

'Abortion?' I gasped. 'That's not what it was.'

'I was using the medical term for a pregnancy that ends without warning,' she continued. 'It's upsetting, of course. But at least you now know you can get pregnant, unlike some. Wait three months and then try again.'

Three months? It felt like for ever. But that's what they advised in those days.

I made my way home alone down Oxford Street, still feeling wobbly after the internal. Tom had returned to the office. The Christmas lights had recently been switched on. Wide-eyed children were looking through the windows of Selfridges at life-size plastic reindeer. There was a little girl with blonde plaits, pointing. I wanted one like that. I almost felt like running towards her and carrying her off. Why hadn't my own mother treasured me more? Then maybe she wouldn't have gone out in a car without me.

No. I wouldn't allow myself to think about that dark time. Yet I couldn't stop. My mind went round and round until, by the time I reached Tom's front door – I still saw it as 'his' and not 'ours' – I was desperate for a drink. They told me to cut out booze while we were trying to get pregnant. But sod it. Tom wouldn't know. Not if it was vodka and didn't smell. I sank half a bottle and then fell asleep.

At some point during the night, I was vaguely aware of him coming in. He kissed me gently. Almost immediately my body melted at his touch, as it always did. I turned towards him.

'Shouldn't we wait?'

But I couldn't. It was so comforting to hold each other and be one. Even though we should have been three.

When all the Christmas decorations had been packed away, I found I was pregnant again.

'It's too soon. We should have waited longer before trying,' I told Tom.

'Nonsense,' he said, beaming. 'We have another baby on the way. Isn't that wonderful?'

I didn't want to admit that I'd been drunk on vodka when we'd had sex (something he hadn't seemed to notice in his passion), so I didn't mention it again.

Then, one morning, while I was finishing off a charcoal sketch of the square outside, I felt a nagging ache down below. I went to the bathroom and there it was. A glaring pool of bright red blood in my knickers. Anger surged through me. 'I told you,' I said to Tom when I rang. 'I said we had to wait like the nurse advised.'

'I'm sorry,' he said quietly at the other end. 'I'll come with you to the hospital.'

'No,' I snapped. 'I'll go there myself.'

But really I was as upset with myself as much as him. Perhaps I was being punished for drinking.

I got a cab to Casualty, where they scanned me. 'There's no need for a D&C this time,' they said. 'The foetus has expelled itself. Your womb is quite clean.' They spoke as if it was something I should be proud of.

I didn't allow myself to cry until I left. I thought of that little pair of white bootees I'd bought from the craft shop in the Scilly Isles (just in case) without telling Tom and wept even more.

'Are you all right, love?' asked a woman next to me on the crowded bus. Everyone else was chatting, laughing, talking about what they'd bought at the January sales for their kids. Carrying huge parcels and laden down with Hamleys carrier bags.

I nodded, unable to speak. But I wanted to ask if she had children and if the same thing had ever happened to her. If only I had a mum to talk to, or a friend.

'You should have called me,' said Tom when he came home. He held me in his arms but I wriggled away. I didn't deserve his love.

'We'll try again,' he said later, after supper, which I couldn't even swallow because I was so upset. 'Did you know that one in three pregnancies . . .'

'I don't want to hear any more bloody statistics!' I screamed. We were in the kitchen. He was painstakingly drying up each piece of cutlery on the draining board and his deliberate actions and words made me want to explode. 'Figures aren't going to make me feel any better when my breasts are sore one week and normal the next. They're not going to stop me looking at another woman on the street who's six months pregnant and thinking "that's what I thought I was going to be by now".'

I began to sob uncontrollably. 'You *will* have a baby,' said Tom awkwardly.

'But we don't know that, do we?'

He had no answer for that. Why should he? No one did.

We tried again. And again. I had two more miscarriages. Each around eleven weeks.

I tried to distract myself by decorating the house. I

bought a blue-and-orange rug from a stall but Tom didn't care for it. 'It's too bright,' he said.

That was the whole point. This place needed waking up. Everything here was chrome or beige. At first, it had felt luxurious compared with the dumps I'd been living in. But now it felt hostile.

Hardly anything in this house was mine.

My body didn't feel like mine either.

Then, as the shops were putting up their *Merry Christmas* signs again, it finally happened. The blue line that said I was expecting.

'It might well be all right this time,' Tom assured me.

'I don't want to talk about it,' I snapped. 'You're not to tell anyone. Especially not Hugo and Olivia. We're going to act as though I'm not pregnant so that when it goes wrong, I won't have got my hopes up.'

'But . . .'

'*Tom!* Please respect my wishes.'

He did. We didn't tell a soul. Not even Hugo, or so Tom said, although who knew what they talked to each other about when they played tennis on Sunday mornings? My intuition told me not to trust that man. I was sure he had led Tom on during that terrible bullying business at school.

Amazingly, I got to twelve weeks. I had a scan and there it was, wiggling on the screen in front of me. 'Everything seems perfectly healthy to me,' said the doctor.

At sixteen weeks, it was a struggle to do up my jeans. The daffodils were coming out in the garden. 'You'll be fine,' said their jaunty little heads, nodding merrily.

Not long afterwards, we were invited to Olivia and Hugo's for supper. I'd been refusing all their invitations since the second miscarriage, but now I decided I could face them. Olivia was stirring something on the cooker when we arrived. The smell made me want to be sick.

'It's lemon sole,' she said. 'I do hope you like it.'

'Excuse me,' I blurted out, rushing to the loo.

When I got back, I could tell from Olivia's expression that Tom had told her.

'What wonderful news,' she said, giving me a hug.

'We weren't going to say anything for a bit longer,' I retorted meaningfully.

'But it's all right now,' said Tom. 'Most miscarriages happen before twelve weeks.'

He said the word 'miscarriage' as if it was a scientific term. Not the gut-wrenching loss of a living, breathing child. *Our* child.

'Mummy,' said a little voice coming down the stairs. 'I'm not sleepy.'

I gazed enviously at Olivia and Hugo's elder daughter. She had her mother's beautiful strawberry blonde hair and a little turned-up nose.

'Nice try, Clemmie,' said Hugo, scooping her up. 'But you need your sleep and we need our time to ourselves.'

'Hello,' I said.

'Who are you?' she demanded.

'My name's Sarah.'

Her eyes widened. 'Sarah who's looking for a meal ticket?'

There was a shocked silence.

'Clemmie!' said Olivia faintly. 'That's terribly rude.'

'But that's what Daddy always says about her. It's why we couldn't be bridesmaids.'

'Nonsense!' Hugo was looking as if he wanted to be anywhere else but here. 'Children get so much wrong. It's quite funny really.'

'I don't think so,' said Tom stiffly.

We left shortly afterwards.

'Don't worry about Hugo,' he said, although I could tell that he was furious.

'I'm not,' I lied.

'In his book, anyone who didn't go to public school or doesn't speak like Olivia isn't one of us.'

'And what about you? Do you see me as an outsider?'

Tom stood still in the middle of the street. He cupped his hands around my chin and pulled my face towards him. 'You are a breath of fresh air,' he said simply. 'And I adore you for it.'

I had another scan at twenty weeks. I could actually hear the heartbeat! Our baby was sucking his thumb. Or hers. This was real. It wasn't make-believe or hope. I was carrying a child!

'I could tell you the sex if you like,' says the doctor.

'Yes,' said Tom.

'No,' I said.

'But it will make it so much easier to buy clothes and decorate the nursery if we know,' said my husband.

'I'd rather have a surprise,' I cut in. Yet what I really meant was that I couldn't allow myself to get too attached. If I had to lose this one too, I would rather lose a baby than a son or a daughter.

At twenty-two weeks I decided it was time. When he was out at work, I began to sketch a mural on one wall of the third bedroom. I hadn't been able to draw or paint as

I used to since we got married. It simply wouldn't come. But now a tree took shape. And then a sun. A park came into view. My hands couldn't work fast enough. I leaned – slightly to the right – to put in the duck pond. The chair wobbled. I righted myself for a second. Wobbled again. And then tumbled onto the floor.

I was shaking so much. Something didn't feel right. I was aware of a heaviness inside that hadn't been there before. A pulling downwards.

Spots of blood.

'No,' I screamed. 'Go away.'

Blood was coming out faster now. I went cold. Clammy. I crawled to the phone. I couldn't remember Tom's office number. I couldn't even, in my terror, remember 999.

'*Help!*' I called out. 'Please someone. *Help me!*'

9
Tom

If a neighbour hadn't heard and come in through the unlocked back door, I don't know what would have happened.

It wasn't the fall, they said at the hospital. It looked like the miscarriage had already started before that.

'Maybe,' I said when Sarah came home from hospital, pale and drawn, 'we should forget about having children.' She had been there for over a week; I feared that the trauma of delivering our stillborn baby was something she would never fully recover from.

Sarah stared at me with horror. 'What are you talking about?'

I thought she might say this. So I was prepared. 'Hear me out. Please. We could still have a good life together. Think about it. We could do all the things we wouldn't be able to if we had kids, like go on adventurous holidays and . . .'

I stopped. The truth was that travelling had never been high up on my agenda. I was the kind of person who liked what I knew. But I thought it might appeal to Sarah.

'You don't get it, do you?' Her deep brown eyes were wild. In fact, I'd go so far as to say that they were piercing into me.

'I *need* to get pregnant!' she yelled. 'I have to have a family.'

She looked almost deranged. It scared me. Had I married a madwoman?

'I didn't have a proper family either,' I pointed out, deliberately keeping my own voice calm. 'And I'd be quite happy with just you in my life.'

'You've got your precious friend Hugo.'

We'd been over this so many times. I'd been very cross with Hugo after Clemmie's 'meal ticket' comment. 'You must have used that phrase in front of her,' I'd said.

But he'd assured me that his daughter had got it wrong: 'You know kids. They pick up words and use them in different contexts.'

I knew he was lying, but after Chapman, it would take more than that to stop us being friends.

Now Sarah burst into tears. She looked so awful; a shadow of herself.

For a minute, I remembered my mother. No one had even told me she was ill. I vaguely recall her having to lie down a lot. But then I was sent away to stay with an aunt. And when I came back, she wasn't there.

'Your mother had cancer,' said my father. 'These things happen. I'm sorry.'

It was the closest he'd come to emotion.

'Men have to look strong even if they don't feel it underneath,' my father had told me after we'd viewed my waxen-faced mother in her coffin. Her jaw had slackened in death so that she looked like one of those elongated images found in fairground mirrors.

I accepted that advice as if it was as solid as my

multiplication tables. So I never told anyone how I felt about seeing her bare dressing table, devoid of all the little knick-knacks. It had been swept bare. Her clothes had gone from the wardrobe.

It was as if my mother had never existed.

What if I lost Sarah too? I tried to hold her hands across the kitchen table but she pulled away from me.

Unlike the previous consultants who had examined her, the latest one had picked up that my wife had scarring on her fallopian tubes. They thought it might be from when she had had her appendix out as a child. It was a 'possible' reason for her miscarriages.

Sarah had been furious. In fact, her face had scared me. 'If my aunt had listened to me when I said I felt ill, this wouldn't have happened.'

If it hadn't happened . . .

If we hadn't done it . . .

Both were phrases that came up frequently in my Wednesday group.

Now I tried to concentrate. 'I'm sorry. But the thing is . . . that's in the past now. We've got to be realistic about the future. He said you'd been lucky to have conceived so many times.'

'Then there's no reason why I can't do it again,' she snapped back. 'It will be all right next time. I know it.'

But weeks and then months went by. By November, it still hadn't happened. Sarah had become listless and miserable. She'd started drawing again. They were big horrible grey abstracts.

Then one evening, when I came back from the office, I found my wife sitting on our bedroom floor. Her beautiful long black hair was now short and spiky. The rest of it lay in uneven chunks on the carpet next to a pair of kitchen scissors.

'What did you do that for?' I asked.

She stared back at me as if it was obvious. 'It was either that or my wrists,' she said. 'I don't want to go on if we can't have a baby.'

I got down on the carpet and put my arms around her. 'Come on. It will be all right.'

'One go at IVF,' she said. 'That's all I want. Please. Think about Hugo and Olivia's children. Wouldn't you like one like Clemmie or Molly?'

I thought back to the early days when I was so looking forward to being a father. But I didn't realize it could be as hard as this to make babies.

'It's not only the money,' I said slowly, 'although we'll have to take it out of my emergency fund. I'm worried for you. And I don't know if it's good for us to go through all that again.'

She moved away from me. 'What do you mean, "good for us"? Do you think we're going to split up?'

'No. Of course I don't. I love you.'

'Then give me this. Please.'

'All right,' I said awkwardly. 'We'll try IVF. Just the once.'

'Thank you.' Sarah flung her arms around me. And instantly, peace was restored. I had my sweet-natured wife back. How can any rational person go from being so miserable to so happy in such a short space of time? It made me feel like I didn't know this woman – my wife – at all.

For the first time, I wondered if I had made a mistake.

10

Sarah

I was lying on my bed when the doorbell sounded, still wretched after another argument with Tom. We'd tried the IVF and it had failed. I had been begging him to give it one more go, but he was refusing.

He really didn't get what I was feeling. And why should he? I'd fallen in love with a man who had been brought up to hide his emotions.

The doorbell rang again. Who was it? None of my old friends knew where I lived. I'd made sure of that.

I dragged myself down the stairs. There on the doorstep was a beautiful woman with a flawless complexion, bright blue eyes, strawberry-blonde hair and an enormous bouquet of stargazer lilies. In my surprise, I didn't recognize her for a moment. Olivia.

'Did Tom send you?' I demanded.

She nodded. 'Yes. But to be honest, I was thinking of coming round anyway. These are for you.'

She pushed the flowers in my direction and then, totally unexpectedly, enveloped me in a big hug, almost crushing the bouquet. 'I'm so sorry,' she murmured. 'You've had a shit time. And I'm sorry, too, for not being friendlier to you.'

She was inside the house now, even though I hadn't

asked her in. Why did women like Olivia feel they had a natural right to do what they wanted?

'It didn't help that your daughter accused me of looking for a meal ticket,' I pointed out.

'That was Hugo, not me. He can be an utter twat.' Then she put her hand to her mouth.

Something about her being so rude and the sheer awfulness of the situation set me off then. A laugh that was almost a wail burst out of my mouth.

Briefly, Olivia looked shocked, and then she laughed too. Soon we were hysterical, leaning against the wall to stop ourselves from falling to the floor.

Finally, she grabbed my hand. 'Tell you what. Let's hit the town and get blitzed. I know this super little lunchtime bar in Soho. We can have a girly chat and dish all the dirt on our men.'

We were out of the house before I had time to think of an excuse. Within seconds, Olivia had flagged down a cab. 'This is nice, isn't it?' she said, patting my hand as we sank into the back seat.

'Why,' I asked her, 'are you suddenly being so friendly? Is it because you feel sorry for me?'

'Yes, partly,' she admitted. 'But also because I admire you.'

'Admire me?'

She shrugged. As she did so, I caught a wave of perfume. It smelt expensive.

'You're not afraid of standing out,' she continued. 'You wear what you like and you paint nudes.' The taxi driver glanced at us in the rear mirror. 'I can tell you, you're the last person we'd have expected boring old Tom to have married.'

I felt a rush in his defence. 'Actually, he's not boring.'

'Oh, come on!' Olivia made a poker face and put on a rather good imitation of Tom's voice. 'If you divide the calculus of thirty by the logic of ten and minus it by ninety-eight, what do you get?'

'I've absolutely no idea,' I said, snorting with laughter again. It was like something had broken loose inside me.

'You see, the trick about getting your own way in marriage is to pretend that everything is their idea,' Olivia was explaining half an hour later in the bar. 'You tell Tom that you're happy to have a break from IVF but that you want him to take some time off for a week or two away. Then, when you're there, you go back to being a honeymoon couple again. No pressure. No nagging. Then slowly, very slowly, you drip-feed the idea of having another go.'

I was both impressed and slightly shocked. 'Is this how you handle Hugo?' I asked.

Instantly, her expression clouded. Only for a second but it was enough. 'Some men are different,' she said.

I wanted to ask more but didn't feel I knew her well enough. Maybe she sensed this too, because she immediately changed the subject. 'Now tell me,' she said in a girlish way that reminded me of the cool crowd at school. The one that shut me out. 'We've talked about Tom's past love life. What about you? What attracted you to Tom? You two are so different.'

Hadn't I asked myself this question over and over again?

'We fancied each other, actually,' I burst out.

Olivia laughed delightedly. 'I always suspected Tom

was good in bed. It's often the quiet ones who have hidden depths.' Her eyes glinted. 'Tell me more!'

'He's steady.' I took another sip of wine. 'That's what did it, really. I knew he'd never let me down.'

'Ah,' said Olivia, clinking her glass against mine. 'I wondered if it was the old stability thing. So who hurt you, then? Come on. You can tell me. It's what girl chat is all about.'

I wanted to point out that 'girl chat' had never been my thing. Not even with Emily. There was too much in my past that I didn't want anyone to know.

'What was his name?' persisted Olivia. Her words were slurred. She'd had too much to drink. So had I. But I was better at holding it.

'I don't want to say,' I said.

'Still that raw, is it? Bet it was your first love, then. They always hurt the most.'

How did she know?

'*It will be safe, Sarah,*' he whispered, unzipping my skirt in my bedroom when my aunt was out. '*Honestly. I promise . . .*'

'How old were you then?'

'Sixteen,' I said.

Olivia raised her eyebrows. 'That's quite young. Mine was when I was eighteen. He was French. My parents knew his and we all went on holiday together in Cannes.'

Her voice went dreamy. 'My mother would have killed me if she'd known we weren't really "going for a walk" in the evenings.'

Now it was my aunt in my head.

'*You dirty girl,*' she'd shouted, coming in on us unexpectedly. '*Just like your mother. No better than a slut.*'

'Did Tom mind?' Olivia asked now.

'I don't know. We haven't talked about it.'

The truth was that Tom had once asked if I'd had a boyfriend before and I'd said there had been one or two, but they hadn't meant anything. He'd seemed pleased not to pursue the conversation. Which had been a relief.

Olivia summoned the waiter over for another bottle. 'If I were you, I wouldn't bring it up. Men like Hugo and Tom like to think they're cool, but they're very traditional really. Hugo wouldn't have married me if he'd known I wasn't a virgin.'

'Really?'

'Yes. Honestly.' She took another large sip and stared into the distance. 'Sometimes I think I've missed out on life.'

'So why did you marry him?'

Her eyes widened as if I'd asked an obvious question. 'Because he was the right kind of man. You know. He'd gone to a good school. His parents were like mine. And he earned a lot. My mother used to say "Marry where the money is. If love is there too, that's a bonus."'

'But that's awful!'

'Not really. It's practical. Besides, I did love Hugo when I married him.'

She stopped.

'And now?' I asked.

A small smile flickered on her lips. 'We've got the girls. It's different. You'll find that out when you have a baby. And don't look like that. You will. I know it. I'll make it my mission that you see the right specialists. In fact, there's this brilliant man who helped one of my other girlfriends get pregnant after years of trying.'

Other girlfriends? Did that mean I was her friend now?

She wasn't anything like Emily. But maybe that was good. No one could replace Emily, with her kind eyes.

'There's only one catch,' she said.

'What?'

'You've got to make me godmother.'

I smiled. 'It would be an honour.'

'Now,' she said, standing up and swaying, 'we ought to get a cab home. And on the way we can decide where you and Tom are going to have that break. Paris or Vienna?' Then she clapped her hands excitedly. 'I almost feel as if I am going myself! Gosh! Is that the time? Just as well someone else is picking up the girls from school. I'll need to sober up.'

I came home feeling happier and more optimistic than I had for a long time. It was going to be all right. I could feel it in my bones.

11

Tom

In another of her dramatic mood swings, Sarah came back from her lunch with Olivia full of beans. She even suggested we had a mini-break somewhere.

'Good idea,' I said. 'I'm due for some holiday.'

'I was thinking about Paris or Vienna,' she said.

'I can't take that long off. And besides, there are so many beautiful places in the UK.'

My mind went back to one of the few childhood holidays I remember with my parents. 'When I was about seven, we went to this lovely seaside town near Exeter,' I said. 'My mother loved it. She swam every morning in the sea near the hotel.'

'Then we'll go there,' said Sarah. 'Can you recall what it was called?'

'No. But I do know that Queen Victoria had stayed there as a baby. My father used to make me recite all the names of the monarchs.'

'At seven?' she asked.

'He expected a lot,' I said tightly.

'Then we should be able to find it. Leave it to me.'

And she did. It was amazing how you could remember things from so long ago. As soon as we parked outside this pretty hotel with its lovely old arched leaded windows with stunning views over the beach, I felt as though my mother's presence was with me. Strange, really, given that I was not usually a sentimental type. Yet as we sat in the dining room, I could almost imagine my mother being with us at the same table. She would have loved my wife, with that smile and sing-song voice that was so like hers.

'I feel so comfortable here,' said Sarah as we walked along the seafront, admiring the beautiful Regency architecture. 'It would be a perfect place to bring up a child.'

I made a noise that I hoped sounded like I was in agreement without encouraging further conversation. But there was no denying that I was beginning to think, more and more, that we would be happier if we didn't have this huge pressure on us. Some couples simply couldn't have children. It might not be fair but maybe it was the right thing, in view of everything. Yet, at the same time, I knew Sarah wouldn't be happy without a child. Every time we saw a family out and about, Sarah's eyes would always be drawn to the little ones, skipping along, holding their parents' hands, gazing up at them adoringly.

The simple fact was that I was not enough for her. Maybe I had to try harder to convince her otherwise.

'Tell you what,' I said. 'I'll go roller skating with you if you want.' We'd noticed some people doing it on the beachfront.

She laughed.

'But you're "challenged when it comes to coordination",' she teased.

'That doesn't mean I won't try,' I retorted. 'Remember the ice rink?'

'Then I'll take you up on it.'

What on earth was I doing? When, once again, I fell over for the umpteenth time, she conceded that I was right. 'But at least you tried,' she said, putting her hand in mine after we'd changed back into our proper shoes.

Afterwards, we made love. Frantic, passionate, uninhibited love while the sea shone through the window. This woman – my wife – was amazing. Until we'd met, I'd never imagined sex could be like this. Once she'd accepted the disappointment of not having children, we'd be all right. I was certain of that.

But things never work out how you expect.

'Pregnant? How can you be?' I asked a few weeks later.

'Isn't it amazing! Completely naturally too. Well, almost.'

'What do you mean?'

She flushed. 'Olivia gave me a few tips, like taking some supplements and having acupuncture. She has this brilliant woman who I've seen a couple of times.'

'I didn't know that.'

'I didn't want to tell you in case it didn't work. Of course, I'm not going to get my hopes up.'

Five months passed. Sarah blossomed. She'd always been beautiful but now her skin had taken on a striking brightness. A small bump had formed. The latest scan showed that everything was 'perfectly normal'. The new consultant, who had insisted on a scan every month, said that perhaps the original diagnosis of internal scarring had been 'over-exaggerated'. We'd hugged each other with excitement.

One July afternoon, we went for a walk. I hadn't wanted us to because I thought she should rest. But she'd insisted. 'It's a beautiful day,' she said. 'Perfect for a Saturday stroll.'

So we went to see the proposed site for the new London Eye. 'Imagine!' said Sarah. 'When it's finished, we'll have our baby!'

My heart swelled with pride. Our baby! I was beginning to see how much I'd wanted a child. It had only been the fear that everything would go wrong again that had put me off.

Sarah dragged me to Camden market, one of her favourite haunts.

'I thought we'd buy some baby clothes,' she said, tugging my sleeve. 'Look. There's a stall through here.'

This was a good sign. Apart from those white baby bootees, which I'd discovered when looking for something in our bedroom a few weeks ago, my wife had refused to buy anything in case it was 'tempting fate'.

'We'll get a blue jacket and a pink,' she babbled excitedly. 'To cover all eventualities. Mind you, I'm sure it's a boy. Olivia did the ring test on me.'

'The what?'

She blushed. 'I kept it quiet because I thought you'd think it was stupid. It's probably a bit of an old wives' tale. But someone holds a gold ring attached to a piece of cord and holds it over your stomach. It starts to rotate. If it goes one way, you're having a boy. If it goes the other, it's a girl.'

'That sounds highly unscientific to me,' I said.

'Maybe!' My wife was laughing. 'But it was good fun. Olivia's lovely. She's even given me some ridiculously expensive cream so I won't have any stretch marks afterwards.'

We took a cut down a side street. 'Spare a couple of quid, mate?' asked a woman squatting on the pavement. She had dreadlocks and a hard look on her lined face.

Then she said something that would haunt me to this day.

'Sarah? It's you, isn't it? Sarah Vincent.'

My wife looked down as I watched her face go very still. Then she grabbed my hand and pulled me on.

'Who was that?'

'I don't know.'

'But she knew your name,' I said, confused.

'I don't know why.' Sarah was walking faster. 'Maybe she was a student of mine at the centre. I can't remember everyone. Come on.'

'Sarah,' called out the woman. 'It's Kelly. You remember. Don't ignore an old mate.'

She was running up behind us now. How dare she grab Sarah's arm like that?

'Get your hands off my wife,' I said angrily, 'or I'll call the police.'

'The cops?' The woman threw back her head and roared with laughter. Her teeth were stained, with big gaps between them. 'Sarah wouldn't want that, would you, love?'

My chest tightened. 'What do you mean?'

'Shall I tell him, Sarah love? Or will you?'

12

Sarah

'I think,' said Tom, after he'd handed over a crisp ten-pound note and ushered me into a local café, 'you'd better tell me everything.' He glanced at my tummy. 'I need to know.'

It wasn't too late, I told myself. I could argue that Kelly had been drunk or high or both and didn't know what she was talking about. But at the same time, I felt relief. Perhaps the best thing to do was come clean.

'I've been wanting to tell you for a long time, Tom,' I said, stirring my coffee carefully. 'But there's never been the right moment.'

His face crumpled.

I realized then I should have kept quiet. He'd leave me and the baby. We'd be on our own. But I had to say something. I took a deep breath.

'I never had friends at school. People tended to shy away from you if you had no parents. It made you different.'

There was another half-nod from Tom. Slightly encouraged, I continued. 'But at art college, you didn't get questions about where you'd come from. All we wanted to do was draw and paint and be expressive. I felt accepted for the first time.'

He nodded again.

'I fell in with what some people might call the wrong crowd although they didn't seem like that to me. I also had other friends too from a more privileged background. There was one in particular. Emily. We were best friends.' I wanted to tell him more about her, but was afraid of letting too much out.

I shut my eyes. I'd gone so far that it was impossible to stop. I could see her face now in front of me. Golden curls. China-blue eyes. Her manner of listening with her hand on her chin. To calm myself, I tried to concentrate on the noise around me. The chatter at neighbouring tables. The clink of cups. A clattering noise that suggested someone had dropped a tray somewhere. My thudding heart.

'One night, when I was at a party, someone handed me a pill.'

Tom groaned.

'They made me feel so good about myself,' I whispered. 'After a while, my friends said they couldn't keep giving me drugs. I had to pay for them. So I started dealing too. You have to understand, I didn't know what else to do, and it was only for a year or so. That woman – Kelly – she was someone I used to know back then.'

Tom was fiddling with his empty cup. He couldn't even look at me.

I stood up. This was no good.

'Where are you going?' His voice was sharp, but his face looked like a worried little boy's.

'Home to pack.'

He gave a short laugh. 'Is that it?'

I shrugged, trying to keep my voice steady. 'Looks like you've already made the decision.'

'I didn't mean "Is that it?" like that,' said Tom. 'I meant "Is that it?" in the sense of "Have you told me everything?"'

Now was the time. This was where I could confess the lot.

I looked down at my small bump. The miracle that was growing inside me.

Despite the miscarriages, I had a good feeling about him. I knew in my heart he was a boy. I owed it to my son to give him a good life. I had to make sure his father stayed. I didn't want him to feel different for having just one parent, as I had done. Times have changed now but, back then, an absent father was a big deal.

'Yes,' I said. 'I've told you everything. What about you?'

I'm not sure why I said the last bit. Maybe it was to try and stop him asking any more awkward questions. I certainly didn't expect what came next.

'Actually,' he said. 'I have some things about *my* past that I ought to have shared with you before.'

Now it was my turn to feel confused. 'What do you mean?'

'My father died of liver failure because he was an alcoholic.'

'Why didn't you say before?' I asked.

I'd never met Tom's dad. He'd died shortly before we got together. I'd tried to encourage Tom to talk about it but he wouldn't.

'I was ashamed,' he said. 'It made me even more determined not to drink. As for drugs . . .' He gave me a 'how could you?' look. 'I've always thought they were evil.'

There was a short silence, then Tom continued. 'I

sometimes think I'd have been a very different person if my mother had been around when I grew up. I was very close to her.'

He was speaking in an almost dreamy way that I'd never heard before. 'She had a wonderful smile. Rather like yours, in fact. When she went . . .'

He stopped.

There were actually tears in his eyes.

I wanted to reach out, but something told me to stay very still or he would clam up. I knew instinctively that Tom needed to get this out.

'When she went, it was as if a light had gone out in the world. It was the last time I had felt truly loved. Until I met you.'

I couldn't help myself from talking now. 'That's lovely,' I whispered. 'But I'm so sorry you had to go through all that.'

Big mistake. My words appeared to pull him out of a trance. He shook himself. Back came the Tom who couldn't show his feelings. 'It's fine. These things happen. That's when I went to boarding school. Best thing for me, probably. Otherwise I'd have been at home with my father and his new wife.' He made another 'hah' sound. 'Didn't take them long.'

'You know,' I said softly. 'We've been more honest with each other than we've ever been before. We should have had these conversations earlier.' I reached out for his hand. 'I'm sorry.'

'I'm sorry too,' he said. 'I don't approve of what you did. But, well, I can sort of see how it might have happened.'

We were going to be all right! My heart lifted.

Then I gasped.

'What is it?'

'I think he moved,' I said. 'Just a flutter! Feel. He might do it again.'

I placed Tom's hand, which I was still holding, gently on my stomach. I felt the flutter again.

Tom's face looked like that little girl I'd seen staring into Selfridges' window a few Christmases ago. Amazed. Disbelieving. As if he'd witnessed something miraculous.

'Do you still love me?' I asked.

There was a short silence. I could barely breathe. 'Yes,' he said.

I knew he wouldn't have said it if he hadn't meant it. Tom wasn't that kind of person.

But he was silent all the way home. This scared me. I needed to get the old Tom back. The one who would have said, 'Yes, of course, I love you,' in a heartbeat.

How could I do that?

Then it came to me. Olivia. She'd know what to do.

'You dealt drugs?' she said when I'd finished. I'd called her as soon as Tom had left the house the next morning. Admittedly, I told her it was 'only' a couple of pills for friends.

'Wow, Sarah!' Then she sounded uneasy. 'Don't tell anyone, but I did a bit of coke once or twice. Tom and Hugo have always been very anti that sort of thing. It's OK, though. We can sort it. I mean, it's in your past, isn't it?'

I took comfort from the 'we'. I wasn't quite sure why Olivia was being so nice but it felt good to have someone to share things with.

'You're going to have to employ all of your feminine wiles to get him back on side,' she added. 'Make him feel good about himself in bed. Tell him what a great father he's going to be.'

'I'll try,' I said doubtfully.

'Hey, come on! You're not the only woman who's had to win back her husband. Hugo and I have been through our bad patches.'

'What do you mean?'

'Oh you know,' she said airily. 'Little niggles; nothing big. How about we grab some dinner next week to plan your strategy and then see a film afterwards? That new Harrison Ford movie is out and Hugo won't go.'

Great idea. How wrong I'd been to misjudge this woman. Olivia was exactly the friend I needed. Someone I could trust.

The rain has started again.
    The tyres are squeaking on the road.
    It feels weird, like this isn't happening.
    I start to shiver.
    He notices.
    'You're not scared, are you?'
    'No,' I say. 'Course not.'

13

Tom

Before Sarah, the only time I had felt loved was when my mother was alive. But my wife had made me feel secure in myself once more.

Until now.

'If you love someone, you don't deceive them,' I told her as we argued again a few nights after I'd found out the truth.

I knew she was trying, because for once the house was tidy, and she'd cooked my favourite dinner: salmon en croute. But I couldn't get it out of my mind. She was just like my father, who never knew when to stop drinking. An addict.

She gripped my arm. 'But don't you see, Tom? It's precisely *because* I love you that I couldn't tell you the truth sooner.' She looked down at her stomach. 'I didn't want you to leave us.'

'I wouldn't do that.'

I meant it. I knew all too well what it was like for a child to be abandoned by a parent. That's how I'd seen my mother's death. I'd felt she'd left me. She should have tried harder to have stayed alive, for my sake. Of course, as an adult, I realize that was impossible.

Yet my head was in such a muddle. There were so many thoughts going in and out. Somehow I had to find a way of controlling my brain and making sense of this situation.

But when I called Hugo and suggested a brief catch-up after work the following week – not that I'd have told him the details of what Sarah had done, but I thought it would be good to blow off some steam – I discovered he had his own problems.

'Olivia wants another baby,' he told me at his club. We were sitting in a secluded corner of the bar where there was sufficient noise around us to permit a conversation like this. 'I reckon that Sarah being pregnant has made her broody.'

'Wouldn't you like a third?'

He snorted. 'No way. We can't afford it for a start. And besides, kids put pressure on you as a couple. There've been times, to be honest, when we've had some pretty heavy conversations about staying together.'

'You two?' I asked, shocked. Olivia and Hugo had married quite young – soon after university, where they'd met. I couldn't imagine either of them being with someone else. 'You never told me this,' I said.

'Well, I don't tell you everything.'

I felt a bit hurt by this. So I stayed silent, watching Hugo drain the double whisky he'd ill-advisedly ordered at the beginning of our conversation. Not for the first time, I was glad I did not drink.

'She got particularly shirty when she found this woman's phone number in my pocket,' he added.

'What?'

'It didn't mean anything. It was just someone I met at a bar. The kids were small then. I wasn't getting any sleep and I felt she was only interested in them. I didn't have an affair or anything like that.'

'Did she believe you?'

'I think so.'

I wasn't sure that I did.

He wiped his forehead. 'We've come through. But there's no way we're having a third and all that pressure again. So she's being a bit cool with me right now.'

Hugo waved his hand at the waitress. 'Make the most of this time before it arrives.'

'Actually, I'm quite looking forward to taking my child around the Natural History Museum and Science Museum when it's older,' I said.

'Hah! Kids have their own ideas on what's fun and what isn't. You'll discover that. As for when it arrives, make sure you get a nanny. And whatever you do, watch out for the R word.'

'The what?'

'R for routine.'

Ah! This was a subject that came up regularly in my well-thumbed books on how to bring up babies. 'You know me, Hugo, I rather like a routine.'

He took another swig. 'You think that now. But her idea of routine won't be yours, if my wife is anything to go by. Ours have to have their meals at the same time every day or you'd think it was the end of the world. Olivia says it's to make them feel secure. But it's goodbye to impulsivity.'

I wasn't very keen on impulsivity myself, so I felt a certain empathy with Olivia.

'And,' added Hugo, who was beginning to sound a little drunk, 'she won't even consider sending them away.'

'We hated boarding,' I pointed out.

'But it was good for us, Wilkins.' He thumped the table

with his fist. An older club member, walking past, threw us a disapproving glance. 'Taught us discipline, didn't it?'

Neither of us mentioned Chapman's name. I still thought of him almost every day. Of his wife and kids.

'Anyway,' continued Hugo, lurching to his feet, 'I'd better go back and pretend to play happy families.' For a second, he looked like he was going to give me one of those manly hugs that some chaps do. I stepped back. That wasn't our style.

'How about you and Sarah?'

'We're good,' I said.

'I have to hand it to you, Tom. I was pretty shocked when you first took up with her. But I've come round. Olivia always said Sarah was a breath of fresh air. I've noticed that she's got really chummy with her. Always talking on the phone and putting it down when I come in the room.' Then his face went dark. 'I hope my wife doesn't get any ideas from her. Your Sarah led a pretty racy life, didn't she?'

'What do you mean?'

'Come on, Tom. She's an artist.'

I breathed a sigh of relief. For a minute I had thought Sarah might have told Olivia about taking drugs; perhaps even the dealing.

That night I couldn't sleep. For some reason, even though Hugo had been really positive about Sarah this time, I couldn't get that slur he'd once used out of my head. The same one that little Clemmie had picked up on.

Meal ticket.

What if he'd been right all along? Sarah had done something awful for money before. What if she was just with me for my money now?

Eventually, around five a.m., I got out of bed.

'Where are you going?' murmured Sarah as I headed for the bathroom.

'I need to be at work first thing,' I said. It wasn't entirely true. But there was always something for me to do. 'Go back to sleep.'

'You're even earlier than usual,' said a voice.

It was Hilary, the actuary we'd taken on last year. She had an impressive CV. Lady Margaret Hall, Oxford. A decent stint with a rival. And now she'd joined us. Like me, she preferred to arrive early and stay late.

'I've got something I need to crack on with,' I said.

'Me too.'

We'd been moved to an open-plan office – something I abhorred. I needed my own space. But I didn't mind when it was only Hilary and me. She didn't engage in conversation or interrupt by saying she was going out to get a coffee and inquiring whether I wanted one too.

Today, however, I couldn't concentrate. The figures that had always been so comforting were leaping around all over the place. All I could think of was that my wife had not only taken drugs. She'd also dealt them.

At one point, I found myself letting out a groan.

'Is something wrong?' asked Hilary. I looked up. She wasn't like the other women in the office who wore heels that were more suited to going out in the evening. Nor did she plaster her face with make-up. She even enjoyed cryptic crosswords. I only knew this because she was finishing one off in her newspaper while we were waiting for the lift up to the offices one morning.

'If you don't mind me saying,' she said now, 'you appear to have the world on your shoulders.'

It wasn't the most original remark, but it comforted me with its old-fashioned familiarity. It also surprised me, somewhat. I'd never gone in for office friendships. You went to work. You did your best. And you kept your private life to yourself.

'Not at all,' I said briskly. 'On the contrary. I'm simply a bit tired. My wife's pregnant and she isn't sleeping well.'

'That's wonderful news,' she said. 'The pregnancy, I mean. I was not aware of that.'

That's because I hadn't broadcast it. No one knew about Sarah's miscarriages or the IVF. I'd deliberately kept it all to myself. The last thing I wanted was someone asking me how I felt.

Yet somehow – and I'd no idea why – I found myself telling Hilary about all of this. Of course, I made no allusion to my wife's unsavoury past.

To my surprise, Hilary did not appear shocked to hear about our attempts to conceive. 'I can understand why you don't want anyone to know, but there are times when it's good to share. Don't worry. I won't mention it to anyone. But if you ever need to talk, I am here. Personally, I think it's wonderful that the two of you didn't give up trying to have a child. But then again, I am not really the motherly type myself. I cherish my independence too much.'

Hilary looked down at her left hand as if making a point. There was no ring on it.

Of course, I never did 'need to talk' with Hilary again. I was too annoyed with myself – and embarrassed – for letting my guard slip. I carried on instead, telling no one about my doubts.

Then one morning, four weeks before our 'due date', as the textbooks called it, I was making a Saturday morning cup of tea for Sarah when I heard a cry from the bedroom.

'Tom! Quick. I think my waters have gone.'

I knew all about waters. I'd become a self-taught expert through textbooks and the classes we'd been going to. But this was too soon.

'Get me to hospital!' she cried. Her eyes were wide with terror. 'As quickly as you can.'

'It's going to be all right,' I said, helping her to the car.

'But what if it isn't?' she sobbed. 'I can't lose this one. I can't.'

I tried to keep my eyes on the road. How would Sarah survive if it went wrong again?

But at the back of my mind there was a thought I immediately tried to banish. If Sarah did lose the child, I would be free to leave.

It must be the fear, I told myself. *You want this. You love her. Even if you're not suited on paper.*

'You have a son,' said the midwife placing a swaddled tiny body in my arms.

Sarah's face was wet with tears.

'We have a baby,' she whispered. 'We actually have a baby. I knew he'd be a boy.'

'Is he all right?' I asked softly, looking down at this small red wrinkled face staring up at me.

'He's beautiful,' said the midwife. 'Bigger than we expected, considering he's early.'

Bigger? He seemed so fragile. What if I dropped him? I was not prone to panic. At least, I didn't like to think of myself that way. But now I felt well and truly out of my depth. Sarah, on the other hand, was holding him as if she knew exactly what she was doing.

'We are taking Baby and Mum next door to do a few checks,' added the nurse.

'Does he have to go onto a machine or anything like that?' I asked, worried.

'No need for that. These checks are routine.'

'Shall I come too?' I asked.

'No, love. You sit there and get some rest.'

She winked at Sarah. 'I like to let the men think they've done all the hard work. What are you going to call him, then?'

'Freddie,' I said swiftly. It's what we'd agreed, whatever the sex. If our child had been a girl, we were going to name her Frederica. It was my mother's name.

I sat down heavily on the chair while the nurse escorted Sarah and Freddie away. I couldn't believe we suddenly had a baby. I was a father! The word, when applied to myself, felt so strange and yet wonderful.

Sarah's notes were on the side. I took a look to check her due date again. They had everything here. Her whole history . . .

I couldn't resist leafing back to her earlier years. And then I stopped.

The words swam in front of my eyes. I wanted to be sick.

'*Is that it?*' I'd asked after that awful afternoon in Camden when we'd met that Kelly woman. '*Have you told me everything?*'

'*Yes*,' she'd said.

But in front of me, I had visible proof to the contrary.

How could she have done this? I had fallen in love with a woman who wasn't what she'd said she was. Who wasn't what I thought.

Slowly, the terrible truth began to dawn on me.

I had a son now. With a wife I could no longer trust.

14
Sarah

As soon as Freddie and I returned to the ward after our checks, I knew something was wrong.

Tom was looking at me in the same way he'd done when Kelly had stopped us on the street.

What was it?

'Ah, there they are,' said the nurse, picking up my notes, which were lying on the trolley. 'I wondered what I'd done with them.'

The blue folder was open. A cold feeling clutched my chest. Instinctively, I knew that Tom had read them.

He knew.

I crawled back into bed, cradling Freddie in my arms. The only person left in the world who loved me. Because Tom wasn't going to. Not now. Not after this.

'Why?' he said coldly after the midwife had left.

'What do you mean?' I asked, playing for time.

'Why didn't you tell me?' Then he repeated the words off pat from my file as though he'd memorized them.

'Treatment for chest infection.' He looked up. 'At age twenty-one.'

My skin goose pimpled. Remembering. It had taken ages to be seen by a doctor. By then, I'd got a really high temperature.

'Yes,' I said.

'But you weren't seen by an ordinary doctor, were you?' he said.

'No.'

I could see the window now in the medical centre. The bars. The officer standing by me. The handcuffs biting into my skin.

'There's a stamp after this comment. It shows where the doctor's "surgery" was. HMP Placton. You were in prison.'

'I can explain,' I said quickly.

'Please do.'

Tom wasn't normally sarcastic.

I took a deep breath. I'd known all along it would come to this. 'There was a party. I dealt some drugs. I got arrested.'

A flash of that night came back to me. Emily's face. Scared. Me screaming as they took me away in handcuffs. *No! Help me! Emily!*

'And you went to prison?'

I nodded.

His voice was incredulous. 'How long for?'

'Six years.'

Six long years. Six years of not breathing fresh air apart from our short daily exercise. Six years of feeling dirty, both inside and out. Six years of living on my nerves, terrified in case someone tried to kill me or rape me or both. Prisoners are not the only ones who break the law inside.

'It would have been reduced for good behaviour,' I said quietly, 'but one of the women beat me up in the bathroom because I spoke out when she jumped the queue. I fought back and she fell, breaking her leg. The other women were her mates and backed her. It was her word against mine.'

I could tell from his face that he doubted my story. But it was true. Yet how could I blame him for not believing me?

I looked down at Freddie in my arms. He was sleeping. Instinctively, I bent down and nuzzled the top of his head. His hair smelt so sweet. So comforting. A million miles away from my past.

'After prison I stayed in a hostel for a time. Then I moved around a lot, sleeping on friends' couches. I even dossed on the streets for a while.'

Tom exhaled heavily. Why didn't he actually say something?

I was dimly aware of a nurse coming in, looking at us and then going away. Reluctantly, I continued.

'Then, a few years later, I got a break. This new arts centre opened. They employed people who'd been inside but couldn't find work. And I got the job.'

Even as I told him, I remembered the thrill. No one can know how good it feels to get a second chance unless it happens to them.

'This was the place where I met you?' asked Tom.

Where I met you. It sounded so romantic. Except that now I'd ruined everything.

'Yes. I'd been working at the centre for three years by then.'

He frowned. 'But you hadn't given up drugs at that point. I smelt marijuana.'

'It belonged to a neighbour who'd come round. That was the truth. It wasn't me. Honestly.'

Again I could see that he didn't believe me. The problem with lies is that they build up a bank of mistrust which never goes away.

'I was doing my best, Tom. I really was. I was getting my act together.'

He took off his glasses, wiped them on the spare linen handkerchief he always carried and put them back again. In one way, it was a comfort that Tom didn't allow a confession as big as this to affect his routine.

'And then you met me and thought I was your way out.'

'If that's what you think,' I said tightly. 'Although don't forget it was *you* who visited the following week and insisted I came back to your place.'

'You were ill. I wanted to look after you.'

He looked at Freddie, nestling up against my breast. 'Just as I wanted to look after our baby.'

'Wanted?' I repeated. So it was over, then. Part of me was almost relieved.

'I can't believe how many lies you've told me. After we met that *friend* of yours in Camden, I specifically asked you to tell me if there was anything else and you swore there wasn't.'

'I was scared of telling you,' I burst out. 'Besides, it was a long time ago. I've learned my lesson. I've paid for what I did.'

Tom shook his head. 'You saw me coming, didn't you? Hugo was right.'

'That's not fair, Tom! I fell in love with you. I hadn't done anything bad since I'd got out. I was ready to make a new start.'

'I used to think that. But now I'm not so sure.' He

laughed hoarsely. The sound made little Freddie stir in my arms.

I bent down and held my cheek against our baby's. So smooth. So unblemished. So pure. Unlike me. In the distance, I could hear an ambulance siren. Even in the midst of my own chaos, I desperately hoped that whoever needed help would be all right.

'Why did you want a baby with me so much?' I heard Tom say.

I looked down at my son again. What would he do when he realized that his mother had made so many mistakes?

'Because I love you,' I said. My voice was cracked with emotion. 'I wanted to create a family. You're a good man. Please don't leave us.'

He said nothing. I could tell he was considering it.

I began sobbing. Freddie's long dark eyelashes were flickering and he was showing signs of waking. He was less than an hour old and yet already I felt as though he had been here for ever. This was our flesh and blood.

Then he began to whimper. I undid my nightdress and he latched on to my breast with a force that said, 'You're mine. I need you, even if he doesn't.'

My husband's voice rang through the air, making us both jump. 'You said you'd never lie to me again.'

Tom's eyes were wet.

'I'm sorry,' I said, pulling Freddie off my chest and holding him out to my husband. 'Hold him. *Please.*'

Our son was yelling now with fury at having his milk taken away from him so abruptly. But I needed Tom to hold him. To bond. To make him stay.

Tom put on his coat.

'Where are you going?' I cried.

He looked as though he was in a daze. 'I don't know.'

Then my husband walked out of my hospital room, leaving the two of us alone.

15

Tom

I walked for hours, as far away from the hospital as I could. My legs marched to a beat. My wife had gone to prison for dealing drugs. And she'd assaulted another woman when she'd been there. Six years. She had a criminal record. One more lie to add to all the others.

I'd told myself that we both had regrets. That I shouldn't judge someone for their past.

But perhaps Hugo had been right all along. Sarah and I had different values. How stupid had I been?

Then I saw Freddie's face. His smooth skin. His innocent eyes. I hadn't held him, but I'd wanted to.

I was a father now. I had responsibilities.

How could I abandon him? I knew all too well what it was like to have an absent father.

And yet I still didn't know what to do.

Eventually I found myself on Waterloo Bridge. A woman in a sleeping bag was sitting cross-legged with a cardboard placard bearing a message in red capital letters.

NO EAT FOUR DAYS.

Did that mean she hadn't eaten for days or she hadn't eaten for four days?

I walked past. Then I spotted a coffee kiosk. I bought a cappuccino and a doughnut and went back to give it to her.

I'd never in my life done this before.

But Sarah's words haunted me. '*I dossed on the streets for a while.*'

The woman looked at me, mumbled something in a language I didn't understand and raised the cup to her lips.

'Be careful,' I said. 'It's hot.'

I walked on swiftly. It took an hour and nineteen minutes to reach the small cobbled lane near Dalston Junction outside the pretty mews terraced cottage that Hugo and Olivia had bought.

The antique knocker was in the shape of a black lion's head. It wasn't as practical as a bell in my view because you had to bang it several times before being heard. On the other side, I could hear raised voices.

'You'll go to bed when I say.'

'Only if I can take my Xbox.'

I knocked again. A clearly flustered Olivia eventually opened the door. Her cheeks were pink and her hair was tied back in an untidy knot. But she still managed to look beautiful.

'Tom?'

'Sarah had the baby early,' I said.

She grabbed my arm. 'Oh my God! Is everything all right?'

'No,' I said. I remained standing on the doorstep.

Olivia covered her face with her hands. 'I'm so sorry. What happened?'

'Did you know she'd been in prison?'

I'd intended to tell Hugo this. Not Olivia. She looked stunned.

'No. Why? What's going on?' She was leading me into the kitchen. Plates with leftover food were still on the table. I slipped on a piece of pasta on the floor and only righted myself in time by grabbing a chair.

'It's complicated.'

'But is the baby all right? And Sarah?'

'Oh yes.' I heard myself laugh hoarsely. 'It's me that isn't.'

'Uncle Tom! Uncle Tom!' Clemmie had come running down the stairs and was now jumping up and down in front of me. 'Have you bought us a present?'

'Clemmie! That's very rude. Now go to bed. Your godfather and I need to talk.'

'Actually,' I said, looking round. 'I wanted to see Hugo.'

Olivia rolled her eyes. 'He's out playing squash.'

'He hates squash.'

'Well, he likes it now,' she said sharply. 'Unless of course it's an excuse.'

'I need to go,' I said, turning round.

'But you only arrived a few minutes ago. And you haven't told me about the prison . . .'

I looked at Clemmie meaningfully. Olivia took my point. 'Go and play with your Xbox thingy, in the sitting room, darling.'

She turned back to me.

'Sarah's on her own in hospital,' I said. 'Well, not actually alone. She has the child with her.'

I was scared of saying 'Freddie'. His name made him too real. Too hard to walk away from.

'Perhaps,' I said to Olivia, 'you could drive her back when they let her out. The baby too.'

'Why don't you?' she asked.

'Because, as I told you at the beginning of our conversation, my wife has told me things that have made me re-evaluate our relationship.'

'What exactly did she do?'

'She went to prison for dealing *drugs*.'

There was something about the look on Olivia's face that told me she wasn't that surprised.

'Listen.' Olivia took me by the arm. I moved away quickly. 'We've all done things we're not proud of. How long ago was it?'

'She started her sentence when she was nineteen.'

'There you are, then. She's changed. Like we all have. The thing is, Tom, that whether you like it or not, your son will bind you together for life. And, trust me, kids need two parents. Why do you think I've stayed with Hugo for so long?'

I thought about what Hugo told me about the woman who had given him her number.

'Please collect her from the hospital.' I gave her a piece of paper with the address on. 'I just don't feel able to.'

She looked confused. 'Where will you be?'

'I don't know.'

'And I don't know how you can do this.' Olivia's eyes were hard. Damning. I'd never seen her like this before. 'Your wife has just had a baby and you're walking out on them already?'

'I need to think before I make my final decision.'

'Do you know what?' said Olivia, following me to the front door. 'I used to try and make allowances after what you and Hugo went through at school. But it's thanks to the pair of you that your friend shot himself.'

I was on the doorstep now. 'That's not true.'

'He didn't tell you? Hugo rang Chapman the night before he died. I overheard him on the phone. "If you write about what happened at school," he said, "Tom and I will deny it. We'll drag your name through the mud."'

I went still. 'He couldn't have done.'

'Ask him. It wouldn't surprise me if that's what made the poor man finish himself off.'

The door closed behind me.

Stunned, I called Hugo's mobile but it went through to voicemail. I never cared for leaving messages. You could not retract words if you said the wrong ones.

So I walked on, thinking about Sarah's confession.

Olivia's words also thumped through my head. '*But it's thanks to the pair of you that your friend shot himself.*'

I rang Hugo's number again. This time he picked up. 'Is it true?' I asked. Then I told him what Olivia had said.

'I had to.' Hugo's voice was immediately defensive. 'Can you imagine what it would have done to us, Tom, if he'd written about what we did? About what happened to us. I didn't know the stupid idiot was going to kill himself.'

I cut him off in anger and disgust. Not only with him but at myself too. What if Olivia was right? By implication, I too might have tipped Chapman over the edge.

I kept walking, no idea where I was going.

After a while, my office loomed up before me with its

very high roofline that made it stand out in the street. The lights were kept on, even through the night. There had been several board meetings about that but it had eventually been decided that it was worth the expense because it reminded passers-by that our firm was there.

'Working late?' asked the security guard.

'Yes,' I replied briefly.

It was a relief to get into my office. Everything was in its place here. The night cleaners had already been and gone. There was a canned fresh-air smell. My desk was ordered. My box of wipes was next to the keyboard.

'Tom,' said a voice.

I started. 'I didn't realize anyone was here,' I said.

Hilary's desk was slightly hidden behind a pillar. The others were on full display. I'd sometimes wondered if she'd chosen this one deliberately.

'I'm working late.' She put her head on one side as if studying me. 'We were told you weren't coming in today.' As she spoke, she appeared to pat her skirt, which was spread around her on her chair. It was a red-and-black tartan design.

'I hadn't intended to,' I said shortly.

'Are you ill?'

'No.' I sat down at my computer. Hilary was standing next to me now. I was aware of a flowery smell.

'How is your wife? It's not long until the baby, is it?'

As I've already said, I don't normally discuss my private business with members of staff. But I'd already done so with Hilary before.

'She had the child today.'

'That's wonderful!'

I opened my screen.

'It was a month early.'

'Are they both all right?'

Her voice was kind.

'Yes,' I said.

'But *you're* not, are you, Tom? I can tell.'

'I'm perfectly fine,' I said.

To my embarrassment, this came out as a sob.

I heard her pulling up a chair next to me. Her voice was gentle. Understanding. I looked down at the floor, focusing on her sensible flat brown shoes.

She put her hand on my shoulder. It felt surprisingly reassuring. 'Why don't you tell me all about it?' she said.

We're nearly there.

That's what he says.

I don't ask what we're going to do, because I don't want to seem scared.

Anyway, he won't tell me.

It's how he works.

It's part of the game.

And even though this freaks me out, it's exciting at the same time.

Much better than being bored.

Much better than being at home.

16

Sarah

The ward lights had been dimmed. Curtains had been drawn around our beds. I could hear other babies making squeaky and snuffling noises. Mothers reassuring them. Male voices too. Fathers were allowed to stay as long as they wanted. Outside, I could see the city lights.

Tom had been gone for hours. He wasn't coming back.

Two voices competed inside me. *How are we going to manage on our own?* That was the new me. The other was the old me. The one who was used to surviving. *We will be all right.*

If only I'd known then what was to come, perhaps I would have listened to the second voice.

Or rather 'voices'. We. That was the difference between the past and now. There were two of us. I looked down at Freddie, curled up in my arms, my milk dribbling out of one corner of his rosebud mouth. My breast was still bare from when we'd both fallen asleep after the last feed.

His eyelashes were so long! Just like Tom's. Mine too. His skin was paler than mine but darker than his father's. There was something about his little ears . . . they didn't have any lobes. Not that it mattered, of course.

'Whatever happens,' I told Freddie, 'we'll get through. I've done it on my own before. So we'll be fine.'

Then I stopped. Who was I kidding? A child needed both parents. Look what had happened to me.

Freddie gave a little jump in his sleep. Instinctively, I bent my face down and felt his soft cheek against mine. He smelt right. That might sound a strange thing to say but it was the only way I could put it. I breathed him in hungrily. Then I found my eyes filling with tears.

'Got the weeps, I see,' said a nurse bustling in. I liked this one. She'd helped Freddie latch on, although he already seemed to 'know the way', as she'd put it. 'Very normal. Now, where's that nice husband of yours?'

'Gone,' I said shortly.

'Needed a walk, I expect.'

'No,' I said. 'He's left us.'

She shot me an uncertain look. 'It can be a bit of a shock for some men when they're a dad for the first time, especially when baby is early like this little one. Still, he's doing very well, isn't he?'

'It took us years to have him,' I sniffle. 'And now Freddie's only going to have me.'

The nurse squeezed my hand. 'It's amazing how you can get through hurdles in life. I was actually coming in to tell you that your friend Olivia is here to see you. It's a bit late for visitors, but I can bend the rules briefly if you like.'

Olivia? Tom must have told her and Hugo.

Hot tears began to roll down my face just as Olivia glided in, wearing impossibly tight jeans and a beautifully cut suede beige jacket. In her hands she had a little box with twirly blue ribbons and a card.

'Sarah,' she said, sitting down at the side of my bed. 'I'm so sorry. Tom came to see us. He told us about you being in prison and he, well he asked if I'd take you back to your place when you're discharged.'

'Did he say he was leaving us?'

Olivia hesitated. 'He said he needed time to think.'

My heart plummeted. 'That's male-speak for "yes" then,' I whispered numbly.

'Not necessarily . . .'

Then she caught sight of Freddie. It was almost as if she'd remembered why I was here. 'Oh,' she breathed. 'Isn't he absolutely perfect? I'd forgotten how tiny babies are. May I hold him?'

But Olivia, with that innate self-confidence of hers, was already picking him up.

Freddie began to yell. 'You want Mummy, don't you?' she said, gently placing him back in my arms. 'And quite right too.' Then she turned to me. 'Why didn't you tell me you'd been in jail?'

'Shhh,' I said. Olivia's plummy tones weren't exactly quiet.

'I thought we were friends! I told you loads of things about me.'

'This is different,' I pointed out. 'I thought you'd be shocked.'

Olivia shrugged. 'I had an uncle who went down for fraud. We all knew about it but when he came out, my parents told us we had to pretend he'd been working abroad.' She leaned forward with a definite glint of curiosity. 'What was it like?'

Where should I begin?

'Horrible.' I shuddered. 'Most of the women either hated me or they wanted to have a relationship.'

Olivia's eyes widened.

'And the prison officers were worse. They'd have their favourites and turn away if one of them did something wrong.' There was a surprised sound from the bed next to me but I couldn't stop myself. 'When I confronted a woman for trying to jump a queue, she beat me up. I fought back to save myself but I hurt her and one of the officers took her side. I got slammed into isolation for six weeks.'

Perhaps it was the intensity of having given birth plus the anaesthetic, but all the old memories were spilling out. 'I didn't see anyone. They just left food in my cell. I thought I'd go mad.'

'You poor love,' said Olivia, taking my hand.

'But I deserved it. Drugs are bad. They kill people.'

'Yes, but you were young. You'd been through a lot.'

Instinctively, I squeezed her fingers. This was what I'd always needed. Understanding. Not judgement.

'Shall I tell you something too?'

I nodded.

'After you and I got talking about our first loves, I searched Facebook for that French boy I told you about.'

'Did you find him?'

'Yes. He was fat and hairy and twice divorced with six kids! So obviously I didn't get in touch.' She roared with laughter. Since getting to know her better in the last few months, I'd noticed that Olivia had an infectious laugh that I'd never seen when she was in her husband's company. It made me feel better. For a split second. Then I looked down at Freddie.

'What are we going to do on our own?'

'You're not on your own.' Her eyes sparkled. 'Tell you what. Instead of me driving you home, spend a few nights with us when you're discharged. It will make Tom miss you.'

I gasped. 'I couldn't do that.'

'Of course you could. Don't you see? You do it like this.' She paused. Her eyes dropped. It was as if I was watching an actress changing roles. Then she lifted her head and her eyes were doleful. 'I understand this has been an awful shock for you, Tom. I should have told you what I did before. Of course, I want you to stay with us. But not just because we have a son. I want you to stay because you really do love me.' Her voice almost sounded like mine! I'd never have guessed that Olivia was such a good mimic.

'But that would be a huge gamble,' I whispered. 'What if he didn't want me to come back?'

Olivia shrugged. 'Then you know where you stand. He'll see you right with money. Tom's a decent man.'

'But you didn't do that with Hugo when you found that woman's number in his pocket.'

She shrugged. 'That was different. I didn't have proof. But do you really want to be with a man who feels he's obliged to stay? He'll be begging you to come back, though. I promise. When he visits you at our place, he'll see what's he's missing out on. The girls and I will look after you. I told you. I'd love another baby in the house.'

'What about Hugo? Won't he mind?'

'I'll sort him out. Don't worry.'

Freddie let out a little cry as though he wasn't at all sure about this. Nor was I. But right now my mind and my hormones were all over the place.

144

'Oh. And there's one other thing!' Olivia's eyes rested on my son sucking at my breast. 'Don't forget you promised to make me godmother!'

After she left, I unwrapped her present. It was one of those expensive designer gift box sets of lavender soap and bath oil. How wonderful it smelt! I held the bar next to my nose and breathed it in. For a few seconds, I felt calmer. Could I – should I – really do what Olivia had suggested?

Freddie started sucking again, as if determined to get every drop. It reminded me of what one of the women in my wing had said about breastfeeding when she'd been in her last prison. 'Bloody drained me,' she said. 'I'd have gone for the bottle if it weren't for the fact that they have to give you decent food when the kid's on your boob.'

'I love feeding you,' I told Freddie, looking down at his long dark eyelashes. 'It makes me feel as though you are still attached to me.'

Then I was aware of someone coming in and standing over us. It was Tom. I wanted to tell him to piss off and cry with relief at the same time.

'How are you doing?' he asked awkwardly.

'Great, thank you,' I said stiffly. 'The doctor says we can leave the day after tomorrow if your son continues to do well.'

I said the words 'your son' pointedly.

'Good. I'll get everything ready.'

As if he'd heard, Freddie stopped sucking and took his little mouth off my breast. Tom was watching with an expression that reminded me of a small boy witnessing something magical. Then I laid our baby against my body, stroking his chest in small gentle upward motions to wind him, as the nurse had taught me.

'I gather you've told someone all about my sordid past,' I said.

He gave a start. 'What do you mean?'

'You know perfectly well. Olivia and Hugo know everything.'

Tom seemed relieved. Maybe he was glad it was out in the open.

'She suggested,' I continued, 'that Freddie and I went back with her for a few days.'

He frowned. 'Why?'

'Because it's clear you don't want us with you.'

'That's not true.'

'You asked Olivia to drive me home because you needed time to think.'

'I changed my mind,' he said. But I went on.

'So I'm giving you that time. Let's face it, Tom. I'm not the person you thought you were marrying. I lied to you. And I'm sorry. But I don't want you to feel you are shackled to us because of our son.'

'I don't.'

He said this in a small voice. I wasn't convinced. 'I think you do,' I said quietly. 'In fact, I'm surprised you're here now. So we're going there for a week or two. Olivia says she'll show me what to do with a new baby. And you can make up your mind while we're gone.'

This was, I knew, one of the bravest things I had ever done. Or the most stupid.

'All right,' he said. 'If that's what you want.'

No, of course it isn't, I almost screamed. But I needed

146

to make sure that our baby was going to be brought up in a solid home without any doubts on either side.

'Can I drive you there tomorrow morning?'

'Don't worry,' I told him. 'As I said, Olivia's picking us up.'

Tom was hesitating. I could see the doubt in his eyes. Olivia had been right. This was forcing him to work out how important we were to him.

'May I hold him?' he asked carefully.

'Of course. He's your son.'

Almost reluctantly, I handed our warm baby over to my husband. Immediately, my body felt empty. I yearned to snatch him back. Yet I knew this was essential.

'Am I doing this the right way?' His eyes looked scared.

'Yes,' I said. Already, in only a few hours, I felt surprisingly confident. 'Just move your hand here. That's right.'

'He's beautiful,' he said.

'He's got rather weird ears,' I said. 'They don't have any lobes.'

Tom gave a little start. 'My father didn't either. It was a family trait, apparently.'

He was warming to Freddie. I could feel it.

Then my husband looked at me. 'Those things I read on your notes. Was that it? Have you told me everything now?'

I glanced at our son with his long eyelashes lying contentedly in his father's arms. 'Yes,' I said firmly. 'Of course I have.'

17

Tom

Of all the words in the English language, 'friend' is surely one of the most confusing. Was Hilary a friend? Or was I making a huge mistake?

Either way, for some reason I'd found myself telling this sensible woman with the flat shoes and flowery smell what I'd just discovered about my wife. It wasn't like me to be so open and I can't explain why I did it. There appeared to be no logic in my actions.

'You know,' she'd said, when I'd finished. 'You can't really leave your wife on the day she's had your baby. You're too nice a man. You would feel guilty about it afterwards.'

'But look what she did,' I pointed out. 'Taking drugs is one thing. Dealing is another. And then prison. It's been one lie after another.'

Hilary shrugged. 'I had an aunt who was in Holloway for fifteen years.'

'Really?' I was taken aback. My colleague did not seem the type to be related to a felon.

'She murdered a man.' Hilary's voice was surprisingly matter of fact.

I didn't know what to say. I was still trying to find the right words when she continued to speak.

'She was having an affair with him. He kept promising to leave his wife but then the wife got pregnant. So she attacked him with a knife. She didn't mean to kill him, apparently, but unfortunately she sliced an artery.'

'That's awful.'

'It was.' Hilary's head bobbed up and down in agreement. Her hair was shorter than it had been before, I noticed, but not unflatteringly so.

'No one spoke about it for years. I only found out at her funeral. I'd always wondered why she hadn't been around during my early childhood but they said she'd gone to Australia. The odd thing was that she was such a kind woman.' Hilary gave a half-laugh. 'You wouldn't think she had it in her.'

I was almost on the point of telling her about Chapman and how Hugo had betrayed me but then she continued talking.

'The thing is, Tom, that none of us is perfect.'

I liked it when she called me by my name. I was not sure why. I just did.

'One of life's lessons,' she continued, 'is learning to do the right thing.'

'I can see that,' I said slowly.

She shrugged. 'However, if you find, later on down the line, that you and Sarah are not compatible, then that's something else.'

She'd said the name 'Sarah' as though she was familiar with it. In fact, I rarely mentioned my family in the office. Hilary kept quiet on that front too, I'd noticed.

'I don't want to detain you,' I said. 'Perhaps you have someone to go home to.'

That was daring on my part. The truth was, I was curious.

'No,' she said. 'It's why I'm choosing to work late.' She tapped my shoulder in an almost chummy way. 'Are you going back to the hospital or not?'

'Yes,' I said.

But I didn't, I'm ashamed to say. Not straight away. I marched briskly for miles down streets I knew and streets I didn't. By the time I'd reached the hospital, I'd decided that Hilary was right. I did need to stay with Sarah, because I wasn't the kind of person who could shirk my responsibilities. I did not want to be like my father.

So when Sarah said she wasn't going to come home and was going to stay with Olivia for 'one or two weeks', I was completely thrown.

I wasn't expecting this. What if I lost my son for ever?

Something inside me actually hurt. It hadn't done this since my mother had died. I'd felt myself melt when I'd picked up my little boy. This child was my flesh and blood right down to his missing earlobes. She had no right to take him away from me.

'I'm not very happy about having a screaming baby in the house either,' said Hugo when I rang. 'But Olivia is determined. And when my wife gets something into her head, there's no changing her.'

Freddie should be living with me, not my so-called best friend. Should I have been more understanding about Sarah's past? If I'd never read her notes, we'd have been home together now and I would have been none the wiser. But was that any way to live a life? Besides, she should have told me the truth right at the beginning.

Then I wouldn't have married her. And we wouldn't have had Freddie.

This was all so confusing. I didn't like the way my head was muddled.

That night I didn't sleep. At 5 a.m. I got up and went into the office. Hilary was already there. If it wasn't for the fact that she was wearing a blue dress instead of a tartan skirt, I might have thought she'd been there all night.

'Aren't you taking a day off to be with your son and wife?' she asked.

I was slightly surprised by her formal voice. There was no one else there, so we could speak freely.

'She's going to stay with friends of ours so we can decide on our future,' I said. 'She says she wants to be sure I love her enough to commit.'

Hilary looked me firmly in the eyes. She reminded me of a sympathetic but no-nonsense teacher. 'And do you?'

'I don't honestly know yet.'

It was amazing how openly I could speak to this woman.

'Then I'll let you get on with your decision,' said Hilary. She turned back to her keyboard. 'But don't forget there's a young child involved here. If I were you, I wouldn't allow yourself to have any distractions.'

I'd never been much good at reading women's minds. Was she suggesting that there might be something between *us* if Sarah wasn't there? The thought was not unpalatable. Indeed, it was comforting. But then I thought of Freddie and how my mother would have loved so much to have held him in her arms.

'Thank you,' I said carefully. 'You're a good friend.'

She carried on typing. 'Always here to talk,' she replied over her shoulder.

The day dragged. It didn't usually. I kept thinking about Olivia collecting Sarah and Freddie from hospital. It should be me.

I'd missed out on one of the most important times of my life.

How could my wife have deprived me of this experience? Of course, I'd been upset when I'd read her notes. But what had she expected if she was going to hide the truth from me?

Then again, I'd hidden Chapman from her.

On the other hand, if this was a mathematical equation, my wife's prison record surely outweighed my mistake, didn't it?

'When is your wife due, exactly?' asked my immediate boss at the beginning of an important conference call in the afternoon.

So Hilary hadn't told anyone. I was glad about that. It showed I could trust her.

'She gave birth last night, actually,' I said.

'Last night?' His face was puzzled. 'Then why are you in the office? You should have taken some time off.'

'Sarah knew this meeting was important,' I said quickly. 'Besides, she's out of hospital now and someone is looking after her.'

'Ah, you've got a maternity nurse. Very sensible.'

I neither denied nor confirmed this.

'Is everything all right?' asked someone else.

'Fine, thanks.'

'Did you have a boy or girl?'

'A son. Freddie.'

The questions were coming thick and fast. I'd never divulged so much information about myself before.

'Well,' said the boss, 'take a few days off if you need it as part of your holiday entitlement. This is a very special time. I've got three myself. All girls. Wouldn't be without them for the world.' He actually clapped my shoulders. 'Well done, Tom! Just be prepared for some sleepless nights!'

During the rest of the day, cards and little gifts for Freddie began to appear on my desk from colleagues. 'Thank you,' I said numbly. But all the time I was trying to concentrate on my work, I kept thinking about my son. What kind of start had he had? I began to wish I'd never read those bloody hospital notes in the first place. I rarely swear. It was an indication of the state of my mind.

At lunchtime, I rang Sarah. There was no reply.

So I tried Olivia. 'Are they with you?' I asked tersely.

'Yes, Tom. They're sleeping.'

Her voice was without its usual warmth.

'Can I bring round all the things they'll need,' I said, suddenly thinking of the stacks of nappies, the carrycot and all the little Babygros we'd bought in the last few months.

'There's no need,' she said. 'I've still got the girls' crib and I've already bought nappies and breast pads and anything else we'll need.'

Breast pads? I had a vision of Boudicca's suit of armour from history books at school.

'You can come round after work, if you want,' she added. 'I'm sure you must be dying to see your son.'

'Yes,' I said. 'Of course I am. And I want to see Sarah too.'

I waited for Olivia to tell me that Sarah would like that as well. But she didn't.

'Shall we say five p.m.?' she asked. 'Please don't be late. We're trying to get Freddie into a routine. I've also got the girls to look after.'

I remembered what Hugo had said about the R word. Five o'clock! I never left the office as early as that. But today I would make an exception. On the way there, I stopped at a toyshop and bought an enormous teddy bear. Then I purchased some stargazer lilies for Sarah. Her favourite.

It felt odd, going to my friends' mews cottage to see my day-old son. He should be at my house.

'Do come in,' said Olivia formally when she opened the door. 'Sarah and Freddie are in the kitchen with the girls.'

I could hear the laughter before I went in. Clemmie and her sister were gathered around Sarah and Freddie was in her arms. 'Can I hold him?' pleaded Clemmie.

'He needs to be winded first,' said Sarah. Then she put him on her shoulder and gently patted his back.

'Remember what I said?' came Olivia's voice behind me. 'You need long sweeping actions from the bottom upwards.'

'Thanks,' said Sarah. 'The nurse said the same. I should have remembered.' Then she saw me.

Immediately, she flushed. 'Tom. I didn't know you were coming.'

'Didn't Olivia tell you?'

My friend's wife gave a little laugh. 'I wasn't sure you'd be able to leave work on time.'

Ignoring this barbed comment, I reached out my arms. 'May I?'

Sarah seemed to glance at Olivia as if for approval. 'I did it last night,' I reminded her.

Almost reluctantly she passed the child over.

I bent my cheek down so it rested on his.

'Isn't he lovely, Uncle Tom?' said Clemmie. 'He's going to live with us for a bit.'

'I know,' I said tightly. 'Sarah, can we talk in private?'

My wife gave me one of those lovely smiles that had drawn me to her in the first place. 'I'm a bit tired, Tom. I'd rather stay here.'

She looked exhausted, I have to say. But she also looked stunning. Her hair, an even glossier black than usual, was curling onto her shoulders. She was also wearing a really pretty pale blue nightdress that I hadn't seen before, with a matching dressing gown.

'Would you like a cup of tea, Tom?' asked Olivia.

It all felt so formal.

'Yes, please.'

'You'll need to give Freddie back to your wife, then. You can't have a hot drink in your hand at the same time. You might burn him.'

I'd never thought of that.

'Is everything going well?' I asked Sarah. I had to shout over the girls' noise. They were fighting over who should hold Freddie next.

'Yes thank you,' said Sarah. 'Olivia's been amazing. She insisted on watching Freddie for a couple of hours after lunch so I could get some sleep.'

'That's nice,' I said.

I was beginning to feel increasingly redundant. This should be Sarah, me and Freddie together at home, getting to know each other. That's what all the baby books had said. I reproached myself now for leaving her in the hospital. And even though nothing had happened with Hilary, I felt guilty.

'Well,' said Olivia, glancing at the clock on the wall. 'We need to give Freddie his bath now, before bedtime.'

'Can I help?' I asked.

'You might get your smart suit wet,' pointed out Olivia coolly.

'It doesn't matter,' I said.

'Actually, Tom,' said Sarah. 'Olivia's going to teach me how to do it. It might be best if you watch tomorrow night.'

But bath time was one of those rituals that parents ought to share, according to my parenting manuals. Then again, there'd been nothing in them about discovering your wife was an ex-convict.

Olivia nodded in approval at Sarah's suggestion. 'Yes, why don't you call in tomorrow night on your way home from work?'

I shouldn't need an invitation to see my own son, but what choice did I have?

'Very well,' I said.

I stood up and brushed Sarah's cheek with my mouth. She smelt different from usual. She didn't respond. Then I stroked Freddie's cheek with my finger. I was not an imaginative man generally but it felt as smooth as silk.

'See you tomorrow, then,' I said.

As I walked down the road, I spotted Hugo driving

past. He waved to me but didn't stop. Maybe it was unwise to do so with the traffic, I reasoned.

How odd it was to go back into my own house and see the nappies and the mobile and the various things we'd chosen for our baby. It didn't feel right, being here without them.

Impulsively, I rang my wife's mobile. 'Why don't you come home?' I asked. 'Please.'

'But can you forgive me?'

I thought about it for a minute.

'You see,' she said softly. 'You're still not sure, are you?'

'It's been a shock,' I said. 'I need time to process it.'

'I know . . . and that's why we can't come back yet.'

I could hear Freddie crying in the background. I wanted to hold him and tell him everything would be all right.

'Goodnight,' she said before I could express my feelings verbally. 'See you tomorrow?'

She'd put the phone down before it dawned on me that she'd phrased the statement as a question.

Too late, I realized I should have replied.

18

Sarah

I'm not sure how I would have managed without Olivia in those two weeks. I'd like to say I missed Tom, but actually I knew he'd have been upset by all of it. He needed to be in control.

'Why is Freddie screaming like this?' I asked on that first morning when nothing seemed to pacify him.

'It's usually because a baby is hungry, needs his nappy changing or has wind. Let's see. You've fed him and I've burped him. He's also nice and dry now, aren't you, little one?'

'But how do I know he's not ill?'

'I've thought of that, but he isn't warm and he doesn't have a rash. Mind you, *you* look a bit flushed. Let's see. Gosh! You have a temperature. Do you feel achy?'

'Yes,' I said.

'Bet you've got mastitis.'

'What's that?'

'Don't panic. It's an inflammation of breast tissue, which sometimes happens when you're breastfeeding. Milk usually comes in on the third day for a first baby but yours seems to have arrived early. Are your breasts sore?'

'Agony.'

'I'll ring the doctor.'

I was prescribed antibiotics and told by the visiting midwife to gently squeeze out excess milk. I felt far more comfortable and Freddie began to settle.

'Babies pick up on vibes,' said Olivia.

'Honestly, I don't know what I'd do without you.'

She looked pleased. 'You'd get it eventually. But it does make it easier to have someone else around. I had a maternity nurse, but it wasn't like having a close friend.'

A close friend? Is that what I was?

Emily!

No one else could be like her. During the student carnival she had dressed up as one of our tutors who had striking orange hair. The tutor in question had been flattered rather than upset. It was a mark of the affection that Emily brought out in everyone. And look how I had repaid her . . .

Olivia could never be the close friend that Emily had been. I didn't want that. Yet Olivia's words made me feel warm inside.

'Why don't you have a little nap?' Olivia said to me the following day after I'd been up most of the night, walking Freddie up and down and trying to make sure he didn't wake up the rest of the house. Hugo had already made it clear, with various huffs and puffs whenever Freddie cried, that he wasn't thrilled by our presence.

'You're clearly shattered,' she added. 'I'll look after Freddie.' She was cradling him in her arms, looking down at him lovingly, almost as if he was her own. 'I'm your godmother, aren't I? At least I will be when Mummy and Daddy arrange your christening. Aren't you a handsome little boy? Yes you are! You are!'

Freddie seemed to listen to her voice. For a few seconds, I almost felt jealous. She was so good at settling him. How would I ever manage?

'It feels wrong to go to bed in the day,' I said.

Olivia's eyes rolled. 'You've had a baby. If you can't rest after that, when can you? Most of my friends have power naps in between massages and Pilates while the kids are at school. Just take an hour or two. I'll wake you if he needs feeding again. Promise.'

So I did. The guest room was incredibly comfortable. The bed was to die for. Really deep, with big fluffy cushions and that sweet little crib at the bottom that had belonged to the girls.

Almost instantly, I fell into a deep void. The kind where you sink so far down that, when you wake, it's like coming out of a general anaesthetic.

My first thought when I opened my eyes was that the crib was empty. Of course it was, I remembered. Olivia was looking after Freddie downstairs to give me a break, wasn't she? I washed my face and went into the kitchen. Freddie's Moses basket was there on the table but it was empty.

'Hello?' I called out.

The house was silent. It was a school day, so the girls weren't around, even though there was a pile of shoes in the hall, empty cereal bowls still on the kitchen table and a stack of washing in a laundry basket waiting to be sorted.

My heart began to pound. Where was my baby? Was he ill? Had Olivia taken him to the doctor? My breasts began to leak. They needed to feed him.

I ran to the front door. Olivia's car was still there. That

was something. So was the pram. Where were they? By now my heart was seriously beginning to pound. All kinds of things flooded my mind. Someone had broken in and kidnapped them. Tom had come round and demanded that Freddie went home with him. Or maybe . . .

As I stood there in the street, still in my nightdress, the front door of the house opposite opened. Out came Olivia, holding Freddie. 'Thanks for the coffee,' she called out over her shoulder. 'Yes! He is lovely, isn't he?' Then she caught sight of me. 'Oh, Sarah. There you are. Did you have a good sleep?'

I could barely talk from relief. I ran over the cobbles, barefoot, and took Freddie from her arms. Instantly, he began screaming. 'I didn't know where you were,' I said.

Olivia's face seemed confused. 'I only took him over to show a neighbour. I also thought you'd sleep better if we were out of the house. I'm sorry. I should have left you a note.'

Yes. She should have done. But I didn't want to be rude. Olivia had done so much for us.

'Come on, Freddie,' she said. 'Don't start crying on Mummy. You've been such a good boy.'

'Maybe he's hungry,' I said.

We were inside now. I undid the top of my nightdress and Freddie immediately zoomed into my right breast, sucking as if there was no tomorrow.

'Don't forget the knee trick!'

Olivia had shown me how to put him tummy-side down on my knees to soothe him.

'You're a fast learner,' said Olivia. 'Now that he's satis-fied, how about a girly lunch? You need to maintain your calorie input to keep the milk going. I've got a lovely play mat with a pretty mobile that the children used to like. Freddie can lie on the floor and we can watch him while we eat.' She gave a little sigh of contentment. 'I must say, it's so lovely having a baby in the house again.'

'Hugo doesn't seem to think so,' I pointed out. 'I heard him asking you yesterday when we were going to leave.'

Olivia waved her arms as if batting my words away. 'Don't pay any attention to him. He's not great with tinies. You can stay as long as you want.'

Something didn't feel quite right. 'I thought the point was to make Tom realize he needed us.'

'Well, yes, it is. But I hope I'm being helpful. Having a small baby can be so scary when you don't know what to do.'

'It is. And you *are* helpful. Thank you.'

I didn't want to be ungrateful, but waking up to find Freddie gone like that had been terrifying. I almost said as much but, then again, I was a guest in her house and she was being so kind.

'Anyway,' added Olivia, 'Tom rang to see if he could come round tonight. I didn't want to wake you but I said yes. I hope that's all right.'

'Sure,' I said. But my heart began to flutter. 'Thanks.'

'Don't thank me. He's your husband. He has every right to see his child. I've told you, you must treat our place as if it's your home.' Then she ran an eye over the blue nightdress she'd lent me, which I hadn't bothered to change out of yet. There didn't seem any point. Freddie was always being sick over me when I burped him.

'We need to get you into some different clothes,' she continued. 'I've got a few outfits that will fit. And we must also work on those postnatal exercises. Don't worry. You'll be trim in no time.'

Then she reached out and smoothed my hair. 'It's such a lovely colour isn't it? A wonderful raven. And I can see it's natural. But it docs need conditioning. I've got just the stuff. My hairdresser makes it herself. People would kill for the formula!'

I hardly recognized myself by the time Olivia had finished with me. I was wearing a simple navy shift dress that hid that post-baby bulge and looked, I have to say, surprisingly good, considering how far a cry it was from the long floaty dresses or baggy jeans I was used to wearing. She also lent me a pair of kitten heels and gave me some earrings that she assured me were brand new. 'I've got loads of them,' she said. 'Pearls suit you.'

I'd never seen myself as a pearl girl – usually I made my own earrings out of beads and wire hooks from the market. The look on Tom's face when he arrived was worth it. Freddie was fast asleep in his carrycot but woke at the sound of the voices. I picked him up quickly and held him against my shoulder, rubbing his back the way Olivia had taught me. He quietened and I turned him round. He seemed to study Tom's face intently. I hadn't realized that babies could look like old people. So wise. What was he thinking, I wondered, as Olivia left the room to give us some privacy.

'Here. Hold him.'

Tom seemed as stiff as he had done when holding Freddie before.

'Try talking to him,' I suggested.

He looked taken aback. 'What shall I say?'

I was glad Hugo and Olivia weren't there.

'Anything. Hum to him, if you like.'

To my surprise, Tom began to sing. I'd never heard my husband sing before. It was a low soothing lyric with words I didn't recognize. 'My mother taught it to me when I was a child,' said Tom when he'd finished. 'Her parents came from Wales.

'Well, it's worked,' I said. 'Look at how happy he is.'

He frowned. 'Well, I'm not happy. It doesn't feel right, you not being at home.'

'On the night he was born, you weren't even sure you wanted us,' I pointed out.

He appeared genuinely upset at this. 'I'm sorry. But it was a shock. If you'd only told me the whole truth instead of me finding out from your notes.'

'I know,' I said quickly. 'I've said I'm sorry.'

'Can we try again?'

Olivia had warned me this might happen. 'Don't go home too fast,' she kept saying. 'Let him sweat. Make sure he really wants you back and that he isn't doing it out of obligation.'

'Not quite yet,' I said carefully. 'I need time to think about this as well.'

He nodded. 'Of course. May I come round tomorrow night?'

'Sure.'

When I told Olivia about this after Tom left, she'd nodded approvingly. 'You did the right thing. Of course, you can stay as long as you want.' Then she laughed. 'For ever, if you like. We love having you here. Hugo has to behave and it's wonderful for me to have baby cuddles.'

Looking back, those days with Olivia were very special. I told her things I'd never been able to tell anyone about before. Like other things that had happened while I was in prison.

We were both sitting on her enormous, cosy sofa, bought from some swanky place in Chelsea, snuggled up under a duck-egg blue cashmere throw; each with a glass of wine in our hands. I hadn't had a drink since finding out I was pregnant, but Olivia assured me that a small one wouldn't hurt now.

The girls had gone to bed. Freddie was asleep in his crib upstairs and Hugo was out at a 'work do'. Olivia had rented out a DVD for us to watch. It was a drama about a woman on the run with her son. My heart began to quicken when we got to a scene where she was arrested and thrown into a cell while her screaming child was taken away from her by social workers.

'I don't think this is for me,' I said, looking away.

'I'm sorry, I didn't realize it was going to turn out like this.' She turned it off. 'Are you OK?'

I shivered. 'It brought back memories. My cellmate had been separated from her son. It's only now as a mother that I can see how terrible that must have been for her.'

'What happened to mothers if they had kids?' said Olivia. 'Were they allowed to see them? What if they were pregnant when they went in?'

'They could keep them in the prison until they were eighteen months old. But then they had to go to family or foster parents.' My eyes blurred. 'I remember one woman on our wing crying all night for months after that happened to her.'

'How awful!'

'I know. She carried this picture of her son everywhere with her. It was one of her twenty-six.'

'Twenty-six what?'

'Twenty-six possessions. That was the maximum number of personal things you were allowed to take in.'

'What did you have?'

'Not much.'

I almost, but not quite, told Olivia about the photograph of Emily that I'd pinned on my wall. Every time I looked at her kind eyes, it hurt as much as if I was cutting my own arm.

'I wanted to keep my mother's pendant. But they wouldn't let me in case I strangled myself with it. Still, at least they gave it back to me when I was released. Some people's possessions would go "missing".'

I reached for my neck and touched it now for comfort.

'What was your cell like?'

'It was a small room with a draughty window that had bars across it. The bed was about two feet wide.'

'Where did you hang your clothes?'

I had to laugh. This was such an Olivia question!

'We had a cardboard box under the bed. It's where the pot was, too, in case we needed to go in the night.'

'No ensuite?'

'Are you joking? There was one lavatory down the corridor for fifteen of us.'

'So why didn't you go there instead of using this pot?'

'We were locked in at night.'

She shuddered. 'I couldn't have borne that.'

'I didn't think I could either. But you just had to get on with it.'

'What did you do all day? Sew mailbags?'

I laughed. 'Not exactly. We had a rota of jobs. The worst was when I was on laundry duty and had to wash and fold the sheets. You often found poo in there.'

'Ugh.'

'The first few times I vomited. Then I sort of got used to it. You couldn't always wash properly because there wasn't enough hot water. Sometimes you'd cut yourself by mistake on rusty razor blades that others had left in the shower.'

Olivia's face was a picture. 'Couldn't you complain?'

'I did, but that made it worse. One of the girls said I stabbed her with my fork at tea. In fact, she did it to herself but the officers didn't believe me. I got sent to isolation again.'

Olivia let out a low breath. 'Oh, Sarah. Poor you!'

'I deserved it for what I did.'

She made a 'well, yes' face.

Then something occurred to me. 'What's the worst thing you've ever done?'

She thought for a minute. 'Parking on a double yellow line when Clemmie was born. I needed to run into a pharmacy to get her some medicine. When I got back, the warden was giving me a ticket. She didn't seem to realize this was an emergency.'

And my friend didn't seem to realize that the shocking

bit was leaving Clemmie alone in the car – not the parking ticket. But I didn't like to point this out.

'Anything else?'

'I don't think so.'

'That makes me feel like shit.'

'Nonsense.' Olivia squeezed my hand. 'OK, drug dealing is wrong. But that part of your life is over now.'

'Yes, but . . .'

I stopped. Part of me wanted so badly to tell Olivia the rest of it.

'But what if something happened that separated me and Freddie one day?' I said quickly.

'We all worry about that. It's what mothers do. My fear is that I might die young. Then who'd bring up my girls?'

'I'd help.'

'That's very kind. But Hugo would marry again and then someone else would have them and they'd forget me . . .'

'No they wouldn't.'

She took a slurp of wine. 'I hope not.' She gave herself a little shake. 'Anyway, let's find something else to watch, shall we? How about this chat show? Wow! Look at Russell Crowe. What a hunk!'

But I couldn't concentrate. 'I'm going to check on Freddie.'

'He's fine.' She pointed a manicured fingernail at the baby monitor. 'He hasn't stirred. Never wake a sleeping child. It's one of the first rules of motherhood.'

'I need to check,' I said.

I tiptoed up the stairs and into the guest room, where Freddie's crib was at the bottom of my bed. My son's small chest was rising and falling gently. His skin was a healthy pink and his little rosebud mouth twitched silently in his sleep as if he was feeding from me.

'I love you so much,' I whispered. 'Everything's going to be all right. I promise.'

Tom came round each evening. Sometimes Freddie screamed blue murder but each time I managed to calm him using the techniques Olivia had taught me. One night, when she and Hugo had gone out for the evening, Freddie wouldn't stop.

'Maybe you might have more success,' I suggested to Tom. It was a gamble and I held my breath. Tom would take it personally if Freddie carried on screaming.

He didn't stop yelling completely but he did seem to be a bit more settled.

'See,' I said to my husband. 'You can do it.'

'I've been thinking,' he said, looking down at our son. 'Maybe it was a good thing I read your hospital notes. I mean, it's brought it all out in the open. Neither of us has any more secrets. That's a comforting feeling. Isn't it?'

'Yes,' I said, forcing myself to sound as if I meant it.

'So come home. It's been over two weeks now. Please, Sarah. I need you. Our son needs me.'

'If you're sure.'

He put his arm around me. 'I am.'

'I'm going to really miss you,' I said to Olivia when it was almost time to leave. We were standing in the hall with our cases around us, full of clothes and toys and equipment that Olivia had pressed on me.

My friend hugged me. I could smell her perfume. It

was the same one that she'd insisted on getting for me when we'd gone shopping. She'd helped me choose 'the right kind of outfits' – pale blue pedal-pusher trousers and a smart black dress with a loose waist until I 'got my figure back completely'. It was as though I was a different woman. I rather liked it. A new Sarah. Goodbye to the old. I felt a strange sense of déjà vu – but this time I wasn't going to mess up my fresh start.

'I'll miss you too,' she said. 'Then she glanced down at Freddie in my arms. 'And I don't know how I'm going to manage without this little one.'

'Would you like to hold him?' I asked.

'May I? Thank you.' She took him in her arms. 'You are so special, Freddie. Do you know that?' Then she carefully handed him back to me.

The girls came running in. 'Don't go, Auntie Sarah,' pleaded Clemmie followed by her sister, Molly. 'We love having a baby here. He's so sweeeet!'

'You must come over to play with us,' I said.

'Thank you,' said Olivia. 'We'd love that. Now, don't forget, I'm taking you to my old baby group on Tuesday. It's invitation-only. I'll introduce you to the lovely woman who runs it.'

I wasn't entirely sure about that – it sounded too exclusive for my liking – but I didn't want to show my doubts. What would I have done without my new best friend?

'If I can ever do anything for you, you must let me know,' I said quietly so the girls didn't hear.

Tears glistened in her eyes. 'I will. Ah, look. Isn't that Tom's car?'

It was. We were going home.

19

Tom

I admit it was partly embarrassment that made me beg Sarah to come back. I couldn't face telling my colleagues that my wife and I had broken up just after having a baby.

And, of course, I loved him. In fact, I was surprised at how much I cared for this little creature with that mop of black hair and my father's ears. My son. My son!

'Glad to see you're not leaving too late,' said my boss when I began packing up my things at 6 p.m. 'How is it going at home?'

For a minute I hesitated. Did he know that Sarah had been living away?

'What do you mean?'

'Are you in a routine yet?'

That word again!

'In a way.' I could hardly tell him that I'd only collected Sarah from my best friend's the night before and that this was our first proper evening together.

As I walked to the station, I glimpsed Hilary a few yards ahead. Her tweed hat stood out in the crowd. I increased my stride to catch up. 'I can't help feeling rather nervous,' I said. I'd told her a couple of days ago about my decision.

'You're bound to.'

Her voice was kind and sympathetic.

'Thank you for your advice,' I said.

'I didn't give you any,' she replied. 'I simply pointed out the facts. There are times when we all need to see them more clearly. It's what good friends are for.'

Good friends? I was pleased. But a part of me also felt strangely disappointed.

We'd reached the Tube station now. Her line went in one direction and mine the other. 'See you tomorrow,' she said.

I watched her go with an odd feeling in my chest that was hard to describe.

When I got home it was so nice to see a light on. There was a pram in the hall and boxes of nappies. Yet the mess no longer seemed as irritating as it might have done before. Music was playing in the kitchen – jazz – and my wife was cooking.

'Hi,' I said, awkwardly. Sarah turned round. She gave me a kiss on my cheek. I thought about giving her one back but she'd moved away.

'Where's Freddie?'

'In his Moses basket.'

She gestured at the kitchen table.

'He's fast asleep.' I was almost disappointed.

'Yes but don't worry. He'll wake soon for his feed.'

'What if he rolls out of the basket and onto the floor?'

'He can't yet. He's too young to turn over.'

Sarah seemed to know so much. I felt as though I had skipped the baby induction course.

'Dinner's almost ready.'

It wasn't salmon en croute, my favourite. But fish pie was a close second.

No sooner had we sat down to eat than there was a

loud yell. 'He always does that,' said Sarah. 'Olivia says it's usually because they need changing or are hungry. There, there.'

For a minute I thought she was trying to reassure me.

Then she picked up Freddie and sat down, while opening her blouse. I watched, amazed that she could do everything at the same time. Somehow she was feeding him and eating! I tried to eat myself but I couldn't concentrate. This felt so strange.

'Olivia says that when you have kids, you have to learn to do things with your toes as well as your fingers,' she joked.

'Did your day go well?' I asked.

'Yes thanks. Olivia came over to see if she could help. She held him while I had a shower.'

Sarah seemed different, I have to say. She looked very fresh and smelt nice. I liked her outfit too – casual jeans with a nice smart turquoise top. They were the kind of clothes Olivia wore. My wife also had her lovely smile back. It reminded me of the woman I'd fallen in love with.

'What about you?' she asked.

I thought of my work, and of Hilary.

'Fine, thanks.'

My eyes were still fixed on Freddie, who was sucking so intently. The veins on Sarah's breasts were standing out. Was that normal? I didn't like to ask.

'Would you like to wind him?'

I tried to remember what she'd taught me at Olivia's.

She handed him over before I could reply. It meant putting down my knife and fork. 'That's right. Low sweeping actions from the base of his spine upwards.'

Freddie let out a huge burp. It made me jump.

'Well done! You did it. Tell you what, could you hold him while I get pudding together?'

I wasn't sure about that. Supposing I dropped him?

But Freddie seemed quite happy to be in my arms. Gradually, I could feel my confidence growing. It took me back to my first day at work.

'Fabulous. Thanks. I thought we might give him a bath together now.'

I thought of our Jacuzzi tub upstairs.

'Isn't he too small?'

'I've got a special baby one that Olivia lent me. You might want to change out of your suit first.'

I hadn't realized how complicated this procedure was.

'Hold him under the shoulder with one arm, like that. Brilliant! You're a natural.'

I didn't feel like one.

'Now gently rinse his little head, like this. You've got it. Well done.'

I felt quite chuffed. All my working life I'd been confident, because I knew where I was with figures. They either added up or they didn't. But babies were unpredictable. Sarah's encouragement made me feel as though I was really getting somewhere. I patted my son's head with the towel. 'Excellent,' she said approvingly.

Was that a pang in my chest? It seemed such a miracle that we had created a life together. I wasn't one for poetic thoughts but I suddenly felt quite overwhelmed.

By the end, I was exhausted. So was Freddie. 'He's going to sleep again. Is that all right?'

'Some babies sleep a lot and others have longer gaps. They're all different.'

'There should be some kind of classification.'

'Very funny, Tom.'

I meant it. But I couldn't help having huge respect for my wife. She seemed amazingly capable. How would I ever catch up? And what if I did something wrong that hurt Freddie? He was so small and vulnerable.

'I hadn't realized that being a parent was such a huge responsibility,' I whispered to Sarah as we got into bed that night. She was already there before me. In fact, I'd taken longer with my shower, almost hoping she would be asleep. Then we wouldn't need to have any awkward conversation.

'It is,' she agreed, nestling her head into my shoulder. 'But you're here with us now. We're going to manage this together, Tom. I know it.'

Slowly she stroked me below. I felt myself stirring. 'You can't make love to me until after my six-week check,' she whispered. 'But I can help you . . .'

Then, at the point of climax, I thought of her in prison. Had she worn one of those orange boiler suits like you see on television? How many hours a day had she spent behind bars? Why hadn't I asked this before? Now was too late. I'd lost the urge.

'It's all right,' she said, reassuring me. 'These things take time.'

Then Freddie woke. He was in his crib next to the bed because Sarah wanted him in the same room. 'Olivia says it's best,' she'd said.

'What do we do now?' I asked.

'He wants feeding.'

'Again?'

'It's all right. You go back to sleep.'

I nodded off. But it was an uneasy sleep. This time, in my dreams, Sarah was running through a prison with Freddie in her arms. Someone was chasing her. I couldn't see who.

When I woke it was only 5 a.m. She was feeding Freddie again. 'How do you know he's not getting too much?' I asked.

'He'll stop, or he might be a bit sick.'

'Isn't that dangerous?'

'Many babies regurgitate some milk, which is why it's important to watch them.'

This whole baby thing seemed littered with pitfalls. Yet it was also strangely addictive. I kept looking at Freddie. This was my son. My son! How incredible was that?

I left for work early. I could get more done that way and then I might be able to come home earlier for bath time.

'How is it going?' asked Hilary, who, as always, had arrived before me. We were the only ones there.

'It's all right, actually,' I said.

'Good.'

I had been slightly worried that the confidences I'd entrusted Hilary with might affect our relationship, but they hadn't. She treated me now in precisely the same matter-of-fact way she had done before. The only difference was that, whenever there was some kind of work-related event, such as a birthday or leaving party, the two of us generally found ourselves sitting next to each other at the pub or wine bar or wherever the occasion was being held. We were the only two people in the group to ask for non-alcoholic drinks. Our conversation was never personal. We talked about things like Gordon Brown's spending policy. I was pleased to find that Hilary's political views were similar to my own.

But shared views were one thing. A shared child another.

When Hugo rang a few weeks after Sarah and Freddie had come home, to suggest a drink or a game of tennis, I told him I was busy.

'You're not still upset about Chapman, are you?' he said. 'I didn't know he was going to kill himself.'

But I *was* still angry. Not just with him for threatening the man but also with myself. For the terrible truth was that part of me felt relief that Chapman could no longer tell the world our secret. Never, I vowed, would I allow my son to be put in such a position. I would always be there to give him the fatherly advice I had not been able to ask for myself. I was going to be the best dad I could possibly be. And the best husband too.

20

Sarah

And so we started again.

I tried my hardest to be the woman Tom wanted me to be.

Rather nervously, I rang Olivia's expensive Mayfair hairdressing salon, using the number on the card she had given me before I'd left. I was shocked when I asked for the price in advance. I'd never spent that amount on anything in the past! Olivia was delighted when I told her I'd made an appointment. 'I'll look after Freddie for you. You go and enjoy yourself.'

'Are you sure?' I said. I'd never been away from Freddie before.

'He'll be safe with me. Don't worry.'

But I couldn't help it. What if he cried for me? I'd expressed some breast milk but there was no guarantee he'd take that from the bottle.

'May I suggest removing the pink-and-blue highlights for madam?' asked the senior 'technician'.

I was so concerned about Freddie that I would have agreed to almost anything.

Two hours later, a glossy, chic black bob stared back at me in the mirror. Part of me rather liked it, in the way you might admire a picture of someone else. But the other part of me felt uneasy.

Who do you think you're kidding? my reflection seemed to say. *You can change your colours on the outside. But not on the inside.*

I also went through my wardrobe, with Olivia's help. 'I think these have seen better days, don't you?' she said, throwing my old market jeans onto the rubbish pile by the bed.

When she'd gone, I put them back. They'd be useful for painting, if nothing else. But I also went shopping, with Freddie in his pushchair, and bought a peacock blue jersey dress from Selfridges as well as some tailored trousers. I wore the dress that evening, along with the pearl earrings Olivia had given me, for when Tom came back from work.

'That looks nice,' he said approvingly, tucking into the pork chop I'd grilled. At Olivia's suggestion, I'd tried making more of an effort to cook meat dishes for him, even though I couldn't face them myself.

On another evening, I wore his mother's diamond necklace. His eyes actually misted up. 'My mother would have been so pleased.'

Then he stopped. We both knew what he was thinking. She would have been shocked and disgusted by my past.

All I could do was try and make up for it now. We socialized with Hugo and Olivia. Sometimes, I sensed Hugo looking at me in a certain way. *Yes,* I wanted to say to him. *I messed up. Big time. But I was young. Stupid. Naive. Besides, everyone's allowed a second chance, aren't they? This is mine. Well, maybe my third, which we won't talk about in the hope it won't be discovered. But I won't mess it up again. I'm a mother now. I've learned from my mistakes.*

During the week, I spent some of my time at the rather exclusive baby group that Olivia had introduced me to.

Everyone there had names like Posy or Anastasia, with double-barrelled surnames. They talked non-stop about which prep school their children had been put down for and which designer baby shops were best. But when I got to know them, I found they had the same worries as me about things like weaning and fussy eating and not sleeping.

Very few of them worked. Their husbands all did something in the City. 'You're an artist?' someone said when I mentioned I'd gone to art school. 'How amazing!'

'I don't have much time at the moment to paint,' I said.

'I don't have much time to go to the loo,' said another.

That made us all laugh.

After the first few days, Tom was rarely back from the office before 8 p.m. but that suited me. Freddie and I could be ourselves without him fussing over the 'mess' caused by toys everywhere or food flung on the floor.

I say 'ourselves' because that's what it felt like. Freddie and I were one. He panicked every time I was out of sight so I had to take him with me, even to the loo. He clung to me with such love and determination that I felt naked without him. I would walk around with him on my hip as if he was surgically attached. I would continually dip my head down to inhale the scent of his hair and skin.

As well as Olivia's exclusive playgroup, I also signed up for one at a local hall. That one was far more casual; there, I was able to relax. One day, I began chatting to an older woman who turned out to be the grandmother of the child she was with. 'Does your mum or dad help with the baby?' she asked.

In the past, any reference to my mum would have made my eyes swim, but this time I felt an alien emotion in my heart. Although I'd loved my mother – and still did – I can now see that she hadn't been that responsible. In the commune, we'd run wild, eating mushrooms from the forest and peas from the vegetable garden or dry cereal at odd times; there had been no routine or security.

It hadn't seemed unusual then or different. But now I had the responsibility of a small child to love and care for, I began to feel angry with her. It made me determined to be the best parent I could possibly be.

Like many artists or writers with children, I was torn between my two passions. When Freddie was still young enough to have daytime naps, I would seize my charcoal sticks and start feverishly sketching. Often I would draw my child as he lay asleep before me, his little chest rising and falling. The birth of my son, I would marvel, had saved me from my old life. He was my guarantee that I would always live a better one. I had to, because mothers had to be good examples, didn't they?

A few weeks later, two of the mothers from Olivia's baby group came back for a coffee. They saw my sketches and asked if they could pay me to draw their children too. Olivia helped to spread the word and, before I knew it, I was receiving more commissions than I could deal with, often ending up working into the night.

'You don't need to do this,' said Tom sleepily. Freddie, by this stage, had gone into his own room next door. I was glad to be back with my husband, but I had to admit that I found it odd sharing the bed with someone again. I also had a constant ear out for the baby monitor, which I kept switched on during the night even though Tom complained that the light disturbed him.

'I can increase your allowance, if you want.'

'It's not the money,' I told him. 'It's about doing something for *me*.'

'Isn't motherhood enough?' he asked.

'It's not as simple as that,' I protested. 'I need to paint and draw as well.'

He'd gone to sleep by then. Yet I knew that even if he'd been awake, he wouldn't have understood.

Olivia also asked me to draw her girls. Of course, I said I'd do it for free, but she insisted on asking what my going rate was. 'You could charge more than that,' she told me. 'I know someone who runs a gallery off Sloane Square. Have you got any pictures you want to sell?'

Three went within the first month, followed by more commissions, but I still wasn't getting the satisfaction I used to get from teaching at the arts centre. Perhaps it was because I didn't go out to work. (I generally took, or asked for, photographs of the subject and then did the portrait at home. This was best for children, I'd discovered, because they didn't sit still for long periods like adults!)

Now Freddie was on the move, I felt like I had to keep my eye on him at all times. He was growing up so fast. Just look at how he was hauling himself up on furniture! He was talking as well. 'Mum' was his first word.

'He'll say "dad" soon,' I told Tom. But I could see he was hurt. I would have been as well, to be honest.

I lived and breathed Freddie. He was everything to me. I couldn't imagine life without him. Sometimes I would be overcome with terror that something awful would happen. 'All mothers have these fears,' said Olivia when I told her. 'It's natural.'

But every now and then my fear got so bad that I was almost too scared to leave the house. 'It will be all right,' Tom assured me. 'I've done some research into it. It's normal for new mothers to be anxious. I'm here for you, Sarah. We're in this together so there's no need for you to worry.'

He gave me a cuddle. I nestled into his chest but still couldn't get rid of those 'what if something happens?' flutters in my chest.

I began to avoid playgroups because they were probably full of germs. We were safer in our home. We could play games. We could do hand printing. We could dance! Our beautiful son had such an ear for music! Did he get it from my mother? I remembered her dancing with me once.

One night, I woke to hear Freddie making strangled cries on the baby monitor.

'We need to get him to hospital,' I told Tom.

'Are you sure?' he asked sleepily. 'I think he's merely chesty after that cold.'

'No! We have to go.' I had a horror of missing something important, like my aunt had missed my burst appendix. Call it a mother's intuition but I knew something was wrong.

I was right. As soon as we got there, Freddie was rushed into special care. He had suffered an asthma attack.

'It will all be OK,' said Tom, as we sat by our son in the darkened hospital room watching the monitor rise and fall with those awful bleeping noises. Freddie looked so help-less with that ventilator mask over his mouth. My eyes could barely focus from all the crying.

'What do you know?' I demanded. 'You're not a doctor. You weren't joined to him by an umbilical cord. You almost . . .'

I'd made myself stop then. But we both knew what I'd been about to say. '*You almost left us after he was born.*' Still, I had to put that out of my head. On the whole, Tom had been really caring since Freddie and I had come back from Olivia's. He'd changed. I'd changed. It was going to be all right. Just as long as our son got through this.

And he did! The following day, Freddie was better, sit-ting up and beaming at us. How could children be so ill one minute and then all right the next?

'Is there asthma in the family?' asked the doctor.

'Not on my side,' said Tom, who had taken a day off work, although he was constantly going outside to make business calls.

'I'm not sure about mine,' I said slowly. It wasn't as if I'd been raised in a family that ever visited a GP. But I do vaguely remember one of the other women bringing round a poultice of dried herbs for my mother when she had a bad chest. There was no way I could find out. My aunt and uncle had not been in touch since my trial. When I wrote to tell them about my marriage and Freddie's birth, the letter came back marked *Return to Sender*. Clearly, they wanted nothing to do with me.

Olivia was brilliant. She put me in touch with a special-ist and sat with Freddie when he napped so I could get some sleep.

'It's no trouble at all,' she said. 'It's my only chance to have a little one in my life. Hugo is still adamant about not having another.'

Tom wasn't keen either. 'It took us so long to conceive Freddie – do we want to go through all those ups and downs again?' he said.

But I was hoping he'd come round to it. That terrible night in the hospital when he'd read my notes now seemed almost like a distant memory. We had Freddie to look after now and Tom was a good father. He played number games with him. We had some great family trips to a city farm, where Freddie loved to feed the goats and sheep. We would snuggle up in bed, the three of us, on Saturday and Sunday mornings when Tom didn't have to go to work. We were a proper family. It was all I'd ever wanted.

If only it could have lasted.

21

Tom

I've never been one of those people who spend time analysing themselves. There doesn't seem much point. You are who you are.

The trouble is that you never really know who *others* are. I certainly hadn't known who Sarah was when we'd met but, then again, she hadn't known everything about me, either.

Freddie, however, was our clean slate. We were going to make a success of parenthood. I knew it. And although, like many young couples (according to my reading matter), we were stressed with the strain of having a baby, I also felt closer to this woman who had given me a son.

But as the weeks went by, I began to feel more and more exhausted. Freddie only wanted his mother, especially at night. It didn't help that Sarah insisted on taking Freddie into our bed if he woke in the night. It was impossible to get enough sleep with all his little noises that ranged from mewing sounds to full-blown yells. I even began to make the odd mistake at work, which I had never done before. 'Why don't you sleep in the spare room to get some rest?' Sarah had suggested after a few weeks of this. But when I left for work in the morning and peeped through the door to see Freddie fast asleep in Sarah's arms, I felt shut out.

I did my best to get back home at a reasonable hour such as 7 p.m. instead of 9 p.m. Sometimes Freddie was asleep by then. This was a mixed blessing. It meant I got to eat dinner in peace. But at the same time, I didn't want to miss out on him. I loved holding him in my arms and stroking his cheek with my little finger.

At the weekends, we often went for walks in the park. 'You push the buggy,' my wife would say to me. At first I was a little nervous but then I got the hang of it. Freddie began to reach out his arms to me as well as Sarah. This filled me with an unexpected warmth. I found myself laughing more than I had done for years.

Often, older people passing would look at us and give us what seemed like approving looks. It made me feel good. I was a father! I felt special. I would defend my little family with my last breath.

'We're so lucky, aren't we?' I would say to Sarah during those walks, taking her hand in mine.

'Yes,' she'd say, with that sunny smile that had captured my heart when I'd first seen her in the arts centre. 'We are.'

After a few weeks, I suggested we tried sleeping together again, but I couldn't rest if Freddie was in bed with us. I was scared of rolling onto him.

'Maybe you're right. Perhaps you had better go back to the spare room. Just for a while.'

The 'while' led into more weeks and then months. It wasn't perfect. But I felt better with more sleep and Sarah was a different woman now she was a mother. Freddie definitely recognized me at last and made 'excited' noises when I came back from work.

'We've missed you,' Sarah would say, nestling into my chest.

Occasionally I thought back to that night in the hospital where I'd been on the point of leaving for a different life.

Thank goodness I'd made the right decision.

I look down now at the barrister speaking and the judge's intent face as she makes the occasional note. I cannot bring myself to look at the man in the dock.

Of course, Hilary doesn't know I'm here – in court – today. She thinks I'm at a conference. Hilary has been helping me. She didn't know I was going to the trial because I was ashamed, but when I came home after the first day, I had to tell her everything.

'You didn't mention that before,' she said last night, after supper.

'Didn't I?' I replied, carefully folding up my newspaper.

Another lie.

To add to all the others.

22

Sarah

When Freddie was two, I allowed Tom to take him to the local playground. This was Olivia's idea. 'You need to let Tom take charge sometimes. I know you're worried in case he takes his eye off him. I feel the same with Hugo. But it shows them what hard work it is to bring up kids instead of the doddle they appear to think it is. It will also give you a break.'

Mothers nowadays seem to think nothing of men looking after children. Yet back then it wasn't so common. And I couldn't help feeling nervous about letting my son out of my sight.

I should have listened to my gut instinct. When the two of them came back, Freddie was crying inconsolably and holding his arm.

'He fell off the slide,' said my husband sheepishly, taking off his glasses and wiping them.

'Where were you?'

'At the bottom, waiting. It wasn't my fault. Boys do things like that. It will toughen him up.'

'Were you on your phone?'

'I was taking a quick work call. But I was still watching him.'

'You can't do both,' I snapped.

Freddie wouldn't stop crying. 'My arm,' he kept saying.

'It doesn't look right,' I pointed out. 'We'd better get it X-rayed.'

'Don't you think you're fussing –'

'No! I don't!'

I was right. Freddie had something called a buckle fracture.

'How did that happen?' asked the doctor sharply. It was a time when there were frequent newspaper reports about parental abuse.

'He fell off a slide when my husband was watching him,' I said, unable to keep the anger out of my voice.

Tom's face looked like thunder.

'Why did you blame me in front of the doctor?' he demanded after Freddie's arm had been set in a plaster cast.

'Because it was *your* fault.'

'Keep your voice down,' hissed Tom. We were leaving the hospital now but people were coming in and out of the main doors. 'You're not exactly perfect,' he said coldly as we headed for the car park.

'That's got nothing to do with this,' I retorted. 'Besides, we agreed to put all that behind us. Didn't we?'

'Don't argue, Mummy and Daddy,' pleaded Freddie.

Tom fell silent. But the answer to my previous question was obvious. That was the trouble with lies. Once they came out in the open, they could not be buried again, however much earth you tried to shovel on top.

After our son's accident, everything changed. I became scared stiff that Freddie would get hurt again. It had taken us so long to have him. He was so precious. But with this incredible gift came a weight of responsibility. How could I live if anything happened to him?

Then, one night, Tom came back even later than usual.

'Where have you been?' I asked, cross because he'd woken Freddie by not shutting the front door quietly enough.

'I had a meeting that went on late. We all went out for drinks afterwards.'

I was so besotted with — and exhausted by — Freddie that I didn't even think to question him about who was there. 'How are we going to conceive another child if you come back late, too exhausted for sex?'

Tom sighed. 'We've already talked about this. Look at what we went through to get Freddie. It caused so much strain. Let's be grateful for what we've got.'

I should have left it there for another time when he was less tired. But I didn't. 'I just want him to have a brother or sister,' I pleaded. 'Neither of us had that.'

'He can have friends instead,' said my husband.

'It's not the same,' I retorted, turning my back.

As time went by, I kept hoping Tom would change his mind. Freddie was coming up to three now and everything around him seemed brand new. 'Look at the sky!' he said one day when we were walking down the high street, his little hand firmly in mine. 'It's lots of different colours!'

He was a fluent talker for his age – something I was immensely proud of.

'It's called a rainbow,' I said, kneeling down and putting my arm around him while pointing up at the arc. 'It happens when it's raining and sunny at the same time.'

'It's magic!' he said, his eyes wide.

If Tom was here, he'd go into the scientific facts. 'Yes,' I said. 'It is.'

'It's like a smile,' he added. 'The rainbow is happy!'

He was right.

'Shall we paint it when we get home?' I suggested.

Freddie was a natural artist. I could tell that from the way he noticed things around us. He held a pencil as if he had been born with one in his hand. He even tried to scoop up the pictures from the pages of his books with his fingers, trying to get hold of them. I remember doing the same myself as a child. 'That's good,' my mother had said, smiling. 'It shows you've got a great imagination.'

He was cheerful, too. He had a smile like mine. Everyone said so. He always saw the bright side of everything. Once, when we got caught in a shower on the way back from the shops, he opened his mouth wide to catch the drops. 'I love the taste of rain,' he said.

We used to dance as well. Oh how we danced! Round and round to one of my favourite albums, *Ziggy Stardust*.

Sometimes, if Tom was going to be even later than usual – something that was happening more and more – I would delay Freddie's bath time and take him for an evening walk to see the stars. 'That one is called Orion's Belt,' I said, pointing out the line in the sky. 'Do you see that shape over there? What does it look like to you?'

'A saucepan,' he said.

'Exactly!'

'Is there a Starman up there?' he asked. 'You know. Like the music we dance to?'

'Maybe.'

I hugged my little boy close to me, breathing him in. Yet I also felt a terrible sense of impending loss. Before long, Freddie would be too old for these magic moments.

I simply *had* to have another child. It wasn't just the maternal longing. It was, as I'd said to Tom, really important for our son to have the company. How much easier life might have been for me if I'd had a brother or sister to share it with.

I would do anything to get one for him.

23

Tom

After the playground accident, I completely lost my confidence. I wasn't fit to look after a child.

Sarah didn't exactly say that. But I knew what she was thinking. That's why I was so cross with her. It's all too easy to take out one's own anger or disappointment on someone else. The truth is that if I had not been on the phone, I might have been more observant of my son.

Hilary did not adopt this point of view, although I have to confess that I left the 'talking on the phone' bit out and just said that I 'took my eye off' Freddie for a short time. 'It's impossible to watch a child all the time,' she said. 'It was one of those unfortunate accidents. One could argue that it will teach your son to be more careful. Little people have to start learning at some point in their lives.'

Hilary had a nephew with asthma so she understood about that too. In fact, she was very encouraging. 'He has grown out of it now,' she said. I noticed that Hilary often said 'he has' instead of 'he's' or 'I have not' instead of 'I haven't'. I liked that. The English language can be so sloppy at times.

It was comforting to have a sensible female perspective, especially as I was beginning to feel more and more that Sarah and Freddie were against me. When we went for the final hospital check-up for his arm, the doctor questioned me again. How exactly did it happen? Was anyone else there to see it? I almost began to believe I had hurt him myself deliberately.

Of course, I'd never do that. Freddie was my son. Yet I now made up excuses not to be in charge of him alone again. What if he had another accident? It was partly why I didn't want another child. We had enough pressure to cope with as it was.

Sarah's incessant nagging not only affected my mind. It also meant I was unable to perform in bed. 'It doesn't matter,' said Sarah one night. But I sensed the disappointment in her voice.

This made me feel inadequate as well as frustrated. I had my urges, like any man. To my shame, I found myself thinking of Hilary instead and getting relief that way. Afterwards, I felt awful. She was only a friend. I wasn't the type to be unfaithful. Besides, it had only been in my head.

It turned out, as the next three years went by, that Hilary was right. Freddie did grow out of his asthma. But he remained what they called at the hospital a 'chesty child'. His behaviour also became erratic, even though Sarah claimed he was 'very good compared with other children'.

At times, he would play quite happily with me. Our favourite was the electric toy train set I had bought him. But sometimes he could be impossible. One morning, when I was helping him to put together a three-hundred-piece jigsaw, he actually punched me on my arm because I placed a piece of the sky in before him.

'How dare you!' I shouted. 'That hurt me and it's also very rude. I was trying to help you. Go to your room.'

'No.'

My son was standing there, his hands on his hips, glaring at me as though he was an adult telling off a child instead of the other way round.

I would never have dared to say no to my father and I had no intention of taking it from my son. He needed to be taught a lesson.

'MUMMY!' roared Freddie. 'Daddy smacked me on my bottom.'

'What?' Sarah came running in. 'Why did you do that?'

'Because he hit me on the arm for helping him with his jigsaw.'

'And you think that smacking is going to teach him a lesson?'

'Well, someone has to teach him right from wrong.'

'I do that, Tom. I reason with him.' She turned to Freddie. 'You mustn't hit Daddy. It's wrong.'

He pouted. 'The boys at school do it.'

'Then they shouldn't. It's not kind.'

'All right, Mummy.' He was cuddling up to her now while sending dark looks at me.

'There you are,' said Sarah. 'He understands now.'

'Is that it?' I said.

'No, actually, it isn't. I don't ever want you smacking him again. How can violence stop violence?'

'I wasn't being violent,' I pointed out.

'My bottom hurts,' whined Freddie.

'Let me see.' Her voice rose. 'There's a red mark on it. How hard did you hit him?'

Both of them were staring at me accusingly. 'This is ridiculous,' I pointed out. 'He's the one who stepped out of line. Besides, everyone got smacked in my day.'

'Well, I didn't.'

'Then maybe you should have been, Sarah. It might have stopped you getting into trouble later on.'

There was a cold silence. Had I gone too far? Then again, it was true.

'We're going out,' she said to Freddie, ignoring me.

'Fine. If that's the way you want to play it, go ahead.'

I expected them to come back soon and apologize. But they didn't. I tried to do some work to clear my head but it didn't help. I was tempted to ring Hilary to tell her what had happened or Hugo. But I was too ashamed to tell them I had a child who hit his own father. What kind of son did that? Yet underneath it all, I felt mortified. Was it my fault? Could it be that Freddie had inherited that terrible bullying streak of mine from school?

By the time my wife and son returned, two hours later, laughing and chatting to each other about their time on the swings in the park as though nothing had happened, I felt a cold distance between me and them.

I was beginning to feel more and more like an outsider. Freddie continued to behave badly towards me. One evening, when Sarah was out on a 'girls' night' with Olivia, he refused to stay in bed and kept coming downstairs. 'You've got to behave,' I kept saying.

Then he'd smile at me as though he was enjoying the fact that he was making me annoyed.

Despite my earlier conviction that I'd made the right decision to stay, I found myself wondering what might have happened if I hadn't asked Sarah to come back from Olivia's after Freddie's birth. We might have got divorced. We'd have had to sell this house to afford separate homes.

Or maybe a judge would have ruled that Sarah and Freddie would stay until he was older and I'd be out on my ear. Freddie would have come back and forth between the two of us. No, I told myself. That wouldn't have been right. Things would get better when he became older.

'I don't feel well today,' he said a few weeks later. 'Do I have to go to school?'

'Is this something to do with the maths test?' I asked.

He had one every Tuesday at school. I'd spend time helping him prepare every week. But the child just didn't have a head for figures. At his age, I was doing long multiplication. He had problems adding simple single figures like nine and four.

'No.' Freddie gave me that look again. It was as if I had done something wrong. 'I feel sick.'

'Oh dear,' said Sarah. 'Perhaps you should stay at home then.'

'He seems all right to me. Have you taken his temperature?'

It was normal. 'Better play safe,' said Sarah firmly.

When I got home from work that night, the two of them were sitting at the dining-room table, crayoning.

'Better, then, is he?' I asked pointedly.

'Your son's right here,' said Sarah. 'You can ask him yourself you know.'

'There's no need to be hostile.'

Sarah, for her part, was only interested in him, or so it seemed. She hardly ever asked me about the office. Instead, it was Freddie this and Freddie that. 'I'm worried he's not making enough friends at school,' she said. 'He never gets asked back to play with others.'

'Maybe there's a reason for that.'

'What do you mean?'

'Well, perhaps he's not very nice to them, like he's not nice to me.'

'Oh grow up, Tom. It's not all about you, you know.'

In the end, I took the plunge and confided in Hugo during one of our tennis games. 'Join the club,' he said. 'I feel it's Olivia and the girls against me all the time. So I've given up. I let them do what they want. I don't interfere with her ways of child-rearing. We almost live separate lives during the week. I have dinner on my own now when I come back from the office. She says she can't wait so eats with the kids.' He slapped me on the back. 'Don't worry. You'll get used to it.'

'An acquaintance of mine suggested some family therapy.'

'That's a sign of failure, in my book.'

'She says that —'

'She?' Hugo stopped. 'A female acquaintance? Are you not telling me something, Tom?'

'Of course not.'

'You're going red.'

'It's just a woman in the office. She's simply a friend.'

'But you don't have women friends.'

'Forget it, can you?'

'What's her name?'

'Actually I don't feel like playing that third set. I think I'll go home now.'

Hugo grinned. 'Suit yourself.'

Even though I hadn't done anything wrong, Hugo made me feel uncomfortable. My friendship with Hilary was the only thing that helped the situation. We had some intelligent discussions about current affairs. Occasionally, I would mention things that had happened at home. But I stopped short at confiding in her about Sarah's past. That felt too much like a betrayal.

Then, of course, there were my Wednesday evening meetings, which I still went to. 'Thanks, Tom,' said one of the group members when we left. 'You've really helped.'

This made me feel better. If only I could help myself in the same way.

Another two years passed. Freddie was seven now, almost eight. It was perfectly clear that he preferred Sarah to me. Sometimes I'd come back from work and find the two of them engrossed over a book or some arty thing. 'Say hello to Daddy,' Sarah would prompt.

But often he wouldn't even look up.

'He's tired,' my wife would say.

'It doesn't matter,' I'd reply, going upstairs to change out of my suit and into a pair of corduroy trousers. But it did. It hurt more than I could say. All I'd wanted was to create a family. No one had told me how hard it was to be a good father when your own child wanted nothing to do with you.

There were times when I yearned to pull Sarah to me and say, 'I'm so unhappy.' But I couldn't do that. Men had to be strong. Besides, I'd made my bed, so I had to lie in it. I was not going to behave as my father had done.

I began to work even harder, getting in earlier and staying later. It was so much calmer in the office. There weren't any Freddie tantrums or Sarah telling me off for being 'too strict' towards our son. If I put something down on my desk, I knew it would be there the next day when I got back.

If I did the same at home, it would go missing. Like one of my favourite fountain pens that I later discovered in Freddie's 'craft box' with the nib all bent and twisted. 'He was using it for some pen-and-ink work we were doing,' said Sarah. 'Sorry. I'll get you another.'

My extra hours in the office resulted in a promotion. 'We're extremely pleased with you, Tom,' said my boss at my annual review. 'As a result, we'd like to offer you a promotion and an increase in salary.'

It was nice to be valued. But at the same time, I felt guilty because it had come at the expense of my family.

'Well done,' said Sarah when I told her that evening. I was at one end of the sofa and she was at the other. 'I suppose this means we'll see even less of you now.'

'Do you and Freddie care?' I couldn't resist saying.

'Of course we do.'

'It doesn't feel like it.'

'Tom,' said Sarah, sighing. When she didn't smile, she looked completely different. 'I'm doing my best here to bring up our son single-handed.'

'Single-handed?' I repeated. 'What do you mean?'

'Well, you haven't seen him for four days. You've been home too late to kiss him goodnight at bedtime.'

Guilt made me defensive. 'I'm working for the family. For us.'

I didn't add that it was better than being at home with two people I didn't understand.

Meanwhile, Hilary had also been promoted. Sometimes I found myself getting some lunchtime fresh air in the park, where she also ate her sandwiches. Cucumber and Cheddar were her favourite too. 'So,' she'd say to me, 'what do you honestly think about this new "broadband" idea for the internet? Do you think it will eventually replace dial-up connections altogether?'

It was so refreshing to talk to someone who genuinely seemed interested in me and wasn't always breaking off to talk about schools or nits.

Since Freddie had been born, our love life – which had once been so much a part of us – had dwindled down to almost nothing. I've already said how I found it hard to . . . well, perform. Besides, by the time I came to bed, Sarah was often asleep. And when she painted late, I would turn out the lights in our bedroom because I was exhausted. Unlike my wife, I had to work the next day.

So I was surprised and embarrassed to discover that when I was in close proximity to Hilary, I sometimes wondered what it would be like to kiss her. Even – with her permission, of course – to take off her clothes.

Then one day it all changed. 'I've been headhunted,' she said to me, carefully unfolding a napkin to place on her lap. It was a proper linen one that she'd brought to work with her, along with her neatly cut sandwiches and flask.

'Really?' I said, chewing the tuna rolls that Sarah had cobbled together for me that morning because I was running late after an early morning call from a client. 'By whom?'

I put lunch to one side. The news had left a feeling of emptiness in my stomach.

She named the firm; it was one of our competitors.

Then she told me about the position they were offering. 'What are your views?'

'It might be a good move, career-wise,' I said hesitantly.

'I thought so as well.'

I waited for her to say that she might miss my company. But she didn't.

I chose not to attend Hilary's leaving party. Instead, I walked up and down the Embankment, staring out at the dark water illuminated by the reflected streetlights. What would it be like, I wondered, to board a boat and head off to sea. 'What are you thinking of?' I reprimanded myself. 'You have a moral duty to your wife and child.'

Two more years went by. Freddie was almost ten and at the local primary. I'd favoured a prep school at the end of the Bakerloo Line but Sarah had wanted him to be in a 'non-exclusive environment'. I'd lost that argument.

I'd hoped Sarah would become less anxious by now but, if anything, she became tenser, always fussing about whether he was 'happy'. She was also in a panic about swine flu, which had been declared a pandemic.

'If you take into account the statistics relating to our particular area,' I told her, 'we only have a low to moderate risk.'

'Low to moderate?' she'd repeated. 'That's not good enough. How do you think I could live without Freddie?'

What about me? I wanted to ask.

Meanwhile, I was concerned that our son was unable to understand long division. In fact, he still showed a distinct lack of interest in numbers, preferring to read or make nondescript shapes with felt-tip pens that had the irksome habit of ending up on the walls. I tried to bond with him by making up fun maths games. 'Maybe you'd like to be an actuary like me,' I said.

'I want to paint instead.'

'But art isn't going to get you a proper job.'

'Thanks,' said Sarah, overhearing.

'I didn't mean it like that.'

'I think you did.'

'Don't argue with Mummy,' scowled Freddie. Then he picked up a cricket ball that was on the floor and threw it across the room, cracking a window.

How dare he? Almost without thinking, I smacked him on the bottom. I hadn't touched him since the last time. The boy yelled even though it wasn't very hard.

'I told you not to smack him again!' screamed Sarah.

'I'm trying to teach him a lesson. I wouldn't have to if you controlled him properly.'

'Well, you're going about it in the wrong way.' She turned to Freddie. 'You're too big to do things like that now, darling. Apologize to your father, please.'

'I didn't mean to smash the window.'

'But why was there a cricket ball in the house anyway?'

'Because I was sorting out his sports kit,' flashed back Sarah. 'Say sorry, Freddie.'

'No.' He glared at me again. 'It was an accident.'

'Now what are you going to do?' I demanded, quite reasonably, I thought.

'Well, I'm certainly not going to hit him.' I used to love my wife's deep brown eyes. Now they flashed at me in a manner that could only be described as hostile. 'Violence breeds violence,' she spat.

'Well, you'd know all about that after your experience inside,' I couldn't help retorting. Too late I regretted this and a sick twist of shame began to screw up my gut.

'Inside where?' asked Freddie.

'Nowhere,' said Sarah quickly. 'Your father didn't mean to say that. Did you?'

I didn't answer. That night, I slept in the spare room and went to work early.

Sarah appeared to have finally accepted my decision that it wouldn't be sensible to have any more children. Looking back, I should have seen that as a warning sign.

'How's it all going?' asked Hugo, when we met for a Sunday-morning game of tennis.

He and I had slowly reached an uneasy truce after my discovery that he'd threatened Chapman the night before his death. I was still furious that he'd implicated me too. But despite everything, we were bound together by the past.

I thought of the office and how empty it had seemed since Hilary's departure. I had glimpsed her once at a conference but we hadn't spoken. She had merely nodded at me across a hall of delegates, and although I looked for her when we left, she was nowhere to be seen.

'Everything is fine,' I said, in reply to Hugo's question.

'Freddie well?'

'At the moment. He's very active. The other day he broke a window by throwing a cricket ball across the room.'

Hugo grimaced. 'Welcome to parent world. How's that gorgeous bohemian wife of yours doing?'

I chose to ignore the 'bohemian' part in the interest of

our friendship. Hugo often referred to Sarah in these terms and he knew I disliked it, especially as her appearance had now become more conventional. 'She appears well, if a little tired,' I replied stiffly.

'Must be all that sex! I bet the two of you are at it like rabbits.'

I refused to be drawn though, so I merely shrugged.

'Olivia and I haven't done it for years now. Probably getting it somewhere else.' Hugo said this in an odd sort of casual voice that meant it mattered more than he cared to say. Rather like my reply to Hilary when she had told me she was leaving the firm. '*It might be a good move, career-wise.*'

'Do you really think she's having an affair?' I asked, in what I hoped was a neutral voice.

'Maybe.'

'Then why don't you talk to her?'

'Because I don't want to rock the boat and lose at least half of my assets, like so many of my friends. Besides, I've had a few flings myself.'

'You once mentioned a girl who worked in a bar,' I said slowly. 'There were others?'

'They didn't mean anything. It's what people do to keep their marriage going.'

'I don't.'

'What about that woman you mentioned in the office?'

'Hilary's just a colleague, as I said.'

'*Hilary?*' He grinned that wolfish smile again. 'So that's her name.'

'If you're going to talk like this, I'm off.'

'Wait. I'm sorry. I know you're not the type to mess

about. Now how about coming back to my place after the game and having a few beers?'

When we got there, I was shocked by Olivia's reception. 'You were meant to have been home an hour ago,' she said to Hugo, flinging a pair of oven gloves at him. 'You can make your own lunch and look after the kids. I'm going out.'

Hugo gave me a 'See?' look.

'Mum, don't be horrid to Dad,' said Clemmie. She was a teenager now. In my view, she had been easier as a child. And that was saying something.

Her sister started crying.

'Now look what you've done,' said Hugo. 'You've upset the kids again.'

'I think I'd better go,' I said. But no one seemed to hear me, so I left.

When I got home, there was no one there. Homework and paints were littered across the floor. On the table was a note: *Gone for a walk in the park*.

I walked around, trying to tidy up. But I kept thinking about how unhappy Hugo was and how he and Olivia had once seemed the perfect couple.

Perhaps I needed to try harder. So after I'd sorted out the house, I put on my outdoor shoes and went to find them. As I approached, I could see my wife and Freddie. Their dark heads were close together as they bent over something on a bush.

'Hi!' Sarah seemed surprised. 'Look, Freddie. It's Dad. Show him what we've found.'

'It's a red admiral,' he said. Then he ran off towards the slide, clearly uninterested in pursuing the conversation.

Sarah offered her cheek to me. I brushed it with mine. Skin on skin. I'd forgotten how that felt.

'Did you have a good game of tennis?'

'Yes, thank you,' I said. 'How was your walk?'

'Lovely, thanks.'

The three of us walked home together, with Freddie running ahead. To an outsider, we might have looked like the perfect family. But the truth was that I was the odd one out. The part of the equation that didn't quite fit.

I could still hear Hilary's words from the night of Freddie's birth. *'However, if you find, later on down the line, that you and Sarah are not compatible, then that's something else.'*

But we hadn't reached that point, I told myself.

I owed it to my wife and child to stay.

I would do what I knew best. Work hard. Provide for them. And accept that I didn't belong to their little twosome.

24

Sarah

Tom seemed to think that staying at home with a child was easy. But I can tell you that it wasn't. Not where Freddie was concerned, anyway. No sooner had one stage finished – like the earlier toddler tantrums – than another took its place.

One sunny August morning during the school holidays, Olivia suggested we took the children on a walk along the Thames. Freddie was ten and desperate to keep up with the girls, who were racing ahead. 'Not so fast,' called out Olivia. 'Honestly,' she said. 'My girls are so competitive. Clemmie's livid because her sister has got into the "A" team at school. She takes after me.'

'Freddie isn't that keen on sport,' I said. That was another of Tom's disappointments. Like me, he hadn't been particularly athletic at school. But unlike me, he seemed determined that his son would do better than he had.

For a second I was lost in my anger, remembering the last time Tom had tried to make Freddie play ball.

'*Come on Freddie, don't be such a girl.*'

'Watch out!' called out Olivia.

The children were suddenly far ahead, and looking like they were going to cross the road.

'WAIT!' I yelled.

But Clemmie and Molly had already dashed over. Freddie was standing there, waiting for a gap in the traffic. I began to run. So did Olivia. But I wasn't as fast as her. I could see Freddie hesitating as lorry after lorry went by.

Oh my God! He was edging out into the road between the gaps.

'STOP!' I screamed. 'STOP!'

I wasn't going to get there in time. There was a screech. A hiss of brakes. Someone screaming. At that moment, my life ended. My legs wouldn't work. I sank to the ground, conscious I had wet myself. I knew without doubt that Freddie was gone. My son. My life. Everything was over.

Lifting my head, I saw a purple blur walking towards me through my tears. Olivia. She was struggling to carry something. A body, slung over her shoulder. 'I've got him, Sarah. It's all right.'

Then she gently put him down next to me.

'Mum,' said Freddie, hugging me desperately. 'I'm so sorry.'

The tears streaming down my face now dried into anger. 'How could you have done that? I told you to stop.'

'Auntie Olivia pulled me back. The lorry driver shouted at me and a woman screamed.' I was holding him close to me, breathing him in, flooded with gratitude and fury. 'Thank you.'

'It's all right.' Olivia put her arm around me. 'Put it down to my school athletics training.' She was trying to make a joke out of it, but I could tell she was shaking too.

Then the girls came running back.

'Are you all right? We saw what happened. I thought you were going to get hit, Mum.'

'If you hadn't gone racing ahead, Freddie wouldn't have followed you,' said Olivia sternly.

'Sorry.'

'No,' I said. 'It's my fault. We should have been closer to you.'

Instead, I'd been chatting to Olivia about my marriage. Dwelling on my anger. My friend gave me a look. She knew what I was thinking.

'How can I ever repay you for saving him?' I said on the way back.

'You don't have to.' Then she gave me a shrewd look. 'Are you going to tell Tom?'

'I suppose so.'

'Want my advice? I wouldn't mention it. It's not going to help, is it?'

'But Freddie will come out with it.'

'Ask him not to. The girls and I are always hiding small things from Hugo.'

'But this is different, isn't it?

She shrugged. 'If you ask me, the truth depends on how you see it. Everyone interprets it in different ways, don't you think?'

Olivia had saved my son's life. I was convinced of that. I'd never forget it, I told myself, to my dying day.

It brought us even closer. When the children were at school, we often had lunch together after I'd been painting in the morning. I told my friend things I couldn't tell anyone else about, such as Tom's increasingly distant behaviour and Freddie's strong-mindedness. 'The other day, we went shoe shopping and he refused to wear the only sensible pair that fitted.'

'You have to make them think that your suggestions were their idea in the first place,' offered Olivia.

'Are we talking kids or husbands?'

She giggled. 'Both.'

'Tom is so strict with Freddie.'

'I've noticed. Hugo's given up. He leaves all the disciplining to me.'

'I don't know how you do it.'

She shrugged. 'It's easier with two. They have their squabbles, but on the whole they get on. They entertain each other. Is Tom determined not to have another?'

'Completely.'

'Hugo too.' She sighed. 'I'd have liked a son, but it wasn't to be. If I got pregnant now it would be an immaculate conception.' She gave a dry laugh. 'We haven't had sex for years. Don't look so surprised. When I realized he wasn't going to let me have another, I told him I wanted separate rooms. It was meant to make him change his mind but now, well, we've stayed that way.'

'Do you mind?'

For a minute she looked wistful. 'It's not what I thought marriage would be like.'

'Me neither,' I confessed. 'We don't have sex either. I'm too tired and, well, Tom isn't always able to . . . you know.'

'Hugo too, actually. I wasn't sure if I should mention it.'

We both looked at each other and burst into giggles.

'Look at us,' says Olivia, putting her arm around me. 'We're a right pair, aren't we? To an outsider we might seem as though we have it all. Anyway, I've decided to make a big change in my life. I'm tired of doing what people expect me to. I want to be brave like you!'

For a minute, I felt scared. She wasn't leaving Hugo, was she?

'What?'

'I've got a job!'

Olivia's face was shining. 'You inspired me with your art. I got in touch with the marketing firm I used to work for before the girls were born. Turns out they were about to advertise for someone. I'm going in at a much lower level, but I'm really excited! A bit nervous too, to be honest.'

I was still struggling to get my head around Olivia going back to work. She'd always seemed to enjoy being a stay-at-home mum.

'What does Hugo say?'

She shrugged. 'He doesn't like it. As I'd expected, he went on about how he made enough money and that there was no reason why I should go out to work as well. I told him that was ridiculously old-fashioned. Then he wanted to know who would pick up the girls from school.'

There was a slight hesitation.

'I'll do that,' I heard myself saying.

'Really? That would be amazing. Thank you.'

'It's the least I can do after everything you've done for me.'

But our conversation about sex troubled me. Voicing my problems out loud made me realize that I didn't want Tom and me to be the kind of couple who grew apart and laughed with their friends about it. How could I fix it?

Then I saw an advert for a holiday let in Cornwall and suggested to Tom that we take a break. Tom didn't like going abroad. He came out in a rash when the sun was hot. But he seemed quite amenable to this idea.

The brochure picture hadn't lied! When we arrived, we found a lovely small stone cottage on a beach near St Ives that looked out onto the harbour. Seagulls swooped around. The air smelt different. The change of scene seemed to work miracles almost from the minute we arrived. 'Who wants to go exploring?' asked Tom.

'Me,' said Freddie.

We fished in rock pools with purple crabbing nets we bought on the seafront. On the second day I encouraged the two of them to go out on their own. I felt nervous when they were away in case they fell out, but they returned flushed and happy, chatting to each other.

On the third night we had fish and chips sitting on the harbour wall, watching the boats come in. 'This is lovely,' I said dreamily. 'I wish we could live by the sea.'

'Me too,' said Freddie.

'It wouldn't be practical,' said Tom.

'I know that,' I said, slipping my hand into his. 'But we can dream.'

That night we made love for the first time in years. It wasn't like it used to be. I had to encourage him. But being away from home made it better.

The next day, Tom and I held hands as we watched Freddie swimming. When he got out we bundled him into a large soft towel, both of us rubbing him dry, Freddie grinning amidst his shivers.

Silently, I made a wish that things would stay like this.

And it seemed to come true. At least for a while.

Freddie went to secondary school. There he had an art teacher who was very encouraging. 'It's what I want to do when I grow up,' Freddie kept saying. 'I'm going to be a proper artist, like you.'

I'd started selling at a small local gallery now and had also gone back to teaching at art school. I didn't need to feel guilty about being away from home more because Tom had loads of late meetings in his new role and Freddie spent one evening a week at the school's art club.

I also picked up Olivia's girls from their school as promised and sometimes brought them back to our place for tea. 'I know they're old enough to come home on their own but there are too many weirdos and temptations out there.'

Olivia's hours seemed to get longer and longer but she was always very grateful.

'I love working,' she said, with a flush on her cheeks. 'It's so vibrant. I've discovered the woman I used to be. Thank you so much for helping out.'

'It's a pleasure.'

It was. Her girls added a new dynamic. Freddie seemed to enjoy their company too. And I loved my chats with Olivia.

One evening, she arrived at our house to collect Clemmie and Molly, carrying a large shopping bag. 'I've got us a present each,' she said, handing me a box in a brown paper bag.

'Thank you.'

Then she looked around. 'Where are the children?'

'Watching TV,' I said apologetically.

'Great. You can open yours now, then. But quickly . . . before they come in.'

I removed the box and looked at the picture on it. For a minute I didn't realize what I was holding. Then it dawned on me.

'A vibrator?' I asked.

'Shhh,' she giggled. 'They might hear us. I've got one as well.'

'But why?'

'Isn't that obvious? You and I "don't get any honey", as the Americans say. So we might as well provide our own. I'm doing the marketing for this sex-toy company and we were given some free samples. We can have some fun at last!'

I didn't want to tell her that, actually, Tom and I were now making love occasionally.

'Samples? They haven't been used have they?' I asked.

Olivia screeched with laughter. 'Of course not! Look they're in sealed bags.'

'But what will Tom say?'

'You don't tell him, silly. Keep it somewhere safe and then go up to bed earlier than him. Say you're tired. It's fine for me because we're in separate rooms, but some of my friends play with theirs in the bathroom with the door locked and the radio on.'

'So you know people who use these things?'

'Of course! For someone who's lived the life you have, I'm surprised you're so naive at times.' She gave me a quick hug. 'Don't take that the wrong way.'

We fell about laughing.

'What's so funny?' asked Clemmie, coming in from the lounge.

'Nothing much, darling,' said Olivia as I quickly put my 'present' back in the shopping bag. 'I was just telling Auntie Sarah about something that happened at work. We have to go home now.'

'Thank you for collecting us,' they chorused. Then they each gave me a hug. I really was very fond of them. How I'd have loved a sister for Freddie.

'They've done their homework,' I added as they left.

'Don't forget to do yours too,' called back Olivia with a wink.

'What homework?' asked Freddie.

'That painting I need to finish,' I said. It wasn't a lie. I did need to finish it. The buyer who had purchased a previous one had commissioned this. It was of the sea and I'd done it from a photograph I'd taken in the Scillies during our honeymoon. I almost didn't want to sell it. The turquoise and aquamarine blues drew me in and made me feel as though I was right there, in the water. Away from all this.

That night I did what Olivia had suggested. I often went up to bed earlier than Tom anyway. He tended to hang around downstairs checking emails. The vibrator was easier to use than I'd thought it would be. I felt a surge of pleasure rush through me. Oh my goodness! I hadn't realized it could be like this!

I woke up the next morning feeling – well, glowing, actually. But a part of me was also cross as I looked over to Tom. Using Olivia's present had reminded me of how good we used to be together. We would probably never be like that again.

But, unlike Hugo, at least my husband was trustworthy.

When Freddie started his GCSE course – I could hardly believe he'd grown up so fast – the pressure began to mount. 'You're going to have to concentrate more on maths and proper subjects instead of painting all the time,' Tom said.

'Art is a proper subject,' said Freddie.

'Yes,' I said. 'It is. And we've been through this before.'

'A man needs solid skills to fall back on.'

'That's so sexist,' I burst out.

'Come on, Sarah. You wouldn't be able to support yourself if it wasn't for me.'

'I'm sorry, Mum,' said Freddie later, when we were on our own.

'It's all right,' I said. But it wasn't.

Soon after that I got a phone call from Freddie's school to say he'd bunked off and had been caught smoking with some friends in town.

'Smoking what?' I asked when I was called in. Tom was at work and I felt it was best not to tell him until I knew all the facts.

The head of year had given me an uncertain look. 'Benson & Hedges, I think.'

That was a relief.

'It could have been worse,' pointed out Olivia, when I confided in her later that day after she arrived to collect the girls. She gave me a knowing look. 'It's not like cannabis or crack, is it?'

There were times when I felt Olivia knew too much about me. That was the old me. The one who still kept trying to creep in.

'How did you buy the cigarettes?' I asked my son.

Freddie shrugged. 'We borrowed my friend's brother's ID.'

'But that's illegal.'

'Is it? Everyone does it.'

'You mustn't do it again,' I said. 'I mean it. You could get a caution.'

Freddie shrugged. 'So what?'

'Trust me,' I said, my chest tightening. You don't want to get a police record.'

He laughed. 'I'm not going to, Mum. 'You fuss too much. And you're such a goody-goody!'

What would he think of me if the truth came out? My son might think it was OK to flout the law every now and then, but parents were expected to be perfect.

Then Freddie got suspended for getting into a playground brawl with an older boy. The other kid had come off worse – with a broken nose. There was no way I could hide this from my husband. Especially as Freddie wasn't allowed back to school for a whole fortnight.

'Why did you do it?' we asked him.

'He was rude about you painting naked people.'

'See?' Tom's face said. Later, he had a go at me in that pompous tone of his. 'It isn't fair on either him or us. People will wonder what's in your head.'

I stormed off. Tom was such a prude. Part of me couldn't help feeling flattered that my boy had stood up for me. On the other hand, I didn't want him being ostracized because I was different from the other mums. It made him different too and I knew how badly that had turned out for me at school.

My mind had become such a muddle. Tom was so controlling. Not just of me but of Freddie too. Nothing we could do was ever right.

For a few weeks, thankfully, everything seemed to calm

down. Then, a couple of weeks later, Freddie had a filthy argument with Tom across the dining-room table.

'Finish everything on your plate like I had to at your age.'

'I'm not a kid any more,' Freddie retorted. 'I have a right to eat what I want.'

'Not when you're living under my roof.'

Two days after that, I saw Freddie coming out of the spare room, which Tom had converted into an office. 'Only getting some paper for my printer,' he said.

That evening, when Tom returned home, he couldn't find an important report. 'I'm sure I left it on my desk,' he said. 'Have you been cleaning there?'

'No but . . .' I hesitated.

'What?'

'Freddie did go in to get some paper. Perhaps he took it by accident.'

There was a furious argument. Freddie swore he hadn't touched it. Tom didn't believe him. Apparently the report was irreplaceable. There wasn't a copy on the computer because the material was 'sensitive'.

'You didn't do anything because of that row you had with Dad, did you?' I asked when we were alone.

His eyes widened. 'Of course I didn't, Mum.'

But I felt an uncomfortable niggle inside.

Freddie's behaviour began to get worse at school again. He skipped lessons because they were 'boring' and kept getting detentions. Then he was suspended for a week for 'constant rudeness to teachers'. On one occasion, Freddie got mad and pushed me away when I tried to turn off the television because, in my opinion, he'd watched enough. I slipped and bashed my calf on the side table. He apologized, but it left a bruise. Not just on my body but in my heart. What was happening to my precious son?

Eventually, the year head suggested we take Freddie to an educational psychologist.

Tom was meant to come too, but had a last-minute meeting. I wanted to be totally honest – or as near as – so I didn't take Freddie with me to the first appointment.

'My son is angry all the time,' I explained to the woman, who looked about thirty with a wallful of certificates behind her.

'Do you get angry yourself?'

'No,' I said, uncomfortably. 'Well, I don't think so. I try to reason instead.'

'What about your husband?'

Thank goodness Tom wasn't here.

'He's quite a controlled person but sometimes he does shout at Freddie. Then he goes all distant and hurt. It's almost as if he sees it as a direct insult to him as a father rather than adolescent behaviour.'

The psychologist bent her head. I'm pretty sure I saw a flash of pity in her eyes. Perhaps it wasn't all in my head after all.

She arranged a follow-up appointment with my son and husband, but when I told him about it, Freddie refused to come with us.

'Make him,' said Tom.

'You can't make a teenager do something,' I bit back.

'When I was at school, I did what I was told.'

'And look where that got you,' I replied.

He winced. I hadn't meant it like that. But I didn't apologize.

I cancelled the follow-up appointment. What good would it do? Nothing and no one could alter my husband's conviction that it was Freddie who needed changing and not us.

Instead, I found a release in something else. In the October of that year, I was asked to contribute four paintings to an exhibition at a local gallery. I was flattered. Apparently, they had heard a lot about my work. I was the only artist showing nudes. The rest were abstracts and still lifes.

'Is that a good idea?' asked Tom when I told him. 'Freddie might get teased again. Look what happened last time.'

'I don't ask you if it's a good idea to bury yourself in figures all day.'

'If I didn't do that, we couldn't live here.'

Fine, I almost said. We can manage on our own somewhere else.

The two of us were like chalk and cheese. The very qualities that had drawn me to Tom at the beginning – security and stability – now felt boring and constrictive. One evening he suggested sex but I told him I was too tired. His behaviour had put me off him.

My world now revolved around trying to be the best mother I could and, of course, my art. This exhibition was a big thing. If nothing else, I wanted to set an example to Freddie by showing him that you had to follow your passions in life. I sent out invitations. 'Wouldn't miss it for the world,' said Olivia. 'Oh, it's a weekday, is it? I'll make sure I leave early to collect the girls from you. By the way, I'm really grateful.'

I knew she was. But actually, Olivia had begun to work extra days and there were times when I did feel that having the girls back to our place was getting a bit much. Still, my friend had saved my son's life, hadn't she? There was nothing I wouldn't do for her.

The art also helped me escape the fear that had been slowly growing for the past few years. A huge cloud of fear that was now threatening to suffocate me.

What if Freddie turned out to be like me? 'You're just like your mother,' my aunt had said over and over again.

But she was wrong.

I had done something far worse.

And then, as if I didn't have enough on my mind, there was Zac.

25

Tom

I should have known the past could only stay there for so long.

For her part, Sarah ought never to have agreed to take part in the exhibition. It wasn't fair on Freddie. It might have been perfectly acceptable if my wife specialized in flowers or dogs. But the naked male form made me feel physically sick. Was it surprising, after what I'd been through? I thought she'd understand that.

The model in all her paintings was a young man; one of the students at the art college where she taught.

'Can I come too?' asked Freddie at breakfast on the day of the opening.

'May,' I said firmly. 'Not can. "Can" implies a physical ability to do something. "May" requires permission. And the answer is no. You know we've been through this before.'

Sarah had organized a babysitter; something else that Freddie resented because he considered himself 'too old' to have one. She'd gone ahead of me. I'd already explained I might be late because of a national actuarial conference.

When I arrived at the hall where the arts exhibition was taking place, there was quite a crowd. At first I couldn't see my wife. Then I spotted her in the corner, her head close to a man with spiky red hair. They seemed engaged in conversation, oblivious to anyone else around them. He was touching the small of her back.

'Hello,' I said, approaching.

Sarah was clearly awkward, fiddling with her hair in that way she did when she was nervous. She'd done something to her eyes. There were black lines around them, which made them even more beautiful. And she was wearing the same shade of red lipstick that had struck me when we'd first met.

'Tom,' she said. 'This is Zac. He was at art school with me.'

I took in this skinny man with tattoos on his neck and a denim jacket. Had he been one of her druggy friends like that woman on the street? 'How do you do?' I said coolly.

He took this as an invitation to shake my hand. His grip was firm. 'Thanks, mate. Your Sarah has some great stuff here.'

I looked up at the painting on the wall. Sarah hadn't shown it to me before. She wanted it to be a surprise, she said. It looked like congealed scrambled eggs. Then I realized it was a couple with their bare limbs wrapped around each other. 'Very . . . very unusual,' I said.

'So you don't like it,' said Sarah. There was a snort in her voice, suggesting she wasn't surprised.

'I didn't say that.'

'I know what you meant.'

'I'll leave you two to it,' said Zac. 'Nice to meet you.'

As soon as he'd gone, Sarah turned on me. 'Why do you always put me down?'

'I don't.' I watched the man make his way across the room. 'Does he know you went to . . .'

I couldn't even say the word 'prison' but she knew what I meant.

'Yes.'

'So, do others here know too?'

She glanced across to a pretty woman – also with bright red lipstick – clutching a mug of tea instead of booze. 'Maybe Crystal. She was in my year at art school. I didn't expect her to be here either. She lives in Florida now and, before you ask, she was one of the good girls.'

Then my eye fell on that man again. I couldn't help feeling jealous. 'What about this Zac?' I asked. 'Did you two go out with each other at art college?'

She flushed. 'For a while. But it was just casual.'

Her voice was defensive, in the way that some people speak when they are accused of something true.

'He was touching your back.'

'It was a sign of friendship. Nothing more.'

People were beginning to look at us.

'You've told enough lies in the past,' I said, more quietly.

'Don't you think I know that? But, as you say, that was the past. I'm different now.'

Then someone came up and tapped my wife on her shoulder. 'I love that painting of the old lady in the corner. Could you tell me more about the inspiration behind her?'

I was beginning to feel distinctly uncomfortable with all these people talking in what felt like a different language. Where were Olivia and Hugo? They had both promised to come.

So I left.

I could have gone home. But I didn't.

What was I doing, I asked myself, as I walked towards Hilary's apartment. This was totally out of character for me. Or was it? The numbers seemed to have finally added up. The way in which Zac had touched my wife's body had definitely suggested a certain familiarity.

But it wasn't just that. It was Freddie too. My son and my wife were ganging up on me. Whatever I suggested was wrong. I felt as though I was the odd one out with those two against me.

'May I help you, sir?' asked the porter.

'Er, Miss Morton . . .'

I hesitated. Hilary might not even be in.

'Miss Morton,' repeated the porter. 'Apartment twenty-four. She's at home, I believe. I could ring her, if you like.'

'That would be very kind,' I said in as casual a tone as I could muster.

I tried to calm myself as I listened to the man on the phone.

'She says to go straight up,' he said. 'Level Two.'

'Thank you.'

My heart was beating as I stepped into the lift. It wasn't too late, I told myself as the doors closed. All I had to do was press the button marked *Open*. I could leave, ring Hilary from outside and concoct some excuse. But my hand wouldn't move. I stayed in the lift as it began to ascend. It stopped on the second floor.

I didn't believe in fate but I felt my feet were taking a preordained path towards her. I rang the bell.

Hilary was wearing a pretty blue floral dress. Her face looked worried. 'Is everything all right, Tom?'

'Yes and no,' I said.

She gestured me to enter. 'That's not like you to be uncertain.'

'I know,' I said, closing the door behind me.

'But how did you know where I lived?'

I felt myself blushing. 'I'm afraid I made a note of your address from the office files some time ago.'

And then – unable to stop myself – I bent down and kissed her.

'We're here,' he says. 'Are you ready?'

I try to find my voice. But it won't come out.

'It's cool!' he laughs. 'You'll see. No one's going to get hurt. I promise.'

My heart is pounding. My stomach clenching like I'm going to be sick.

But what choice do I have?

26

Sarah

I haven't told you about Zac before, but it was true what I'd said to Tom. It had just been a fling. And everything that came after that had made me blank out most of my life at art college. So Zac had disappeared along with the rest.

What a shock it was to see him again after all those years! He said he'd spotted my picture in the local paper, alongside a listing of the exhibition, and guessed it was me.

He was still wearing baggy jeans and had the same spiky red hair and nicotine-stained fingers. But he looked like a middle-aged man trying to be young. I'd fancied him, of course, when we'd gone out, but now I wondered what on earth I'd seen in him.

I decided I'd be nice for a few minutes and then make an excuse. But he wouldn't leave me alone. He kept putting his hand on my back. It made me uncomfortable, yet I was scared he'd say something if I showed it. That's when Tom came up to us. I knew he'd read it the wrong way. And to be honest, I couldn't blame him. So I wasn't surprised when I found my husband had left without telling me. I had to stay late, helping to tidy up. Then I realized with a sickening feeling that Zac was still there. Eventually, I realized I'd have to talk to him.

'Lovely to see you again.' I smiled in what I hoped was a dismissive way.

'Your husband isn't the kind of man I thought I'd see you end up with,' he said.

'Why do you say that?'

'Pretty staid, I'd say.'

'He's a good man,' I said shortly.

'But does he give you the space to paint? Does he understand you on the inside?'

'We have a son. He means everything to me.'

'That's not what I asked. I know you, Sarah.'

'No you don't. You knew the old me.'

He reached out and touched the side of my face. 'Do you know what I see?'

I flinched. 'No.'

'I see the old Sarah.'

'Please, Zac. Go.'

'It wasn't all your fault, you know. Emily was to blame too. She wasn't quite as naive as you think.'

'I'm leaving now.' I raised my voice and one of the attendants looked over.

'Fine, fine. I'm off. But be true to yourself, Sarah. If there's nothing else I've learned in life, it's that.'

I was shaking as I walked home.

When I got back, I found the sitter asleep in front of the television. So Tom still wasn't home?

I checked my phone for messages. Nothing from Tom or Olivia to explain her non-appearance. I didn't care about Hugo, who hadn't turned up either, but I was disappointed by my friend. She knew how important the exhibition was to me.

'Everything all right?' I asked the sitter.

'Fine,' she mumbled, clearly trying to pretend she hadn't dozed off. She was one of the receptionists at the arts centre. I'd asked her twice before and Freddie seemed to accept her because she was 'cool', despite his previous objections about being too old for a sitter.

'Freddie went up to bed as good as gold at nine o'clock,' she continued, stumbling to her feet and stretching. 'I haven't heard a peep out of him since.'

An uneasiness crawled through me. The house was very quiet. My son usually blasted out loud music from his room. Tom was always having a go at him about it. 'I'll just get some money from upstairs,' I said. But I headed for Freddie's room first. His door was shut.

'You've got to knock, Mum.'

It was his latest rule. I understood that. I'd never had much privacy when I was a teenager. My aunt was always barging in and out.

When I went in, the duvet was rumpled and there were CDs and books and T-shirts strewn on the carpet. But no Freddie. Maybe he was in the bathroom? No.

My heart skipped a beat. I ran down. 'Are you sure he didn't come downstairs?' I asked the sitter.

She frowned. 'Quite certain.'

Maybe he was in the kitchen, making a cheese toastie; that was something we did together as a late-night treat when Tom was working over.

But he wasn't.

The downstairs loo?

No.

If my son had a mobile, I'd be able to ring it. But Tom

said it might distract him from homework even though I'd been on Freddie's side from a safety point of view. 'It means I can get hold of him,' I'd argued.

'We didn't have them in our day and we managed perfectly well without,' my husband had answered back.

Then I realized. My son's black hoodie that he'd made me buy him instead of a smarter jacket that I preferred, had gone. So too had his trainers.

'He must have sneaked out,' I said tightly. 'Didn't you see him?'

'No.'

'Then maybe you shouldn't have bloody well been asleep!'

I didn't normally swear. Not any more. But I could feel hysteria rising. Freddie had never done this before. Where had he gone? And where was Tom?

I rang my husband's mobile. It went straight to voicemail. I tried again. The same.

'Freddie's gone missing,' I said, hearing my voice rise with panic. 'Ring me.'

'Is there anything I can do?' asked the sitter. She sounded worried, as well she might.

'Stay here in case he comes back. Ring me if he does. I'm going out to look for him.'

'But I really need to get home.'

'And I need to find my son who *you* should have been looking after,' I snapped. Seeing Zac earlier and then finding Freddie had gone missing was bringing all the old fear and anger back. If anyone had touched my son, I'd kill them.

I ran out into the cold night air. The clocks had recently

gone back, and although it had been dark now for some time, it felt even blacker than usual. I'd forgotten, in my panic, to put on my own coat as I'd dashed out of the house but I wasn't going back now. 'Freddie!' I yelled out. 'Freddie!'

A dog walker passed. 'Have you seen a boy in a black hoodie?' I asked urgently.

'Sorry.'

I ran on, looking to my right and left as I went. Freddie had been going on about a dog ever since he was little. '*I want one, Mum.*' But Tom vetoed it. '*They moult. It might make Freddie's childhood asthma come back. They're a tie.*'

If I find Freddie, I told myself, I will make Tom allow us a dog. Where the hell was my husband? I rang his number again without stopping and almost slipped over the edge of the pavement into the road. '*Please leave a message . . .*'

My stomach began to freefall with panic. I could already hear the sirens. The searches with the dogs. A body in the woody part of the park . . .

'Freddie?' I yelled out again. 'Freddie!'

27

Tom

I woke around one a.m. to find six missed calls from Sarah followed by numerous texts. I rang the number, wondering as I did so how I was going to explain my absence. It went through to my wife's voice message.

'What is it?' asked the voice beside me.

'Freddie wasn't home when Sarah got back,' I said, leaping out of bed. I don't normally leap but the message had shaken me. 'The sitter said he'd sneaked out.'

'Is he back now?'

'I don't know. Sarah's phone is going through to voice-mail. I need to go.'

'I understand.'

Hilary sounded as calm and understanding as she had when I'd come round the previous night. I hadn't meant to sleep with her. I might not have done it I hadn't seen her again at the conference, which was why I'd been late for Sarah's art exhibition. And I might not have gone round to hers if it hadn't been for Zac and the thought that he and his arty friends might be laughing at me. I could just imagine what they'd be saying. *Have you seen the geek that Sarah's married? Chalk and cheese, aren't they? Wonder if he knows . . .*

It was the last straw after everything else. But now the

guilt was overwhelming. I was a husband. A father. What had I done? I was no better than my own father.

'I shouldn't have done this,' I said, pulling on my trousers. 'It was a mistake. I'm sorry.'

'It was wonderful.' Hilary was sitting up. Her breasts were unashamedly on show, hanging gloriously over the duvet; each perfectly proportioned without a third nipple or any other blemish.

'But also wrong.' She bit her lip. 'I've never slept with a married man before. I feel appallingly guilty.'

'It's not your fault,' I said quickly.

'And it's not yours.'

Her voice was sad. 'The thing is, Tom, that you married the wrong woman.'

How very true.

I was in a lose–lose situation. If I left Sarah, I'd feel terrible for the rest of my life. It meant breaking my marriage vows and abandoning my son. Even if I saw him for access, it wouldn't be the same.

But if I stayed, it meant putting up with Freddie's awful behaviour until he went to college, and living with a woman I had nothing in common with.

'If only I had met you earlier,' I murmured, pressing my lips on the top of her head.

'I know,' she said. 'I wish that too. Now go home and check your son is all right.'

'Can I see you again? Just as friends?'

'No. We both know that wouldn't be the right thing to do. Don't we?'

She turned away, but not before I glimpsed tears in her eyes. 'Have a good life, Tom.'

28

Sarah

I had to find my son.

I was crossing a park now. A man was sitting on a bench, his toothless mouth gaping open in sleep. He was snoring. There was a bottle of whisky lying at his side. Could he have seen him? I stood over him, wondering whether to wake this stranger. This could have been me once. I had been on the verge of being homeless again when Tom had rescued me. And now look at us. How could my life have gone so wrong again?

Must find Freddie.

There were more benches. More people asleep or drinking. 'Lost your bloke, have you, love?' slurred one.

'My son,' I said.

'Oi!' He put his fingers to his lips and whistled. 'Listen up, everyone. This lady's lost her boy.'

'How old is he, love?' said a woman with a red beanie pulled down over her forehead and a cigarette in her hand.

'Fourteen,' I said.

'Got black hair, has he?'

'Yes!'

A bolt of fear and relief shot through me.

'I saw him over there with Angus, a while back.'

A man? So he'd been taken. My legs gave way and I

sank down to the ground. Oh my God! A paedophile had got him . . .

'It's all right, love.'

The woman with the beanie was speaking. She was helping me to my feet. 'Angus is OK. He won't hurt your boy. Come with me. We'll find him.'

Her hand – the one without the cigarette – was clasping mine like a claw. Her nails were biting into my palm.

'You said he was all right. Is he dangerous?'

'No. Just sensitive, like. Life hasn't been kind to him. There he is. See? Is that your kid?'

Tears rolled down my face as I ran towards the figure sitting close to an old man on a bench. There was a black sleeping bag spread across their knees. 'Freddie!' I screamed.

He looked up at me. 'Mum?' His voice sounded surprised.

'What are you doing here?' I panted.

He shrugged as if I'd asked a silly question. 'I told you before. I'm too old for a sitter. She told me to go to my room and I got bored. So I went out. Then I met up with Angus.'

'You're not meant to talk to strangers,' I hissed.

'He's *not* a stranger. Are you, Angus? I say hello to him every day on the way back from school. He used to live here when he was a boy. In fact, he's been telling me stories about what it was like in those days.'

'That's right.'

I'd never heard Freddie sound so articulate before. In fact, those were the longest sentences he'd uttered for . . . I don't know how long. Then I got it. Freddie felt like an outsider. Exactly as I had at his age. Maybe this Angus did too. The two of them had bonded.

'You've got a bright boy here,' the man said.

'Thank you. But we need to be getting home now.'

The conversation felt incongruously polite.

'Can't Angus come with us?' pleaded Freddie. 'He gets cold here at night and his rheumatism is playing up.'

Tom would have a heart attack if he came back to find a homeless man on our sofa.

'I'm sorry.' I took from my pocket the twenty-pound note that I had been going to pay the sitter with. 'Buy yourself some breakfast with this in the morning.'

Angus snatched it swiftly. 'Ta.'

Whenever I'd given people money on the street, Tom always said it would be used for drugs or drink and that I was helping to fuel their habits. (His only exception had been to 'pay off' Kelly.) But I'd known what it was like to be cold and hungry. And if my money was going to allow this poor man to get through another night, what was the harm in that? Besides, Freddie was safe.

'You must never do that again,' I said as we walked home.

'Why?'

There were times when I thought my son was old beyond his years and others when he appeared almost like a child. 'I've told you before. You can't always trust strangers.'

'But everyone's a stranger until you get to know them. Aren't you always saying that, too?'

'Yes . . . but as you get older, you learn to tell who is good and who isn't.'

'Does that always work?'

No. It didn't. But how could I explain that?

'Please don't go out of the house again without telling me. You've already been suspended from school. Isn't that enough?'

'Are you going to tell Dad?'

His voice was small. Worried. Tom's tongue could be scathing.

'I have to.'

But my husband still wasn't picking up his phone.

'He'll be mad when he finds out.'

'No he won't. I'll explain it to him.'

I reached for Freddie's hand but he pushed me away. 'I'm not a kid any more.'

'Then don't act like one.'

'I needed to get outside.'

I knew exactly what he meant.

'Tell you what,' I said. 'How about if we get you a dog. Would you do what you're told then?'

'Yes!' Freddie actually clapped his hands. I hadn't seen him so excited since he was a little boy. 'Of course. When can we get one? Can I walk him on my own? Can he sleep on my bed?'

What had I done? Tom would go nuts. But he wasn't here, was he? He wasn't the one who had to roam the park at night, looking for our son as I'd just done. He was never around when I had to sort out issues at school or persuade Freddie to do his homework. He was always at work.

'We'll see.'

The sitter was still at the house, but there was still no

sign of my husband. Maybe he wasn't in the office at all. Perhaps he was with Hugo in some bar, the pair of them moaning about their wives.

'You've got him,' the sitter said, clearly relieved that her own skin was saved. 'Why did you go out like that without telling me, Freddie?'

My son shrugged. 'You were asleep.'

She flushed. 'I wasn't!'

'Yes you were. You'd nodded off on the sofa.'

I was too angry to even engage in this conversation. I wanted this woman gone from my house. 'Get out!' I said.

She looked cross. 'I need my money.'

I rounded on her. 'I'll drop it off later, even though I could have you for negligence for not checking on him. Leave, will you?'

'Cool, Mum,' said Freddie, as she slammed her way out of the house.

'As for you,' I said. 'You're never to do that again. Do you understand?'

Glowering, he stomped up the stairs.

Then I tried Tom again. He still wasn't picking up. *'Please leave a message after the –.'*

Sod that. He'd see all the missed calls anyway. Surely he would know something was up.

But then I saw Zac had texted:

Great to see you again. Fancy catching up for a drink?

I deleted Zac's message and had a shower. I still got pleasure from knowing that the water would be hot every time. It soothed me. Cleansed me. Then I slipped into bed between the crisp sheets, curled up like a baby in my nakedness. But it was too cold, so I slipped on one of Tom's newly washed flannel tennis shirts — the nearest piece of clothing to hand.

Some time later I was aware of being shaken awake. 'Sarah! Is Freddie back?'

Tom. At last!

'He's in his room,' I mumbled sleepily.

'What happened?'

I eased myself up on my elbows. 'I found him in the park with some homeless people.'

'What?'

'He's all right. Why didn't you answer your phone? Where were you?'

'I went for a long walk.'

'At this time? Why didn't you tell me?'

'You seemed busy with your arty friends.'

'That's right. Turn it round on me.'

I was awake now, even though my clock showed it was 3 a.m. 'I've had enough of this. You need to be around more. Then Freddie will have a male role model.'

Something gave in his face. 'I'll try. But my work . . .'

'Your work is not more important than our child. There's something else too. We're getting a dog. Don't say no because I've decided. Freddie's been asking for one for ages.'

He shook his head. 'Then you'll be rewarding him for bad behaviour.'

'It will teach him responsibility. Anyway, there's been another burglary in the street and a dog will be good security.'

Tom looked as though he was going to argue, but instead he sighed. 'All right.'

'You know,' I said, 'seeing Freddie on a bench with that homeless guy terrified me. Kids suffer when their parents break up. Both you and I had horrific childhoods in our different ways. Do we really want to repeat that pattern?'

'No.' He spoke slowly as though the thought had only just occurred to him. 'You're right.' Then he took in what I was wearing. 'You've got my tennis shirt on.'

'I was cold.'

He frowned. 'I'll have to wash it again now. It will be all sweaty.'

That was so typical of Tom. Our son had gone missing and now he was back, all my husband was worried about was what he saw as 'imperfection'. I got out of bed.

'Where are you going?' he asked.

I pulled off his stupid shirt and threw it at him. 'To sleep on the sofa.'

He shrugged. 'If that's what you want.'

My mobile rang as I'd almost drifted off to sleep. For a moment, I thought it was Tom from upstairs, apologizing. But it was Olivia.

'Are you alone?' she whispered.

'Yes. What's wrong?'

'Hugo and I had a massive row before setting off for your exhibition.'

'What about?'

'He found a message on my phone.'

'From me?'

Olivia and I were always sending each other messages. Sometimes they were moans about our respective husbands. Hugo wouldn't like that.

243

'No.' She gave a small laugh. 'From this . . . well, this colleague of mine at work.'

A sinking feeling went through me. 'Do you want to tell me more?'

'I would have told you before. Honestly. But it took me by surprise. And I wanted to make sure it was serious first. We worked together before I married Hugo and . . . and we hit it off all over again. Before you ask, he's not married. Well, not any more.'

'But you are.'

'I know. And that's it. You understand what it's like being married to Hugo. I've told you enough times. You feel the same about Tom.'

'But we've always agreed that we'd stay in our marriages for the sake of the children.'

'Yes, but life doesn't go on for ever, does it? And it's bad for the girls to see Hugo and me arguing all the time. Look, I can't be long. I've had to go into the bathroom to make this call. The thing is, I need you to tell Hugo I was with you last Wednesday evening. Can you do that?'

'OK,' I said slowly. Wednesday evenings were when Tom always had a late work meeting. If it came up, I'd simply say that Olivia had come over to our house. He'd be none the wiser.

'Thank you. You're great.' Olivia sounded dreamy. 'It's so lovely to have a man who thinks I'm attractive. Someone who understands me.'

'Olivia,' I said, 'have you thought this through? What about the girls?'

'I'd never leave them,' she said. 'If I went, they'd come too. Alex knows that.'

Alex. So that was his name.

'It sounds as though you've got it all planned.'

'I need to think ahead, don't I? Got to go. Thanks so much. I owe you.'

We're back in court after our break. The barrister is shuffling his papers. The judge is taking a sip of water. The jurors are looking self-important.

More evidence is being given.

'This young man has proved time and time again that he is incapable of following decent rules. He has committed several offences, including the theft of valuable jewellery and money.'

I'm not sure I can hear much more. But I have to.

Freddie's life – and mine – depend on this.

29

Tom

If it wasn't for my guilt over Hilary – not to mention my absence when Freddie had gone missing – I'd have made more of a stand over the dog.

'In my day,' I pointed out to Sarah, as we drove along a country lane, with Freddie sitting in the back, 'we punished children for doing wrong. Not rewarded them.'

We were on our way to a farm in Essex. Against my advice, my wife had found an animal refuge. If we had to get a dog, I'd rather it came from a breeder. But apparently a farmer had taken in a pregnant Labrador that had given birth to five puppies and wasn't able to keep them.

'We've been through this before,' she said quietly. 'Don't go on about it.'

I glanced in the mirror. 'Freddie's nodded off. He can't hear us.'

It amazed me that teenagers could sleep so much. We wouldn't have been allowed to.

'I'm not asleep,' said a voice in the back. 'I'm just pretending to be so I don't have to talk to you two.'

'Freddie,' said Sarah, 'that's rude. Now come on. We're almost there. Let's think of a name, shall we?' She had put on her smiley everything's-all-right voice. 'There are four black puppies and a chocolate one, apparently.'

'Bonzo?' I suggested.

'That's so boring, Dad.'

'Thanks.'

I couldn't help feeling really hurt. Why could I never say anything right to my son?

But the glow on Freddie's face as this little chocolate Labrador walked towards us shakily was almost worth it. It reminded me of when he was small, back when things were better.

'He's perfect,' he whispered. 'May I pick him up?'

The volunteer nodded. I watched my son hold the dog to his nose. 'He smells right,' he breathed.

Sarah gave me a look. 'See,' it said. 'All we needed to do was find him something to love.'

'You'd have to be responsible for him,' she said. 'You'll be in charge of walking him when you're back from school.'

'I will,' said Freddie. 'I will.'

'What do you think, Tom?' asked Sarah.

I shrugged. 'It's up to you two,' I said.

Part of me wanted to hold this little puppy too. But I couldn't. Everything I loved seemed to turn against me.

Sarah and I had drifted so far apart. And that, I reminded myself as I thought of Hilary, was partly my fault. Still, at least I'd had the courage to break that off. I hoped Sarah was telling me the truth about Zac. I'd noticed she kept getting texts that she deleted before I could see them.

'Well, I think he's wonderful,' said Sarah.

'Jasper,' said our son suddenly. 'That's what I want to call him.'

'Jasper?'

One of those new-fangled names!

'It's the name of the singer in a band I like.'

'I see.'

On the way home, I glanced in the mirror. Jasper was sitting on our son's lap. He was looking down on the puppy with a rapt expression on his face.

I glanced across at Sarah. There was an almost identical smile on her face too. Another reminder, as if I needed it, of how similar my wife and son were. 'Sweet, isn't he?' she said. 'It will be the making of Freddie. I know it.'

Then her phone pinged. She glanced at it.

'Who's that?' I asked.

'No one,' she said.

'Really?'

'Look at it, then.' She thrust the screen in front of me, even though I was driving.

'Happy now?' she asked quietly. 'Just a spam message.'

'Don't argue,' said Freddie's voice from the back.

'We're not,' we both said.

I drove on.

But I couldn't get Hilary's sentence out of my head. *'You married the wrong woman.'*

30

Sarah

I rang Olivia back as soon as I could. I had to pretend I needed to drive to the pet shop for more dog food so I could have some privacy. That 'Ring me urgently' text of hers that had come through in the car had worried me. Thankfully, I'd managed to show Tom an old spam message I hadn't got round to deleting.

I'd learned a bit more about Alex since Olivia had asked me to cover for her. She'd also asked me to do the same a few more times; twice overnight, when Hugo had been away at conferences. I hoped that he didn't mention it to Tom when he came back.

'He makes me laugh,' she said, her eyes shining, when she came to collect the girls after the last occasion a week ago.

We'd spoken quietly in the kitchen while the kids were watching television. She'd had her lovely long strawberry-blonde hair done, I noticed. It was a bit shorter now at the back, tapering down at the front. The style suited her.

'I feel like a real person with Alex. He wants me to leave Hugo and live with him instead.'

'But what about the girls?'

'He's always wanted children of his own. His wife wasn't a family person.'

'But they're not his own,' I tried pointing out.

She'd given me a baleful look. 'I thought you'd understand, Sarah.'

'I do. I just don't want to see anyone hurt.'

'But we're hurt already. Don't you see that? Wouldn't you
be tempted if someone came along and offered you love?'

'Maybe,' I said. 'But I know what it's like to come from
a family that's been broken.'

'Your mother died,' she said.

'Exactly. And divorce is a type of bereavement too. I
couldn't let Freddie suffer.'

'I see.' Her voice was cold. 'I'm sorry you feel that way.'

I reached out for her. 'I'm not saying I disapprove. I'm
worried for you all.'

'I know.' She gave me a quick squeeze back. 'But it was
you who inspired me.'

'What do you mean?'

'Remember how you stayed here after Freddie was
born?'

'How could I forget? You were my lifesaver.'

She gave me a hug. 'And you showed me some things
too. I loved having a baby in the house. I was jealous of
you, to be honest. But Hugo hated the crying at night and
the disruption. I realized he couldn't cope with a third, and
that made me turn away from him even more. Then when
I saw how you were so unhappy, trying to keep the balance
between Freddie and Tom, I realized life was too short to
keep struggling when a relationship is obviously failing.'

So it was my fault. Or partly. That made me feel even
worse.

'You won't tell Tom or Hugo, will you?' she asked.

'Of course not.'

I didn't like the deceit, but I owed Olivia.

'Thanks. You're a good friend.'

And now there's this 'Ring me urgently' text.

She picked up immediately. 'We've left,' she said. Her voice was breathy and excited and scared, all at the same time.

'What?'

'The girls and I. We've moved to Alex's place.'

I was still trying to take this in. 'Does Hugo know?'

'I've said I'm with a friend. He'll ask you things. You promise not to say, won't you?'

'Of course I won't. But Olivia, you need to tell him.'

'I will, soon. Just leave it for me to do in my own time.'

'OK.' I felt awkward about it, but what could I do? Then it dawned on me. 'This all seems to have happened so quickly, Olivia . . .'

'Not really.'

'You started seeing him earlier than you said, didn't you?'

'I told you, Sarah. We worked together for years, before I even married Hugo.'

That wasn't my question and she knew it.

'This is the right thing to do, Sarah. I feel as though a weight has been lifted off my shoulders.'

'But what about the girls?'

'They can see their father whenever they want. They're almost grown up now. Soon they'll both be at university.'

I thought of how lonely I'd felt at eighteen. 'Children need parents, however old they are.'

'So, are you and Tom really going to be miserable until the end of your lives because you don't want to upset a middle-aged Freddie?'

I hesitated. I'd always thought that if parents were going to split up, it was best to wait until their children had left school. But now I wasn't so sure. Children didn't suddenly become responsible adults at some magical, pre-defined age. They needed stability for as long as possible.

'I don't know,' I said. 'It would need something big to happen before I did that.'

'And being unhappy isn't big?'

'I don't want to be selfish.'

Her voice changed.

'Is that what you think I am?'

'No.'

She didn't believe me. I didn't believe myself either.

'What about Hugo?' I asked.

'Hah! Now there's someone who really is selfish and only concerned about himself. Look what he did to that poor man from their school.'

'Yes, but he was young. And those terrible things that were done to them were far worse . . .'

'It isn't that on its own, Sarah. It's everything. I couldn't take it any more. Look, I wanted to tell you because you were such a good friend. I'll be in touch.'

And she put the phone down.

Were such a good friend, she'd said. Not *are*.

Perhaps she was calling to make sure I wasn't going to blab. Perhaps our friendship wasn't what I had thought at all.

But Olivia had shown me something. I couldn't break up my little family in the same way my friend had shattered hers.

Somehow, Freddie, Tom and I had to find a way forward.

31
Tom

If only I'd known that this was to be the last of our happy times. The last before Freddie changed for good.

He got up early before school every day to take Jasper for a walk and he did the same when he got back. He was politer to us both.

'It's teaching him some responsibility,' Sarah said.

My wife was being much friendlier now, too. She listened more attentively when I talked to her about work. She sat down with me to eat when I came back from the office, however late, instead of having her meals earlier. She made me apple crumble on several occasions – my favourite pudding. And she watched television with me instead of drawing. This made me feel even guiltier about Hilary. Well, that was over now. True to her word, Hilary hadn't tried to contact me once.

I was thinking about all this the following week when my mobile rang, after leaving Old Street station on my way to work. I knew as soon as I heard Hugo's voice that something had happened. It carried the same cold fear from our schooldays.

'What is it?' I asked. One of those motorbike couriers shot past me as I spoke. The noise was so loud that I had to ask him to repeat his reply.

'Olivia's left me. She's taken the girls.'

Hugo was actually crying. It took me back to those awful nights in our dorm. 'She says she needs time to find herself. I've asked her if there's someone else but she won't tell me. She said she was staying with a "friend" until she sorts herself out. I don't know what to do without her, Tom. I really don't.'

I tried to comfort him as best as I could. But how could I give advice? Hadn't I committed adultery with Hilary? I was no better than him.

That night, I made a concerted effort to leave work early, even though others were still in the office.

When I told Sarah about Olivia leaving, she was clearly shocked.

'Where is she staying, then?' she asked.

'I thought you might have an idea.'

'No,' she said. 'I don't.'

'We ought to have him over for dinner,' I said. 'He's completely lost.'

'Of course. But I'm Olivia's friend too, so I'll stay out of your way.'

Hugo was very quiet when he arrived the following evening, but livened up a bit after a few drinks. He spent most of the time talking to Freddie about rock bands. They kept discussing someone called Blink.

'It's Blink-182, Dad,' laughed Freddie.

'Yes,' said Hugo, rolling his eyes and helping himself to the bottle of whisky he'd brought with him. 'Keep up, Tom.'

This was not my area. I hadn't realized it was Hugo's either. I wondered whether you ever really knew someone.

Sarah left us alone, as she'd promised, but somehow we didn't get round to talking about Olivia. I thought he was avoiding it and I didn't exactly want to discuss it either. But as I saw him to the door, he turned to me. 'You're a lucky bastard, Tom,' he said, giving me a slap on the back. He stank of drink. 'I'd give anything to go back to having a family again. You and Sarah seem to have patched things up. By the way, what happened to that woman in the office you were always talking about?'

'Nothing,' I said shortly. 'She was just a colleague.' Luckily we were on the doorstep, well out of earshot. The whisky had clearly loosened his tongue.

'You're a dark horse, Tom. Always have been.'

'That's not true,' I began.

But he was already stumbling down the path towards the taxi that I'd had the presence of mind to order.

In the night, I woke and made love to Hilary. It was only when I finished that I realized I was dreaming. I looked across at my wife sleeping soundly, a strand of her dark hair across her mouth.

I got out of bed and went downstairs and into the garden with my mobile. It was not like me to be this impetuous but I could not help myself. I needed to talk to her.

'*Hello. You have reached Hilary. Please leave a short message after the tone.*'

It was so good to hear her calm voice even if it was her answerphone message.

'About that night,' I said. 'I wish I could have stayed for ever. I really do. But I have to remain with my wife for our son's sake. I simply want you to know that I miss you.'

I kept hoping she might cut in and say something. But she didn't. So I went back to bed and tried to sleep.

After that, I worked even harder at being a good father. I helped Freddie with his homework. Even though he simply could not comprehend equations, I made a big effort not to sound frustrated when I had to explain basic algebra to him again and again.

We also went on family walks with the dog. 'You don't need to wipe your hands on a tissue every time you pick up his ball, Dad,' said Freddie one afternoon.

'What if it's got muck on it?'

'Your father has always been fussy,' said Sarah, coming towards us.

They laughed. This time I didn't feel as though they were laughing at me. It was a kinder 'daft dad' type of laugh. Rather nice, really.

Freddie's work at school improved. He got better grades. I began to hope that we were through the worst of it.

When Freddie turned fifteen, we took him to the local Italian restaurant to celebrate. 'Do you want to bring a friend?' I asked.

'No thanks. You might embarrass me by cleaning the cutlery with a napkin when you think the waiter isn't looking.'

That wasn't fair. I didn't always do that.

But in fact, the meal with just the three of us went better than I'd expected. Freddie was very pleased with his birthday present, a mobile phone. That was Sarah's idea. I still wasn't convinced. In my day, if we needed to communicate, we used the landline or made an arrangement and stuck to it instead of changing plans at the last minute, as so many people appeared to do nowadays.

As the weeks went by, there weren't any dramas at school. When I felt the urge to ring Hilary, I reminded myself of my obligations. I had a wife and son. Right now, they needed me around.

That was when the idea occurred to me.

Hugo had moved on. Or so he said. He'd already found someone else – another woman he'd 'come across at a bar'.

We rarely met up now. Only the odd brief chat on the phone. We had very little left in common. He was seeing the girls every other weekend, but apart from that he was living the single life. Drinks with the 'boys' from work who were also divorced. And 'clubbing', although he was reluctant to go into more details.

'I've been trying to ring Olivia,' Sarah told me as we sat down for dinner one night, still waiting, as usual, for Freddie, who was playing loud music in his room. 'I left several messages but now it's saying number not recognized. She must have changed her number.'

Sarah sounded hurt.

'She has. Hugo told me.'

'Can you ask him to give it to me?'

'Hugo says she doesn't want to talk to anyone. She's only given him the number for emergencies. Apparently she wants to "move on".' I took a deep breath. 'Perhaps we ought to do so as well.'

'What do you mean?' said my wife.

'We could move house.' I'd been thinking about this ever since I'd seen how much a similar property over the road had sold for. But the last few months had reinforced my decision.

'It's what we need,' I continued, feeling even firmer about it. 'We've never bought a house together. You are always saying that you would like to put your own stamp on a place. This can be our new start.'

'Where?' She sounded almost excited.

'The country. There are some lovely spots at the end of the Metropolitan Line.'

'The *country*?' said Freddie in an appalled voice. I hadn't even heard him come in. 'But I've got my friends here. How can you ask me to start somewhere new where I don't know anyone?'

'Think about it, Freddie,' said Sarah, placing a hand on his arm. 'Maybe we could go to the sea instead. You loved our holidays in Cornwall.'

'It's a long way for me to commute,' I said.

'How about Dorset?' I suggested. 'That's nearer.'

Freddie scowled. 'I'm not leaving London and that's that.'

He walked out and slammed the door.

So much for thinking we'd turned a corner.

'We can't let him tell us what to do,' I pointed out – not unreasonably, I thought.

'Maybe he'll come round,' said Sarah. 'Give him time.'

'Why don't we make a start at house hunting?' I said. 'I like your idea about Dorset. But let's have a bit of a holiday first. Somewhere like St Mawes. Remember driving through it? I'm due some holiday. I'll take three or four days off.'

Sarah sounded dubious. 'We can't leave Freddie that long.'

'Do you know any of the parents of these friends of his?'

'No.'

'How about Hugo?'

Sarah made a face. 'Are you joking?'

'He is his godfather.'

I was quite pleased with my idea. Hugo was always saying he missed his own children, even though they were virtually grown up. In fact, when I put the proposition to him the following day, Hugo seemed quite keen. And, surprisingly so did Freddie. 'We'll have some boy time together,' said my friend.

'That woman from the bar won't be around, will she?' I asked.

'Don't be daft.'

To be sure, I asked Hugo to stay at our place. It also meant he could look after the dog.

St Mawes, on Cornwall's Roseland Peninsula, was beautiful. Those white houses in layers on the hills were even more stunning than the pictures online. Sarah took her sketchpad. The weather was perfect. Every time I thought of Hilary, I tried to blank her out.

On the second day, I got a headache. It wouldn't go away. I was physically sick. 'Perhaps I have a bug,' I said weakly.

'You don't feel as though you have a temperature,' said Sarah, putting her cool hand on my forehead.

'Then maybe I'm reacting to the shellfish from last night.'

'I had them and I was all right. They were delicious.'

But it got so bad that by the evening, all I wanted to do was go home.

'I'm sorry,' I said. 'I've never had anything like this before.'

Privately I wondered if it was stress from work combined with that longing for Hilary which wouldn't go away.

'It's all right,' said Sarah. 'We'll cancel those viewings in Dorset tomorrow. Better ring Hugo and tell him we're returning early.'

There was no answer from Hugo's mobile. Freddie wasn't picking up either. 'It's late,' said Sarah. 'They've probably gone to bed.'

But as we drove into the street, I could see that every single window in our house had the light on. As we got out, we heard music blasting. It was the kind that made your teeth grate and your ears feel they were going to explode.

What was going on? The front door was open. Kids were squatting on the doorstep, looking at me as though I was the intruder instead of the homeowner. Inside, the dining table was upside down and two boys were jumping over it from one side to the other as though they were infants. There was a sweet smell that immediately brought me back to that first time I'd visited Sarah. Glasses everywhere. Spotty-faced couples entwined on the sofas.

'Freddie?' I shouted. He was nowhere to be seen. I marched upstairs. There was a condom (used) on the bathroom floor. I shuddered with revulsion.

His bedroom door was locked. 'Open up,' I yelled, rattling the handle. A face appeared. It wasn't my son's. I'd never seen this kid before. Freddie was sitting on the floor with a glass in his hand.

'What the hell is going on?'

'It wasn't my fault,' he said, in that challenging tone that he always used on me. 'I told one of the boys at school that you were away and he said we should have a few friends round.'

His speech was slurred. His eyes looked bloodshot.

'What about Uncle Hugo?' I demanded.

Freddie shrugged, an action that caused the drink in his glass to slop out onto the carpet. 'He didn't know I was coming home. He went out for the evening but he hasn't come back.'

I must have been mad for trusting Hugo. He'd have gone to see that woman.

'You're drunk,' I said, shaking my head.

'You're also stoned,' said Sarah behind me.

Freddie burst out laughing. 'How do you know, Mum? Were you a dope head too, in the old days?'

I couldn't help it. I grabbed Freddie by the scruff of his neck. 'This is it. I mean it!'

'Stop!' Sarah flew at me. 'Don't hurt him.'

I pushed her away. 'This is your fault. I told you we should have been stricter.' I whipped round to the crowd of kids in the doorway. 'Now get out of here. All of you.'

I was glaring at Freddie now. 'You've gone too far this time.'

'Where's Jasper?' said Sarah suddenly.

The front door had been open when we came in, I remembered. He could have run out. The back door was open too.

'Jasper!' called out Sarah running downstairs.

Freddie joined in. 'JASPER!'

'He's only a bloody dog,' I said, catching up with them. Of course, I didn't mean it but I was upset.

Freddie rounded on me. 'That bloody dog, as you put it, means more to me than you do.'

'You know that's not true, Freddie,' Sarah said quickly.

'Yes it is.'

'Freddie. That's really unkind.'

Then a shape loomed up at us, bounding across the garden.

'Jasper,' said Freddie, burying his face in the dog's fur. 'You're all right! I'm sorry, boy. Really sorry.'

I stormed back into the house and up to our bedroom. 'You see,' said Sarah running after me. 'Freddie *can* show remorse.'

'Oh, Sarah,' I said. 'You really don't get it, do you? That child is killing me. And you. We've got to act. Before something really terrible happens.'

'Then make sure it's not *you* who does that terrible thing, Tom,' she said quietly.

'What do you mean?'

'You can't hit him again.'

'I wasn't going to. But something has to make him behave.'

'It's a stage, Tom. He'll be all right.'

'It's always a stage with Freddie.'

'I'm going to make sure that all the kids are going,' she continued. 'Can you check our bedroom please?'

The books on the side of my bed were as I had left them, neatly arranged. That was something. There were no visible signs of the bed having being used, thank goodness.

But then my eyes fell on Sarah's dressing table. Her jewellery box was open. It was empty.

'My mother's diamond necklace,' I shouted, running back out to the landing. 'Where is it?'

Sarah came rushing in. 'It was here when we left.'

Suddenly I was eight years old again, looking down at my mother's slackened jaw in the undertakers.

'No,' I whimpered. 'No.'

Don't look, he tells me.
  It's part of the game, he says.
  So I cover my eyes with my hands.
  I can hear a noise.
  He's talking to someone.
  I want to look through my fingers.
  But I don't dare.
  A car door slams.
  We drive on.

32

Sarah

'I'm sorry, Dad. I really am. I didn't know the party was going to get out of control like that.'

Tom's eyes were red. He was staring at our son as if he was an intruder.

'That necklace,' he said very slowly, 'was one of the few possessions I have from my mother.'

'I know but –'

'Listen to me. She died when I was eight years old. *Eight years old*. Do you know what that means to a child?'

Freddie was looking at the ground. 'I get it.'

'No.' Each of my husband's words so far had been laden with slow fury and contempt. Especially this one.

'You can't "get it", as you put it, Freddie. No one can unless they've been through it themselves. No one can replace that necklace. No one.'

'I know it's awful, Tom,' I said gently, 'but Freddie didn't do this on purpose.'

'He invited people to our house.' He sounded as though he was being choked now. 'That's hardly accidental.'

'Your dad's right,' I said to Freddie. 'But maybe we can get it back. It can't have disappeared. Have you any idea who might have taken it?'

'No. None of my mates would do anything like that.'

'Are you sure?' I asked.

'I want the phone numbers of each "guest" who was here tonight,' said Tom.

'I didn't know everyone there! Honestly, Dad. Are you really going to ring them and ask if they nicked a diamond necklace?'

'I bloody am.'

I'd hardly ever heard my husband swear.

'You can't embarrass me like that, Dad. They'll never talk to me again.'

'I don't care! Don't you get it, as you said yourself just now? I want my mother's necklace.'

'Tom,' I pleaded, putting my hand gently on his arm. 'Maybe I could ring them . . .'

'No!' shouted Freddie. 'Neither of you are. I won't let you.'

'Where's your phone?' roared Tom.

'I'm not giving it to you.'

'It's in your pocket isn't it?'

Tom made a dive for it.

'Get off!' screamed Freddie.

But Tom had it. 'What's your password?'

'I'm not saying.'

My husband looked as though he was going to lunge at Freddie's neck.

'Stop it, both of you,' I begged. 'Let's think this through carefully. We'll tell the police. They'll look out for it if we give them a picture.'

Tom gave a sarcastic laugh. 'Do you honestly think that's going to be top of their crime list?'

'It might do something,' I said. 'Freddie, you can put something out on Facebook. That way, it's not aimed at any particular person. We could even offer a reward.'

Tom snorted. 'Reward someone for stealing?'

'It's not going to work, anyway,' said Freddie. 'No one's going to want to get into trouble or point the finger at someone else, are they?'

'So what do you suggest?' spat Tom. His fists were raised. I grabbed them but he pushed me away.

Freddie's face was red. 'Don't you dare hurt my mother.'

'I wasn't going to.'

It was only a gentle push but it had shocked me. At the same time, I could see why Tom had lost it. His mother had been everything to him.

'I want you to realize what you've done,' said Tom, more quietly now, as if knowing he'd gone too far.

'What do you want me to do?'

'Like your mother said, put a notice out on Facebook.'

'All right. I will. But if I lose friends through this, I'll never forgive you.'

Then he stomped up to his room and locked the door. I followed him.

'Freddie,' I hissed through the lock. 'Your father's desperately upset.'

'Don't you think I am too?' he said.

I could tell he was crying.

'He's really sorry,' I said to Tom as I came back down. My husband was standing by what he called one of the 'occasional' tables, holding a silver-framed picture of his mother. She was in an evening dress with the missing diamond necklace sparkling around her neck. It was a rather stiff pose that looked as if it had been shot in a studio. I was never allowed to dust it. Tom preferred to do that himself.

'We could use that picture to give the police,' I said.

Tom said nothing.

'You pushed me away. You looked like you were going to hurt him.'

'I'm sorry,' he said dully.

'It wasn't his fault, Tom. Why do you always blame him? His friends caused the trouble and besides, Hugo should have been here.'

'I know that and I'm going to have it out with him, don't you worry. But Freddie has to pay too.'

Then he turned to look at me. His eyes were dark and his mouth was a tight straight line. Sometimes there was a side of my husband that scared me.

'The sad thing is, Sarah, that you make too many excuses for him. All that boy does is think of himself. The sooner we get out of here and make a new start, the better. Let's hope that it works because if not . . .'

His voice tailed away.

'If not, what?' I asked.

'If not, I don't know what we're going to do.'

Nor did I.

But unlike my friend Olivia, I had to keep my little family together. The stolen necklace was terrible. Yet maybe it would teach Freddie a lesson. Tom was right. A move to another part of the country would give us that fresh start we so desperately needed.

*

A few days later the estate agents rang to see if a couple could come round in an hour to view the house. 'In an hour?' I questioned. But I didn't like to turn them down.

I dashed around, trying to tidy up. Tom had gone out to play tennis with Hugo – something he hadn't done for a while. He'd offered to stay and help but I'd encouraged him to go, telling him that I could sort out the house. He'd left without saying a word, his face set. Ever since the party he'd barely spoken to me or Freddie. Needless to say, the police didn't hold out much hope of recovering the diamond necklace.

Freddie had come down briefly to take some cereal back to his room.

'Have you had any replies to your post on Facebook?' I asked. He'd finally put it up last night.

'Yes.'

'Can you show me?'

'You don't believe me?'

'I do.'

'You don't, do you? Come up to my room and I'll show you.'

I waded my way through the mess on his floor and stared at the screen. 'That's not very nice,' I said eventually. Freddie had indeed put out a plea for the necklace. But the replies were horrible.

What the fuck? was one. *Are you accusing us of being thieves?* And *I don't want to go back to your house ever again. Those drawings of naked people are weird. Your mum must be some kind of perv.*

'What do you expect?' said Freddie. 'I told Dad this would happen. They all hate me now.'

'Well, someone took it.'

'Not my friends. Or rather the people who used to be my friends.'

'Then they can't be very nice, can they?'

'You don't get it, do you? How can I show my face again at school?'

'Your dad is very upset. That necklace meant everything to him.'

'I know. You keep saying so. But I can't bring it back. Now please, Mum. Give me some peace.'

Then he went back to his room and once more I heard the bolt being drawn across.

I felt as though I was being sawn in half. My heart ached for Tom's loss, but I also felt sorry for Freddie. He'd made a stupid mistake and now he'd lost friends. I knew what that felt like. Olivia hadn't tried to get in touch once since that last phone call, telling me she had left Hugo. I'd covered for her – even pretending to sound surprised when Tom said she had left. Part of me felt used, to be honest. I thought I'd meant something to her.

The betrayal of a friend could be as painful as the betrayal of a husband. Not that Tom would ever do anything like that. He simply wasn't the type.

Freddie was still in his room when the estate agent arrived.

'I'm sorry it's a bit of a mess,' I said apologetically, watching the young couple's nose wrinkle at the stench of body odour in my son's room. The man was carrying a baby in a sling. Tom used to do that with Freddie in the days when he was such a sweet baby. If we could only go back to that time and start again.

They left soon afterwards.

'It might be helpful if you could tidy up that third bedroom,' said the estate agent when he rang the following day to say the couple had found somewhere else.

That was all very well. But I couldn't guarantee it. Not if Freddie refused to do it himself or allow me in.

The terrible tight atmosphere that had settled over our home simply wouldn't go away. Something had to happen. Even if we did move, it wasn't going to change Freddie, was it? Or Tom's attitude. We had more rows. We said the same things. Over and over again.

'I don't understand why you aren't stricter with him,' said my husband the following week. We had finished lunch in the dining room. I'd made a vegetarian lasagne. Freddie had refused to eat with us and had taken his back to his room.

I wanted to scream with exasperation at my husband's comment. Did Tom expect me to wave a magic wand or perform some sort of lobotomy on our son? He was who he was. Hopefully, he'd mature one day.

'You simply can't go on protecting Freddie,' he continued, drumming his fingers. When my husband began to rant like this, he did not stop. It was as though he was treating me like a member of his team at work. 'What he needs is someone who can force him to get into line. In my view, there's only one answer. Boarding school.'

'You want to send our son away?' I gasped.

'You make it sound as though I'm suggesting Siberia.'

'But you *hated* boarding yourself. So did Hugo. Look what it did to the two of you.'

'Schools have changed since then. I've been doing some research. Look.'

He got up, went out of the room for a moment and then came back, thrusting a brochure in front of me. 'It's got a good art department. Freddie would like it. And, let's face it, it would help us as a couple.'

Tears pricked my eyes. 'Freddie's going through the teenage stage,' I said. 'He's not bad. He's simply made some wrong decisions, like you and I did when we were younger.'

Tom's mouth tightened. 'Simply? Is that what you call it?'

'Look what you did to that boy Chapman at school,' I said. 'That was worse than a stolen necklace.'

He winced. 'How can you bring that up?'

'But it's true, Tom, isn't it? I know Freddie isn't easy, but I can't bear the thought of waking up every morning and not having our son under the same roof. It would be like living without half of myself.'

'Don't be overemotional.'

'I'm not. It's true. And supposing he gets into drugs there?'

'He's hardly avoiding them here. Besides, I asked them that and they've got a zero-tolerance policy.'

'You've spoken to them already?'

Tom put on his defensive look. 'I wanted to find out more before we discussed it.'

'Discussed what?' said a voice.

It was Freddie. He must have come downstairs without me hearing. Then his eyes fell on the prospectus in my hand.

'Boarding school? You want to get rid of me?'

'It's not like that,' said Tom quickly.

'Fuck you!'

The front door slammed so hard that the walls reverberated. Now Freddie would think this was my idea and not his father's. I burned with indignation and fury.

'Well done,' I said to Tom.

He stared at me hard. 'You know what? I give up.'

A cold feeling crawled through me. 'What do you mean?'

'I'm going out,' he said quietly.

The front door clicked. I was alone in the house with Jasper.

I opened my mouth and screamed. Jasper looked up at me. 'It's all right,' I said, kneeling down and burying my face in his soft fur. 'It's all right,' I repeated.

But it wasn't. I knew that then. And I know that now.

33
Tom

It was wrong. But I couldn't help it.

Hilary's apartment – in a smart 1960s block – was near Russell Square. She'd bought it outright, she told me, with money that her mother had left her. It had been a shrewd investment. There was even a twenty-four-hour porter on the desk, which seemed sensible for a woman on her own, even though Hilary appeared to be perfectly capable of looking after herself.

The man appeared to recognize me from my previous visit, which was slightly embarrassing. 'Afternoon, sir,' he said. 'Or should I say evening. It's getting that way now, isn't it?'

I'd walked for two hours around London before coming here.

I hadn't liked to ring Hilary on my way. She'd never returned that message I'd left on her answerphone some weeks earlier. It might be better, I rationalized, if I just turned up, even though spontaneity wasn't my usual habit.

'Would you be good enough to call Miss Morton's apartment, please?' I said.

'Certainly.'

My fingers drummed against the desk. It was an anxious habit from childhood that my father had always disliked. But old habits die hard.

'Miss Morton says she will come down to the lobby shortly.'

Ten minutes passed. Fifteen.

Perhaps she was teaching me a lesson.

The lift doors opened. Hilary came out, wearing a blue striped jumper and jeans. The latter surprised me, but then again it was a Sunday. There was her familiar flowery smell as she walked towards me.

'Tom,' she said, coolly. 'This is a surprise.'

I was aware of the porter's eyes on me. 'Did I disturb you?' I asked.

'I was doing my accounts.'

She didn't seem pleased to see me. I began to feel nervous. 'Could we talk somewhere more private?' I asked.

Hilary gestured to the green leather sofa in the foyer.

'I meant,' I said in a low voice, 'could we go upstairs?'

'No, Tom.' Her voice was steady but calm. 'I don't think that would be a good idea.'

'Do you have someone there?' I asked.

'No.' She appeared to find this question amusing. 'Although if I did, I hardly think it is any of your business.'

'You're right,' I said hastily, keen to make amends. 'I'm sorry.'

She looked at her watch pointedly. 'I've got things to do, Tom. Do you have something you want to tell me?'

I felt silly now, rather as if I was a schoolboy again. 'Freddie had a party recently when we were away,' I blurted out. 'He wrecked the house and one of the so-called guests stole my mother's necklace.'

To my deep embarrassment, I was unable to hide the catch in my voice.

Her eyes softened. 'I'm sorry. That's awful. What did Sarah say?'

I swallowed hard to make myself sound normal again.

'That I'm not being understanding enough.'

I'd hoped she'd make a comment along the lines of 'That is not fair' but she said nothing.

Slightly unnerved, I continued. 'I want to send Freddie away to boarding school, but Sarah won't hear of it.'

Surely Hilary would see my point of view. She had boarded from the age of eight as well. It had been 'the making' of her, she'd told me at least once before.

'Well . . .' Then she stopped. An older man came in to collect his key from the porter. He tipped his hat at Hilary, who gave him a warm smile. I felt a flash of jealousy. She waited until he'd passed before replying.

'I haven't got any experience in this field, as you well know, but it seems to me, Tom, that your son needs professional help.'

'We've tried that – well, Sarah has – and it doesn't work.' I was even more aware that I was sounding desperate.

Her cool grey eyes focused on me. 'I still don't understand what this has to do with me, Tom. Why are you here?'

I glanced at the porter, who, seeing my look, instantly began shuffling papers around on the desk. 'I thought you'd understand.'

'Because your wife doesn't?'

'Look,' I said urgently. 'You're angry with me. I get that.'

'No, Tom. I feel angry with myself for getting involved

with a man who is married with a child. That's against my moral code, as I told you before.'

'And mine.'

'Yet here we are.'

Any minute now and she would ask the porter to see me out. I tried to think of a way to make her stay. No one understood me like Hilary. She didn't allow emotions to get in the way of living. Everything was black and white to her.

I used to think it was the only way too. But then I became a parent.

'I'm not right for Sarah,' I burst out. 'And she's not right for me. If it wasn't for Freddie, we wouldn't be together.'

'I understand that,' said Hilary. 'Then again, children grow up. Freddie's not going to be at home for much longer, is he?'

'No,' I said, thinking of Hugo's girls. 'Are you trying to say something here?'

'Isn't it obvious, Tom?' Hilary touched my arm briefly. 'If you're serious about us . . .'

'I am.'

'Then maybe you should consider leaving Sarah when you've sold the house. It will be a clean break. You simply divide your assets down the middle.'

'But what about Freddie? It's a difficult time for him. He'll be starting his A-level course shortly.'

'Will it make it any easier for him if both his parents are miserable together?'

I thought of Freddie's behaviour now. Of my mother's necklace, which hadn't turned up and probably never would. His habit of locking himself into his room. The way he seemed to hate everything I said or did.

'Maybe not.'

Hilary sighed. 'I don't want you to think I'm giving you an ultimatum, Tom. Far from it. I'm merely suggesting, as a friend, that you might take a broader view of the picture.'

'Will you wait for me?' I asked.

'No,' she said firmly. 'That would make me feel I had something to do with you and Sarah splitting up. This has to be a decision you make without having me in the equation.'

'But will you be there for me if – when – that happens?' I persisted.

She looked up at me with those calm grey eyes. 'I hope so, Tom. At least in the platonic sense.'

Then Hilary reached up to kiss me on my cheek. It could have been the sort of kiss one might give to a friend. But it meant much more and I knew she knew that too.

'Let me know when you're free,' she said softly. 'Until then, I think it's best that we don't see each other again. It's the right thing to do.'

As I left, I felt the porter's eyes on me again. How much had he heard? Then again, did it matter? Part of me felt light and happy in a way I hadn't for goodness knows how long. Hilary cared for me. But she was also a moral person. That meant a lot to me too. Of course, she didn't know about Chapman. At some point I would need to tell her, but until then, what was I meant to do?

As I walked back, I tried weighing each option against the other. Would staying together help Freddie through A levels? Maybe not. Besides, there was no guarantee he would stick them out.

What if we didn't stay together? I'd feel guilty, but Sarah and I would both be happier. That would be better for Freddie, surely?

Naturally, I'd take my responsibilities very seriously. I'd make sure Sarah did not want for money.

But when I opened the front door, Sarah flew into my arms.

'I was worried,' she said. 'I didn't know where you'd gone. You didn't answer your mobile. Freddie's come back and he says he's sorry for shouting. I think he's had a chance to think about things. Please, Tom. We need you.'

This wasn't what I'd been expecting. My head was now in a terrible muddle.

I thought of my father. I thought of Hugo, who was struggling without his family. I thought of Hilary, who didn't have children and, with the best will in the world, didn't know what it was like to grow up without a parent or be one. I thought of how I knew I wouldn't be able to live with the guilt of walking out on my family. Hadn't I sworn to myself I would do the right thing in life after school – and even more so since Chapman's death?

I wouldn't make this decision now. I'd wait until Freddie had his A levels under his belt. Surely I'd be entitled to my own life then. Maybe with Hilary.

'We'll give him one last chance,' I heard myself saying. 'But I mean it, Sarah. If he does anything else, Freddie is going to boarding school. It will be the best thing for him. And for us.'

That night I couldn't sleep. After, when my wife was gently snoring, I went out into the garden and rang Hilary's number. It went through to answerphone. 'I'm sorry if I caused offence before,' I said. 'But I want you to know that I love you, Hilary.'

Then I went back to bed.

34

Sarah

What had happened to my little boy who had thought rainbows were magic and that they smiled? To the child who saw everything around him as an exciting adventure. Constantly exploring. Regarding everything with wide-eyed curiosity and wonder. It reminded me of Emily and her innocence. She'd have loved Freddie. I would have made her godmother instead of Olivia. She would have taken her duties more seriously. I could see Emily now, taking Freddie to a gig or down to her family's house to ride the pony and pick plums in the orchard.

But Emily was gone. And Freddie had turned into this impossible teenager who seemed to hate both me and his father.

Where did I – we – go wrong?

'You've got to behave,' I told Freddie the following day, before he went to school. Tom had already left for work.

'I said I would, didn't I?'

I spot something on his bare arm. It's a word. PEACE.

'Is that a tattoo?'

'I just wrote it on my arm with a Biro.'

That's a relief. I remember doing the same when I was at school, although ours were smiley faces.

'Why "peace"?'

He shrugged. 'Thought we could do with a bit of it in this house.'

Maybe he was right. 'I do my best,' I began. 'But your behaviour hasn't helped.'

'I know. But Dad doesn't understand me. He doesn't understand you, either.'

Sometimes our children see us much more clearly than we realize.

Freddie had left his door unlocked. Good, I'd be able to clean, though I'd have to be careful to leave everything as I found it. I remembered all too well how my aunt would take things from my room. I'd never forget my mother's photograph that had 'gone into the laundry'. I wasn't going to invade his privacy as she had done mine.

The doorbell! Very few people called round now. The playgroup and school mums I'd known from the past had all merged into their own little sets. I had nothing left in common with them. I'd lost touch with most of my art friends too, because I knew Tom disliked them. I had to do my best to make sure there were as few arguments as possible. It wasn't good for Freddie.

Jasper ran towards the door barking. The estate agent was here.

'I do hope you don't mind,' he said. 'I was in the area with a client and I wondered if I could possibly show them round.' He looked back at his car where a man was sitting. 'He's a cash buyer.'

'Can you give me a couple of minutes?'

I ran back upstairs to Freddie's room to open the windows and make a start. To my surprise, it didn't look too bad, even though I could see he had simply shovelled everything under the bed. *See*, I told myself, *he's trying.*

I looked in on Tom's study too. He was usually very tidy, but there were some papers that had fallen down a crack between his desk and a filing cupboard. I pulled them out. Wasn't this the report that my husband had accused Freddie of stealing?

I rang him at the office, something he didn't like, but this was important.

'Yes,' he said after a slight pause when I read out the opening words. 'It is.'

'Then I think you owe Freddie an apology.'

'After all the apologies he owes *us*, you mean?'

Tom had an answer for everything.

Shortly after the viewing, the estate agent rang me. The house was exactly what his client had been looking for. Subject to survey, he wanted completion to take place as soon as possible.

'Excellent news,' said Tom when I told him that night. Now, unusually for us, we were all eating dinner together at the same time. I'd made a leek-and-cheese bake but I could only pick at it.

'We haven't got anywhere to move to,' I pointed out.

'We'll rent. It will put us in a stronger position to buy.'

'I told you before,' scowled Freddie, pushing his plate away. 'I'm not moving.'

'Too bad,' snapped Tom. 'You don't own this house. The decision is up to us.'

Couldn't he see this wasn't the way to handle our son?

'Have you told him about the missing report?' I asked my husband pointedly.

Tom shrugged as if it was no big deal. 'Your mother found the document I'd mislaid when she was tidying my office.'

'The one you accused me of taking?' demanded Freddie.

'I didn't exactly –'

'Yes you did.'

Too late, I wished I hadn't raised the subject. I should have known that Tom wouldn't apologize.

'Getting back to the move,' I interrupted quickly. 'We'll make sure you like wherever we go.'

'But I want to be in exactly the same area, Mum.'

'I can't promise that,' began Tom. 'Why do you only think of yourself?'

'That's not really fair,' I began. Then I stopped. Was it?

'You know what?' said Freddie, flinging his cutlery down on the plate, 'you can move without me. It's clear that you don't believe anything I say, Dad, let alone even *like* me.'

'Nonsense,' said Tom.

'Is it? I told you I hadn't taken that bloody report of yours. You haven't even apologized properly.'

Scraping back his chair, Freddie stormed out, slamming the door behind him.

Tom shrugged. 'It's not his decision. We're the adults.'

'Are we going to drag him kicking and screaming out of here, then?' I asked.

His mouth set in that straight, narrow line. 'If necessary.'

My heart chilled at the thought. What if it really did come to that?

Through the agent, we found a house to rent a few streets away until deciding whether to move further away or not.

'You'll still be near your friends,' I said to my son a few days later, when I broke the news. Tom was at work. Freddie had just come back from school and was sitting in front of the television, munching his way through a packet of crisps even though dinner was almost ready.

He gave me a sulky look. 'I don't have friends any more. Not after the fuss you and Dad made over the party. You really embarrassed me.'

'Have you forgotten about the necklace?' I said. 'It doesn't compare with your embarrassment. It broke your dad's heart.'

'I apologized, didn't I? But you two don't seem to realize how horrible it is that no one wants to hang out with me.'

There it was again. That little-boy face. How could he switch so fast from being a near adult to a child again?

'You know,' I said, putting my arms around him and trying not to say anything about the sweaty smell, 'you can tell me anything you like. I was a teenager once.'

'Get off, Mum.' He pushed me away. Of course he would. He was fifteen, wasn't he? I could remember what a difficult age that had been. But that had been due to my uncle and aunt. Freddie had *me* to talk to.

Not for the first time, I couldn't help feeling hurt. And angry too. If Tom had handled Freddie's childhood misbehaviour in a calmer way, maybe it wouldn't have got this far.

Our last night approached. The packers had been and everything was in boxes by the time my husband got back late from work.

'Have you cooked dinner?' he asked.

'The pans have been put away. I thought we'd get an Indian.'

'You know I don't eat rice.'

This used to be a joke between us. In the early days, I'd loved the fact that Tom had staunchly eaten his way through a large bowl of the stuff because he didn't want to hurt my feelings. But now it didn't seem romantic any more. Briefly Rupert flashed into my head. What might life have been like if I'd married him instead?

There was the sound of thudding down the stairs. Freddie was heading for the front door. 'Where are you going?' I asked.

'Out.'

'We can see that,' snapped Tom. 'Your mother asked "where".'

'Nowhere.'

'Don't be rude to your father,' I said.

Tom snorted. 'It's a few years too late for that.' Then he held up his hands as if he'd given up and stormed into his study, shutting the door behind him.

I tried a different tack. 'Who are you going out with?'

Freddie made a sulky expression.

'A mate.'

'You said you didn't have any.'

'Did I?'

He knew he had. Unless he'd been lying. I tried again. 'What's his name?'

'Why? You don't know him.'

'Is he a school friend?'

'No.' Freddie rolled his eyes and made a "duh" sound. 'If you really want the truth, I met him in a pub.'

'But you're too young to drink.'

'C'mon, Mum. Didn't you ever do anything illegal when you were my age?'

Yes, I wanted to say. And that's why I'm worried about you.

'It's a school night,' I tried. 'You can't go out. What about your homework?'

'I've done it.'

'Please be back by eleven. The removal men will be here really early tomorrow.'

'How about two a.m.?'

'Don't push it, Freddie. I'm trying to be reasonable here. Let's compromise with midnight, and not a second later.'

He sighed. 'If you say so.'

I gave him a hug, breathing in my boy. It always amazed me that the miracle of giving birth to a child was often forgotten. Every person was once created by two others. How incredible is that?

He opened the front door. There was a gust of wind. The rain lashed in. 'You need a jacket,' I said, eyeing his T-shirt with I HATE THE WORLD written in red capital letters.

'Bye.' My son brushed my cheek with his. He hadn't done that for some time. His rough jawline – he'd been shaving for a few months now – left a slight redness on mine as I saw when I glanced in the hall mirror, but it didn't matter. I was grateful for the brief affection.

'Wait,' I said, catching sight of something red on his inside wrist. 'Is that a tattoo?'

'I haven't got time for this, Mum.'

'Ziggy?'

'You know, Mum. After the David Bowie album. It's what I want to be called now.'

'Why?'

'Why not?'

'Is it a pen drawing like the other one?'

'Sure. I did it a few weeks ago. You just didn't notice.'

And then he left.

'Come on, then,' he says. 'What are you waiting for?'
My legs won't move.
'Don't you trust me?' he asks.
I don't know.
But I nod.
I mustn't upset him.
You don't want to mess with blokes like Knuckles.

35

Tom

'Tom,' said Sarah's voice. At the same time, I felt her prodding me. 'Freddie still isn't back.'

I woke immediately. It was a habit left over from school that I had purposefully retained in order to get to work early.

'What time is it?' I asked, fumbling for my glasses.

'Gone three o'clock! He promised to be back by midnight.'

We argued about our son for a while.

'Who's he with, anyway?' I asked sharply.

'A friend,' said Sarah. She sounded fearful.

'But who?'

'I don't know.' I could see in the half-light from the lamppost outside that she was twisting her fingers. 'He wouldn't tell me.'

'You should have made him. Or got this friend's number at the very least.'

'He wouldn't give it to me.'

'I'm going back to sleep,' I said, glancing at the clock. 'I've got three hours and fifty minutes until I have to get up for work.'

At some point, I woke up again because of Jasper barking. So Freddie was home. About time.

I heard Sarah getting up. Best to leave her to it. I'd have words with him later; not that that would do anything.

I lay in bed in that half-stage between being awake and asleep. Then Sarah's phone bleeped.

I picked it up.

I need to talk to you.

It was a text message. From Zac.

I went cold. So she really wasn't to be trusted.

Finally, I felt Sarah sliding into bed.

'Freddie back?'

'Yes.'

'That's all right then.' I was going to confront her about the text. But she'd only lie. What was the point? I must have dozed off briefly, only to hear voices coming from the bathroom. The empty space beside me suggested Sarah had got out of bed again. Didn't they know how late it was? I made my way there, intending to give them both a piece of my mind. And that's when I heard Freddie's confession.

'Mum. I've killed someone.'

An ice-cold chill passed through me.

'You've what?' asked Sarah.

'I've killed someone.'

'Killed someone?' I barged in. Freddie was slumped on the floor, his head in Sarah's lap. I grabbed him by his denim jacket, trying to lift him off the ground. 'What the *fuck* do you mean?'

'Don't hurt him!' called out Sarah.

'Then he'd better bloody tell me what's going on.'

Freddie was blubbering, shaking, snot running down his nose. 'I can't say.'

Sarah and I tried to get more out of him, but he refused to talk. There was only one thing I could do.

'Where are you going?' cried Sarah. Her eyes were wild.

'Where do you think? To ring the police.'

Freddie started to howl. Downstairs, the dog did the same.

'No!' Sarah shouted. She grabbed my pyjama top and almost ripped it. 'Not yet.'

'Sarah,' I said, shaking her off. My lips felt numb. It was as if I was talking in slow motion. 'Don't you see? It's the only thing to do.'

We stared at each other for a second. Then Freddie's voice cut in. 'Does Mum know you're having an affair?'

I stopped still. My wife looked at our son and then at me. I felt cold sweat dribbling down my neck and a hot flush rising in my cheeks.

'I don't know what you're talking about,' I said.

'I heard you on the phone in the garden ages ago.' Freddie looked at me in the same way my father used to when he collected me from boarding school; an inconvenience. 'You were talking to someone called Hilary and you said you loved her.'

I'd always known this moment might come one day. The probability of an affair being discovered is high, although it's hard to put an exact figure on it because people generally lie when asked. I just didn't expect it to come now.

'It isn't what it sounds like,' I said quickly to Sarah. 'It's over. I chose to put you first.'

'Put me *first*?' she repeated, with a strange laugh. Freddie wrapped his arm around her. The two of them glared at me as if I was the enemy.

'All right,' I said. 'I was wrong. But don't tell me you haven't had affairs. What about Zac?'

'Who's he, Mum?'

'Only an old friend. He keeps trying to contact me but I ignore him.'

'Even if you are telling the truth, surely we're missing the point here!' I yell. 'Your son has *killed* someone. Yet you want to protect him.'

'*Our* son,' she retorted.

'Exactly. It's why I'm going to do the right thing and phone the police. I'm not protecting a murderer.'

'Really?' she screamed. 'Well, you've been married to one for years.'

I froze. 'What exactly do you mean?'

36
Sarah

It slipped out in anger and fear. But now I couldn't take it back.

'What do you mean?' I'd never seen this look on Tom's face before.

'I told you how I was inside for six years. But I was lucky not to get longer.'

'What did you do?' Tom whispered.

I looked down at the ground, unable to face him. 'My best friend Emily took drugs that belonged to me.'

I paused for a few seconds. If I continued, there would be no going back. But I had no option. I'd gone too far already. Besides, the weight of this final lie – the biggest – had tormented me for so long that I could no longer carry it.

'They were a dodgy batch. She had a reaction and . . . and she died.'

'Shit!' said Freddie.

For once, I didn't tell my son off for swearing.

Tears were pouring down my face now. My voice was choked. My words were blurred, running into each other in my fear. 'Emily was so sweet. So kind. I'll never forget the look in her parents' eyes at the trial. If it wasn't for me, their daughter would be alive. And nothing I could do would ever put that right.'

Tom had taken a step back, as if my proximity revolted him.

'That's really why I went to prison,' I burst out. 'Not only for dealing. But for manslaughter.'

Freddie let out a cry. 'You couldn't have, Mum. You wouldn't hurt a fly.'

I sobbed even louder. 'But I did.'

'Has *anything* you've ever said to me been true?' asked Tom quietly.

'Yes!' I grabbed his sleeve. He pulled away. I grabbed it again, forcing him to come closer so I could look into his eyes and show him I was telling the truth. 'It's the last thing. I promise. Prison was worse than I can describe, Tom. I lived in fear of my life. So, don't you see? I won't allow Freddie to go through the same thing. You've got to help me. We have to do this as a family. Please!'

37
Tom

I could hardly believe what Sarah had told me. Who was this woman standing in front of me? Had I ever really known her?

'But if Freddie's killed someone, he has to be punished,' I said. 'Just like you had to be.'

'And what about you!' fired Sarah. Her tears had stopped now and she was glaring at me. 'If it hadn't been for you and Hugo, that poor man Chapman might still be alive now.'

'What are you talking about, Mum?' Freddie's eyes were going from his mother's face to mine in puzzlement.

'Nothing,' I snapped. 'It was an unfortunate incident that is not comparable to this.'

'Isn't it?' Sarah said quietly. 'Are you sure, Tom?'

'I'm going to call the police right now,' I said, ignoring her question.

I took out my mobile. Before I could stop her Sarah had grabbed it and thrown it down the lavatory.

'No!' I fished it out but the screen had gone blank. I threw it on the floor.

'Tom, please don't.'

I ignored her and went to the kitchen. I picked up the landline. It was dead. The new owner had wanted it disconnected.

I could have – and should have – walked straight out of the house there and then and driven to the police station.

But something stopped me. It was as though I couldn't move any more.

Sarah was right. If Hugo and I had stood up to the masters, Chapman might still be alive now.

Maybe I was no better than my wife or son.

Then another thought crept into my head. One that I was not proud of but which, nevertheless, could not be ignored. What would Hilary think of me if she knew what Freddie had done?

I went back to the bedroom. For a while I sat on the side of the bed, staring blankly at the wall. I would leave in a minute. Then somehow, partly because of that stress headache which had returned again, I found myself lying down.

'I'm sleeping in the spare room,' I heard Sarah tell Freddie.

One more minute, then I would go.

Some hours later, I woke to hear the removal men knocking on the door. I'd overslept. Never had I done that before. Then it all came back to me.

My son had killed someone. My son had committed murder.

Swiftly, I got out of bed. I needed to contact the police. Of course, they'd want to know why I hadn't rung them last night. I would just have to tell them the truth. The phone. Being overwhelmed. Freddie would be questioned. Probably arrested. We'd need to find him a lawyer. Someone who would coax the truth out of him.

What would people say when it all came out? What

would my bosses say when it hit the newspapers? We'd be blamed. I could see the headlines now: *Actuary's son accused of murder*. The implication would be that if a criminal came from a professional class, it was the parents who were at fault.

And what about the poor parents of his victim, whoever that was? I couldn't even think about them. It was too awful.

'Sarah!' I called out.

There was no answer. The neatly made bed in the spare room suggested she hadn't gone there after all.

I went to Freddie's room. The door was open. His drawings were still on the wall. But no sign of my son.

I rushed down to the kitchen.

The dog wasn't there.

And nor was my wife.

The radio was on. It was the local station. Sarah's favourite.

'*Breaking news. The body of a man has been discovered in a petrol station on Long Road. Police are searching for a youth wearing a denim jacket, who was seen last night running from the scene and into a waiting car. We'll be updating you as soon as we know more.*'

'Quick!'
  'No, we have to wait.'
  It's not long enough.
  We're off. Speeding round the corner.
  I want to be sick.
  What have we done?
  I wish I'd never come.
  It was supposed to be a bit of fun.
  But we hit him.
  And he didn't get up.
  'Drive. DRIVE!'

38

Sarah: Truro Crown Court

'All rise,' says the court clerk.

My knees knock together. Try as I might, I'm unable to stop them. My teeth judder. Sweat runs down from my armpits.

I think back to a different trial. To my trial. To Emily.

Emily . . .

Her parents had been there, watching me, along with Rupert, Emily's older brother. I used to fancy him. 'He likes you too,' Emily had giggled when she'd asked me to stay at her parents' farm at Christmas during our first year.

After that, I'd been invited back at Easter and over the summer too.

'You're one of the family,' her mother had said. I loved being in their warm, cosy kitchen. It was huge, with a great big black Aga and Pony Club rosettes on the walls.

Emily's mum was making breakfast pancakes. Wow, they smelt delicious! 'Have another, dear. You need a bit of fattening up.'

'You're so kind to me.'

'Nonsense. We love having you here. It gives me peace of mind to know that Emily has a good friend like you. We were worried about her going to art school, weren't we, Doug?'

Emily's father nodded. 'Our daughter's a lovely girl. But she's too nice sometimes for her own good.'

We swam in the river. Rode ponies bareback. Sat late into the night drinking Pimm's in the garden and playing Leonard Cohen songs. One evening, Rupert's hand had slid into mine. He'd kissed me after Emily had gone up to bed. It had blown me away. (Only one other person ever kissed like that after him and, ironically, it had been Tom.) My body yearned for him but he had pulled back. 'Not here,' he'd said. 'Later. I'm coming up to stay with Emily at the end of term.'

I couldn't wait! 'Wouldn't it be wonderful if you fell in love and got married,' Emily said dreamily. 'Then we'd be sisters-in-law.'

Life was always beautiful in my friend's head. But then again, her parents gave her plenty of money. She didn't have to do what I did to make ends meet.

For a while I managed to keep it from her. It wasn't difficult – she was so innocent. But one night, at a party, she asked if she could have one of my spliffs. 'Your roll-ups smell so enticing,' she said.

'Better not.'

'Why?'

'Because they're not ordinary cigarettes, Emily.'

She laughed. 'I know that. They're weed, aren't they? I'm not that stupid, you know.'

'I didn't say you were. But it can mess with your head sometimes.'

Her eyes widened. 'Then why do *you* do it?'

'Because sometimes I want to forget what's in my brain.'

'Just one little puff.' Emily snatched it out of my hand.

'Mmm,' she said, 'That's nice.' Then she began coughing violently.

'Are you all right?'

'Of course I am.'

After that, Emily began smoking regularly. I couldn't stop her. She was a grown-up. Besides, I told myself, it was only weed.

But one evening she was at my place when a regular came round unexpectedly.

'I've got someone here,' I told him.

'Don't mind me,' trilled Emily.

If I hadn't been so desperate for the cash, I'd have told him to come back another time.

Instead, I handed the package over at the door and stuffed the money he gave me into the back pocket of my jeans.

'It's OK,' said Emily. 'I know you sell tablets.'

'What?'

'One of the others told me. What's it like?'

'Dangerous. I could be arrested at any time.'

'So why do you do it?'

'For the money.'

'I could give you some, if you need a loan.'

I hugged her. 'That's very kind, but I couldn't let you do that.'

'What if I bought some from you?'

'No way.'

'But I want to try one myself.'

'Absolutely not! I don't even do them myself any more.'

'Sarah,' said Emily, taking my hand. 'Don't you see? All

my life I've been cosseted by my parents. I want to live. I want to experiment. I'm a grown-up.'

'Sorry,' I said. 'Not with me you don't.'

Then before the end of the Christmas term, we went to a party. I took my stash with me. They were a new batch. One of my regulars had offered to pay over the odds for them and wanted to meet me there later. It would give me enough money to see me through the next term.

I wore a glitzy dress I'd found in a charity shop and took even more care than usual with my eyes, putting on blue and silver sparkle. Rupert was driving up later that night to take us back to the farm the next day. I wanted to look my best.

We got to a tall, Victorian student house where the party was being held. There were overflowing dustbins outside and ragged net curtains. It seemed like a right dump, but Emily thought it was 'cool'.

Someone gave us a glass of sharp white wine and we found a place on the sofa.

'What's that?' asked Emily, when I opened my bag to check the package was still there. Of course it was, but I was nervous. This was the biggest deal I'd ever done.

'Nothing,' I said, closing it quickly.

I looked at all the others crowding into the room. As far as I could see, my regular wasn't there.

She shrugged. 'I'm going to dance. Want to come?'

'Actually, I need the loo.'

Maybe my regular was hanging around there, I thought. But he wasn't.

When I came back, even more people had arrived. The air was full of smoke. Everyone was dancing. Some close-up, some in circles, waving their hands, half-stoned. Then, to my surprise, I saw Rupert coming in.

'I thought we were meeting you back at halls,' I said, trying to hide my dismay. I didn't want him here before I did the deal. He might see me.

'The traffic was light. Emily gave me the address, in case I changed my mind. So I made my way here instead.'

He spoke so beautifully. And he was so handsome, with that floppy brown fringe and blue velvet jacket. Then he gave me an admiring stare. 'You look gorgeous, Sarah.'

Stepping towards me, he gave me a long kiss. Oh my God! It was as wonderful as last time. Emily's words came back to me. *'Wouldn't it be wonderful if you fell in love and got married? Then we'd be sisters-in-law.'*

We stayed there for ages, just snogging. Never had I felt anything like this before. Rupert was different. He was a man.

'So, where is my little sister?' he asked when we finally pulled apart.

'Dancing.'

We both peered through the crowd of sweaty bodies writhing up against each other.

'I can't see her.'

'Nor me.'

My eyes began streaming with the smoke. I needed a tissue. And that's when I realized. My bag had gone.

'Excuse me a minute,' I said. 'I think I've left something in the loo.'

'I'll look for her. She's got to be here somewhere,' he smiled.

The toilet door was locked. I had to wait ages before someone came out.

'Did you see a bag in there?' I asked.

'Sorry, no.'

My chest filled with panic. There were over fifty pills in that bag. Supposing someone had handed them in? I'd get done. My personal details were inside. And what about the money I'd spent on them? I needed the cash to pay my supplier back.

I dashed back out into the corridor and bumped into a girl from my real-life art class. 'Emily was looking for you. Someone found your bag and gave it to her.'

Thank God for that. Then another thought struck me. She wouldn't have taken one, would she? Surely not.

'I think she's in the kitchen.'

But she wasn't. I checked the bedrooms too, although I knew Emily wasn't that sort. Instead, I interrupted a couple who were making out. 'Sorry,' I said and then shut the door quickly.

I went back into the sitting room. Something was wrong. People were gathered around someone on the floor. It was a girl. Lying on the ground. No. It couldn't be.

I drew closer. Rupert was kneeling over her. 'Emily. Emily, what's wrong? Can you hear me?'

Emily was thrashing about. Her eyes were rolling. It was as if she was having a fit. My bag was next to her.

'Get an ambulance, someone!' shouted Rupert.

We didn't have mobiles in those days. At least, people like me didn't. Someone gave me theirs. My fingers shook as I pressed the numbers. 'Ambulance,' I yelled. 'Quick!'

Emily's face was turning blue. I got down and began

pumping her chest with my hands, desperately trying to remember the first aid I'd learned at school. Then I breathed into her mouth.

Nothing.

'Emily! Help!' I screamed. 'Someone help!'

Suddenly, the music stopped. There was a deadly hush.

I looked down at my friend's beautiful, heart-shaped face. Her startlingly-blue eyes were rolling upwards towards her eyelids. Saliva was dribbling out of her mouth. 'Emily, Please don't go. How many did you have?'

'What are you talking about?' yelled Rupert.

Before I could answer, he glanced at my open bag by Emily's side. You could see tablets in it.

'I wouldn't let her have any!' I screamed. 'But she must have taken them from me.'

'What the fuck have you done, Sarah?'

'I didn't mean to. I didn't. Emily! No!'

Emily died five hours later. I was already under arrest. The autopsy revealed that the batch had been contaminated. One tablet had been enough to kill her.

At the trial, my fate was a foregone conclusion. In fact, I wanted to go to prison. I needed to pay for what I had done.

But the worst punishment of all was the look on Emily's parents' faces, and on Rupert's. Tears were running down his face. He had never seemed the kind of man who would cry.

'*How could you have done it? How? How?*'

I've carried that guilt and pain since that day. I'd give anything to bring Emily back. Apart from one thing. My precious only son.

That's why I'm here today.

I look down on the defendant in the dock, who is shifting awkwardly from one foot to the other. For a minute, my mind fools me into thinking that this young man is him.

He even looks like Freddie. The build is stockier, but he has that same black curly hair.

This is the man who must go to prison. Not my son.

All I have to do is stay silent.

PART TWO
Sarah

39

'Quick,' I'd hissed to Freddie when I was sure that Tom was asleep. I'd crept out of the spare room, where I'd been lying wide awake, to peep through the door at my husband. His chest was rising and falling in a steady manner as though nothing had happened.

This was the man who had always accused me of hiding things. Yet he'd been having an affair. For how long?

It didn't matter. My husband was a hypocrite. And now he was going to hand in our son. My Freddie couldn't have killed someone. He was incapable of it.

But you killed Emily, said that voice in my head. *If you hadn't left your bag behind, she'd never have taken the pills.*

My son was face down on his bed, sobbing quietly. The rain outside was lashing against the window.

I glanced at the clock. 4.30 a.m. We didn't have long. Tom could wake up any minute. I'd been amazed he hadn't walked there and then to the nearest police station after Freddie's revelation. '*I killed someone.*'

'Quick,' I repeated, more urgently this time. 'We need to go.'

Freddie's voice was muffled against the pillow. 'Where are we going?'

'To the sea,' I said.

Until the words came out of my mouth, I hadn't had a plan apart from getting as far away from here as possible.

But right then a memory had flashed back into my head of the only time when we'd been happy as a family: that summer in Cornwall.

I remembered thinking, as we'd walked along a remote cliff edge back then, that this was exactly the place to hide in if you wanted to lose yourself. We wouldn't go to the same spot, in case Tom guessed, but we could head in that direction. We'd find somewhere quiet. Perhaps Freddie was wrong. Maybe Freddie had just *thought* someone had died.

Of course, I wanted to ask him more. But I knew that, if I pressed him for details, he might not come with me. He might even run off. I wouldn't know where he was. I'd be one of those mothers who are always searching. The thought made me sick. I'd rather die.

We had to act fast.

'Get your stuff together,' I instructed, pulling my son off the bed. For once, he didn't try to fight me.

I'd already packed a bag of necessities – including our passports – in preparation for the house move.

'What about Jasper?' asked Freddie.

'He's coming too of, course,' I said.

Freddie was standing motionless next to the bed. I began to sweat. We were running out of time.

'They'll put you in prison, Mum, if you help me.'

I shrugged. 'I'll deal with it if they do.'

'Did you really kill someone too?' he asked in a small voice.

Too. I felt sick. 'It's not so simple. I'll tell you later. Now, come on!'

Somehow – I don't know how – I got him and Jasper out of the house. We kept our heads down in the rain, glancing up every now and then to see if we were being followed. I'd expected the streets to be empty but another dog walker crossed our path. I didn't recognize him. Besides, he was speaking furtively on the phone and looked as if he didn't want to be seen any more than we did.

A lorry went by, its wheels shushing in the wet as it slowed down. Had the driver clocked us? Would he, when he heard the news later this morning, tell the police that he saw a woman, a boy and a dog walking through the streets of north London?

The train station, when we got there, was closed. 'We'll walk to the next one,' I said. 'It will be open by then and it won't be so local. Hopefully, no one will see us there.'

Freddie gave me a strange look. 'I didn't think you were like this, Mum.'

'Like what?'

'Deceitful.'

I shuddered. My aunt had called me that when I was a teenager. It still hurt. But I wasn't trying to save my own neck here. What mother wouldn't do this for her son?

A good parent, said a nagging voice in my head. *Someone who isn't a murderer.*

'What exactly happened?' I asked, as we carried on walking.

The rain had stopped, although we were, by now, soaked. I could feel it dripping down the collar of my jacket – the last thing I had seized by the door when we left. Jasper was walking at our speed instead of stopping to sniff like he usually did. It was as if he knew this was serious.

'I can't say.'

I took a deep breath. I'd learned from years of

experience that you couldn't push Freddie. Yet this was different. 'When you came back home, you told us you'd killed someone,' I said carefully.

I wanted him to deny it. But there was silence.

'Is that true?' I asked. I was really scared now.

'There's more to it than that. You wouldn't understand.'

'Try me.' I was conscious that I was sounding impatient now. 'This is serious, Freddie.'

'Don't you think I get that?' His voice is scathing, almost unkind. 'But I can't say because, if I do, you could get into even more trouble if we're picked up. I'm trying to protect you. Then you can say you didn't know anything.'

If Tom was here, he'd accuse Freddie of being manipulative. This was his way of avoiding the truth. To pretend he was protecting me instead of himself.

'I don't care. I just need to know. What happened? How did it happen? Otherwise, I can't help you.'

'You can't help me?' he repeated. His voice sounded like a little boy's. 'But I'm your son. You're not like Dad. You'll stand by me.'

He understood me too well.

He grabbed my arm. His fingers dug into me. 'All I can say is that I didn't mean it.'

I had a burst of hope. 'So it was an accident?'

'Sort of. I didn't think anyone would die.'

'Do you know for certain that anyone did? What if you . . . you just hurt them by mistake?'

'You should have seen him.'

So it was a man, then.

'No one could have survived it.' He burst into tears. 'I don't want to go to prison, Mum.'

My mind was going into overdrive. 'You might not have to. Not if you tell me the truth. We'll find a good lawyer . . .'

'No one will believe me, Mum. No one ever does.'

'I do.'

'That's because you're my mother. It doesn't count.'

He was right. Maybe not in a court of law, anyway.

The next station loomed up before us. It was open. I could see the lights. This was madness. I couldn't hand my son in. But we wouldn't get away with this. The consequences would be worse if we tried to run.

'Perhaps we should go to the police after all,' I said, hesitating.

'Please, Mum,' said Freddie. His voice was scared. Like a child's rather than a teenager who was always pretending to be older. 'Don't let them get me.'

This was it. The point where I had to make a decision that could save us or break us. Some poor man had already died. Nothing we could do would bring him back. Yet what kind of lesson in deceit was I giving my son?

'Please,' he repeated.

I saw my mother's face, the last time I'd seen her. I could not leave Freddie to fend for himself, as her death had left me to do. I saw my aunt with her disapproving expression. '*No better than your mother.*' I was back in the prison that day when the alarm had gone off.

An announcement had come over the tannoy to say we would be locked in our cells until a 'situation had been contained'.

'I've been waiting for that to happen,' said my cellmate.

'For what?'

'That bitch next door. She always gets the new ones.'

'She's stabbed her?'

'Raped.'

'But how? She's a woman.'

'She's got fists, hasn't she?'

'I don't understand?'

My cellmate snorted, her almost toothless mouth grinning. 'Where've you been all your life?'

I wanted to be sick on the spot.

'You're lucky you were slammed up with me and not her,' she continued.

'She's done it before?' I asked weakly.

'Loads of times. But the staff let her get away with it.'

'Why?'

'We reckon it turns them on.'

The very thought made me feel sick again as my mind returned to the present.

How could I let Freddie go through any of that?

I went up to the ticket office, pulling my hat down over my eyes. 'Two singles to Truro please.'

We'd have to go via Paddington, but it would be safer to get our tickets from here. They might be on the lookout for us at the mainline station. Tom would have discovered we'd gone by now. He'd have rung the police. Given them photographs so they could identify us. The police would be looking at CCTV on the trains.

'Where the hell is Truro?' asked Freddie as we sat on the station bench, waiting. It had begun to rain again. Jasper was by my feet, looking up at us trustingly.

'Far away,' I said.

The train arrived. 'You sit by the window,' I said.

Freddie slid his hand into mine. He hadn't done that since he was at primary school. It was bigger than mine. Despite everything, I felt warmth spreading through me. He was only fifteen. The age when children pretended to be adults. The age where they still needed protecting.

'I didn't mean to hurt anyone,' he whispered.

'I know you didn't.'

'Will we be all right?' he asked.

'Yes,' I said, crossing my fingers.

We sat in silence for a while, watching the houses go by. Safe houses with lights just being switched on. Normal families inside. 'Of course we will.'

40

All the way to Paddington, I waited for someone to tap me on the shoulder. Whatever had happened, I was as much to blame now as Freddie. Well, almost – I was an accomplice.

But nothing happened. By the time we got off, I was literally shaking with nerves. Freddie, on the other hand, was composed. Too composed. As though he had done something like this before. Or maybe he was just putting on a front to hide his distress. 'Can I buy a magazine?' he asked as we went past a news kiosk.

'No,' I said, feverishly scanning the departures board. The fewer people who saw us, the better. Jasper tugged at his lead. It occurred to me, too late, that he would make us stand out. Yet I could not have left him behind.

I was feeling angry now, more with myself than with Freddie. The enormity of what I was doing was gathering weight on my shoulders. My temples were pulsating. It was like Emily all over again, just in a different way.

The Penzance train was packed, mainly with business people from the look of their briefcases and feverish tapping on laptops. We should have reserved seats, I realized. But then again that might have drawn attention to us. Better to sink into one of the few free doubles that remained and keep our heads low. Jasper settled down in the gap between my knees and the seat in front. It was as if he knew we had to be quiet.

No one spoke to us, thank goodness. If they had, I'd worked out a story. We were going to visit an aunt who was ill. We had left in a hurry. Keep it clean and simple. Stick to the facts.

A couple of stations in, the train stopped but didn't depart again. After ten minutes an announcement from the train manager informed us there was a problem with the engine and we all had to get off and wait for a replacement. 'Do you think it's a trick?' asked Freddie in a voice that was too loud.

'Shhh,' I said, looking round furtively in case anyone had heard. But they were all too busy making their way out and grumbling about yet another delay. At least it gave Jasper a chance to have a wee.

At last, another train came. The manager announced that we were now doubling up as a local service. That meant more passengers, so we had less room and more chance of being noticed. It stopped at small stations that hadn't been on the original route. I looked out of the window, wondering what life would have been like if I'd grown up in one of these country towns with my mother and not my uncle and aunt in their neat, semi-detached house on the edge of North Harrow. Life was such a lottery. If Mum hadn't died, I might not have got caught up with drugs. If Freddie hadn't gone out last night, we would be moving into the rented house today. Yes – and he and Tom would be at loggerheads again.

But now what? Where were we going to live? My mind went back to the time I was released from prison. My probation officer had arranged a place for me at a hostel. But it was cold and damp. The lavatory was always bunged up.

At night I had to push the table against the door because people would try the handle. Everyone was doing drugs – apart from me. I'd learned that lesson, at least.

Then the hostel closed. I had nowhere to go. I had to sleep on the streets. My fingers were so cold that I couldn't feel the tips. Was that what was going to become of Freddie and me now?

No, I told myself. *Get a grip*. I had money. Or I would have, when the house sale went through. It would go into our joint account.

But Freddie had killed someone, just as I had killed Emily. Money wouldn't save us. They'd be after us.

How had my life changed so much in the space of a few hours? Yesterday, I'd been a mother and wife living a fairly ordinary life. Now we were on the run from the law. Any minute now, Tom would tap me on the shoulder. 'You're having another bad dream,' he would say.

If only that were true.

I shivered. There was a gnawing pain in my stomach from hunger even though I knew I'd retch if I ate something.

But murder didn't seem to have blunted my son's appetite. 'Can I have a sandwich?' asked Freddie, eying the trolley as it rattled down the carriage. 'I'm starving.'

I opened my purse. There was a hundred pounds inside. Luckily, I'd been to the bank two days earlier. If I got more out through a hole in the wall, we would be traced. I'd have to make this last. But then what?

I looked at my watch. It was just past nine a.m. The funds from the sale of the house would be in the joint account now. Half exactly. That was only fair. That's how a court of law would see it after a long marriage like ours. Swiftly, I transferred it using my mobile phone app into my own account. I never had much in it – just the proceeds from my paintings, which Tom insisted I kept. 'You've earned it,' he said. There were times when he could be very even-handed.

The thought of my husband gave my stomach a little jolt. But, I reminded myself, it wasn't the Tom I knew now who I missed. It was the old one. The man who had fallen in love with the old me all those years ago after art class.

'Look out of the window, Mum,' said Freddie, nudging me. I gasped. The sea was right beside us. My son's voice sounded entranced, just as when he'd been a toddler and told me that he liked the 'taste' of rain.

On and on we went. The coastline gave way to hills at one stage and then back down to the sea below again.

Some of the stops had names I'd never heard of, let alone knew how to pronounce. The train went down at one point into a valley with miles and miles of fields around. The sort of place where no one would visit. It pulled up at a tiny station. Talk about being off the beaten track.

I felt my feet move. 'Get your bag,' I said to Freddie. 'This is us.'

'But I thought you said we were going to Truro.'

'I changed my mind,' I said quickly, hanging on to Jasper's lead. 'This is our destination.' I'd almost said 'destiny'.

We got off. No one else did. We watched the train depart. The wind struck right through us and we both shivered. 'What do we do now, Mum?'

'We walk.'

There was no one to check our tickets as we went out.

No automatic barriers, like London. I was right, it would be easier to hide here.

A seagull swooped overhead. We almost had to duck. Beyond the fields, I could see the sea glinting. Wild blue flowers lit up the hedgerows. It was as if we'd stepped through a door, and found another land.

'I'm hungry,' said Freddie, bringing me sharply back to the present.

'You had a sandwich on the train.'

'That was hours ago. Jasper's hungry too.'

I wanted to ask him again about what happened last night. But maybe he was right. That way, I could honestly tell the police, when they found us, that I didn't know anything.

Besides, I needed to persuade myself that my Freddie didn't mean anything to happen. If he told me the truth, I might not be able to do that. I resolved to keep quiet.

This place was deserted. The lanes were thin and twisty. The hedges were so high it was almost like being in a tunnel. A Land Rover coming round a bend hooted as it barely missed us.

'It's dead here,' said Freddie.

I winced. 'Don't say that word.'

'I know, Mum. Don't rub it in.'

So much for my earlier resolution not to discuss it.

Yet there was one way of finding out. I'd thought of it before but I kept putting it off, like you might delay opening a letter that you know will upset you.

'What are you doing, Mum?'

'Checking the London news on my phone.'

'Don't . . .'

Too late.

I gasped.

'What?' said Freddie quietly.

'Well,' I said, brandishing the screen at him. 'Which one was it? There are three stabbings and a young man who throttled his ex-girlfriend's new partner.'

'Stop it, Mum,' said Freddie. 'I'd never do anything like that. Don't you know me at all?'

Good question. Did I? Do I? Would I ever truly know this child of mine?

'If I find out you lied to me, I'll . . .'

I stopped.

'You'll what?' asked Freddie.

'I don't know.' Tears began to roll down my cheeks. I looked at my phone again.

'You're not going to ring Dad, are you?' asked Freddie. He looked scared now.

'No,' I said. Then I lifted up my arm and flung my phone over the hedge.

His mouth hung open. 'Are you mad?'

I held out my hand. 'Give me yours.'

He hung on to it tightly. 'No way.'

I grabbed it, chucking it in the same direction that I'd sent mine. 'What did you do that for?' yelled Freddie. 'You're nuts, Mum.'

'No I'm not,' I retorted. 'I'm trying to save our lives. Phones can be traced by the police. I should have thought of it before.'

We walked and walked. Neither of us talked, as if by some unspoken agreement. What was there to say? Only the unspeakable.

'What's that noise?' asked Freddie at exactly the same time as I heard it. It was like a whirring. A yellow helicopter hovered overhead. Jasper barked. Grabbing my son, I pulled the two of them into a hedge. My teeth chattered. My body shook. Slowly, the helicopter moved away.

'I'm sorry, Mum,' said Freddie quietly. I looked down at the ground where he was staring. There was a puddle. He'd wet himself. Like a toddler.

'Are they after us?' he asked plaintively.

Gone was the earlier anger. His voice was so needy that I almost felt grateful. 'No,' I said. 'They can't know we're here. I just panicked, that's all.'

But that might not be true. What if they'd seen us? It could have happened so easily. Someone at the station. That dog walker we'd passed. The lorry driver. A passenger on the train who would have spotted us from the pictures that must by now be circulating.

'I should have handed myself in,' said Freddie quietly. 'Now I've got you into trouble as well.'

'It was my choice too,' I reminded him. I wasn't going to patronize him by denying either of his statements. We were both responsible. Even if we did surrender ourselves, it wouldn't stop Freddie being charged.

'Tell me more about that girl who died from taking your drugs,' he asked.

My mind went back to the day I met Emily. My incredible warm, sweet friend. She'd knocked on my door shortly after I'd moved in to our student hall.

'Just wondered if you'd like a piece of chocolate cake,' she asked. 'Mum made it for me. I can't possibly eat it all on my own.'

Emily had also asked some other students on the corridor to share it. She stood out with her thoughtfulness towards everyone. I've often noticed that people who look lovely on the outside aren't always that nice on the inside, but Emily was both. She resembled an old-fashioned doll, with blonde curls and those bright china-blue eyes: so unlike my dark looks.

And like china, she was capable of being broken.

'I don't want to talk about it,' I said. 'All I can say is that I didn't mean to harm her.'

He nodded. 'I get that, Mum.'

'How? Tell me,' I can't help myself asking.

His lips tightened. 'I've already said. It's best that I don't.'

We started walking again. Our steps were getting slower.

'What did Dad do?' he asked. 'You mentioned someone called Chapman last night.'

'You'll have to ask him yourself,' I said.

'Fat chance of that.'

'He talked about someone called Zac.' Freddie looked at me sharply. 'Is he really just a friend like you said?'

'Yes. I promise.'

'OK.'

A wind had whipped up. It was colder here in the country than in London. There had to be a shop somewhere we could buy some food.

'Look,' said Freddie tightly.

A large red tractor was blocking our way. The engine cover was open. A man had his head inside with a tool box at his feet. He looked up at us. Too late to hide.

'Afternoon,' he said in what I took to be a Cornish accent.

'Afternoon,' I replied, trying to sound normal. Freddie stayed silent.

'You've picked a blowy day for a walk.'

'Actually we're a bit lost,' said Freddie.

I shot him a 'What are you saying?' look.

'On holiday, are you?'

'House hunting actually. We only got down today and we're meeting my dad later.'

I was shocked at how easily the lie came out of my son's mouth, even if the first bit was possibly true. Still, the 'dad' bit was clever. If this farmer heard anything on the news about a woman and teenager on the run, it might throw him off the scent.

'Picked the right part of the world, you have. Nothing like it. As I'm always saying to the missus, it's God's own country, with the fields and the sea. Let's get you on the right road, shall we?'

He'd been tinkering with the tractor while talking and now there was a whirring noise followed by the hesitant burr of the engine, which then spluttered into a louder, more confident sound.

'That's my beauty.' He tapped the bonnet. 'Hop in, then. I'll give you a lift.'

'Thank you,' I said quickly, 'but actually we'd like a walk.'

'Don't be daft. Take a gander at that.' He pointed up to the grey sky. 'I give it ten minutes before the downpour they promised us on the radio. There's enough space for your dog too.'

'That's really cool of you,' said Freddie, climbing in. He held out a hand to me. He didn't need to speak. His eyes said it all. It would look too odd if we turned down the lift.

As we trundled along, I braced myself for the inevitable 'Where are you from?' questions. But instead our rescuer only wanted to talk about how beautiful the county of his birth was and how he and his father and his father's father before him had all farmed locally. It struck me, as he rambled on, that the air smelt different here. Fresh. Clear.

Unlike my conscience.

'You wouldn't get me out of Cornwall for anything,' he said. 'Beats me why the young want to leave. See that?' He pointed to a run-down cottage at the end of a rough track we were passing. 'Belonged to Gladys Furwood. Born and bred there. She's moved to a home now. But did her nephew want to live there? Did he not. Buggered off to Australia instead, he did.'

Briefly, he paused for breath. 'Now it's on the market and they can't sell it for love nor money. Bloody shame. It's not the only one. There are quite a few places like this. You just have to look in Jim's window to see that. He runs the town's estate agency. Most grockles decide to come here cos of the low prices and the scenery. But they miss the bright lights, so they leave after a year.'

'What's a grockle?' asks Freddie.

There was a snort. 'A holidaymaker. You can spot 'em a mile off, you can.'

It was so insular here, I thought. Freddie and I would stand out like two sore thumbs. Or maybe this could work for us. People might be more interested in what was on their doorstep than a crime that had been committed in London. By my own son.

'My husband works abroad a lot,' I said carefully. 'My boy and I thought it would be nice to live by the sea while he's away.'

'Is that so? Then Jim's your man. I can drop you off there, if you like.'

'Thanks.'

'Mind you, you'll want to wait for your husband first, I suppose?'

This was getting complicated. 'When my son said we were meeting my husband later, he meant in a few days,' I said quickly.

'Yeah,' said Freddie. He jerked a thumb at the pub on our right. 'He'll need to sound that out, won't he, Mum?'

Tom wasn't much of a drinker. Either Freddie was trying to build up a picture of someone completely different to throw this man off the scent or else he was imagining someone he'd have liked as a dad. One who took his son out for a pint when he came of age.

The man chuckled. 'Well he won't find better bitter than the brew at the Lamb and Flag on the high street.'

I remained silent, quite happy to hear him chatter on in a running monologue – luckily without asking more questions – until we reached what appeared to be the outskirts of a village. There was a community hall with the date 1891 engraved above the door and a small petrol station opposite.

Outside was a news placard. I could hardly bring myself to look but I forced myself: *Plans for new sea defences underway.*

Nothing about us. Perhaps it was too soon.

The tractor driver noticed me looking. 'About time. If they don't get a move on there'll be nothing left of our coastline, what with all the erosion. Discovered Shell Cove, have you? No? It's a real little gem. Mind you, it's a bit nippy for swimming at the moment. You have to be careful with the currents. The Coastguard helicopter's already been out once today. I saw it coming back not long ago.'

So it hadn't been looking for us after all. I felt a flood of relief.

'Did they save the people?' asked Freddie.

'I believe they did, young man.'

Freddie's question gave me hope. If my boy was worried about strangers being drowned, surely he couldn't have killed someone himself?

There was an old-fashioned department store on the right now. It looked strangely comforting, with its floral patterned duvet covers and notices advertising a sale of 'ladie's slacks'. Normality in the middle of this nightmare. The displaced apostrophe almost felt reassuring, perhaps because we were displaced too.

'My Brenda works there,' said our tractor driver. 'Loves it, she does.'

'Is that your wife?' asked Freddie. I wished he wouldn't talk so much. He might let something slip.

'Lord no! She's got her hands full with the farm. Brenda's me granddaughter. Seventeen, she is. Getting married to one of my farm workers next month. With any luck I'll be a great-grandfather before the year is out.'

This man, with his bright blue eyes and agility, didn't look old enough to be the grandfather of a teenager.

'Here we are!'

The tractor stopped outside an estate agency that appeared, from the signs outside, to double up as a post office. 'Tell Jim I sent you. And make sure that husband of yours tries out the local beer when he arrives.'

'Thank you so much.' I felt in my pockets. 'I'm afraid I don't have anything to give you.'

'I don't want nothing.' He looked hurt. Instantly, I realized I'd done the wrong thing. 'Happy to help. Hope you have a good time.' Then a thought seemed to occur to him. 'Not at school then, lad?'

'No.' Freddie's reply was smooth and fast. 'I've left. I'm going to be looking for work.'

'Good on you. Well, if either of you need anything, ask for Blockie. Everyone knows me. What's your name, love?'

'Sarah. Sarah Vincent. And this is my son, Freddie.'

'Why did you give him your maiden name?' Freddie asked when he'd gone.

'Why do you think? It might disguise us if people come looking for us.'

'They'll still be looking for a Sarah and a Freddie. You should have gone for something completely different.'

He was right. I hadn't thought. But Freddie had. Who was this person?

'Why did you say you weren't going to school any more?' I asked.

'I can't, can I? They'll ask questions.'

Although I'd told myself the same earlier, I felt my chest slump. So that was it, then. The end of my son's education.

Freddie's face tightened. 'Besides, I'd rather do something than hide away until they find us.'

'Shhh.' I looked around quickly to see if anyone could have heard. 'They might not find us.'

Freddie made a 'Don't be daft, Mum' face. 'But they will, won't they? We can't hide for ever.'

And I knew he was right.

Before long, someone *would* find us.

41

Truro Crown Court

'Almost exactly five years ago,' says the barrister, 'an innocent man died.'

My ears are buzzing. I need to stand up now. Tell them everything. Otherwise I'll be breaking the law. But I can't. My mouth is frozen. I cannot speak. Just listen.

'*Help me, Mum. Help me.*'

I can hear Freddie's voice as clearly in my head as if he was here now. I've been waiting, every day for the last five years, for the knock at the door. Waiting for a policeman to ask where my son is. And now it's someone else's son on trial.

I look at the man in the ill-fitting suit behind the glass screen. The accused. The defendant who is described on the charge sheet as Paul Harris, also known as 'Knuckles'.

So that's his real name, then. The one that Freddie had refused to give me until his phone call yesterday. The name sends shivers down my spine. Presumably it's a reference to the things he does with his hands to other people. I steal another look at him. He must be, at a guess, six foot three or more. The same sort of height as my son, although Freddie is slighter.

Knuckles's eyes are searching the public gallery, almost as if he knows I am here. But he can't know. As far as I'm aware, he's never seen me before.

Besides, no one from my old life would recognize me. I've gone back to my 'alternative look', as Tom used to call it. I've grown my hair long again. I wear floaty pink and purple dresses from charity shops. I am fitter and browner from the long walks along the beach when I'm not at my potter's wheel. I meditate daily, which helps me to be calm. Though, right now, I'm twitching all over.

'We will argue,' continues the prosecuting barrister, 'that Paul Harris told his cellmate in HMP Downwood that he had killed a man in a hit-and-run in London five years ago, and that he had "got away with it".'

Downwood was near Truro. I was sufficiently aware of judicial procedures to know that defendants were generally tried near the place where the crime took place. Maybe it was simpler to try him near his prison – especially as some of the witnesses were fellow inmates or staff.

But why would Paul Harris make this confession?

Perhaps he'd been boasting. When I'd been in prison, there'd been women who had claimed they had done some terrible things. One had allegedly slashed her mother-in-law's throat and watched her bleed to death, giving her status and making others more afraid of her. That way, they might be less likely to be attacked by other prisoners. It was how it worked. It still gave me nightmares.

The man next to me mutters something about hoping 'the big bastard gets his just deserts'. I wonder why he's here. Is he a reporter? Or simply a voyeur? Judging from the chatter on the way up to the public gallery, there are quite a lot of people who simply enjoy watching cases. What would they say if they knew the wrong man was in the dock?

*

'The defence will declare that Mr Harris was merely present but not involved,' continues the prosecuting barrister. 'He denies that he was the killer and claims that a friend, someone called Ziggy, was responsible for the crime.'

My fingers tighten as I recall the tattoo on Freddie's wrist. My son's 'new' name.

'Unfortunately, the CCTV evidence offered by the defence is, as you will see, insufficiently clear to permit identification of the perpetrator, so we only have Mr Harris's word. Despite an extensive manhunt, the police have been unable to find any evidence to support the claim that this person exists. It is the prosecution's intention to prove that no such person exists, and that Harris acted alone.'

This is where I should get up and find a court official. To tell him that my son had confessed that he had 'killed someone'. That it wasn't just this giant of a man, Paul Harris, with his shiny suit, slicked-back hair and furtive look.

But then my boy will go to prison. And I know all too well what that is like. The noise. The claustrophobia. The hunger. The constant threats from other prisoners. The taunts from staff.

Freddie's life will be ruined.

I will not – cannot – allow him to go through what I did.

I make a low groan. The man beside me gives me a curious look. I turn it into a cough.

'*Tell the court.*'

That's what Tom would be saying if he was here. But he isn't. He's with Hilary. Or maybe he's moved on to someone else by now. It's just me. Alone. This is not something I can share with friends from the new life I've made for myself. I am scared.

'Then we shall proceed,' declares the judge.

A murmur ripples through the court. Papers are shuffled. The prosecuting barrister leans forward in anticipation of the kill. Paul Harris thrusts his hands together defiantly. He no longer appears frightened. He seems angry.

It's time for the prosecution to begin.

'Kieran Jones. You have been sharing a cell with Paul Harris, the accused, for the past eighteen months. Would you please tell the court what he told you regarding the deceased, Hassam Moheim, and the unidentified person known as Ziggy?'

The huge, meaty man in the witness box is the type I would usually swiftly cross the road to avoid. Now, though, he is my saviour. If his evidence helps to send Harris/ Knuckles down, the case will end. My boy will be off the hook.

'I already told the police.' He has large hands, which he is waving around indignantly. What crimes have they committed, I wonder.

Did this Kieran have a mother who refused to believe his crime? Or had she taught him everything she knew about breaking the law?

'Please tell the court what you told the police, Mr Jones.'

'OK. But it's repeating myself, innit?'

He's looking nervous. Had someone got to him? Maybe Knuckles had threatened him. *'Grass me up and you won't wake up in the morning.'* I'd heard that phrase often enough in prison.

'It doesn't matter if you repeat yourself,' says the prosecutor with a hint of impatience in her voice. 'We just want to know the truth.'

This bear of a man shrugs in an 'It's your call, guv' way. 'OK. We was talking about the worse things we'd done that we'd got away with. I told him about the old lady. Not the one I'm in for but another.'

There's a chilled silence in the court. Sometimes, as I knew from the women in prison, the most disturbing crimes are the ones where you don't know the details but can imagine all too well.

'And then he said he could top that. I never believed him at first. Thought he was just pissed up. We'd made some hooch, see. Anyway, he came out with this stuff about running some geezer over in a garage and not stopping. "No one saw us," he told me.'

'Us?' repeats the barrister. 'So, even then, he was claiming that someone else was with him?'

My heart freezes.

'I dunno. I didn't ask who it was. We was just talking about what we'd got away with, see.'

I feel like I can't breathe. My mind goes back to those news stories on my phone when Freddie and I had gone on the run. '*Which one was it?*' I'd said. '*There are three stabbings and a young man who throttled his ex-girlfriend's new partner.*'

All this time I'd thought he must have had something to do with one of those. Though after we parted ways I just tried not to think of it at all. Of course, I know differently now.

'Did he say why he didn't confess?'

There's a sound of disbelief. 'Would you hand yourself in if you'd run a bloke over and no one knew who did it?'

'It's the law, Mr Jones.'

'And we're criminals.'

There was a disapproving sound from a couple of people on the jury.

'Did he say anything else?'

'Yeah. He said he'd nicked the car an' all. "Went like shit off a shovel, it did." Those were his words. "Or else we couldn't have got away."'

'Did he say where he stole the car from?'

'Nah.'

'Thank you, Mr Jones. That's all for the time being.'

'That's it, then,' whispers the man next to me in the public gallery. 'Clear-cut case. That Knuckles bloke is as guilty as hell.'

But he's not! It's Freddie who should be in the dock. My mind goes back to my son's call last night.

'Mum. I have to tell you something awful. I ran a man over. It was a mistake. But we left him there.'

Paul Harris was already in prison for running someone else over in cold blood – I knew that from looking him up online. He was obviously evil. So what was wrong with him getting another sentence?

Because it is *wrong,* says my inner conscience. Because he didn't do it. My son did. He didn't mean to. But he still ought to be punished.

'Don't you think?' says the man next to me.

I started, jolted out of my thoughts.

'Think what?'

'That this Knuckles bloke is guilty.'

I dig my nails into the palms of my hands.

'It looks like it, doesn't it?' I hear myself say.

I almost believe myself.

42

Jim the estate agent seemed very pleased to see me when I told him I was looking for a three-bedroom house. 'My husband will be joining us,' I added. 'He's working abroad at the moment.'

'Really? Whereabouts?'

'All over the place,' I said. I only mentioned the 'abroad' bit to fit in with what I'd told the farmer and hopefully throw them off the scent. A single mother with a teenager might stand out too much in a rural place like this. Perhaps we should have gone to a city after all. But what if Freddie made friends and told them what he'd done? At least here I had more chance of keeping an eye on him.

'What sort of price range are you looking at?'

'I've no idea. I'm not familiar with rental rates here.'

His face fell. 'You want to rent rather than buy?'

'I'm sorry. Didn't I mention that?'

Buying somewhere was totally out of the question. It would leave more of an identity trail. I'd already worked that out in my head. But my mind wasn't my own. It hadn't been since Freddie had come home, soaking wet, and confided that he'd killed someone. Could that really only have been last night?

The agent glanced at Jasper, who was sitting upright on the floor next to us, perfectly behaved. 'I've only got two rental houses on my books and neither will take dogs, I'm afraid.'

'Why not?' asked Freddie, bristling.

I threw him a 'Don't talk' look. We'd agreed before-hand that I would handle this.

'They had some problems with scratched floorboards and nasty messes left in the corners.' His mouth was raised at the sides in distaste. I suspected he wasn't a dog owner.

'Jasper is trained,' said Freddie indignantly. I could see a familiar steeliness behind my son's eyes. He was up for a fight. Woe betide anyone who criticized his dog.

My son could be like that. Warm and loving one min-ute, hard and cold the next. But capable of murder? No. Please, no.

'Sorry I can't be of more help. I'll keep my ears out. You'll need to provide references, of course, if something comes up.'

My mouth went dry. References? I hadn't thought of that.

'Of course,' I said smoothly. 'That's not a problem.'

'Would you like to fill this in?' He pushed a form towards me. I could see that it asked for a previous address.

I glanced at my watch deliberately. 'Actually, I'm in a bit of a rush so I'll come back later,' I said.

'Now what?' asked Freddie, as we got back onto the high street.

'I don't know. Maybe we'll move on to somewhere else.'

'Jasper's tired. So am I.'

Tired? Some man might be lying dead in a morgue. He could be a father. A husband. A grandfather. And my son was tired?

'Then you shouldn't have got yourself into this mess,' I snapped back.

'I know. I'm sorry, Mum.' He was back to that little-boy version of himself.

There was a hotel at the end of the high street. We could book in there, but it was smart-looking. The kind where you'd have to leave an address for their files. If I forged it, they might check and be suspicious. Was it always going to be like this? Looking over our shoulders wherever we went? Maybe it would be best if we handed ourselves in right now.

'The pub's got vacancies, Mum! Look at the sign in the window.'

We went in. Freddie ordered half a pint at the bar with such ease that it was clear he had done this before. He was under age. I knew I should stop him. But an argument might draw attention to us.

Jasper made himself at home under the trestle table next to the fire with a bowl of water and two packets of pork scratchings that Freddie had bought him.

I had a bitter lemon. I'd have liked a large red wine, but I needed to keep my wits about me.

'Jim see you right then, did he?' asked a voice.

It was Blockie, our tractor driver.

'I'm afraid not. I decided rented would be best, but none of the owners on the agent's books would take dogs.'

He made a "pah" sound. 'Some people don't know what's good for them. Dogs are better than many a human being, if you ask me. Not a bad bone in their body, unless you treat them wrong. If a dog doesn't do what it should, it's the owners' fault. Like parents.'

He raised his hand to wipe the foam off his chin.

Then he leaned towards us. 'I could ring Gladys, if you like.'

'Who?'

'Gladys. The old dear who owns that cottage we passed earlier on. Her nephew used to live there but like I said, he's in Australia now. She'd be glad to have it occupied. Mind, it's a bit damp.'

'Will she want references?' asked Freddie.

Talk about sounding suspicious. Why couldn't he have kept quiet?

'I don't know.' His eyes narrowed. 'Is that a problem?'

'Of course not,' I chipped in quickly. 'But it might take a bit of time to get them.'

'I'll ask her. Only thing is, the place is a tip. How fast do you want to move in?'

'Now,' said Freddie.

'As soon as possible,' I add. 'I've got money to pay someone to clear it.'

'Have you? Well, maybe some of my lads might like to earn a bit of spare cash on the side.'

In a normal life, I'd have asked for two or three quotes. But that would have meant more exposure. More questions. More people to recognize our faces when it all came out.

'Tell you what. Why don't we go and look at it now, before the dark sets in?'

This is crazy, I told myself. They'd find us sooner or later. I'd given the police enough trails. We should keep running. On and on. *But you can't leave*, says another voice in my head. We needed to sit and take stock. Maybe we would end up handing ourselves in. But not just yet. I needed to be with my son for a little longer. To savour every minute. To hold his hand. To prepare him – and myself – for what might lie ahead.

Gladys's cottage door was open when we arrived. It was a faded marine blue – one of my favourite colours – which seemed to work well in contrast with the old stone. 'No one locks their door in these parts,' sniffed Blockie.

There was a wood burner with charred logs inside. In the kitchen was a dirty cream Aga, which was cold to the touch. The floor was filthy with rat droppings. There was mildew on the walls.

'The garden's a jungle!' said Freddie, pointing through the window to nettles about six feet high.

'Used to be Gladys's pride and joy. Gone to weed now, it has. You can't see it, but there's a hut at the bottom. Still got her kiln and wheel in it.'

'She's a potter?' I asked.

'Certainly was. Made these. Look.'

He pointed to some earthenware pots that were lining the kitchen dresser. All were covered with dust.

'I used to do pottery for a bit,' I say quietly. 'Back at art school.'

'Then you might get it going again. Gladys would like that.'

'I'll take it,' I said.

'Really? It's a bit out of the way, especially if you change your mind about going to school. I know you said you wanted to work, but had you thought about sixth-form college?'

He looked pointedly at Freddie.

'Not interested,' I said. 'He's sixteen now and I've learned there's no point in pushing him academically.'

Freddie was beaming. It wasn't true. He wouldn't be sixteen until his next birthday, although he looked older.

But if I'd given his real age, it might look odd that he wasn't at school.

Blockie was scratching his chin. 'I could do with a hand on the farm, if the lad really is looking for something.'

'I'm up for that,' said Freddie unexpectedly.

No! I wanted to say. Someone might ask questions. Freddie might say the wrong thing. And what would happen when the newspapers came out with our photographs? We'd both be arrested.

Yet a crazy part of me, the other bit that pretended everything would work out, piped up. 'That would be great,' I said. 'Thank you.'

'Where are you staying tonight?' Blockie asked.

'I was going to book into the pub or the hotel,' I said.

'You can stay at one of our farm cottages, if you want,' he said. 'So happens we've had a cancellation. Going cheap as it's off-season.'

It was too easy.

Now all I had to do was wait for something to go wrong.

It wouldn't be long. I could feel it in my bones.

I have to blank it out of my head.
It's the only way.
But I didn't mean it to happen.
I promise.
Honestly.
You've got to believe me.
You do, don't you?

43

Had we really been here for a whole week?

For some reason, the farmer had taken the two of us under his wing. Perhaps it was because he'd overheard Freddie worrying about what would happen 'if Dad found us'.

One morning as we came downstairs we both jumped as we realized our new friend was standing in the hallway.

'Sorry,' he said. 'The front door was open so I just came in. It's what we do round here.'

'It's fine,' I said.

Freddie had shot back upstairs.

'Everything all right?' he continued.

'Great, thanks.'

'Your husband not here yet, then?'

'No.'

'Right.' He hesitated. 'Look, it's none of my business, but if you're in any kind of danger, you'll let me know, won't you? I had an employee whose husband was violent. I wouldn't want to see another woman going through the same thing.'

Tom's not violent, I almost said, although he did smack Freddie when he was younger. But if the farmer wanted to see it this way, then maybe he'd be more likely to keep quiet about us being here.

'Thank you,' I said. 'That's very kind.'

Meanwhile, Blockie, as he kept reminding me to call him, got his men to sort out the missing tiles on the roof of Gladys's cottage and give it a lick of paint. He even managed to find the right marine blue for the door and I helped to paint the window sills in the same shade too. It was amazing how it transformed the place. I'd always hated the neutral beige and browns that Tom wouldn't let me change in the London house.

What was I doing, thinking about colour, when my son had killed someone?

They also cut the grass and got the Aga going.

'You'll soon get the hang of it,' said Blockie when he saw my doubtful expression.

But the flame kept going out and it was so difficult to reach in through that tiny little window and light it.

'Let me have a go,' Freddie said one evening.

Amazingly, his hands succeeded in positioning the taper so the blessed thing lit up. It would take a few hours to get warm, but at least we had it working.

'Well done!' I started to raise my hand in a high five, as I had done when my son was younger. He did the same. Then our eyes met. For a minute, the task of lighting this strange cooker in our new kitchen had distracted us from the monstrous black weight that sat on our shoulders. But now it had come back.

A man had died.

Every now and then, I couldn't help pressing Freddie to tell me the truth.

Each time, his answer was more or less the same. 'You wouldn't understand. And anyway, I need to protect you. If you don't know, you can't be accused of hiding the facts.'

Each time I reconsidered going to the police, I found I couldn't do it. It wasn't me I was worried about. I'd have taken my sentence on the chin, as I'd done before. But Freddie was different. He had his life before him. Whatever he'd done, it had to have been an accident.

My son was no cold-blooded murderer.

Yet the niggling thought *What if he is?* simply wouldn't go away.

Over the next few weeks, we fell into a rhythm. During the day I kept myself busy in Gladys's shed with Jasper sleeping by my side. My old art-school lessons had come back to me. I would make a clay pot! We used to do this by hand, without a wheel, making a flat round disc and then rolling a series of sausage shapes, one on top of the other, to get height.

I do this now. It struck me as I did this that life itself is like a coil pot. The layers represent different stages in our lives. Each one builds up to create a whole. Unless you choose to self-destruct. Like me.

Then, with Gladys's wheel, I worked in a different way by placing a ball of clay in the middle and carefully pulling up the 'walls' of the pot, as the wheel turned. But every time I got anywhere near making what looked like a decent shape, I squeezed the clay too fiercely between my hands so it was shapeless. Then I started all over again, wishing I could do the same with history.

In another life, this would be paradise. Living near the sea. Just Freddie and me and Jasper, without Tom to nag us. But this was real. Not make-believe or a bad dream. Sick with constant fear, I was unable to concentrate on anything. Any second I expected a knock on the door with a policeman standing there. Every minute I waited for a phone call from my farmer friend to say that Freddie had been arrested at work. Every day I bought a national newspaper from the village shop, scanning it with a dry mouth for a story about a fifteen-year-old, suspected of murder, and his mother who was on the run with him.

But there was nothing. Maybe our story had died down. Maybe it hadn't been big enough in the capital's scheme of things to warrant any newspaper coverage. I found that both tragic yet also, selfishly, a huge relief.

By the time Freddie came back at around five every evening from his farm work, I had a hot meal ready and waiting. At first I cooked chicken or chops, which had always been his favourite. The Aga flame was still going some days later. It not only kept the cottage warm but also gave food an entirely different flavour.

'Sorry, Mum,' he said, pushing his plate away. 'I don't think I can face meat any more. Not after . . .'

'Not after what?' I asked quickly.

I could see tears glistening in his eyes. 'It doesn't matter.'

After that, I cooked macaroni cheese or baked potatoes or vegetable casseroles. 'You must eat,' I kept saying.

But neither of us had much of an appetite. How could we?

Only Jasper seemed settled in the dog basket, next to the warm Aga.

'Why don't you go and draw in your room?' I suggested.

He shook his head. 'I can't any more.'

'Nor me,' I said quietly. 'But somehow pottery is differ-ent. Maybe you could find something else to do.'

'It's why I like working on the farm. It stops me thinking, because it's nothing like the stuff I used to do. I can pretend I'm someone else. And the routine takes me out of my head.'

I got that.

Since we'd arrived here, Freddie had changed almost overnight from being a difficult teenager to a young man with a drawn expression and blistered hands from hard work. He was polite. He actually offered to wash up every night. 'That lad of yours is a grafter,' said the farmer when he came round with some big brown fresh eggs one day. 'He's a natural on the land.'

I almost wanted to ring Tom and tell him. '*See*,' I'd say. '*All he needed was to find something he enjoyed doing*.'

And all *I'd* needed was to get away from the repressive atmosphere at home. It wasn't anyone's fault. The truth was that Tom and I had never been suited. Even if we had been, our marriage could never have survived after he'd found out what I'd done. I'm not sure I could have survived his infidelity either.

The following night, when I couldn't sleep, I came downstairs to make a milky drink. Freddie was sitting by the Aga, talking to Jasper. 'I didn't mean to,' he said. 'I really didn't.'

Then they both looked up at me.

'Didn't mean to what?' I asked.

'It doesn't matter.' Freddie had his closed face on. I should have pushed him. I knew that. But I was also scared he might go. And, yes, I know that sounds weak.

'You couldn't sleep either?'

'No. But we're going back to bed now.'

Freddie brushed my cheek. His face was a mixture of smooth and rough. A child-man. Too young to be totally self-sufficient. Too old not to know he'd done something wrong.

Then I noticed something. 'I thought that Ziggy tattoo would have washed off by now,' I asked.

'No.'

'Why not?'

'Because it doesn't come off.'

'But you said it was done with a pen like the other.'

'I just said that to get you off my back. I'm sorry.'

Then the two of them went upstairs. If my son had lied about that, what else had he lied about?

A fortnight later, our £100 in cash had nearly gone. Gladys's rent was due. And I didn't want to use my credit card for food at the village shop because that would leave even more of a trail. I would take out one more big amount and after that try to earn my own money.

So, my heart thudding in my throat, I took a trip into the nearest town with a building society. The hole in the wall wouldn't give me enough so I had to go inside up to the counter. I keyed in the PIN code with shaking fingers. The girl studied her machine carefully. 'I just need to ask my manager something,' she said. This was it. Mine was probably one of the cards they'd been told to look out for. Should I run? But if I did, I'd look even more guilty. My nails dug into my hands with tension while I waited for her to come back.

'Sorry,' she said. 'I needed to check something for another customer. Can you sign here on the screen?'

My hands, clammy with relief, could hardly grip the pen.

I took away a substantial amount of cash, which would hopefully last a few months. But who was I kidding? All I'd done, I told myself as I got the bus back to Gladys's cottage, was to buy time. My husband would give the police my maiden name. They'd ask for it. They'd guess I might use it. Then they'd find us. Our running away would only increase the sentence they'd give Freddie and they'd put me back in prison too. My legs started to shake and I could barely get off when the bus stopped. I had to lean against the stone wall for support. 'Are you OK, love?' asked an elderly man who'd got off at the same time as me.

I nodded. 'Thank you, I'm all right.' But inside I wasn't all right. Not at all. All I could hear was the slamming of cell doors, the shouting of the women, the fear of not knowing what your cellmate was going to do next and that terrible claustrophobia because there was nowhere to hide. No fresh air. No humanity. No escape.

'Let's take Jasper out for a walk,' I said the following weekend when Freddie wasn't working. 'We could look for that beach Blockie was talking about. What was it called? That's right: Shell Cove.'

'OK.' His voice had that 'don't care if I do and don't care if I don't' tone that I knew all too well from his teenage days in our old life. But this time I knew that wasn't because of me. It was because of what he'd done. Or said he had.

The sun was unusually warm for April, I thought, as we made our way through the copse I'd found. There was a beaten path and a *Keep Out* notice, so I hoped we weren't breaking any laws. Both of us had done enough of that already. The ground went up some steep slopes at times and then down at others. It seemed to be much further than it looked, but then we finally made it.

'Wow!' said Freddie, as we looked down at the sparkling water that went on as far as the eye could see. Seagulls were bobbing on the waves as if they were surfing. 'Beautiful, isn't it?'

For a minute, he looked like an ordinary teenager without a care in the world. But then his face darkened. As if he remembered.

'I need to talk to you,' I said, sitting down on the shingle.

He sighed. 'Not again. I told you, Mum. I'm not saying.'

'Why not?'

'I just can't. Anyway, what about you? You're just as bad. I've got a feeling you've never told me the full story about this Emily girl.'

My mouth went dry at her name. My son knew me too well.

'Fine. I'll tell you everything,' I said.

Freddie immediately looked curious and then suspicious. 'Just so I'll confess too?'

'Not if you don't want to. I need to tell you about me so you can see I'll understand. You see, your story and mine aren't that dissimilar. I've already explained that I was brought up by strict relatives. But I haven't gone into detail about what happened after my mother died.'

'You said you lived with your aunt and uncle.'

'Yes, that's right. But the thing is, they weren't very nice. They made it clear I was a nuisance. They made me feel like it was somehow my fault my mother had died.'

'That must have been so horrible,' he said.

'It was.' I shielded my eyes against the sun and looked out over the horizon.

'Did you have any friends?'

'It took time. When I was younger, the other kids didn't want anything to do with me because I had no parents. Dad did a runner soon after I was born. In those days, people didn't like it if you were different.'

'They don't like it now,' he said.

'Of course,' I nodded, remembering how he'd taken flak for my nude portraits. 'I'm sorry you got teased about my paintings.'

He shrugged. 'That's OK. I was proud of you anyway.'

'Really?'

'Course.'

'Before we ran away, you said you dealt in drugs and that someone died,' he said slowly.

This was so hard. Parents were meant to set an example.

'I was desperate for friends at art college. Doing drugs helped me get into the crowd. And then my money ran out. I didn't have anywhere else to live. I started dealing just a bit, but my supplier kept pressuring me to sell more. My friend took one of my tablets without me knowing.' I tried not to cry. 'Like I said before, it was from a contaminated batch.'

'That wasn't your fault, Mum,' he said staunchly.

My throat was closing. Wasn't it? I'd been a dealer. 'I left them in a bag in the loo. She found them. So it *was* my fault.'

'Sounds more like a mistake to me. Did Dad know all about this before you got married?'

'Some. Not all. He didn't find out I'd been in prison until after you were born.'

Freddie's face went still. Immediately, I knew I shouldn't have said that bit.

'So he stayed because of me? And that's why he doesn't like me.'

'That's not true,' I said quickly.

'It *is*, isn't it? And what did Dad do? Who was that man you mentioned? Chapman.'

'I told you before. You'll have to ask your father one day. It's not my secret to tell.'

'So he's not perfect either?'

'No one is. That's just the point.'

For a minute, he looked as if he was going to say something else. This was it, I thought, bracing myself. He's going to tell me everything now.

I should have known better.

'So neither of you are great examples, are you? And you wonder why I went wrong.' Then he got to his feet. 'I want to go home.'

'Home?' I questioned. 'London?'

'Course not. The cottage.'

It had been a mistake, I told myself, as we walked back in silence. I'd hoped my confession might make Freddie understand. But now I was scared it was going to change the way he thought of me. For ever.

Freddie refused to eat supper that night. When I went to bed, I knocked on his door. I could hear him talking. But I'd thrown away our phones. He'd promised that he wouldn't get another – not even a pay as you go. Yet he'd clearly broken that rule.

'Who was that?' I asked, opening the door without knocking.

'No one.'

He was stuffing something in his pocket. I was right. It was a mobile.

'Where did you get it from?' I demanded.

'I've always had it. It's a spare.'

'Give it to me,' I said.

'No.'

What was I meant to do? Tackle him to the ground to get it?

'Look, I've had enough.' Fear made me angry. 'I've asked you time and time again what happened. You won't tell me. I risked my own freedom to hide out here with you. And now you're talking to someone. Don't you think I deserve to know what's going on?'

My son looked like he did when he had fractured his arm that day in the playground. His face was raw with pain. In contrast to his anger on the beach, he now looked scared. 'Mum! Don't you get it? You've been in prison before. If you get done again, they'll give you a longer sentence. Now please. Give me some space. I need to figure this out.'

He pushed me – not hard, but hard enough – towards the door.

'I just want to know what you did!' I yelled. 'First you said you'd killed someone and then you'd said there was more to it than that. Tell me the truth. You owe it to me.'

But I could hear the door locking behind me. There'd already been bolts on the inside when we'd moved in. If Tom had been here, he'd have taken the bolts off. Maybe I should have done the same. Of course, it would have caused another argument. And I'd had enough of that. I simply didn't have enough strength. I'd left my home, my husband, everything, to save my son. And now what?

That night I tossed and turned. By the morning, I'd decided. I couldn't live like this any more. I'd been wrong to hide Freddie. I'd set him a bad example. I had to go to the police just as Tom had said we should have done. He'd been right. I could see that now. Better to do it now than wait to be arrested. It might, with any luck, reduce our sentences by a few years.

I showered and dressed. I'd take Jasper for his morning walk. We always passed a phone box. I'd go into it and make the call.

It was only just after six but my son's door was open. Maybe he'd left early for work at the farm. Then I went downstairs. There was a note on the table.

Dear Mum,

I can't risk you going to jail for me. I'm going somewhere where no one can find me. Please don't try. That way you can be honest when the police come.

I love you.
Freddie x
P.S. Burn this.

Rain.
  Black.
  My feet sliding on the wet pavement.
  Falling.
  Picking myself up again.
  Running. I need to go home.
  My parents will kill me.
  But I don't know where else to go.

44

Truro Crown Court

There's a break in the proceedings and I go outside for some fresh air.

Being here freaks me out. It takes me back to what happened after I'd been sentenced.

The slamming prison doors, the kicking of shins in the line-up, the constant fear of attack. One of the women on my wing broke her neck after she 'fell' down the stairs. Not one person saw what happened. Or so they said.

I call Steve. A couple of years ago, I'd finally given in and got a mobile. It made it easier to contact each other. Besides, he was the only person I rang, apart from the odd call to Blockie.

'How are you doing?' he asks.

His gravelly voice still makes me go weak at the knees. 'Oh, you know,' I say, trying to sound casual. 'Busy.'

'Where are you? It sounds noisy at your end.'

'In Truro. I thought I'd go shopping.'

'That's nice. You deserve a break.'

That was Steve all over. Kind. Thoughtful.

'By the way, did you see that rainbow this afternoon?'

'No.'

'Must have been just here then. It reminded me of that Wordsworth line. "My heart leaps up when I behold . . ."'

That's what I loved about Steve. He always saw the bright side of things. But what would he do if he knew where I really was?

'Fancy a drink tonight?' he adds.

'Thanks. But I feel a bit tired. Maybe at the weekend.'

'Sure.'

He sounds a bit disappointed.

I ring off, feeling awful.

More lies.

Don't I ever learn?

Then I go back to the court.

Something tells me that today is make or break.

45

I told Blockie that Freddie had gone travelling.

'Bit sudden, wasn't it?' he said.

'Yes. I'm sorry.'

I felt as though I was responsible. Which, in a way, I was. But obviously I couldn't tell the truth. I was glad we were having this conversation on the phone and not face to face.

'He was really upset about letting you down,' I added. 'It's just that one of his friends from London asked him to go backpacking around Europe at the last minute.'

'Well, I hope he takes good care of himself.'

I hadn't expected such concern. It made my eyes water. 'Me too,' I managed.

'Let us know if you need anything. Your husband not turned up yet?'

'No.' I took a deep breath. Might as well get this bit over and done with too. 'Actually, we've decided to go our separate ways.'

I could almost see his bushy eyebrows rising at the other end. 'Have you now? Well, these things happen. If you need anything, let me know, won't you?'

'Thank you.' A lump came up in my throat.

'In fact, it's the wife's birthday next month. I wondered if you'd consider making her something with that old pot-ter's wheel. She's been hankering for a new milk jug. The last one got broken. Might give you something to do. I'll pay you, of course.'

I came off the phone, deeply touched by his kindness. If only he knew . . .

The house was so quiet. I spent all my time listening out in case the landline rang. Freddie had a mobile. I'd been more concerned about getting him to hand it over so I could see who he'd been talking to. I should have asked him for his number instead. Then again, I didn't know he was going to run away.

Ring, I willed him mentally. *Let me know you're all right.*

As a distraction, I forced myself to tidy my son's room. Not that there was much to do. Unlike his bedroom in London, it was scarily tidy. His work boots were positioned next to a pile of clothes he hadn't taken, no longer with muddy clumps on the sole. He must have cleaned them first. His drawing materials had gone. I was glad of that. It would help him. Just as the pottery was helping me.

As I went down to the shed at the bottom of the garden, followed by Jasper close at my heels, I was haunted by something that wouldn't go away. Although I was worried sick about Freddie, terrified that he'd get picked up or attacked or do something stupid, I also felt a guilty relief.

For so many years, there had always been one Freddie crisis after another. Something that he had or hadn't done. I'd lived with a constant fear that this would set off yet another argument with Tom and that I, in turn, would be told off by my husband for not being able to 'put it right'.

Now, if the police came, I could honestly tell them what I'd told Blockie. My son had gone travelling. I had no idea where he was. 'You know what it's like with these teenagers,' I would say. 'They get in touch when they want.'

Then I stopped. What was I even thinking of? Freddie wasn't your average teenager seeking an adventure. My son had killed someone by his own admission. *'There's more to it than that.'*

Again, I told myself that maybe it was just as well he hadn't told me what had happened. Part of me feared that I might not be able to take it. If I didn't have Freddie to love, my life would not be worth living. Once more his smell came back to me. His skin. His face. His voice. Freddie was a part of me. He'd been in my body. It was easy to forget what a miracle birth was. But you couldn't carry a child for nine months, writhe in agony during labour, become overwhelmed with relief and love when he was born, look after him for all those growing-up years and not grieve when he had gone.

I gazed down at the lump of clay in my hands. Any minute, the police could be here.

The sensible thing, of course, would be for me to go somewhere else. I could move to another part of the country. I could even get a ferry to France or Spain. But then they'd check my passport. What if they were doing the same to Freddie right now? My heart began to beat faster. Why hadn't I thought of that earlier?

Even if I stayed in this country, there would be questions from people in the village. Someone who might put two and two together after reading a newspaper report. Just because I hadn't seen a news story didn't mean one hadn't appeared in a different paper.

There was no escape. Besides, I was exhausted from the trauma of the last few weeks.

Finally, I decided. I'd stay here in the community that had appeared to welcome me. I'd lie low and see what happened.

But all the time, as I went about my new daily routine – working at my wheel on a series of milk jugs so I could choose the best for Blockie's wife, taking Jasper for walks by the sea and buying groceries – the thought kept going round and round in my head.

Someone had died. My son was responsible. I had helped him run away. I was to blame.

More weeks passed. Still nothing from Freddie. I went around feeling as though half of my mind was missing. A yellowy cream rose in Gladys's garden began to bloom early. There was still a weather-worn name tag on it. 'Peace', it was called. Like Freddie's first tattoo. How ironic. How fitting. How impossible. I stroked its velvet petals on my way down to the hut, where the soothing motion of the wheel helped to distract me from the inevitable.

Yet memories kept coming back of a younger Freddie when he'd been so sweet and trusting. The one who had looked at the sky and asked if the plane trail above was like the lines on his Etch A Sketch. My heart ached with loss. I kept reaching up to touch my pendant out of habit – my precious pendant that had been given back to me by the officer when I'd been released from prison – but it no longer gave me comfort. Jasper sensed my distress and would paw at me as if to say 'I'm still here'.

During his short time in the cottage, Freddie had always taken him out for his last night walk. Now I did it, wondering if by any chance my boy might have stayed close, lurking in the shadows.

It was the not knowing where he was that really hurt. When I couldn't sleep, I'd walk up and down Freddie's room, trying to bring him back to me. I'd hold his old T-shirts to my nose, breathing him in. I found myself unable to recall the exact shape of his nose any more. How could that be when he'd only been gone for six weeks? I wished we'd spent more time together. Our talk in Shell Cove hadn't been enough. Supposing he'd fallen in with another bad crowd? What if he'd been knifed by a thug? There was no limit, I told myself, to a mother's imagination. Or determination. Or sheer stupidity.

Every day I would wake with Jasper by my side, with the morning sunshine streaming through the small gap in the fresh lemon yellow curtains I'd run up. Was that the time? Freddie would be late for work! And then I remembered. My boy, who had been with me every day of his life, had gone. And I'd no idea if I would ever see him again.

I threw my distress into painting a wall in the sitting room. Bright purple. Tom would have hated it. Gladys's cottage gave me the chance to make a home in which I felt comfortable. To put my own stamp on it. I made pads for the bay window seat out of a Sanderson remnant I found in the charity shop. I soaked net curtains in cold tea for a sepia-coloured vintage look. I discovered an old patterned rug in the attic, washed it in the bath and dried it on the line. It was a bit frayed but the apricot design gave a softer look to the flagstones in the hall.

Outside, I fashioned a little arch out of wood I came across in the copse. It would support one of the climbing roses that had fallen on its side. I also tried to tackle what looked like a large overgrown vegetable patch at the bottom of the garden. The weeds seemed to go down into the earth for ever.

Just like my sins.

Yet there were moments when I almost forgot the darkness in my mind. I learned to rejoice in the sound of the birds in the morning. The smell of the roses when they burst into bloom. The joy of growing courgette seeds that transformed into yellow flowers and then plump, healthy, green vegetables that I would roast in the Aga along with garlic and ginger. The soothing rhythm of Gladys's potter's wheel.

Then, one day, when I had finally made a milk jug I was happy with, Jasper leaped up from his mat next to me and began racing towards the house, barking madly. It couldn't be Blockie. Jasper had got to know him well enough not to act like this.

My heart beating nineteen to the dozen, I opened the door to find a pleasant, fresh-faced, middle-aged woman with bright eyes. 'My name's Daphne. I live in the village. I'm the publicity officer for the local Women's Institute.'

She pressed a leaflet into my hands. 'We have some very interesting speakers on the programme. Next up is a talk by a retired prison officer who used to work in Dartmoor.' Her eyes sparkled. 'Should be fascinating.'

A prison?

Once more my heart began to beat wildly. More memories came flashing back, shooting pain into my temples.

The smell of the loos. The narrow-eyed looks from prisoners and officers. Razor blades on the floor of the shower. Shit in your shoes.

'It can't be easy moving somewhere new on your own,' said my visitor after I'd felt obliged out of politeness to ask her in. I was aware that I looked a bit scruffy, with my cut-off jeans and hair that had gone all frizzy. The Sarah that Olivia had made me into, with the styled bob and smart clothes, had gone. So had Tom's wife, with that big house and his posh friends like Hugo. Good.

Strangely, I didn't feel any anger towards Tom for his affair. We'd never been right for each other. In fact, it was a relief. It showed that I wasn't the only one who had behaved badly. Even though it didn't compare with murder.

'Blockie said your son had gone travelling,' said Daphne, cutting into my thoughts.

I felt a chill running down my arms. 'Yes, that's right.'

'He'd taken quite a shine to your lad. You must miss your son.'

I tried to gather myself. 'Yes. But my work keeps me busy.'

'I heard you're a potter. Is that one of yours?'

She gesticulated at the milk jug in my hands.

'It is.'

'Perhaps you'd like to come and give a talk one day.'

No chance. I needed to stay in the shadows. Not put myself in the spotlight.

'That's very kind,' I said. 'But I'm not good at public speaking.'

'That's a shame. We're very keen on crafts round here.

Well, I must be off. Let me know if there's anything I can do.'

That reminded me of something I'd been meaning to ask Blockie.

'Actually,' I added, seeing her out, 'you don't know of anyone who sells clay, do you?'

Gladys had left a sealed bag but it was nearly empty now.

'You want Steve Leather,' she said promptly. 'He can get hold of almost anything locally. I'll get him to call round.'

Unexpected visitors made me nervous. 'I'd rather ring him,' I said quickly.

'He doesn't work like that. He operates through word of mouth. Does things in his own time.' Daphne touched my hand briefly. 'You'll soon get used to some of our ways round here. Meanwhile, do have another think about our meetings. It would be lovely to have a new face.'

Part of me was tempted. I'd have liked the company. But I couldn't risk it. I'd gone so far to save my son.

And now there was no going back.

46

Gladys's old wheel was my saviour in those months. The calm rhythmic movement, and the intense concentration required, helped me to block out everything else. For example, the fact that my son still hadn't called.

When Steve Leather finally came round, I had started to experiment with mugs. I'd got to the point I always did when one was fully shaped on my wheel. I took the sharp wire and sliced it neatly between the wheel and the bottom of the clay. It occurred to me that the wire was surely capable of throttling someone. Where had that thought come from?

Very carefully, I lifted it up. If I crushed this one, there wouldn't be time to dry out another.

'Looks like you're a keeper,' I said out loud.

'Thanks,' said a voice at the door. I'd kept it open because it was warm. I almost jumped out of my skin. 'Sorry. Did I scare you? I did knock but there was no answer. Your dog came round the side and brought me down here.'

Jasper was nosing the bottom of my visitor's trousers; a worn brown corduroy.

I looked up, taking in this tall, slightly stocky, tanned man with cornflower blue eyes, rather wild chestnut brown hair and cowboy boots. 'He usually barks,' I said, trying to gather myself.

'Seemed as if he almost knew me.' He put out his hand.

His grip was brief, but warm and firm. 'I'm a cat man myself, but I like dogs too. The name's Steve Leather. I believe you're out of glaze and clay.'

I nodded, still not trusting myself to speak too much. Inside, my heart was pounding from relief that it wasn't the police.

'I've brought some glazing mixes with me, and a couple of sacks of clay are on the way.' He glanced around the shed. 'Good to see you've got this place working again. Gladys will be pleased when I tell her.'

'You know her?'

'Since I was a kid. She's in the same care home that my mum used to be in. They were friends from way back. Often pass the time of day, we do.'

'Please tell her that I love her house and that I'm looking after it,' I found myself saying.

'I will indeed.' He didn't have Tom's boarding-school accent but he didn't have Blockie's strong West Country burr either. I wondered how old he was. A bit younger than me, perhaps. But not much.

'Now, would you like to take a look at some of these glazes?' His voice was deep. It sounded as though it knew where it was going without being bossy. 'I can order in some more if you want something different.'

Even though I hadn't glazed anything since art-school days, the result wasn't too bad. Or so I hoped, as I took the milk jug round to Blockie on the Monday night before his wife's birthday.

'Thanks, my dear. That's proper job. The missus will be well chuffed. What do I owe you?'

'Nothing. You've been good enough to us.'

I stopped at the word 'us'.

'It's natural to be upset,' he said, watching my eyes well up. 'I know what it's like when the kids leave home. Especially when you've been through so much together. Has that husband of yours been in touch?'

'No,' I said.

'Well, let me know if he gives you any trouble.'

His kindness made me wish I could tell him everything. But, of course, that was impossible.

'Have you heard from your lad yet?' he continued.

I shook my head, not trusting myself to say more.

He paused a second, then seemed to decide on a new course of action. 'Now, I've got a proposition for you. The missus wants to set up a farm shop. All part of diversification, they call it now. I was wondering if you could make us some more jugs like this and maybe some mugs. Steve tells me you're doing some of those too.'

Was nothing secret around here?

My first instinct was to say no. I didn't want the commitment. But then again, it would give me something to do. I was nearly out of the cash I'd withdrawn a few months ago, despite barely spending anything. Some money on the side would come in useful. That's if I wasn't arrested first.

'Thanks,' I said. 'How many would you like?'

'A couple of dozen to start off with perhaps? Then we'll see how they go.'

Good point. I might be back inside for harbouring a suspect by the time I'd finished. And, let's face it, I deserved to be.

*

370

It was a hot summer. The hottest, said the woman in the post office, for as long as she could remember. 'Global warning,' she nodded her head knowingly. I resisted the temptation to correct her. I was beginning to learn the ways around here. Showing up people who'd lived here all their lives wasn't one of them.

Almost without knowing it, I had become one of the newcomers Blockie had referred to when Freddie and I had met him. Once more, I wondered if I would have been better off hiding in a town. Maybe I should move on. But the truth was that I was tired. I didn't want to keep running.

Was that what Freddie was still doing? It wasn't fair. He could have rung the landline. I know he wanted to protect me, but didn't he realize what agony he was putting me through? Anger was beginning to replace worry.

I tried to concentrate on small domestic tasks to distract me from the bigger things. I found a surprising satisfaction in digging: putting in bulbs and lifting out weeds with those long white roots. If only I could uproot my past in the same way.

One evening, a few days later, I was in the kitchen making jam from the currants in the garden when there was a loud knocking at the door. Jasper went nuts. My heart started thumping overtime. It was gone nine o'clock. Everyone around here had closed their doors and drawn their curtains by now.

It was the police. It had to be. They'd finally traced me through the building society. I steeled myself as I opened up. At least I could tell them hand on heart that I didn't know where Freddie was.

But it was Blockie.

My chest continued to thump as if the *you're safe* message hadn't got through to my head.

'Sorry to drop in rather late,' he said. 'But the wife thought you might like this.' He handed over a fistful of notes. 'Someone came in today and bought all of your mugs. Wants some more too. Opening a tea room somewhere and liked the colours. Said they reminded him of the sea.'

So much for my intention to keep myself to myself after Freddie had gone. Blockie seemed to have made it his mission to keep an eye on me. I was pretty convinced that the mug-selling idea had initially been out of the kindness of his heart.

'Thanks,' I said, the fear starting to wear off. The cash was welcome. I was trying to be careful so I didn't have to take out any more. The fewer risks the better.

'Heard anything from your lad?' he asked, sitting at the kitchen table as I put the kettle on.

'Yes. He rang for a quick chat recently,' I said, in as casual a manner as I could. But my hand shook with the lie as I placed the teapot on the Aga to warm it.

'Where is he now?'

'Somewhere in eastern Europe,' I said, struggling to keep my voice even. 'He did say where but it didn't mean much to me.'

It could be true, I reasoned. He might be in Europe. Or he might be in the UK. Or he might be lying dead somewhere. *No! Don't think that.*

'Maybe he'll bring back a foreign bride.'

'I don't think so,' I said with a half-laugh. 'He's too young to think of marriage at the moment.'

'Not round here it's not. Many of the kids are married by twenty-one.'

Maybe that was the way to do it. Stay close to your family roots. Marry someone you've known since childhood so there are no nasty surprises. Keep life simple.

I put the teapot on the table. I was quite pleased with the jaunty blue stripe I'd glazed around the middle. 'This one of yours?' asked Blockie, eyeing it.

'I thought it might make a change from mugs.'

'We'll have some of those as well, then.'

'You don't have to,' I said.

His eyes narrowed. 'I'm not taking your stuff as charity, Sarah. I'm doing it cos the customers want them.'

Instantly I realized I'd misjudged him.

'Thanks,' I muttered.

We kept our conversation to business after that, talking about prices and which colours were popular. 'The wife wants you to put your signature on the bottom,' he suggested. 'It'll give a personal touch.'

'I'd rather not,' I replied, swiftly hoping he wouldn't ask why. I could hardly tell him I was scared of being traced.

He shrugged. 'Your call.'

After Blockie left, I felt uneasy. If I'd misunderstood his motives about ordering my mugs, what else had I misunderstood? Was it possible that the police had been asking around after all? Had he put two and two together about Freddie? Was that why he was asking so many questions about him and also me?

But what could I do? Nothing. So I buried myself in more work. It was all I had left now.

47

A few weeks later, I woke up realizing it was my birthday. I was fifty. This time last year, Tom had taken me out to dinner. We'd sat in near silence through an expensive meal at a local Italian bistro. He'd given me a voucher to spend at John Lewis.

Freddie had made me a birthday card. 'I know I should have got you a present, Mum,' he said. 'But I thought you might like this instead.'

It was a graphic cartoon of a mother telling her son off for not tidying his room. 'It's meant to be funny,' he'd said. 'Open it up and read the words.'

My disappointment that he hadn't bothered to get me something – anything, just to show he cared – immediately dissolved with the words.

> To the best mum in the world
> I just want you to know that I love you very much
> cos I'm scared sometimes you might forget.

I'd carried the card everywhere with me after that. Luckily, it was still in my bag when we'd left. I took it out and traced the writing with my finger. Where was my boy now? Even though we never got any post, I hoped today might be an exception.

But no card came tumbling through the letter box. The

landline didn't ring. Surely, of all days, my son would get in touch today. Had Freddie forgotten my birthday? Or had something happened to him?

To distract myself (again), I made my way down to Shell Cove. I'd been deliberately avoiding it because the last time I'd been here was with Freddie. Yet today I was drawn to it for some reason. I'd brought a beach towel to sit on, but not my swimming costume; still, what the heck! There was no one about to see. I peeled down to my undies and then tentatively made my way in. Despite the blazing sun, the water was shockingly cold and I gasped out loud. But once I'd braced myself to dip my shoulders in and then strike out with my schoolgirl breast stroke, it was surprisingly all right. In fact, it was more than all right. It was exhilarating.

The water was almost flat, beautiful, like a still lake. When I finally got out, I felt on a high.

'Beautiful isn't it?' said a voice.

I whipped around. It was Daphne, the woman from the WI who'd called to see me about the prison talk.

She was folding her clothes into a neat pile on a flat, clean rock. 'I'm about to go in myself.'

'It's lovely,' I said warily.

'I heard your lad had reached eastern Europe.'

I began to shiver as I wrapped my towel around me, and not just because I was cold.

'Blockie misses him,' she added. 'Still, that's to be expected.'

'What do you mean?'

'Well, Johnny was your Freddie's age, wasn't he?'

'Who was Johnny?'

'Didn't you know? He was Blockie and his wife's

youngest. Lovely boy, he was.' Her face clouded over. 'He had a tractor accident four years ago this October. Turned over in the field. Crushed. He died instantly.'

'That's awful.' I can't even bear to think about it. 'Wasn't he too young to drive a tractor?'

'You're right. But Johnny was a bit of a hothead. There was an inquiry into it and Blockie was lucky to escape without being prosecuted. Turned out he knew his boy drove it but turned a blind eye because he thought the lad could handle the tractor. He's blamed himself ever since.'

My heart was aching with sadness for poor Blockie and his wife.

'He won't talk about it now,' she continued. 'But his wife does. She says she needs to keep his memory alive. The whole village knows, of course. It's why I thought you would too. Hazel told me how her husband had taken a shine to your lad. Reminded him of Johnny, with his hard-working ways and determination.'

So I'd read the farmer wrong. He wasn't prying into Freddie's whereabouts because he was going to hand us in. He simply cared. My mind went back to what Blockie had said about parents being responsible for the way their children turned out. The guilt was clearly continuing to haunt him. At least Freddie was still alive. Please may that be true. *Please!*

Daphne had somehow got into her swimming costume without exposing herself. 'Have you had any more thoughts about coming to one of our meetings?' she asked.

The question, so hard on the heels of her shocking revelation about Blockie's son, rather threw me.

'Maybe. Sometime, perhaps.'

'There are still some spaces left for that prison talk,' she said.

'It's not for me,' I said quickly.

'That's a shame. We all need to educate ourselves. We're not as backward around here as you might think.'

'I don't think that,' I said. Oh dear. She had taken offence.

'Good,' she said sharply. 'The WI was a lifesaver for me after my divorce.'

'I didn't know –' I began, but she cut in.

'There are a lot of things we don't know about each other. Still, if the talk isn't for you, I can let you know what else is going on.'

'Thank you.'

I walked home deep in thought. As I rounded the corner, I saw a shiny black four-by-four outside the cottage. My skin broke out into beads of sweat. My knees buckled. A man got out.

It was Steve. My heart ballooned with relief at the sight of his chestnut hair and cowboy boots.

'Where's the van?' I asked.

He grinned ruefully. 'Broken down. I've borrowed this from my brother. Not my kind of thing, but it's got enough space. I've brought you that clay delivery and something else too. I found it in the skip and reckoned it was too nice to leave. Might be useful for you to get about in.'

He lifted a bike out of the boot. It was one of those old-fashioned ladies' bicycles with a wicker basket on the front. Just like the one I'd 'borrowed' when I first knew Tom.

'Wow!' I said, running my eyes over its cherry-red frame. It was slightly scratched, but I rather liked that. 'Are you sure no one wants it?'

'It was going to be chucked away, like I said. If it's not to your taste, I'll find someone else.'

I needed to stop questioning what people said around here. Unlike those I'd known in my old life – including myself – they generally had no hidden agenda.

'No,' I said quickly. 'I love it.'

I was already climbing on.

'The saddle needs lowering a bit.' Steve was so close I could smell a slight scent of wood and maybe oil. Embarrassed by our proximity, I got off, watching while he did something with a bolt.

'Try that.'

'It feels good. Thanks. What do I owe you?'

'Nothing. The skip people sometimes charge, but they gave this to me. Even if they hadn't, I wouldn't have asked you for anything.'

His voice was edgy, as if I'd offended him, just like Daphne's had been earlier.

Why did I find it so hard to read people properly? I'd never thought Tom would have an affair. I'd been suspicious of Blockie's friendliness, not realizing he was trying to help because my child reminded him of his son. And as for Freddie, I still didn't know what to think.

'*I killed someone . . . There's more to it than that.*'

Steve cleared his throat. 'On another subject, I was wondering if you fancied going to the cinema in Truro this weekend? There's a good film on. Can't remember the title but everyone's talking about it.'

378

He was, I could see, blushing. Moving from one foot to the other.

I felt sorry for him. I knew what it was like to be embarrassed. To want someone to like you.

Don't get me wrong. I did like him. Although I hadn't known him long, I suspected that Steve's character was rather like his surname. Leather: dependable; strong; warm. *Stop right now, Sarah,* I told myself. Now was not the time to even contemplate another relationship.

'Sorry. I can't. I'm not exactly free. You see, my husband . . .'

I stopped.

'It's OK,' he said quietly. 'Blockie told me. You've split up.'

Was there anything they didn't know around here?

'Yes.'

'Are you divorced now?'

'Almost,' I said. Instantly, I regretted the lie but I had said it now. Besides, we were as good as. I never intended to see Tom again.

'And at the moment,' I added, 'I need time to myself.'

'Sure, I get it.' His voice was slightly clipped. 'I'm the same, except I thought . . .'

He stopped. 'It doesn't matter. Now, about that clay. There's this new brand that you might find better value next time.'

That's when I heard the phone ring from inside the house.

'Sorry,' I said. 'I've got to get that.'

I raced in, almost tripping on Gladys's frayed rug in the hall. Jasper was running after me.

Surely it couldn't be Freddie. Maybe I should leave it. Perhaps it was the police. Or Tom had tracked me down somehow. Or more likely it was Blockie with a new order. Daphne perhaps with another WI invitation . . .

'Yes?' I gasp.

'Mum?'

I sink to my knees. Tears of relief pouring down my cheeks.

'Are you all right?' I whisper.

'Yes. Are you?'

'I'm OK. But I miss you.'

'Me too.' His voice was edgy. As if scared he might be overheard. 'Look, Mum. I can't be long. I wanted to wish you happy birthday.'

'Thank you.' I could barely talk with emotion. 'Where are you?'

'It's safer if I don't say. But I'm fine. I just had to let you know. I'm throwing away the SIM card after this. So no one can track me.'

I had to grab this chance. 'Freddie,' I blurted out urgently.

'Yes.'

'Please tell me the truth. What actually happened that night? Did you really –'

There was a click. He had gone. I pressed the number to return the call. There was a dead noise.

I sat on my heels for a while, rocking back and forth. My son was alive. But he'd refused to tell me what had happened. That meant he was guilty. Or did it?

Eventually, Jasper's persistent licking brought me back to the present. I went outside to thank Steve but he had gone. There was a noise behind me. The window latch had come undone in the breeze and was knocking against the wall. It must have been open all the time without me realizing.

How much had my visitor heard?

48

Truro Crown Court

A prison guard is being called as a witness.

She looks too small to be in charge of murderers. But her words suggest a tough side: a force to be reckoned with.

'I was cleaning the corridor outside the cell. It was a real mess because one of them had puked on the floor. Right disgusting it was. That's when I heard him speak.'

'Could you say exactly who you mean, please?' asks the barrister.

'*Mister* Harris.' She pronounces 'Mister' sarcastically. 'Or "Knuckles", as we know him. He told Kieran Jones that he'd mown down some bloke in cold blood.'

'Yet the defendant is now denying this. Why do you think that is?'

'Because they're a load of bleeding liars. And some people here look up to murderers. That's why.'

There is more evidence against the accused. It turns out that there are surprising similarities between this Paul Harris (aka Knuckles) and my boy.

Both got into trouble at school.

Both had difficult relationships with their fathers.

It's almost as if I am being given a gift.

All I have to do is keep quiet.

But what about Knuckles's mother? What kind of agony is she going through? Is she here now? I look around the public gallery. There are no obvious candidates. I can only see the man who'd already spoken to me and a row of students who are taking notes.

Even so – and this is the cruncher – can I, as a mother, let someone else's son go down for what my own boy did?

Then there's a sneezing noise from the other end of the gallery, behind the students. I glance across. And freeze.

It can't be. It just can't. Why hadn't I noticed him before?

He's older, of course. And his hair appears thinner. But it's the eyes that are the dead giveaway. They are pinning me down with the same disdain that they did when my old cellmate had called out to us from the pavement.

It's Tom.

I can't take in what is being said now by the prison officer, or indeed by the person who came after him to give evidence.

All I know is that my husband is here. The man I haven't seen since Freddie and I did a runner five years ago.

The game is up.

49

When Steve returned a week later with the new clay, I apologized for having abandoned him before to take the phone call. Obviously, I didn't say who it was from.

'No problem,' he said.

What I really wanted to know was whether he'd overhead any of my conversation. I could hardly ask that outright. So I tried a different way.

'Did you wait for long before giving up on me?'

''Fraid not. I left when you went in. Didn't want to disturb you and, anyway, I was just about to go surfing. The sea was beautiful. Perfect for catching waves. You should try it.'

'I don't think it's for me,' I said, laughing off his suggestion, 'although I've discovered that I do like swimming.' But really my laughter was to disguise my relief that he hadn't been around to hear my conversation with Freddie. As long as he was telling the truth.

Still, his friendly behaviour didn't suggest anything else. I was glad of that. I'd been worried that I might have hurt his feelings by turning down his invitation to the cinema. We stood for a while, chatting about the garden and the best local beaches and how to get rid of the blackfly on Gladys's roses. Subjects that I would never have been interested in a few months ago. Topics that helped to blank out the constant fear inside me.

As we chatted, it occurred to me that Steve was an easy man to get on with. So different from Tom. But how would he react if he knew what I'd done? He'd go straight to the police, that's how. And I wouldn't blame him. I needed to banish any thought of romance. I didn't deserve any love, after what I had done.

'Well,' he said, glancing at his watch. 'I'd better be going. Time to make some lunch.'

'I've just made a cheese and asparagus quiche,' I said spontaneously. 'I don't suppose you'd like to share it with me.'

What was I doing?

He raised an eyebrow. *Didn't you turn down a date with me?* he seemed to say.

'Just as friends,' I added, blushing madly.

'Of course,' he said easily. 'I'd like that.'

Jasper was jumping up at him. It was clear he approved too. Yet why, I asked myself, as I chopped up some carrots to go with the salad, had I asked him to stay? Why had I taken such a risk? All it needed was for me to make one slip of the tongue and he might realize I was not what I seemed.

Then again, if I continued to keep away from everyone, people might get suspicious of the newcomer who lived a hermit-like existence in Gladys's cottage. And if I was going to make friends, I might as well do so with people I genuinely liked.

Over lunch, I found that my guest was relaxing company. Our conversation didn't have any of those awkward pauses. We also discovered that we both enjoyed listening to the radio. 'I like the plays,' he said. 'I also read a lot on my own in the evening. Short stories are my favourite. I can dip in and out. And I love poetry.'

'Me too,' I said, thinking about the anthology I'd been reading on the night when Freddie had come home. The night we'd run away.

'"I must down to the seas again, to the lonely sea and the sky",' he said.

'John Masefield!'

'Amazing, isn't he?'

'Wonderful. Mind you, some people say it's "I must go down", not "I must down".'

'I prefer the last.'

'Me too.'

Then I told him a bit about my painting, before coming here. 'The pottery is a bit of a break,' I said.

He nodded. 'We all need changes from time to time. My brother says I'm good with my hands.' He gave a laugh that sounded rather sardonic. 'It's his way of saying that we can't all be high-flying solicitors like him.'

He didn't pry into my past, as if sensing I didn't want to talk about it. He, in turn, didn't tell me much about his, save the fact that he'd grown up here, went to London for a while, didn't like it and came back.

I purposely didn't ask him where in London, in case that led to more questions on his part about my origins. I'd already told him more than I'd meant to.

Steve had a surprisingly good sense of humour. He was also musical. When he insisted on helping me wash up, he began humming a Beach Boys song. 'You've got a good voice,' I said.

He made a mock bow. 'Thank you.'

When he left, he invited me to lunch at his place the following Sunday. As the weeks passed, this became a tradition. No strings. Just congenial company.

My new friend didn't constantly criticize the government whenever a news item came on the radio, as Tom used to do. He took joy in simple things like the colour of the sunset or the crisp autumn leaves underfoot when we took Jasper out. He helped me clear the vegetable patch and brought me seedlings that his big hands would gently plant in the ground. 'Hear that cooing?' he'd say, putting his head to one side. 'It's the pigeons. We need to get these covered. I'll bring you some hoops and netting.'

Steve also appreciated my work. Like me, he was a pescatarian, and he didn't drink either. 'I did too much of that in my old life,' he said, without giving details. I wanted to ask but, again, I feared that he might reciprocate with questions of his own.

In return, my own body relaxed when we chatted. I never felt tense or inadequate or downright nervous, the way I did with other people. In other circumstances, it might have been different. I would have accepted that earlier offer of a date. I might even, I realized, have asked him out myself.

This surprised me. Steve wasn't my type. And even if he was, the last thing I needed in my life right now was another complication.

'Has your divorce come through now?' he asked casually one day.

'Yes,' I lied.

Why had I said that? Perhaps it was because his

question took me by surprise. Maybe it was wishful thinking on my part.

But even if I had been divorced, I knew it would still be better to remain 'just friends' with this good, kind man, because one day that knock from the police would surely come. Then my life would fall to bits all over again.

At times, the tension was unbearable. At others, I almost forgot about it. Then the hard facts would come to me out of the blue when I was setting the kiln to the right temperature for firing, or when I was carefully trimming the edges of the clay while it was still wet for a smooth finish. My son was on the run. He had killed someone. I could be arrested at any time.

There were no more calls from Freddie, but I hadn't expected any. He didn't want to endanger me, he'd said. Or else he'd put me to one side and moved on. This last possibility brought a lump to my throat.

More time passed. The post-office lady put up Christmas lights in her window. The village school had a banner outside with a picture of Santa Claus and Dick Whittington, announcing the annual pantomime. I got a pang in my chest when I remembered how I would dress up Freddie for nativity plays when he was a child. Tom had never managed to get to them. He was always busy at work.

'Written your Christmas cards yet?' asked Steve when he called round one day to drop off a glaze I'd run out of. It was the azure blue, which went down very well at the shop. I was under pressure to make some more for the festive rush.

'I don't send them any more,' I said.

'Nor me. I'm trying to do my bit for helping the environment. Cut down on paper and all that.'

'Exactly.'

How could I admit that, even if I had anyone to send them to, the postmark would announce my location to someone hunting for me?

'Is your son coming back for Christmas?'

'No,' I said quickly. 'He's spending it with friends.'

It could be true. I'd vowed to tell as few lies as possible from now on. The problem was that the big lie made this difficult. One untruth leads to another. And then another.

'What about you?' he asked.

'Jasper and I are going for a long walk in the morning and then we'll snuggle up by the fire.'

'Sounds like a good plan. I'm going to do something similar, although without a dog.'

I couldn't help feeling slightly disappointed. I'd half expected him to suggest we spend the day together.

'I was married once,' he blurted out suddenly.

'Really?'

'Yes.' He was examining his fingernails as he spoke. 'It didn't work out. It wasn't her fault. It was mine.'

I wanted to ask why but didn't like to.

'It reminds me of that wonderful poem "The Young Man's Song" by Yeats,' he continued. '"Oh, love is the crooked thing / There is nobody wise enough / To find out all that is in it".'

'I don't know that one,' I said. Steve's memory for poems constantly amazed me.

'Anyway,' he continued, 'it was better for her in the long run. She's married now with kids.'

'Do you wish you'd had them yourself?' I couldn't help asking.

His reply was off pat, as if people had asked him this before. 'Yes and no. I loved the idea but they're a big responsibility.'

Even more reason, I told myself after he'd gone, why he wouldn't understand about my boy.

Then, early on Christmas Eve, there was a knock on the door. Jasper didn't bark as he usually did, which meant it must be someone he knew, like Blockie or . . .

Steve was standing there, wearing a smart brown checked jacket instead of his usual waterproof, and brogues instead of cowboy boots. There was a serious look on his face. 'Sorry to bother you, but something's happened. There's someone who needs to see you.'

A shot of electric terror bolted through me. Tom had turned up. The police had found me. But why would Steve know? In my rush of panic, anything seemed possible.

'Gladys has taken a turn for the worse. She keeps talking about her cottage and how much she misses it. I've told her that it's being well looked after but she wants to see "the person who lives there now", as she put it. Would you mind?'

Relief flooded through me, followed by compassion. Poor woman. Of course I'd come. I just hoped she wouldn't ask about the references. I was meant to have given those to Gladys's solicitor, ages ago, but so far he hadn't chased me. Maybe people trusted each other more around here.

We set off in Steve's van along the bumpy track. It was icy, and every now and then, the vehicle skidded. Once, I put a hand out to steady myself and accidentally brushed his leg.

'Sorry,' I said.

'Any time,' he joked. Then his voice became solemn. 'I hope Gladys is going to be all right. Your visit will mean a lot to her.'

'It's the least I can do,' I said. Besides, I was curious to know who had lived in the cottage that now felt so much like home to me. No. It was more than that. It was my refuge.

Gladys's care place was on the outskirts of the village. 'She'll be glad to see you,' chirped a fresh-faced girl, leading us down a corridor with soft watercolour seascapes lining the walls. We rounded a corner to see an elderly lady with powder-white hair, tottering up on her walking frame. She grasped Steve's wrist.

'You came, love,' she said. Then he bent down and gave her a kiss on her wrinkled cheek. We made our way into the residents' lounge with its large TV and various chairs – some upright and others more squashy-looking – and sat down.

Gladys's eyes seemed to glisten as she looked at me. Yet I sensed that behind those tears was a woman of steel. It was as though she could see right through me.

'So *you're* in my little cottage now.'

I felt like a usurper. 'I do hope you don't mind,' I said. 'But I promise you that I'm looking after it. I love it there.'

She nodded. 'Good. And people are being nice to you?'

I found myself flushing. 'Yes.'

'Steve and I go back a long way,' she said. 'He brought me all my supplies when my husband died. I hear you're a potter too.'

'Yes. I used to paint and draw, but then I changed mediums.'

'Why?' Her tone was both sharp and interested.

Her direct question threw me.

'Something changed in my life,' I said hesitantly.

'Ah.' She nodded. 'That makes sense. I had a friend at art school who started off making murals but changed to sculpture when something big happened to her too.'

I waited for her to tell me what, but she didn't. She just looked at me for a long second, a slightly quizzical smile on her lips.

'Now, tell me more about my home. I want to know it's all right. Is that Aga playing up? You'll need to teach it who the mistress is.'

Before long, I felt as if I'd known this woman all my life. She was less like a landlady than a grandmother. The sort I'd always wanted. Kind, but also on the ball. Not afraid of giving advice, but also curious about me. I needed to watch my step and not give too much away. 'My son is travelling abroad,' I said carefully, when she asked if I had children.

'That must be hard for you, especially at this time of the year.'

Her kind words brought a lump to my throat. I had to fight hard to stop tears welling up. 'Yes,' I said.

Every now and then, Gladys stopped and panted. 'It's my chest,' she said. 'The doctors are keeping an eye on it, so don't look so worried, young Steven.'

I had to smile at the 'young' bit. I was aware that I'd begun, very slowly, to smile more often in the last month or so.

'You might laugh, but you're both young to me,' she said. 'You've got your lives in front of you. Mine is running out, but I've had a good time.'

'Don't talk like that, Gladys,' said Steve, with a catch in his voice.

'But it's true, boy, isn't it? Now, do me a favour and get me some more lemonade from the pantry along the corridor.'

As soon as he'd gone, she turned to me. I saw that flash of steel again. 'Steve's told me about you,' she rasped. 'I can see you've been hurt. It's why you're being cautious. But I can tell you this for free. He's a good 'un, that one. You won't do no better than him. Yet he has his own burdens to bear, which makes him different from some other men. Give him a chance.'

I wondered what kind of burdens. Still, that wasn't really the point. The real issue here was that Steve wouldn't want anything to do with me if he knew what I'd done. But before I could say something non-committal and neutral, Steve returned. We spent a bit longer with Gladys, but it was clear she was tired. 'Come back soon,' she told me, grasping my wrist and pulling me down so my cheek brushed hers. 'And remember what I said.'

'What did she mean by that?' asked Steve when we went back out to the foyer, where a giant paper snowman was bobbing from the ceiling.

I could feel my toes curling with embarrassment inside my boots.

'Nothing,' I said.

'Gladys always means something when she talks. It's what I like about her.'

He was standing close to me, closer than he'd ever done before.

No more lies. Maybe that's why I heard my voice coming out before I could stop it. 'She said you're a good man and that I ought to give you a chance.'

'And will you?'

He was even closer now.

I stepped back. 'Steve,' I began slowly. 'I like you. I really do. But I've done things in my life that I deeply regret. And if you knew what they were, you wouldn't want to be with me.'

He frowned. 'What do you mean?'

'I can't say.'

'Have you killed someone?'

It took me a few seconds to realize he was joking.

I said nothing.

His face went serious now. 'I've done things I'm not proud of either. Supposing we both agree that we'll never ask each other about our pasts?'

'Sounds good to me.'

He shuffled from one foot to the other. 'Sarah, I've never said this to any other woman, including my ex-wife. But I feel comfortable with you in a way I've never felt with anyone else. How about we agree to just get on and enjoy life together?'

Was this a moving-in proposal before we'd even kissed? 'I can't live with you,' I blurted out.

'I can't live with you either! I'm too used to my own company.' He squeezed my hand. It was warm. And it wrapped itself round mine firmly. 'But we can spend time together. Don't you think?'

'That sounds nice.'

And then he did kiss me. It was soft and yet hard. Passionate and yet kind. And I wanted more. It made me think of that first kiss with Rupert. The opening up of possibilities.

'May I come in?' he asked when we reached Gladys's cottage.

There was no need to reply.

50

By the time the wisteria was in full bloom, it was common knowledge that Steve and I were 'together', as Blockie put it.

'Nice to know you're not lonely any more,' he said.

I hadn't said I was. Funny how married couples often assume that about anyone on their own.

Steve and I had our separate houses. We saw each other when we were free, and if one of us wasn't, the other never got the hump.

We enjoyed each other's company but, equally, it was good to have our own space. When we were together, we had silences that felt natural rather than awkward. He helped me tame the vegetable patch, showing me how to plant seedlings for the autumn and thin them out when they got bigger. We bought a second-hand greenhouse that was going cheap from someone Steve knew. I watched his big hands holding the little shoots tenderly as he explained how to pot on, mentally drawing them in my head. It took me back to the time on the commune with my mother, helping her and the others to plant beans and potatoes and cabbages.

The two of us walked Jasper for miles over the fields. Steve taught me to laugh again – really laugh and not just a half-smile – with the unexpected things he did, like dancing around the kitchen with me when our favourite

Saturday radio programme was on – the one with the slot for listeners to thank those who'd helped them in the past.

'Warms your heart, doesn't it?' said Steve one day, when a woman rang into the studio to thank the stranger who had rescued her from a snowstorm thirty years earlier. There were actually tears in his eyes. He saw the good in life and he was beginning to help me do the same. I smiled even more. 'I love it when you do that,' Steve would say. 'It lights up your whole face.'

But despite this blossoming relationship I missed Freddie so much. The what-ifs went round and round in my mind every second when I wasn't busy.

I started to wake up in the night, screaming. Again and again, it was the same thing. Tom yelling at Freddie. Freddie yelling at Tom.

I killed someone.

You killed someone.

I began to swim regularly, although I would only go into the sea when the water was calm. There was nothing, I discovered, like the freezing cold shock of an early morning dip followed by a gush of hot water in Gladys's cranky shower to get you started for the day. One morning I bumped into Daphne again. 'The newsagent sells wetsuits,' she told me. 'You'll be able to go in all the year round then, like me.'

She was right. It made such a difference. I couldn't believe how much I had changed. It was as if I was wilfully turning myself into someone as different as possible from the old Sarah.

'Let me teach you to surf,' Steve said. 'I've got a spare board.'

But every time a wave came towards me, I would scream out, convinced it was going to suck me down as punishment for all the awful things I had done.

'We'll keep trying,' said Steve as he helped me get onto the beach. I was shaking with relief that I was finally on dry land. 'You'll get the hang of it one day.'

'One day' suggested a future. One I could not have. Because, sooner or later, someone, somewhere, would find me. It was only a matter of time.

We started visiting Gladys together; despite the medical odds, she seemed to have rallied. 'I told you he was a good 'un,' she said, looking with approval at my hand in his. 'Come back and see me any time on your own,' she invited.

It was almost as if Gladys wanted me by myself. Maybe it was because we shared the same interests: pottery and her beloved cottage. It became a weekly event – usually on a Friday. 'What beautiful gladioli,' she exclaimed when I brought in an armful. 'That apricot was always my favourite.'

'They just came up,' I said.

'I know.' Her eyes twinkled. 'Bulbs do that.' Then her gaze became dreamy. 'I remember planting those years ago. Your Steve had just got back from living in London. My fingers had become arthritic, so he helped me.'

'He's helping me too,' I said.

Gladys's eyes twinkled once more. 'I can see.'

I felt myself flushing.

Every time I visited, I would bring her a little present from the garden. Sometimes it was something I'd grown myself, such as dwarf beans, and sometimes it was something that still technically belonged to Gladys, like her juicy Victoria plums. 'Delicious,' she said, as we sat in the garden of the home. 'I used to win first prize with these in the village show. Why don't you exhibit them for me this summer?'

'I couldn't. They're not mine.'

'Yes you could. And they are yours. You're the tenant.' Then she giggled. 'You've got juice running down your chin.'

'So have you!'

'Allow me,' she chortled. Then she took out a lacy handkerchief and dabbed my face. I did the same back.

'You know,' she said wistfully, 'this place is all right. But I do miss my little cottage.'

'I'm sorry,' I said.

Then I had an idea. 'What if Steve and I brought you back for a visit? He could get your walking frame in the van.'

'You'd do that?'

'Of course.'

Why hadn't I thought of this earlier?

Gladys's face was a picture when we wheeled her in. 'I love what you've done to it,' she said. 'And just look at my old rug in the hall. It's perfect. I bought that during my travels to Turkey.'

'I wasn't aware you'd been there,' said Steve.

'It was while I was at art school.' Gladys had a glint in her eye. 'Old people have lives too, you know! Now, show me what you've done to my studio.'

I'd been a bit worried about this. My heart pounded as Steve pushed Gladys down the garden path, with her exclaiming at how tidy it all was and how lovely the marrows looked with their yellow trumpet flowers.

Then I opened the door of the old shed.

Gladys's eyes widened. 'I don't believe it,' she said, looking around at the kiln and wheel and the sacks of clay and the ramshackle shelves with pottery pieces and the rug on the floor where Jasper slept.

'I didn't want to change anything, you see,' I said. 'It felt perfect from the minute I went in.'

'Thank you,' said Gladys quietly. 'I'm glad. To be truthful, I thought you might have turned it into some kind of yurt or whatever they call them nowadays.'

Then her eyes settled on my duck-egg blue mugs. 'I love that colour. How did you do that?'

'Why don't I show you?' I said. 'I'm about to mix another glaze in azure blue. It's been really popular. Do you think you could help me?'

'There's nothing I'd like more!'

We had a wonderful afternoon. Steve came in with sandwiches and then tactfully withdrew. 'I can see you artists are busy,' he said.

'Very true,' retorted Gladys. 'But if you've got a bit of time on your hands, I wouldn't say no to some oil for my wheelchair. It's pretty creaky.'

'Already done,' he said.

'That's what I like about this man. He's one step ahead!'

So was Gladys. She taught me to brush on the glaze with a slightly different stroke that gave it a new texture. 'I love that,' I said as I put it into the kiln.

She looked pleased. 'It was a little trick I thought of myself. You know, I think I'm going to have to go now.

The staff are quite strict about mealtimes. But I've had a wonderful day. I'll never forget it.'

'Come again,' I said.

Her eyes were shining. 'I'd love to!'

It occurred to me that I'd lacked an older, nurturing figure after my mother had died.

'I'll bring the mug round as soon as it's dry.'

'That would be wonderful. It would be nice to show the others that I'm still a potter.'

'You always will be,' I said. 'No one can take that away from you.'

She tapped the side of her cheek to indicate that I should kiss it. Her skin smelt sweet and her complexion was surprisingly smooth despite the wrinkles.

'You're a good woman, Sarah,' she said.

If only she knew.

51

Time ticked on. It was now two years since he had gone. I could almost pretend that none of the past had happened, if it weren't for the fact that I was constantly waiting for another phone call from Freddie.

Sometimes there were months of silence. Each time, I'd convince myself that he was dead or that he had moved on. '*Only thinks of himself.*' That's what Tom had said. But then my boy would ring, just for a minute or two. Long enough for him to tell me he was alive. Not long enough for me to question him properly.

'Where are you?'

'It's best you don't know.'

Afterwards, I would go over and over our conversation, trying to remember each word. Holding it in my head like a precious stone. Cementing it in my heart.

'Who was that?' asked Steve one night when he was with me.

'I can't say.'

I didn't want to lie.

'Your ex-husband?'

'No.'

'Do you want to talk about it?'

'Sorry.'

'You haven't got another man, have you?'

He said it half-jokingly.

'No,' I said. 'I can promise you that.'

'OK.'

He put an arm around me. I snuggled back into his chest. Not many partners would be as accepting.

One night, I had the dream while Steve was staying over.

You killed someone.

I woke up screaming. Steve took me in his arms, stroking my hair. 'If something's upsetting you, you only have to tell me,' he said.

But how could I?

A third year went by. Then a fourth. The dreams became less frequent.

It wasn't that I'd accepted it. Anything but. No. It was more of a recognition that this was a terrible thing that both Freddie and I would have to live with for the rest of our lives.

And yes, there were times when I told myself that perhaps Tom had been right: I should have turned Freddie in. But it was too late now. Or so I had convinced myself.

I started having new dreams. Dreams in which Freddie was still here. I'd wake with relief mixed with fear. 'You have to get out of here – go somewhere safe,' I'd call out.

'Shhh,' Steve would say if he was staying overnight.

In the morning, he'd tell me I'd had another dream. I'd pretend I didn't remember. 'What did I say?' I asked, scared in case I'd let something slip.

'I couldn't make it out,' he said.

I hoped he was telling the truth.

In an attempt to stay sane, I continued to throw myself into my work. Distraction is a strange thing. It can be healing, but it can also be like columbine. It fastens itself onto a host and wraps around it with such pretty, innocuous-looking flowers as it strangles the life from it.

Meanwhile, my pottery range had really taken off. I didn't just sell at the farm now. Daphne's sister-in-law had taken some for her craft shop near Lizard Point.

Daphne had also introduced me to meditation classes in the village hall. They helped me to concentrate on the moment rather than the past or future. I began to stop looking over my shoulder when Steve and I went out of the village or made trips to Penzance or St Ives – which I particularly loved. Such light! Apparently, it's why the town has always been so popular with artists: not just recently but going back through the centuries. We swam in Shell Cove too, but I still couldn't get to grips with surfing. I was too scared of the waves.

One bright September day, Steve suggested we try again. Other surfers were out in full force, bobbing around or standing up on their boards. 'The conditions are perfect,' he said. 'I'll be next to you. You have nothing to fear.'

But I couldn't get rid of the thumping dread in my heart or that sense of helplessness when a particularly massive wave loomed up. I watched with horror as it roared towards me, crashing over my head and taking me with it. I felt myself spinning to the seabed, knocking my leg on a rock. My ears sang with the underwater pressure. Then, to my huge relief, I found myself surfacing again.

'I nearly drowned,' I spluttered, gulping in the air.

'No you didn't.' Steve was there, grabbing one of my hands. Leading me back to the shore. 'I promise,' he said.

'I won't let anything happen to you. Surfing just takes confidence. Like life after you've had a few bumps.'

'I want to do it to prove I can,' I told him, even though I was still shaking. 'I don't want to feel scared of anything any more.'

'You'll get there,' he assured me, as he helped me unzip my wetsuit. 'One day you'll fly! Trust me.'

How I loved to feel his hands on my bare skin. His touch made me melt. But what would Steve do if he knew the truth?

Once, I thought I saw Olivia coming out of a hotel on the Roseland Peninsula and my heart stopped. But then the tall, glamorous woman with strawberry-blonde hair turned round and I realized it wasn't her. My chest physically ached. There's something about losing a friend that can hurt in a different way from any other loss.

It's only when we're older, I realized, that we understand how past relationships defined us. How they pointed us down a certain path even when the signpost ordered us to take another route.

Another time, I thought I saw my boy. Steve and I were leaving a pub after a delicious crab salad lunch. A young man was walking down the opposite side of the street in our direction. Dark hair. A T-shirt with some colourful picture on the front. My son's build, with that tall wiry frame. The same sort of age. He would be nearly twenty now. I'd missed out on a quarter of his life.

'Freddie!' I called out.

He looked at me and I could see I was mistaken. There were some similarities but it wasn't him.

'Sorry,' I said. 'I thought you were someone else.'

I felt stupid. Scared. Upset. My hand was clutching Steve's arm.

'Are you all right?' he asked.

I'd told Steve that Freddie was still travelling and that he rang occasionally.

'I know I don't have kids,' he said kindly, 'but I can understand how much you miss him.'

'Actually,' I said. Then I stopped. For one moment there, I was going to confess everything. Steve had become far more important in my life than I'd intended him to be. I couldn't keep telling him lies by omission for the rest of my life.

'Yes?' he said.

If I came clean, I'd lose him. He'd suggest I went to the police, which was the only decent thing to do. I'd be back behind bars. They'd find Freddie by tracing the phone calls he'd made to me. If I was going to have done that, it should have been when it happened.

'Nothing,' I said.

Yet, after that, I kept imagining I saw my son in various places.

Oddly, never did I see anyone who looked like Tom. I couldn't help wondering if he was still with that Hilary woman. Was he happy with her? Was I right to think I'd never really loved him? I'd just been a young woman who needed security after losing her mother and who made some terrible mistakes. Now I too was a mother who had messed up and was trying her best to lead a decent life. Sometimes it seemed like that cold, wet night when Freddie had come home crying, had never happened.

And then, nearly five years after we'd come down here, the landline rang once again.

I'd just got back to the cottage and was drying off Jasper after a lovely walk along the beach. I'd gathered some driftwood for painting: I had thoughts about making a doorstop from this nice square piece I'd found. I'd also picked up some shells, which I intended to paint as decorations for the mantelpiece. But the phone stopped before I could reach it in time.

It would be Steve. He'd said he'd ring to arrange something for that night. Steve disliked leaving messages. He'd call again. And he did, a few minutes later.

Except it wasn't him.

'Mum?' said Freddie, in the same voice he'd used that wet windy night.

My throat tightened. Sweat prickled my back.

'Are you all right?' I cried.

It was always the first thing I said.

'Yes but . . .'

I knew it. Something had happened.

'There's something I've got to tell you.'

'What?' I say hoarsely.

'Two things, actually.'

'Please. Just tell me.'

'The first is that I'm sorry for everything. I know I put you through hell. I feel terrible about it. But I've changed now. You've got to believe that.'

How could I say it was all right? Because it wasn't. My son had, by his own admission, killed a man.

'What's the second thing?'

My body began to judder. Dreading what was coming next.

His voice went quiet. I had to strain to hear it. 'It's about Knuckles.'

'Knuckles?' Even as I said the name, I had a terrible feeling of foreboding. 'Who's that?'

His voice came out like a low moan.

'The person I was with on the night of the murder.'

52

Truro Crown Court

I can't believe Tom is here.

I wouldn't be here myself if it hadn't been for Freddie's call.

Had he rung his father too?

No. Surely not.

But how else would he know about it?

I think back to last night's emotional conversation with my son. He said he'd heard about Knuckles's case being brought to trial through social media – part of a current outcry over the number of undisclosed crimes committed by criminals already serving time. But Tom wouldn't know what name to look out for.

I think about the other things Freddie said. Finally, the truth. He sounded full of regret. But he still wasn't going to do anything about it. In fact, he wanted me to help him again.

'I'm scared that Knuckles is going to mention my name. I need you to go there and see what happens. I can't – I'm living somewhere far away. You might be implicated too. If he tells them everything, you'll need to leave the country. Fast.'

'Where?'

'I don't know, Mum. I just don't want you going to prison for me.'

And so, here I am.

When the barrister had opened the case by outlining the 'facts', I had hardly been able to believe my ears. Even though I knew what had happened from Freddie, it was worse than I'd ever imagined.

'Five years ago,' she'd started, 'Hassam Moheim – a twenty-nine-year-old father of two with an expectant wife – was mown down in cold blood outside the petrol garage where he worked. My intention is to prove that the accused, Paul Harris, who also goes by the name of Knuckles, is guilty of murder: a heinous crime in that he not only ran over the deceased but also left Mr Moheim to die without summoning help.'

I felt sick to the core. So Freddie had spoken the truth. A man *had* died. Not just a man. A father of two. With a third on the way.

'I would also like to read out a statement that Mrs Moheim gave at the time to her local paper,' continued the barrister. 'One can only describe it as heartbreaking.' She allowed a long pause to stretch across the room before she went on.

'"Someone has to know who was at the wheel. My children cry every night for their daddy. Now my new baby will never know his father. He won't ever have heard his kind, softly spoken voice. He will never have been held by him or been soothed to sleep. It is wicked. Someone, somewhere, knows what happened. It is this person's duty to hand the killer in."'

She was right, of course. But that person is me. And I

cannot give up my son. Besides, what good would it do now? Freddie knows he did wrong. Knuckles already has a criminal history. Yet that didn't mean he wasn't sorry or that he was irreparably bad.

The barrister paused before continuing. 'During a police interview, Mr Harris admitted he was in the car but claimed that another boy, known to him as "Ziggy", was the driver.'

My right knee began to knock against my left leg with fear. I tried to stop it but I couldn't. It seemed to have a will of its own.

'Despite extensive searches,' she continued, 'the police have been unable to trace him. It is the prosecution's contention that no such accomplice exists, and that the defendant is guilty of murder.'

Now, as I sit in the courtroom watching the third day of the proceedings, Freddie's words ring through my head once more. *'I killed someone . . . There's more to it than that.'* What if Freddie hadn't told me the truth during his phone call? Supposing he had been at the wheel instead of this Knuckles? Would I still be able to love him? Yes. No. I don't know. This scares me almost more than anything.

I look across the public gallery to Tom. My estranged husband. The father of my child.

The only one here, apart from me and Paul Harris, who knows Freddie is involved too.

His eyes meet mine. They are hard. Accusing. I can read his mind as clearly as if he is speaking.

Tell them, Sarah.

Tell them what Freddie did.

That night the nightmare returns.

When I wake, I find it hard to tell the difference between my dreams and real life.

The rain.

That poor man's scream.

On the outside I might look OK.

But inside, I am shaking. Sick-scared. Waiting for that knock on the door.

53

Any minute now, Tom will surely call out. I can hear it in my head.

'Stop this trial! See that woman there? She's the mother of the boy who really killed that poor man.'

Why hasn't he done so already?

But the judge is ending the proceedings for the day. The court is being dismissed.

The trial is nearly over. Soon, according to my garrulous neighbour, will come the summing up.

I make my way quickly out of the public gallery, hoping to sneak out into the car park before he finds me.

'Wait.'

Tom is behind me. His face is set just the way I remember when Freddie had done something he didn't approve of. But now he has good reason.

'We need to talk,' he says.

He's grown a moustache. It has traces of silver, which gives him a certain gravitas. His lazy eye must have been corrected because both are staring straight at me. No glasses.

'What are you doing here?' I say.

'I read about the trial in the paper. I drove down because the case sounded like it might be connected.'

Such logic is typical of Tom.

'But how did you know what had happened? What Freddie –' I can't bear to say the word 'did'.

'I heard it on the radio. The morning after you'd left.'

Oh.

He gives me a sharp look. 'Why are you here?'

'The same reason,' I lie. 'I read about it in the paper.'

'Is Freddie here too?'

If I admit that Freddie was abroad and that he'd called me, he'd tell the police.

I walk swiftly on ahead, ignoring the question.

He follows.

'Talk to me, Sarah. You owe me that.'

'No.'

I open my car door. I say 'my', but in fact mine is in the garage, so I've borrowed Steve's. A couple of years ago, his old van packed in and he bought this second-hand estate car. Before I can lock the passenger door, Tom gets in next to me.

'You're insane, do you know that?' His face is stamped with fury. 'You could go down. Again,' he adds coldly.

It's the last word that brings out the anger. 'And wouldn't you just love that?' I yell. 'You could tell the world what you've probably already said. That your wife was in prison and that if you'd known this before you married her, you wouldn't have done it.'

'That is not something I broadcast,' he says more quietly. 'Look, there's no point in going over old ground. This is something completely different. You left me, Sarah. You took our son.'

'Only because you were going to hand him in.'

'He deserved it.'

'Is that what you told the police after we'd gone?'

'I didn't tell them.'

414

'What?'

'I never told anyone.' His head is down, as if he doesn't want to look at me.

'Then they haven't been looking for us all this time?' I whisper, even though there's no one to hear us.

'No.'

'I don't get it.'

The possibility of Tom not reporting us had never crossed my mind. He'd been so adamant on that wet, windy night.

'Nor do I. There's more to it than that.'

The same words that Freddie had used.

'Try me.'

He's twisting his hands, the way he often does when nervous. I first remember him doing that when I invited him back to my place all those years ago. 'That boy I told you about. The one I was at school with. Chapman.'

Tom seems to find it hard to say his name.

'Just before Chapman shot himself, Hugo told him that he and I would deny everything if he went ahead with the book. That we'd drag his name through the mud. So I'd played a part in someone's death. Just as our son had.'

'I already knew that.'

'Then don't you see? When I'd had time to think about it, I couldn't call the police to report our son. I was no better than he was. Besides, we hadn't known for certain what he'd done. You know how Freddie used to twist the truth.'

Yes. He did.

'At first,' Tom continues, 'I thought I ought to just let you go. When Olivia heard through Hugo, she got in touch and asked after you.'

Olivia had tried to find me? I'd been so hurt when she'd just gone, changing her number.

'I told her you'd left me,' continued Tom, 'and that you weren't picking up your phone. She didn't contact me again. When the school called about Freddie I told them we were moving abroad in the hope this would stop the education authorities becoming curious. But then something happened, so I tried to find you without actually going to the police. Legally, I couldn't check your account. I suspected you were using the building society one under your old name. But I didn't have access to it, and obviously the staff weren't allowed to give me details. I even employed a private detective, but he couldn't find you either.'

'What happened that made it so important to find me?'

Tom's voice is different now. There's a note of excitement in it. 'A girl turned up at my work one day.'

'Someone else you were having an affair with?' I ask hoarsely.

'No. Not at all. This girl – Flick – said she was pregnant with Freddie's child.' Tom's eyes are actually shining now. It makes him look completely different. 'She had a little girl. She's called Mattie and she's four years old now. She even looks like you! We're grandparents, Sarah! And Freddie is a father.'

54

This is a trick. I know it. What if Tom had lied about not telling the police after we'd left? Maybe they told him to 'get me on side' so I'd reveal where Freddie is. Not that I knew. '*I'm living somewhere far away*,' our son had said. Unless he was lying again.

But a child? Surely Tom couldn't make that up? A granddaughter! My own flesh and blood. Freddie's daughter.

'I don't believe you,' I stammer. 'He didn't even have a girlfriend.'

Tom shakes his head. 'He did. He just didn't tell us.'

Can this really be true? His face tells me it is. Then again he's lied to me before. Just like our son.

'Does she know anything about the . . . ?'

I stop. The word 'murder' sticks in my throat.

His expression darkens. 'No. Apparently she was waiting for him to come round that night but he didn't turn up.'

Tom's voice has grown harder and his mouth has tightened. I notice more lines around it than there'd been before. Once more, I feel as though I am being told off on behalf of our son.

'Freddie has to face the music, Sarah. He's a grown man. You can't keep hiding him for ever. All his life, he's lied. He's stolen. Look at my mother's necklace . . .'

'That wasn't him,' I say quickly.

'As good as. It was one of his so-called friends, wasn't it? But murder. That's different.'

I realize something suddenly. 'That's why you're here, isn't it?' I say, turning on him. 'You'd hoped I might be here as well.'

'I thought there might have been a possibility,' he replies. 'There'd been so much publicity in the media.'

I don't tell him that this had passed me by and that it was Freddie who had alerted me to the case.

'Our son changed after we ran away,' I say softly.

I stop for a minute, thinking about how he'd worked for Blockie. 'He held down a job. He wanted to hand himself in but I wouldn't let him.'

'So where is he now?'

Tom clearly thinks that repeating the same question a little further down the line might trip me up.

'I honestly don't know. We went to Cornwall together and then he left shortly afterwards. He said he was going travelling.'

'And he hasn't been in touch?'

'Once or twice.' I skirt around the truth. 'He'll ring from a mobile and then change the SIM card so I can't ring back.'

Tom is studying me as if trying to decide whether I am being straight with him. 'Sarah, somewhere out there is a little girl who needs her daddy.'

I thought of my father, whom I never knew. And my mother who had meant everything to me. What would I have given for someone to have brought them back to me?

'Honestly, Tom, I can't get hold of him. I just don't know where he is. It's one of the reasons he wouldn't tell me. He said he wanted to protect me.'

'How can you live with yourself? You've already gone to prison for manslaughter. Now you're protecting your son from a murder charge.'

Tears trickle down my face. It had taken me so long to have Freddie. Then Tom had denied me another. Was it any wonder that my whole world centred around our son? No man can truly understand that umbilical cord that knits a mother to her child, invisibly, for the rest of their lives, even when one of you departs this earth. How could he understand unless he had carried that child himself?

'I did protect him. That's true. But I'm not now. How many times do I have to say? I just don't know where he is.'

Tom reaches inside his pocket and hands me a photograph. It's of a little girl who looks a bit like me! But at the same time, she is also the spitting image of Freddie at that age. She has a broad smile, rather like the one I used to have when life was relatively carefree. My granddaughter! I'd never given any thought to being a granny before. But now my heart lurches with such love that I am blown away.

'There's another photograph too,' adds Tom. It's of a young girl with cropped hair and a ring in her eyebrow.

'Her mother?' I ask Tom and he nods.

'I've never seen her before.'

'Nor had I. But Freddie didn't bring friends home. Did he?'

'Not that you'd know,' I bite back. 'You were never there.'

'I'm sorry.'

Tom never apologizes. At least, he didn't used to. But anyway, it's too late now.

'Maybe if you'd been around more,' I say, 'Freddie might have been better behaved.'

He makes a conceding gesture with his hands. 'Don't you think I haven't told myself that enough times?'

The old Tom would have continued piling the blame onto me. Not accepting it himself. I find this slightly disconcerting. Just as I find it unsettling that I am talking to my husband at all.

'I wasn't always at work meetings,' he says suddenly.

'I don't want to know,' I say quickly.

'It's not what you think. For nearly thirty years, every Wednesday, I've been helping out at a charity for teenagers who have been abused. I saw it advertised in the local paper a few years before meeting you. So I volunteered. And now I run it.'

What? I'd never had Tom down as a do-gooder. 'Why did you never tell me?'

'I found it too hard to talk about. We never really spoke about the abuse, did we?'

I am, briefly, lost for words. I realize that I never asked him for details. Perhaps I was too focused on my own pain.

'I just wanted to tell them that they had a right to say no and to get help.' He had his hands shoved in his pockets, as if he felt awkward.

'That's a really nice thing for you to have done, Tom.'

'No. It isn't. Don't you see? I was able to help other kids, but not my own son.'

I almost wanted to squeeze his hand. 'It's often easier to be kinder to people we're not related to.'

'The thing is,' he says slowly, 'those things that happened to me at school . . . well, they gave me the wrong idea about love. I became angry. It's why I couldn't commit to anyone until you. And I think it's also why I didn't allow myself to get close to Freddie. Every time I tried to cuddle him, I thought of that master at school putting his arms around me . . .'

He begins to shake.

I can't help it. This time I do place my hand briefly on his arm in comfort.

'And I also felt that the two of you pushed me away. You were so close.'

Yes. We were. And we still are. Despite everything – and I know not everyone will understand this after his crime – Freddie will always be my beloved son.

'Tell me more about this Flick,' I say. 'Is she coping?'

'Well, I've been helping her out a bit. Hilary has been helping me . . .'

'Hilary? The woman you had an affair with? She's seen my granddaughter before me?'

Tom presses his lips together. This was something else he'd always done that I'd forgotten until now. He nods.

I feel winded. That really hurt. Far more than the cheating. Or rather it was a different kind of pain. She'd stepped in. Usurped me. Taken my role. How dare she?

'So you're together?' I ask.

'Yes.' His voice is apologetic. 'I'm sorry I cheated on you, Sarah. I shouldn't have done. But I was so unhappy.'

'Me too,' I say. 'We were always very different.'

'Yes, we were. But we met at a time of our lives when we both needed each other.'

This sounds rather philosophical for Tom. 'Is that what Hilary says?'

He doesn't need to answer. The flush on his cheek says it all.

'It's true,' I say. 'But I'll never regret it, because we have our son.'

'I'll never regret it either and for the same reason. But don't you see, Sarah? Freddie is a father. So you have to tell him what's happened, wherever he is. He deserves to know he has a daughter. Then it's up to him what he does next. We can no longer protect him. He's a man now.'

And, much as I hate to admit it, I know that Tom is right.

But the jury will be asked to give its verdict soon. Time is running out.

55

Everything has changed now. It's knowing that Freddie is a father that's done it. That I am a grandmother. That this Flick had a child at about the same time as poor Mrs Moheim.

'How was your shopping trip?' asks Steve, when I get back to Gladys's cottage. He was already there because he'd been walking Jasper for me. Our beloved dog isn't as bouncy as he was when Freddie left. But he still jumped up at me with excitement when I came in. There was a delicious smell of roasted sea bream coming from the Aga.

'OK,' I say shortly. I don't mean to sound snappy but I'm trying to hide my shock at seeing Tom and his revelation.

I'm a grandmother, I want to tell this wonderful man. Freddie is a father. It changes everything.

Yet I can't.

We sit down together. I can only pick at the fish. It sticks in my throat.

'Don't you like it?'

'It's delicious but . . .' I try to choose my words carefully. 'Something happened today.'

He puts down his cutlery and looks concerned. 'Do you want to tell me about it?'

Isn't this what I've been dreading ever since Steve and I got together? How I envy people who have always done

the right thing. They will never feel the weight of decep-
tion that hangs around your neck. Sometimes you are able
to forget it. But then something returns – a memory or a
reminder or a decision that has to be made – and brings it
all back.

And now I've reached that crossroads. I can't hide
things any more from this kind, warm, man whom I've
fallen in love with. He deserves to know. Whatever the
consequences.

I take a deep breath.

'I saw Tom. My ex,' I say slowly.

Steve visibly stiffens. 'I see.'

My heart quickens. Is it too late to take it back?

Yes.

'I didn't arrange to meet him,' I add, my heart pounding. 'It was a surprise.'

'Quite a coincidence then.'

Steve isn't normally sarcastic.

'Not exactly. He sought me out.'

His voice is cool. 'You don't need to go into details.'

'But I do. I've been wanting to tell you something for
years but I didn't have the courage . . .'

'Years?' Steve looks stricken.

'It's not what you think.'

'Like I said, you don't have to tell me.'

He's getting up. Any minute now he will go. This could
be my last chance. But when I tell him, he won't want me
any more anyway.

'Freddie killed someone in London when he was fifteen,' I blurt out. 'It's why we came down here. I was
protecting him. Then he went. I don't know where.

Sometimes he calls me. But he'll never tell me where he is because he says he needs to protect me too.'

Steve is standing still. He is looking at me with the same expression as Tom had done when he'd read my hospital notes and seen the name of the prison stamped on them.

'Is that why your ex-husband came to find you?'

'Actually,' I say falteringly, 'we're still married. I know I said I was divorced but the lie just slipped out and then I didn't know how to take it back. The truth was that I was too scared to serve papers on him because he'd then know where I was and turn me in.'

Steve's blue eyes are staring at me. I'd never seen them so cold before.

'I'm really sorry.' I hold out my hand. He ignores it.

'So how did he find you if he didn't know where you had gone?'

'It's complicated.'

'Just explain,' he says tightly.

Jasper is close to me, as if he knows I am upset.

'He found me at Truro Crown Court.'

Steve frowns. 'But you were shopping.'

'That's what I told you. I actually went to the court to hear a trial.'

'Whose trial?'

'Someone who's already in prison is being tried for running over a man and killing him, but the truth is that Freddie did it.'

There's a moment of tense silence. 'How do you know?' he asks.

'Freddie rang to tell me.'

'What exactly happened?'

I think back to that conversation. His voice had been breathy. Scared.

'*The truth is, Mum, that Knuckles dared me to nick something from the garage shop. I had to do it to get into his gang. I wanted to have a friend. No one at school would talk to me after the party because I'd accused them of stealing the necklace.*'

'*Was the car stolen?*'

'*Yes.*'

'*And you knew that?*'

'*Yes. Sometimes we used to go joyriding.*'

'*Oh, Freddie.*'

'*When I came back to the car, the garage man ran after me. Knuckles couldn't see. It was raining. I thought he was going to bump into him. So I grabbed the wheel. But I made it worse. The car went into him. I hit him, Mum. I hit him . . .*'

Just as my actions had accidentally led to Emily's death . . .

'The thing is,' I say to Steve, 'Knuckles bragged to a cellmate that he did it, probably to get jail cred. Now he's denying it. He's telling the truth, that Freddie was involved too, but the jury may not believe him, especially as he's already in prison for running over someone else in a similar situation a few years ago.'

'That's awful.'

'I know. Tom thinks I should tell the police, but I can't.' I am crying now.

'Oh, Sarah.'

I expect him to leave there and then. Walk right out the door. But instead, he stands there. Waiting.

'There's something else,' I sob. I have to get this over. There's no point in hiding anything any more. 'I was sent

426

to prison when I was at art college. I was dealing drugs and my best friend took a tablet without me knowing. It was from a contaminated batch and . . . and she died.'

Steve steps back as if he wants to put as much distance between us as possible.

'How long were you inside?'

'Six years.' This comes out as an agonized cry that doesn't feel as though it belongs to me.

'I see,' he says. 'And you didn't think of telling me any of this earlier?'

'I was too scared.'

He picks up his jacket. A cold fear grips my throat.

'You're going?' I say.

'I think it's best. Don't you?'

I collapse on the sofa, listening to the sound of his car rattling down the bumpy track. After a while, my tears stop. There's just a horrible emptiness in my heart instead.

I've lost the only good man I've ever really loved.

And that's when the phone rings.

Keep quiet.
Say nothing.
It's the only way.
That's what I've been telling myself.
But what will happen now?

56

I pick up the phone. It's Freddie, ringing to see what happened at court. He hadn't said he would, but I'd been hoping. And thank God he had.

'I'm a father?' repeats my son incredulously, when I tell him. 'I didn't even know Flick was pregnant.'

Maybe she hadn't wanted to tell him. Or perhaps she hadn't known herself, the last time they spoke.

'Tell me more about my daughter,' says my son. He sounds eager. Excited. 'What's her name?'

'Mattie.'

'Mattie!' He repeats it in a tone of childish wonder, as if trying it on for size.

Then his voice cracks. 'I can't believe it. I mean I do – but I'm gutted that I've missed so much of her life. She'll think I've abandoned her. What has Flick told her about me?'

I have to confess I didn't think of asking Tom that.

'I don't know. Your father has been helping out, apparently.'

'Dad? How?'

'Money, I gather, and taking Mattie out.'

Neither of us speaks for a moment. Then Freddie starts talking, and his voice sounds completely different.

'I need to come back, Mum. Not just to see my daughter, but to tell the truth. I thought I could live with it, but

I can't. Five years of hiding, of running from one place to another, have taught me that. It's always there in my head. Always sitting on my conscience. And now I know that poor man had a wife and two kids and another on the way, it's even worse.'

Then he gives a cry that reminds me of the younger Freddie. The one who broke his arm. The teenager who beat up another pupil for teasing him about my paintings. 'But I can't. If I do tell them what happened, they might put you in prison for taking me and hiding away.'

So once again it's down to me. I must decide the fate of my son. And of myself.

What verdict do I deserve?

57

When Steve and I had started to become close, about a year after we met, I realized that he was very true to his surname. Strong. Sturdy. Protective.

But my confession earlier this evening had surely changed everything. I couldn't bear it if he put the phone down on me.

Yet I didn't know who else to ring.

'I see,' he says, when I tell him my decision. 'I'll do what I can.'

'Wait,' I say. 'There's something else.'

'Yes?'

'I meant it when I said I was sorry. I really am.'

'I know you are,' he says.

His tone is neutral. There's no forgiveness, but at the same time no hostility either. It's the voice of a distant friend who is simply helping someone else out.

Then he calls back. 'My brother says he'll take you on. He'll pick you up tomorrow morning to take you to Truro police station.'

I begin to shake. 'Will you come too?'

There's a silence.

'If you want,' he says. Again, his voice is neutral.

The two men arrive at eight the next morning. Daphne has agreed to mind Jasper for the day. I merely tell her that I have 'important business' in Truro.

Derek Leather is very different from his brother. Not just in looks but in personality too. He is businesslike. To the point.

'Tell me everything,' he says.

'I'll go,' says Steve. 'Give you some privacy.'

'No,' I say quickly. 'I want you to hear.'

'Then we'll talk in the car,' says Derek.

I tell Derek everything. Absolutely everything. I'm aware as I do so that Steve is listening to each word in the back. He says nothing.

'It's quite possible,' says Derek, 'that you will be charged with assisting an offender.'

My right leg judders up and down.

'How long might I get for that?' I tremble.

'If you asked me to make an educated guess, I'd say we're looking at about two years minimum.'

I make a small moan. Not as long as last time, but it was still prison. Still four walls hemming me in. No fresh air. Fear. Unable to breathe. Not being able to hug my loved ones. How could I bear it?

'What about my son?' I ask faintly.

'Hard to tell at this stage,' says Derek. 'It partly depends on whether he pleads guilty.'

If Derek disapproves, he doesn't show it. When we park and walk to the police station, Steve makes to take my hand.

But I am so ashamed of myself, that I slip mine into my pocket.

'You know,' he says, 'I needed time to think yesterday, which is why I left. Now I take back what I said about not telling me. We did agree not to discuss our pasts.'

'No,' I say. 'You were right. This was too big for me not to have told you.'

'I still love you, Sarah.'

'How can you?' I ask. 'You don't know me. I don't even know myself.'

I walk on ahead.

I make a statement to the police. I am not charged. Not yet. They want to question my son first. 'He'll be landing at Heathrow at lunchtime,' I tell them, repeating what Freddie told me when we spoke again this morning.

It's clear they don't believe me. They demand his details. 'Are you going to arrest him?' I ask.

They don't reply.

Everything I've tried to hide for years is unravelling at an unbelievable speed.

'What about your husband?' I am asked. 'Was he involved in hiding your son?'

'No,' I say. 'He wanted to turn him in.'

'Yet he didn't. Why not?'

But I have no intention of being my ex-husband's executioner.

'You will need to talk to him about that,' I say.

'We will when he gets here.'

So Tom is on his way, is he? I'm not surprised.

'What will happen now?' I ask.

'I suspect,' says Derek, 'that court proceedings will be adjourned until Freddie is found.'

'Found?' I repeat. 'I've already said that Freddie intends to go straight to the police himself.'

'So he says.'

Like the police, he obviously isn't convinced. Am I being naive?

My throat goes dry. I feel sick. There is nowhere to hide. Even if I wanted to. It's all over now.

When Derek and I come out of the interview room, Tom and Steve are both in the waiting area. It's oddly unnerving to see them next to each other.

'What are you doing here?' I ask.

'After our conversation last night, I felt it was right to come to the nearest police station and inform them of my involvement.'

I'd forgotten how Tom always spoke in such a formal way.

'Are you going to be charged?'

'I haven't been interviewed yet. What about you?'

'I've given a statement.' Bile rises into my mouth. It tastes sour. 'But nothing's certain until Freddie arrives to give his.'

'That's if he turns up,' mutters Tom. Just what Derek had said, more or less.

I round on him. 'Why can't you trust our son for once?'

'Because,' says Tom, in that patronizing manner that I had almost forgotten, 'he's let us down so many times. What makes you think he's changed now?'

'He's a father.' The words are falling out of my mouth almost as if they are trying to convince me too. 'He wants to see his child. Freddie is far more responsible now.'

'For pity's sake, Sarah.' Tom shakes his head just the way he used to if I did something that he disapproved of, like leaving out paints on the kitchen table. 'When are you going to take those blinkers off?'

'That's not fair . . .' begins Steve.

Tom's eyes glitter with anger. 'Do you know our son?'

'No. But –'

'Then leave this to my wife and me, will you?'

'Sarah is my partner.' Steve takes my arm. I want to cry with relief as the warmth of his touch seeps through me.

'But you're not her son's father, are you?'

'Fine job you did of that,' I blurt out.

To my surprise, Tom winces. But it was true. There had always been that distance between them. Perhaps it wasn't surprising. Freddie's birth will inextricably be linked with Tom's discovery about my past. The last final lethal piece of the jigsaw. Emily . . . Oh, Emily. Can you ever forgive me?

We both stop talking as a policeman comes over and takes Derek to one side.

'It seems you were right, Sarah,' he finally says. 'Freddie has just flown into Heathrow and handed himself in.'

My boy! My son is finally back! And, just as important, he has done the right thing. At last.

Relief floods through me. Followed by fear.

'I need to see him,' I choke. 'It's been so long.'

'He's being held for questioning at the moment.'

Derek's voice is softer. More understanding. 'But I will personally make sure you see your son as soon as is humanly possible.'

'But can you get him off?'

Derek's tone changes now. It's more measured. 'That entirely depends on exactly what he did. And, just as importantly, on how much he is willing to tell us.'

*

435

We drive seven hours to the police station where Freddie is being held. I cannot say a word. My insides are churning. My son! I am going to see him for the first time in five years. Though this is hardly how I imagined our reunion.

The police station is very close to Heathrow airport itself. Apparently it has everything a police station usually has, such as cells. On our way in, I hear a man swearing that the drugs in his suitcase were nothing to do with him.

We sign in. 'Can I see Freddie now?' I plead.

'It's best that I do that first,' says Derek crisply.

Steve and I sit in the corridor. He puts his arm around me. Am I forgiven, or is he just being kind? It's hard to tell. I cannot stop shaking. Steve gets me some coffee from a machine. It's bitter and I cannot drink it.

'Your son is in good hands with my brother,' he assures me.

'I hope so,' I say quietly.

We sit there for an hour or more. I sweat all over. I pinch my skin with my nails because, in a weird way, the pain seems to help. I realize, with a shock, that I can't remember exactly what my son looks like. Of course, I can recall an overall impression. His dark curly hair. His height – taller than me. But not the exact shape of his nose or his eyes. It's as though he is an out-of-focus photograph. How can that be? I gave birth to him.

Then Derek emerges along with the barrister whom he has chosen to save my son. He apparently 'possesses a strong verbal left hook'.

'The likelihood is', says the latter, 'that Freddie is going to be tried alongside Paul Harris. The problem we've got is you, to be honest. The jury may not take kindly to a man whose mother protected him. On the other hand, you might get someone on the jury who will sympathize because they'd do the same to protect their own kids. Still, you've been given permission to see him for ten minutes.'

I try to take in this new information as I follow the officer down a flight of steps. I go into a room marked *Visitors*. There is a bench secured to the floor (presumably in case anyone tries to lift it up and cause trouble) where I am told to sit, facing a perspex screen. There is no one on the other side. I hold my breath.

Then a tall, rangy young man is led in, handcuffed to an officer.

For a minute, I almost don't recognize him. Where is that thick black glossy hair? He is bald. He's also a good deal thinner. Only the 'Ziggy' tattoo on his arm tells me immediately that this is indeed my son. The one that he had promised was drawn with a 'pen'.

'Mum!' he cries out. I breathe him in through the screen. Inhale his presence. Freddie My son.

'It's so good to see you,' he sobs. 'I've missed you.'

'So have I,' I choke.

Then my son puts his hand up flat against the barrier. I do the same. It is the closest we can get to holding hands. And that's when he tells me exactly what happened.

My maternal instinct tells me he's speaking the truth this time. I know it. Besides, the officer is there. He'll be listening to every word.

'I'm so sorry I've got you into this mess,' he weeps.

'It's all right,' I sob back.

But it's not. And we both know it. Because at the end of the day, whichever way you look at it, a young father died.

'It's such a relief to hand myself in,' he chokes. Then he pats his head. 'I shaved this to make me look less recognizable. But now it's a relief to be out in the open.'

'I used to imagine I saw you in Cornwall,' I say. 'Were you?'

'No. I was hiding in Spain.' His eyes swim with tears. 'I should never have run away.'

'Nor should I,' I say quietly.

When I leave the police station, a young woman is waiting outside. She has very short, spiky, pink hair, plug earrings and purple heart tattoos on her neck. She's holding the hand of a little girl. An olive-skinned girl with bright blue eyes and a sweet, heart-shaped face. She looks a bit like pictures I have of me as a child.

I know who she is. At least, I think I do.

'Mattie?' I ask.

She nods.

My granddaughter! I want to hug her. But it might seem too soon.

'Are you Freddie's mum?' asks the young woman awkwardly. Then she speaks softly to the little girl. 'This is your gran I was telling you about.' Then she addresses me again. 'We wanted to come into the police station but they wouldn't let her in cos she's too young.'

'Hello.' I bend down next to her, consumed with regret that Tom has known our grandchild for four whole years and that I have missed out through running away. What should I say?

'I like your hair,' I blurt out. It's black. Just like mine, with the same wave. I am too nervous to ask if I can cuddle her. I am no more than a stranger to her. I have lost so many years.

Mattie looks at me solemnly. 'Mummy brushes it every night for me.'

'That's nice.' I have a vision of doing the same for her. But that's the sort of thing that a real gran would do. Not a near-stranger like myself.

Then I look up at her mother.

'Flick,' I say. 'Freddie is desperate to see you both.'

I have a sudden fear that she won't let him see Mattie.

'We want to see him too,' she says. 'He rang us when he landed. It's why we're here.'

Relief shoots through me. It would kill Freddie – I just know that – if she refused to let him see his daughter.

'But like I said, they won't let Mattie in and I can't leave her.'

'What about me?' I ask. 'I'm aware she doesn't know me but at least you could see Freddie.'

'Only if the officer in charge gives you permission,' adds Derek.

'Would you stay with your new granny if Mummy is allowed in?' asks Flick.

The little girl stares up at me. 'Will you be long?'

'No.'

'OK.'

I can see Flick hesitating. 'There's something I need to tell you, Mrs Wilkins.'

I haven't been called by my married name for so long that I almost don't recognize it. 'Please. Call me Sarah.'

'Your son didn't know I was pregnant. I didn't know myself until later. By then, I hadn't heard from him for a bit so I reckoned he'd dumped me. I went to your house and found you'd moved. They gave me a forwarding address – it was your husband's office.'

439

I wince at the word 'husband'. I can't even look at Steve. This is exactly the story that Tom had told me. But now the girl is confirming it.

'I lied when your husband asked if I knew anything about an accident. I told him that I was waiting for Freddie to come round that night but that he never turned up. I was too scared to get involved in case they took my baby away.'

I glance at the beautiful little girl next to her who is eyeing me shyly. How I would love to gather her in my arms and breathe her in.

Derek gets permission for Flick to see Freddie 'briefly'.

Mattie and I sit on a nearby bench. I'm not sure what to say. Where do I start? But she begins.

'I want to see my daddy too,' she says.

'He'd like to see you as well but he can't yet,' I say gently. 'You'll be able to visit him before too long.'

I don't add that this will probably be when he's in prison.

'I made him a picture,' she says.

She holds out a piece of paper. There are three stick figures. One tall, one medium height and the other small.

'That's Daddy, Mummy and me,' she says. 'Mummy says that one day, we might be able to hold hands together.'

I can barely speak. But I have to.

'I expect you will,' I say carefully, hoping this is true. 'Do you like drawing?'

'Yes!' she says enthusiastically. 'Mummy says you are an artist and that Daddy liked to draw when she knew him. I want to be like you when I grow up.'

We sit and chat for a bit. About school and her best friend, Seth. Then Flick comes out of the police station.

She's been crying – I can see that – but she's putting on a bright face, just as I used to in front of Freddie when I'd had an argument with Tom.

How did it go, I want to ask.

But I don't know her well enough for that.

Mattie runs towards her. 'Did you see Daddy?'

'Yes,' she says. 'He wants you to know that he loves you with all his heart and that he'll see you as soon as he is allowed to.'

'I forgot to give you my picture for him.'

'Don't worry. I can do that next time.'

So there's going to be a next time then? That's a relief.

'When can I see you again?' I ask.

'In court, I expect,' says Flick. Her upper lip is quivering.

I want to see them before that! But I have to give this girl time. I can't expect her to embrace me instantly.

I watch them go. It feels so surreal. There is so much to take in. My son is back. And I have a beautiful granddaughter I didn't know about until yesterday. Yet I may not get a chance to know her. Not if they put me in prison. Another woman – Hilary – is her grandmother instead.

How can I bear any of this?

I want to talk on the way back but find myself drifting into sleep. I'm aware of Steve placing his jacket over me to keep me warm, a brief stop at a petrol station and a sign for the South West. Then nothing until I hear the crunch of stones on the rough drive leading to Gladys's cottage. 'We're back,' he whispers.

Shepherding me into the kitchen, he makes a pot of tea. I watch him stir in a teaspoon of honey, the way I like it, when my tears start up again. 'I should have handed Freddie in,' I sob.

'Don't look back. I learned that years ago.' He puts the mug in my hands and then wraps his arm around my shoulders. 'Besides, if you had, you and I would never have met.'

'So you forgive me?'

He sits back in his chair and looks at me frankly. 'I can't say I'm not shocked. But you're no criminal. Not in my book, anyway. I'm not a parent myself. However, I do know how far I'd go for someone I love. It's why I'm still here. With you.'

If it wasn't for the circumstances, his declaration of love would have made me cry all over again.

But the fact is that I have broken the law. Again.

And even though Freddie has now returned to face up to his crime, nothing can bring back Mr Moheim.

All we can do is look to the future. And, frankly, I am terrified.

58

Truro Crown Court

I look at the young man on the stand. My boy. My son. The child who I finally gave birth to after all those years of heartbreak, desperate to be a mother. And now he has been accused of murder. After Freddie came forward, the original trial was abandoned and my son and Knuckles (aka Harris) stand jointly accused. Knuckles has already given the jury his twisted version of events. It's time for Freddie's lawyer to call my son.

'Can you tell us how you became involved in this case?'

My heart feels as though it is shedding drops of blood as Freddie begins to talk. His deep voice is shaking.

'I didn't have many friends at school. Not real ones. Once, to try and make myself popular, I had a party. They wrecked the house and stole my dead grandmother's diamond necklace. I felt really bad about it but Mum and Dad made me put something on Facebook to try and get the necklace back. Then my so-called friends started to blank me for suggesting they were thieves. So I began to hang out at a local pub. It was pretty rough. No one bothered to check how old you were. And that's where I met Knuckles.'

His eyes are looking straight at me. It's as if he is telling me and not the court.

'I knew he was the "wrong sort" as Mum would have said. But that's exactly why I wanted to be friends with him. Knuckles said he was starting this gang. I could be one of the first members, he promised. But I had to do something if I wanted to be in it. He dared me to go into a garage shop and nick a bottle of vodka. Of course, I knew stealing was wrong. But it wasn't like a diamond necklace, was it? And I just wanted to be with people who liked me.

'That night, I was really pissed off cos we were meant to be moving the next morning. We were going to rent first and then maybe move miles away for what Mum and Dad called "a new start". I didn't want that. I'd just met Knuckles and things were finally a bit better. I was also really mad with my dad because I'd heard him talking to this woman on the phone. It sounded to me like they were having an affair.'

He shoots me a 'Sorry, Mum' look.

'We agreed to meet up a few roads away. It was raining. Knuckles had recently passed his driving test. At least, that's what he told me. He seemed different that night. I think he'd had a few to drink. I was beginning to have doubts then. The plan had seemed quite cool when we'd talked about it before but now I wasn't so sure. What if I got caught?

'He told me I was being wet. I asked where he'd got the car from and he said he'd borrowed it from a friend. I got the feeling he was lying so I accused him of stealing it. He admitted it, and then said he was going to take it back later that night.

'I should have got out there and then but I didn't want Knuckles to think I was a coward. I was also scared he'd drop me, like the others at school had. We pulled up at the garage so I could do my dare. Knuckles told me to put on his denim jacket to disguise myself. He said my white T-shirt would stand out.'

So that's where the jacket had come from.

Freddie is clutching his head with his hands, staring at the floor. Then he looks up. 'I couldn't see the vodka at first. The bloke behind the counter kept staring at me. My hands began to shake. I wanted to leave but I also wanted Knuckles to be my friend. And then I saw a whole line of them. So I grabbed a bottle and ran.

'I jumped into the car and Knuckles started the engine. But then the man from the garage ran out in front. I yelled at Knuckles to stop, but he wouldn't. He was laughing like a maniac.

'I leaned across and tried to turn the wheel. But in my panic, it went the wrong way. The car ploughed right into him. There was this awful thud. Oh God!'

Freddie's voice comes out as a terrible groan. I know that he is there at the scene in his head. Just as I'd been when I'd told the court about Emily during my own trial.

'Then Knuckles did stop. He was still laughing. I jumped out of the car to see if the man was all right. His face was . . . I can't describe it. He looked dead, but I kept hoping that maybe he wasn't.'

There is a shocked silence in the court. Freddie is weeping. I can see from one or two of the faces on the jury that not everyone believes him. Only I know for sure it isn't an act. My boy is sorry, he really is. But there's something else as well. I can tell he's keeping something back.

'Knuckles drove on,' he sobs. 'When we stopped at

445

some traffic lights, I got out and ran home. I didn't know where else to go. I wasn't going to tell my parents. How could I? But when I saw Mum's face, I couldn't help it. She's one of the few people in life who understands me. So I let out that I'd killed someone. Then I wished I hadn't in case she got questioned later. I didn't tell her about pulling on the wheel cos I didn't want her to start defending me. I felt guilty, even though it was Knuckles driving. Besides, I wasn't sure anyone would believe me, least of all my dad. He overheard me telling Mum and said he was going to call the police. And then . . .'

My boy is staring at me as if scared he's said too much. He doesn't want to get me into trouble. But he has to. When I saw him in the police cell at Heathrow, I told him to tell the truth whatever the cost.

'Then Mum said we had to run away. She kept asking me about the man I'd killed. But I just told her there was more to it than that. I couldn't give details because I needed to keep her out of it.

'We went to Cornwall. This farmer gave me a job. I liked it there but I couldn't stay. I couldn't get that dead man out of my head. I kept expecting the police to come. So did my mum. I saw the strain on her face. I knew that she'd get done for hiding me. So I went. I didn't tell her where I'd gone.'

'And where did you go?' asks the barrister.

His voice jolts me back to the present. Until then, I had been there. With Freddie, right through from that terrible rainy night until the morning I discovered he had gone.

That's if my son is telling the truth. Is it a mother's intuition? Or am I misjudging him again?

'I got a ferry from Plymouth to Santander. Then I made my way to Barcelona, and from there down the coast towards Cartagena. I made some money through giving English lessons. I moved from hostel to hostel, always scared someone would find me. I had a mobile that I used for ringing Mum every now and then, changing the SIM card every time. I kept an eye on social media and the news. That's when I found out Knuckles had gone to prison for another crime but was on trial again for the one we'd both committed. He was bound to mention me – even though he only knew me as Ziggy – and this might lead to Mum getting arrested. So I rang to warn her. I asked her to go to court to hear what was going on, so we could both decide what to do.'

My son wanted to protect me. But he's also made me look as though I am the kind of person who would break the law again by fleeing. Maybe he realizes that now because he shoots me another apologetic look.

'So, let's get this straight,' says the barrister. 'You were not driving the car, as Mr Harris claims?'

'No,' says Freddie stoutly. 'I wasn't.'

'But you felt guilty because it was your intervention with the steering wheel that caused the car to collide with the victim.'

He hangs his head. 'Yes.'

'And that is why, members of the jury,' says the barrister, 'this young man is no murderer. Yes, he was stupid. Yes, he broke the law by knowingly travelling in a vehicle that was stolen and by stealing a bottle of vodka. But he did not intend to play a hand in the death of Hassam Moheim. This unforgivable crime lies at the feet of Paul

Harris, a man who is already serving a prison sentence for a similar offence.'

This isn't always allowed to be mentioned in court but our defence barrister has already explained there are certain 'extenuating circumstances'. Apparently this is one of them.

There is a break. I am suddenly aware once more that Tom is on one side of me and Steve on the other. 'Shall we get some fresh air?' Steve suggests.

I allow him to lead me through the crowded hall outside. Flick comes up to me. Mattie isn't with her. I feel a dip of disappointment. Who knows how many opportunities I will have to see my granddaughter before they take me away? But, of course, she shouldn't be here. A court is no place for a child.

The defence barrister joins us. His face is taut.

'How is it going?' asks Flick. 'I couldn't get here any earlier. I had to wait for Mum to babysit.'

'To be honest, not great,' says the barrister.

My heart plummets. 'But Freddie was telling the truth just then. I know it.'

Tom makes a sound that reminds me of the old days. 'Don't you see, Sarah? He's so good at wrapping you around his little finger.'

'That's not true . . .' I begin. Then I stop. Maybe he's right. He hadn't told me everything that night. Rather like I hadn't told Tom I'd taken that bicycle in the early days. Small fry compared with the other secrets I'd kept . . .

'From reading the jury's faces,' says the barrister, 'I'm afraid they appear to side with your husband on this one. We are going to have to prepare ourselves for the fact that

Freddie will be found guilty of manslaughter. If he'd stayed to face the music, it might not have been so bad.'

'So if I hadn't made him run away with me, it would be less serious?' I ask.

No one answers.

There is no need.

I tried to save my son.

But in doing so, I may well have thrown away his freedom.

And mine too.

I've also done something far worse.

I've lost my soul by doing the wrong thing. Just as I did before with Emily.

59

'To sum up,' says the judge, 'it is clear that there were two young men who were present at the tragic death of Mr Moheim. Paul Harris, who claims he was a passenger although he has declined to give evidence, and Freddie Wilkins, who also claims he was a passenger but admits that it was his hand that turned the wheel, resulting in the car striking the very person he says he was trying to protect.'

My heart is thudding so hard that I feel faint. Steve, as if sensing this, places a hand on my arm.

'Furthermore, I would remind the jury that they should ignore the high-profile nature of this case. The recent report on the number of prisoners who are responsible for undisclosed crimes has no bearing.'

There is a brief, dramatic pause here before she continues.

'It is true that Freddie Wilkins does not have a previous criminal record. Yet he did not, by his own admission, stay to face the consequences. Even if his version of events is correct, both men then fled the scene, leaving the victim to die, for all they knew, although the post-mortem determined that Mr Moheim died instantly.'

A low moan rises from a woman in a sari at the back of the public gallery. I glance back briefly. Could that be Mrs Moheim?

'You must consider the evidence in relation to each person separately as to whether they are guilty. Cases like this sometimes give rise to emotions or sympathy. You must not let such feelings influence you when you are considering your verdict.'

A cry goes up in the air. It reminds me of a film my mother had taken me to once. *Bambi*. I can still remember crying bitterly when Bambi's mother was shot. 'Hush,' she said softly. 'It will be all right.' But it wasn't. I knew, even at that age, she was lying to protect me.

I also realize that this cry I can hear so clearly is coming from my own mouth.

Freddie is looking up at me. Fear on his face. For a few seconds he is once again the little boy who had marvelled at the stars. He is the child who talked about the taste of rain. He is the teenager who told me to fuck off when I asked what time he'd be home. But he was – he is – my son. And that overrides everything.

'Order,' calls out the judge sharply.

And then I hear another voice. A quieter but more assured one, even though it is shaking. A young woman's voice near me in the public gallery.

'Stop,' she calls out. 'I need to say something.'

My legs are like jelly as I pull myself up to a standing position. I can't keep quiet any more.

I won't let Freddie take the blame.

He doesn't deserve it.

I can't allow my daughter to grow up thinking her father is a murderer.

It's time to tell them all about the rain. The black night. The car. The screams. The shock. Running home to my parents because I didn't know where else to go. Keeping silent. Then wondering if this was the right thing to do.

It's time for me to tell the truth.

60

There is a moment of shocked silence.

Both Knuckles and my son look up. Fear written across their faces. *What is she going to say?*

'I was there too. I'm to blame.'

The court bursts into uproar.

'What do you mean?' I demand, as Flick sits back down. Shock makes this come out harder than I meant. So there *was* something else.

But she does not answer. Instead, she sits there, visibly shaking. Her hands in her lap. Her nails, I notice, are bitten down to the quick. She is looking down as though she has said her piece and is waiting for a noose to be put around her neck. She reminds me of myself during my trial. My heart goes out to her.

'Order,' cries out the judge. 'There will be an adjournment while new evidence is being considered for admission.'

Everyone in the public gallery is staring at us, including the man who'd been talking to me at the beginning of the trial.

'Blimey,' he says. 'I've been coming here for years, just out of interest, but I've never seen anything like this before.'

I don't know what to do. Tom appears speechless too.

'We've got to get her out of here to find Derek,' says Steve.

There is no need. He is here already. 'This way,' he says firmly.

Derek leads us down some stairs and into a room. Our barrister is there. 'I think,' he says to Flick, 'you'd better tell us everything. From the beginning.'

I put my hand out and squeeze hers. 'We're here for you,' I say. 'But please, no more secrets. We just want to know what happened.'

She raises her face. It is pinched, and very pale. 'I'll tell you on one condition,' she says. 'That no one takes away my daughter.'

Derek's mouth tightens. 'No one can guarantee that if you give evidence. My advice is that you seek independent legal advice. I cannot give you this myself because it might be a potential conflict of interest.'

'There's no point. I know what I must do.'

I'm impressed by her determined tone of voice.

'Right. Then tell us exactly what happened. Can you do that?'

'Yes,' she nods.

When she's finished, Derek lets out a long breath. 'If you're sure about this, I think we have a crucial piece of evidence. If the worst comes to the worst and . . . well . . . you go down, the courts always make a decision based on the child's best interests. They'll probably try to place Mattie with someone in your family.'

Flick begins to weep. 'But my mum might not want the responsibility. She's always saying she needs a life of her own.'

I cannot help it. I take Flick into my arms. 'It's all right,' I say. 'I'll be there for her.'

But even before I catch Derek's warning eye, I realize this might not be possible. Because when it comes to my day in court, I could go down too.

61

Derek tells us there has to be a second retrial in light of the new evidence. Apparently too much has changed for the current jury to continue. Normally this might mean waiting for several months. But another case was cancelled, leaving a gap. The judge, according to Derek, appears to have taken a personal interest in the case. I've looked her up online. She is a mother herself. Is this a good or bad thing? I can't decide.

A few weeks later, all eyes are now trained on this waif of a girl with the pale face and plug earrings in the dock. The first witness.

Flick speaks so softly that I – like everyone else, to judge from their faces – have to strain to hear her.

'None of this would have happened if Knuckles and Freddie hadn't both been trying to impress me. I met them in a pub a few weeks before . . . before it happened. I didn't get on with my parents so I tried to get out as much as I could. I was fifteen but I'd dress up to look older. I never got asked for any ID. I don't think the staff were that bothered.'

She stops. I think of myself at fifteen. How desperate I'd been to love and be loved.

'Please go on, Miss White.' The defence barrister's voice is kind enough but firm.

'I could see that they both fancied me. I was flattered by that. I hadn't had a boyfriend before. All the other girls in my class had them and they'd keep asking what was wrong with me.'

I can't help feeling sorry for her. Just like Freddie – and me before him – she'd wanted to be part of the crowd.

'In some ways, I liked both of them. Knuckles was older which was cool. But I liked Freddie too. I didn't know he was called Freddie. Nor did Knuckles. He'd said his name was Ziggy because of a singer called Bowie. He said he liked his music. He said it made him think of a time when he was happy as a kid.'

My mind goes back to when I'd seen his tattoo. On the night of the murder.

'*Ziggy?*'

'*You know, Mum. After the David Bowie album. It's what I want to be called now.*'

'*Why?*'

'*Why not?*'

How stupid had I been? It was because it made him feel safe. It had reminded him of dancing around with me as a little boy before all the arguments.

Flick is still speaking.

'He was so good-looking and he had these gentlemanly ways, like walking along the pavement on the outside.'

That was me. I had taught him that from an early age. 'A man has to shield the lady from the traffic,' I'd told him. I can't help glancing at Tom to say, 'See?'

'Knuckles asked if I wanted to join his gang. Freddie was going to as well, he said. I agreed, cos I'd decided I liked him best. He'd told me by then that this was his real name but he didn't want anyone else to know. "I want to be someone different," he said. I got that, cos I did too.'

She flushes. 'That was when we slept with each other for the first time. It was at his house when his mum was teaching at the college and his dad was at work. I got pregnant with my daughter then. Of course, I didn't know that at the time, but I did know I loved him. I just felt it. Here.' She hits her chest with her hand. 'It might sound corny, but it's true. Freddie said he loved me too. Neither of us had done it with anyone else before. It was like it was meant to be.'

She's so young, I think. So naive at times and yet so knowing at others. I can't even bring myself to look at Tom. It feels weird to hear someone talking in such an intimate way about your own son.

'Knuckles said we each had to prove ourselves by stealing something,' she continues. '"It only has to be small,"' he said. '"I just need to know you've both got what it takes."'

Flick gives a little shudder.

'I got a bit scared then. I'd never stolen anything before. But I didn't want to say no because then they might drop me.'

I shake my head. Exactly what I had thought when someone had first offered me drugs at art school.

'I had a big row with Mum and Dad that night,' she continues. 'They wanted me to babysit my little sister but I said I was going out. It was black and raining – the kind that makes your hair stick to your head. I was bored. I wanted to make something happen. I passed other people on the street who were laughing. I wanted to join in. I wanted people to like me.'

Her voice comes out as a small pitiful cry. Once more, she reminds me of my younger self, reeling from Emily's death. I want to wrap her in my arms. But instead, I can only watch, sweat trickling down my back, nails biting into my palms.

'Knuckles had said he'd pick me up in the car. I didn't know where we were going. He said it would be fun.

'The rain stopped. It was pitch black. There weren't any stars. I remember thinking that would be good, cos then we might not be seen so easily. We drove for a bit. I could tell Knuckles liked me but by then I knew I fancied Freddie and not him. The rain had started again. The tyres were squeaking on the road. It felt weird, like this wasn't happening.'

Flick stops then. Her head is down. She looks exhausted, as if she's run a race.

'Then what happened?' asks the barrister.

Flick takes a while to answer. Just as I think she's going to stay silent, she begins again. 'We stopped. Knuckles told me not to look. He said it was all part of the game. But I heard him talking to someone and a car door slam. I was allowed to open my eyes after that. Freddie had got in the back. Knuckles put his hand on my knee and I could see Freddie was pissed off. I was pleased, cos it showed Freddie liked me.'

The games we play when we're young. And, I remind myself, when we're older too.

'Knuckles said we were going to rob a petrol station.

He told me I was going first, but Freddie didn't want me getting into trouble. "I'll do it," he said.

'Knuckles told him to shut up because we both had to do it. They kept arguing all the way. I liked it. No one had ever fought over me before. It made me feel good. Then we stopped in this garage forecourt. Knuckles asked if I was ready.

'I tried to say I was but it wouldn't come out. I could see Freddie was scared too. But I think he wanted to protect me, so he got out of the car before Knuckles could stop him.

'It was raining really hard now. Freddie only had a white T-shirt on. I was worried it might make him show up in the dark. I had a denim jacket that I'd borrowed from my brother. It was too big for me but I thought it made me look cool. I took it off and threw it out of the window to him.'

Freddie had said the jacket had come from Knuckles. He must have lied in court to protect Flick.

Her face looks even more pinched and anxious now.

'We watched Freddie run across the forecourt. Knuckles called him a stupid bastard. I can remember his words dead clear. "There's cameras. He's not keeping his head down." But I knew Freddie just wanted to look after me. It made me feel proud.

'Knuckles and me had an argument then. "What do you want with a kid like that?" he said. "Do you fancy him more than me?"

'I said I did.

'His face went all nasty then. He revved up the engine. "You've got to wait for him," I said. "Look, he's coming."'

460

'Freddie was heading for the front, so I climbed over, into the back. Knuckles revved the engine again. Freddie got in and yelled at him to get going quick.

'There was this bloke running out of the forecourt shop towards the car. Knuckles was laughing. I knew he was showing off. He shot forward, towards the man.

'I yelled out that this wasn't funny. Then I shouted at Freddie to do something. He screamed at Knuckles to stop but he didn't. Then I saw Freddie leaning across and trying to grab the wheel. There was this awful thud. And then . . .'

She begins to cry.

'I don't want to think about what comes next,' she sobs. 'I have to blank it out of my head. But I didn't mean it to happen and neither did Freddie. I promise. Honestly. You've got to believe me.'

Then she raises her head to face the jury. 'Please.'

I certainly believe her. It's how I felt after I confessed about Emily. But I'm not so sure that the rest of the court is convinced.

'Miss White,' says the barrister. 'If you really want the jury to understand, you must carry on and tell us exactly what happened after that.'

She gives another little shudder. And then she continues. I can hardly bear to listen.

'Freddie got out to have a look at the bloke. Knuckles wanted to drive off, but I begged him to stay. When Freddie got back in, he looked terrible. He said, "I think he's dead."

'Knuckles began driving really fast, telling Freddie how he'd made a right mess of things. Said if Freddie hadn't grabbed the wheel, he wouldn't have hit him. That wasn't true, though. He could easily have stopped the car. He was just showing off because I said I preferred Freddie to him.'

Several of the jury gasp when Flick says that.

'Freddie made me promise that if anyone asked, I'd say I wasn't there. Then Knuckles told me I'd bloody better keep quiet or I wouldn't recognize my face in the mirror.

'That really scared me, cos I knew he meant it.

'When we stopped at some traffic lights, Freddie and me jumped out. We ran down a side street and on and on until we were sure Knuckles wasn't following us. Freddie told me to go home and not tell anyone. So I ran back in the rain. I kept slipping on the pavement. I knew my mum and dad would kill me if they found out what I'd done. But I didn't know where else to go. So I just crept upstairs and luckily they didn't ask any questions.

'On the news the next day there was something about a garage man being killed in a hit-and-run. Someone had seen a man in a denim jacket getting into a car. I felt really bad. If Freddie and Knuckles hadn't been trying to impress me, that poor bloke wouldn't have been killed.'

She began to cry again. 'I couldn't believe it when they said he was a dad with another kid on the way. It made him seem real.'

'And then what happened?' asked the barrister.

'I didn't hear anything from Freddie or Knuckles again. I went to the pub a couple of times but they weren't there.'

'So you didn't hear from Freddie again?'

'Yes.'

'Yes you didn't hear from him or yes you did?'

Flick waits. There's a stiffening amongst the jury.

'Please answer the question.'

Her voice is hesitant. Scared. 'Three weeks later, Freddie rang to see if I was all right. He said he was hiding out somewhere and was going to go abroad but that he'd try to ring every now and then. I wouldn't be able to get hold of him, he said, cos he'd need to keep changing his number.'

Was that the phone call I'd heard my son making just before he left me?

'Soon after that,' continues Flick, 'my period didn't come. It wasn't regular anyway, but when it didn't arrive again the month after, I got scared.'

The barrister's voice brings me back. 'You said you were flattered by the attentions of both Knuckles and Freddie. Did you know who the father was?'

'Of course I did! It was Freddie I wanted. I never slept with Knuckles, even though he asked me to. Freddie loved me like I loved him. I know he did.'

Flick began to cry. 'I was desperate to get in touch with Freddie to tell him. And then I remembered that during one of our walks Freddie had pointed out where his dad worked. So I went in and asked the receptionist if I could talk to him.'

That must have taken some nerve, to have walked into a swanky office like that. This girl had guts.

'At first, I just said I was a friend of his son's and that I was looking for him. I didn't tell him about Freddie's phone call and how he'd said he was going abroad, because Freddie had asked me not to. I thought his dad might know the exact address. But it turned out he was looking for him too. Apparently, his wife had walked out on him, taking Freddie.

She stopped.

'Please go on.'

Flick was twisting her hands. 'Tom – that's what he told me to call him – was really nice. He wanted to know when I'd last seen Freddie. I couldn't tell the truth, so I gave him a different day. He asked if I knew anything about an accident that Freddie had been involved in.

'I told him no.'

'So you lied,' the barrister said flatly.

'Well, I had to, didn't I? Freddie made me promise.'

There was another stirring amongst the jury. That didn't sound good.

'Then I told him that I was pregnant by his son. At first, he thought I was after money. But then I explained I was just scared and didn't know what to do because Freddie had disappeared.

'I thought he'd be mad at me, but he was really kind. When I said I was terrified of telling my parents that I was expecting, he offered to come with me. My mum went nuts but Tom said he'd help us financially. Mum said people like that always made promises they couldn't keep. But Tom isn't like that. He's been a really good granddad to Mattie. She loves him.'

I feel a stab of jealousy. Yet at the same time, I am seeing my husband in a new light.

Flick carries on speaking. 'After that night, life changed. Nothing was the same. I cut off my hair because I wanted to be a different me.'

Hadn't I done the same after one of my miscarriages?

'I also changed my phone number so Freddie couldn't get hold of me again. Of course, I wanted to hear his voice, but I got scared that the police might use that as evidence and take my baby away. There are some things you can't hide.' She sobs again. 'Like murder.'

I shift in my seat. I know exactly what she means.

The barrister speaks. 'So what made you change your mind about coming forward?'

'I didn't know Knuckles was being charged with the garage man's murder or that he was already inside for another hit-and-run. I don't bother with the news or social media myself. I'm too busy with Mattie, my little one. But then Tom came round to say that he'd met up with Freddie's mum and told her about us. He said that Freddie was on the run for killing someone in an accident five years ago. He asked if I had anything to do with it and I swore I hadn't. I had to. Like I said before, I was scared they'd take Mattie away from me.'

'So why are you taking that risk now?'

'Because Freddie might go to prison and I know he didn't mean to kill that man. He tried to save him.'

'But how can the jury be certain that you are telling the truth, Miss White?'

There is another silence. This is what we've all been wanting to ask. How do we know that amongst all these webs of deceit, Flick's account is the truthful one? Freddie's barrister, however, looks unconcerned. Clearly, he has asked this question for a reason.

'It was on my phone. It was part of the plan. That's why there had to be three of us in the car. Knuckles was driving and said that Freddie and I had to video each other on our phones when we did our dares. We were supposed to give the videos to Knuckles to prove our loyalty to him.

Freddie never videoed me cos he went into the garage first. But I videoed him.'

There is another stirring amongst the jury. This must be the crucial piece of evidence that Derek had got so excited about.

'And you kept this video?'

Flick shrugs. 'After it went wrong, I realized it might be important. I downloaded it and kept it on a USB stick and then deleted it from my phone. I hid the USB and just tried to forget about it.'

Once more, I can't help feeling both awed and uneasy that this girl is so frail-looking and yet so astute.

'For the purposes of the jury,' says the barrister, 'the video will now be played.'

My skin goes hot and cold. There are three court screens, I suddenly notice, placed at strategic positions around the court.

I can barely look. But I have to. My Freddie is going into the garage. Then he runs out again towards the car, with the garage man following him. There's a shot of Knuckles at the wheel revving up. Freddie yelling at him to stop. Flick's screams, with the same plea. 'STOP!'

Freddie seizing the wheel. 'We've got to avoid him!' The sound of a scream and an ominous thud. The video picture goes all over the place. And then it stops.

A stunned silence settles over the court. Then Flick is asked to continue with her evidence.

'I've been keeping the recording safe in my bedroom all these years, just in case we ever needed it. I did tell Freddie when he came back and I saw him at the police station, but he said I couldn't tell the police . . . he was scared that they'd send me to prison and take Mattie away. But then I felt I had to.'

'For the benefit of the jury,' says the barrister, 'I can confirm that the police are satisfied that the video is genuine.'

Flick turns to the judge. 'I didn't mean it to happen. I promise. Honestly. You've got to believe me. You do, don't you?'

Her eyes glitter. 'I'm not having my daughter growing up and thinking her dad is a deliberate killer. Cos he isn't.'

This young girl has courage, I realize. Then she faces the jury. 'He's a good man. He must be, or else he wouldn't have come back to hand himself in. He loves Mattie and he still loves me. He doesn't deserve to go down.'

62

My heart is in my mouth as my boy returns to the dock. Steve takes my right hand. I feel Tom brushing my left. I don't move away. My husband, for he is still that, needs reassurance. We both do. We may not care for each other like we used to, but there is one bond that will connect us. Our son. And nothing can take that away. Not even murder.

The jury gives its verdict. I listen, stunned.

Then the judge delivers her sentencing.

My mind is in such a frenzy that I can only take in bits.

Evil . . .

Manipulative . . .

Innocent victim . . .

Web of lies . . .

I am back in the dock. Listening to the judge delivering his verdict all those years ago. Emily . . . Emily . . . And I sense Tom thinking that the same words applied to him and Hugo over Chapman's death.

'Paul Harris,' booms the judge, breaking into my thoughts, 'I hereby sentence you to eight years, added to the sentence you are already serving.'

'Freddie Wilkins, I sentence you to five years in prison.'

I let out a cry. I know it could be worse. But five years? Little Mattie has lost her father almost as soon as she has found him.

How I fear for my son in prison. His life will never be the same again. But he deserves it. I know that now. The real victims are the Moheim family.

Next it will be my turn.

Now Freddie has been sentenced, I too must brave the consequences.

The choice to self-destruct no longer lies in my hands.

It will be with a judge.

No jury, because I'm going to tell the truth.

I am guilty.

63

HMP Statton

Things have changed since I was last in prison. This particular one is more modern. There's a lounge with magazines and newspapers, for a start.

That's where I discovered I was front page news.

'Controlling Mother Persuaded Teenage Son to Run Away with Her After Fatal Hit-and-Run', screamed one headline.

'Judge Criticizes Mother for Taking Law into Her Own Hands', declared another.

Then an article about how Knuckles's mother had disowned him. I did my best for my son, but sometimes a parent has to give up.

I have learned not to be judgemental, but I do wonder whether I would have reacted differently if Freddie had been Knuckles. There are different shades of guilty.

'How come you only got two years, that's what I want to know?' demanded one of the women in the lunch queue one day. Her eyes glared with hostility. 'I got five for fraud and no one got killed. It's not bleeding fair.'

She had a point. But it didn't seem like a good idea to say I had an excellent barrister who appeared to be sympathetic when I'd said that I wasn't thinking straight. I had just wanted to save my son.

'I think it's rubbish that your ex wasn't charged,' said another.

I don't agree. I was the one who'd persuaded Freddie to run away with me. Tom had wanted to hand him in. Apparently, he had not committed any criminal offence by failing to report our son to the police. The law acts in strange ways. I hold no hard feelings – what would be the point? – and, besides, our divorce is now going through. No doubt he will marry his Hilary and lead the quiet, untroubled life he has always wanted.

Fortunately, it was decided that Flick had not committed a crime by failing to report what happened and that it was 'not in the public interest to prosecute her in relation to the conspiracy to steal or allowing herself to be carried in the car Knuckles had taken'.

I count my blessings that my granddaughter is still with her mother. I knew all too well what it had felt like to lose mine so young.

Mattie and Flick visit me every month. At first, I was worried about exposing them to prison, but there are family days and even a play area. One day, when the weather is nice, we are allowed to go outside under strict supervision.

'Push me, Granny,' calls out Mattie from the swing.

I can almost pretend that I am an ordinary gran in an ordinary park. Instead of one behind bars.

If it wasn't for this little girl with her sunny smile and glossy black plaited hair, I could not cope. She gives me hope. When I am out – which could be a year, if I behave myself – I will be a better grandmother than I was a mother. I have learned my lesson. Meanwhile, I buckle down with my prison jobs – from digging the garden to cleaning out the loos.

I won't go into details. Trust me, you wouldn't like it.

There's also an education wing with art lessons once a week. 'Done this before, have you?' asks the teacher, a woman of about my age.

'Yes,' I say.

She doesn't press me. It's as if she knows I don't want to talk about the past. But she has hung some of my paintings on the long white walls that line the corridors as I walk from education to my wing, keeping my head down to avoid trouble.

I only hope that Freddie does the same. His letters say he is OK. Who knows what is really happening? I can only hope and pray for the best for my precious son.

'How was Freddie when you saw him?' I asked Flick quietly last time she was here.

She and Mattie visit him every other week. It's not that easy because his prison is further away.

'All right,' she says slowly. 'But he's worried about you.'

'Please. Tell him not to be.'

'You know,' says Flick, speaking softly, so Mattie doesn't hear, 'I'm really sorry about the trouble I caused.'

'You got caught up in something that spiralled out of control,' I said quietly. 'You were also very young.'

I almost felt like telling her about what happened to me, but didn't feel this was the time. Maybe in future years.

'But like I said in court,' she went on, 'if I hadn't wanted to impress both Knuckles and Freddie, it might not have happened.'

'You can't think like that,' I say, although I've spent some time thinking about this too. If I hadn't been desperate to make friends – any friends – at art college, I wouldn't have done the awful things I did. Adolescent insecurities can lead to wicked crimes.

'Knuckles wrote to me from prison,' she adds. 'Can you believe that? He asked if I'd write back to him.'

'What did you say?'

'I didn't answer. I don't want to think about him ever again.'

I want to say that I hope she's more mature now. Freddie too. But who am I to speak? It took me years to grow up and right the wrongs I'd done. I'm not even sure I've done that now.

'Did you know,' says Flick suddenly, 'that Tom does charity work for teenagers who've been abused?'

'I did, actually.'

'He's a good person, isn't he?'

That depends on how you look at him, I almost reply. Then again, there's good and bad in all of us.

And then one day, I receive a visitor request.

It is from Mrs Moheim.

64

How can I not see her? This is the woman who we have damaged beyond repair. An innocent wife, now a widow. A mother.

'You could turn down her request,' says Derek, who is still advising me.

But it wouldn't feel right. I know I have to do this.

I spot her as soon as I go in. She has presence and grace. I can tell that from the way she is sitting there at the table, in that upright position, holding my gaze. But most of all, she is polite.

'Thank you for seeing me,' she says in the crowded visitors' room.

I remember her in court, hearing her moan out loud as they'd read out the details of her husband's death.

Then she looks me straight in the eye. 'How are they treating you?'

I hadn't expected this question. 'It's not too bad,' I say. 'I probably deserve far worse.'

Her face neither agrees nor disagrees.

There is a silence as we look at each other across the table.

'I am so sorry,' I say.

'Why? You were not in that car that killed my son.'

'Your son?' I say. She seems so young. I had thought she was the poor man's wife.

She ignores my question, carrying on as if I have not spoken. 'My daughter-in-law is too distressed to see you. But I wanted to look into your eyes and speak as one mother to another.'

I am lost for words, but I make myself talk. I owe her that.

'All I could think of was how to protect my boy,' I say in a cracked voice.

She shakes her head gently from one side to the other. 'It is what a mother does. I might have done the same.'

'Do you mean that?'

Her gaze holds mine unflinchingly. 'Yes. It's why I wanted to see you. I read those headlines. They were cruel.'

'But I deserved them. Your son died.'

She smooths down her purple sari in a slow, deliberate fashion, as if giving herself time to think. 'I am the kind of person who tries to see all sides. Your son was influenced by that other boy. I have to confess that I am struggling to forgive both of them. But you, you are different. No one else can understand the bond between mother and child apart from another mother.'

The lump in my throat is so big I can barely swallow my saliva. 'Your daughter-in-law and your grandchildren,' I gulp. 'How are they?'

She looks at me with sad eyes. 'How do you think?'

It was a stupid question but I had to ask it. 'Are you managing?' I add.

'We all live together, with my parents and my husband's parents. In my family, we look after each other.' Her voice takes on a hint of disdain. 'We do not send our old people away for strangers to look after them.'

I think of Gladys, who, according to Steve, is doing well. Is he saying that to comfort me?

Then she stands up. 'Goodbye, Mrs Wilkins. I wish you well.'

And she is gone. I know, without her having to say, that she does not intend to return. She has said her piece. And more importantly, perhaps, made her peace too.

If only I could do the same.

65

One of the things about being headline news, even for a short time, is that you get letters from people you don't know. Complete strangers who have read about you in the press, and feel the urge to express their views.

YoU BItCH, says one in uneven capital letters. *YoU MIGHt AS WELL oF KILLED tHAt MAN YoUR-SELF. YoU SHOULD hAVE GIVeN YoUR SoN UP At WUNCE.*

Another, in shaky handwriting, offers to take me out to dinner when I am released. *I like your picture.*

There is one from a woman who says my story has made her wonder what she would do in my position. I get the feeling she might actually be in it right now, in which case I hope she doesn't get traced. Then I catch myself. Perhaps she should be found.

There's a letter from a PhD student who is doing some research into the effect on the parents of murderers. The tone makes Freddie out to be on a par with Jack the Ripper. 'My son is not a killer,' I say out loud in my cell, as I tear the typed letter into shreds.

But the end result had been the same, I remind myself. Death.

There is an envelope with a French postmark. The letter inside is folded so that I can see the signature at the end before I take it out.

Dearest Sarah,

I read about you in the paper. I could hardly believe it! What a terrible thing for you to have gone through. But I'd have done the same for my girls.

Still, at least I know where you are so I can get in touch with you again. I should have tried much harder to find you after Tom said you'd left him, but Alex persuaded me not to, saying I needed to make a clean break with my past. I think he was worried that you might all persuade me to go back to Hugo.

I know what you're thinking. That's not the Olivia you knew. You're right. Turned out that Alex was a bit of a control freak. It's hard to really know what someone is like until you live with them, isn't it?

He wasn't that great with the girls, either. He didn't understand teenagers. But I wanted it to work. I felt too ashamed to say I'd made another mistake with a man. But finally I worked up the courage to leave him. By then, the girls were at uni and so I took myself off to Europe on an adult gap year with only a backpack.

I paused for a moment, trying to imagine my glamorous friend with walking shoes and a cagoule, instead of a fully coordinated wardrobe and a make-up bag bursting with 'essentials'. It made me smile.

Again, I know what you're thinking! That's not Olivia. But it was, actually. I'd found the real me. I'd never been without a man before, yet it was strangely liberating. That year of doing what I wanted and going where I felt like was heaven. I put a few pictures on Facebook, hoping you might see me. I even sent you a message.

I felt a pang of regret. Olivia wasn't to know that I hadn't touched social media when we ran away to Cornwall, for fear of being traced.

But then an old friend got in touch. Remember how we talked about our first loves one night in a wine bar?

I could almost hear Olivia's girlish giggle.

I told you about that handsome young French boyfriend I'd once had — the son of family friends. And how I'd checked him out online and found he was fat and bald with two marriages behind him.

Why do I know what's coming?

Well, he sent me a message and asked if I felt like visiting him in his chateau in the Dordogne. So I thought, why not? And here I am all these years later! In fact, we got married last year. You'd love Dominic. He's funny and overweight and he doesn't care. He loves the girls and they love him and all his six children from those previous marriages. In fact, he's still in touch with his wives and we have these fabulous family barbecues. You'll have to come and visit us when you're out.

I'd been so hurt by Olivia. But I can also understand.

I've never had a friend like you, before. And I never will again. You and I are bound together, Sarah. We each knew what it was like during those long years that we were married to the wrong men, hanging on for the sake of our children. Please

*come and see us. Meanwhile, I hope you are all right in that
awful place.*

> *Sending oodles of love,*
> *Olivia xxxxx*

That's Olivia to a tee. A born survivor. But she's right.
We had been bound together through those years of
bringing up our children. Friendship like ours endures for
ever. I want to see her again. And maybe I will.

And then, a week or so later, there is another letter,
beautifully written in round swirly flourishes, from a
woman called Marigold.

I read it on my narrow bed at night.

The opening line gets straight to the point:

You may not remember me.

*I recognized the pendant you were wearing in one of the photo-
graphs. She made a similar one for me too out of shells and stained
glass. Such a distinctive style!*

What?

*Your mother was my best friend. She and I met at art school – your
dad was in the same year. Afterwards, we formed this group – with
some other friends – to make our own jewellery and sell paintings.*

*You were the first baby to be born on the commune! I'll never
forget it. We were all around you when you were born, chanting and
singing and clapping. Your mum made me your godmother. We
weren't the churchy type, but I took my duties very seriously. I
showed you how to plant courgette seeds when you were quite small.*

Was that why I'd had that feeling of familiarity when I'd taken over Gladys's garden? Her words bring back a vague memory of a woman with golden hair from my childhood. But it's no more than that.

> *I want you to know that your mother loved you very much. But she was young, and none of us were as responsible as we should have been. I encouraged her to go out on a date that night she died. She wanted to stay with you but I said she needed some adult time to herself for a change. If I hadn't, she might not have died in that terrible car crash. I am so sorry. It was all such a horrendous shock. I'll never forget your little bewildered face when I tried to explain that Mummy wasn't coming back. I begged Social Services to let me bring you up.*

My mother's friend had wanted me? My eyes filled with tears.

> *But they didn't think I was good enough. So they arranged for you to go to your aunt instead. I tried to keep in touch with you but she wouldn't answer my letters. I've often thought of you, dear Sarah.*

I swallowed the huge lump in my throat. Marigold sounded so lovely! If only she'd been allowed to have me instead of my aunt and uncle, my life might have been very different.

> *I don't know whether the prison will let you have these, but I'm enclosing a couple of photographs. The bigger one was taken when we all went on a trip to the Scilly Islands. That was such an adventure! We were invited to exhibit some of our paintings there – all expenses paid.*

Another piece of the jigsaw was now slotting into place.

In fact, I still have a painting of the island of Tresco that your mother gave me. I will let you have it when you are released.

The prison officers had permitted the photographs to have gone through because they are inside the envelope. I take them out, one at a time. The first is of a couple. Instinctively I know they are my parents. Mum's very blonde and is wearing a long cream cheesecloth dress. Dad has my jet-black hair and looks like a young Elvis Presley with a denim jacket. They are clearly, from the way they look at each other, madly in love. This is the first time I can see what my dad actually looked like; his departure after I was born had always left a gaping hole in my heart.

The other picture is smaller. It's of a child who is, at a guess, a little older than Mattie. I know that because I remember my mother taking it. 'Smile,' she told me. 'Show me your beautiful smile.'

On the back, in sloping writing, is a note in pencil.

My lovely little girl. How lucky I am!

And that's when I cry. Because Marigold's letter is proof that once upon a time, I was loved. Really loved.

66

Marigold's letter changed everything.

It gave me roots. It confirmed various memories that, until now, had hung like spiders' webs at the back of my mind. It allowed me to begin to forgive myself. What chance had I stood, orphaned at such an age? No one to tell me I was wanted. Of course, there are others who have had far worse starts in life and have not made the terrible mistakes that I did. Nothing can ever bring back Emily.

Yet, for some inexplicable reason, I feel a certain peace beginning to settle over me.

I ask the arts teacher in prison if she can photocopy the photographs so I can send them to Freddie. He and I write regularly, even though the prison post can take up to three weeks or more due to security checks. His next reply carries his usual concerns about me as well as his astonishment about the letter.

It's important for Mattie too, he writes. *I want her to know about her family history.*

Freddie's letter also says something else: *Steve has written to me. He says you won't see him. Please think again, Mum.*

I can't. I am too ashamed. I'd betrayed a good, kind man. I'd been as good as unfaithful to him. Hiding my past was as bad as cheating. Maybe worse, in my case.

Then my eye falls on Freddie's next line.

He says he has something important to tell you.

So the next time a request comes through for a Steve Leather to visit, I accept, although not without apprehension.

It's been four months since I saw him last. Yet I think of him every day. He could have left me as soon as I'd told him what Freddie and I had done. But he hadn't. He'd asked his brother to defend me. He'd held my hand during the court case.

He says he has something important to tell you.

When I go into the visitors' room, I see those cowboy boots below one of the small metal-framed tables. His kind eyes are still the same, although a little tired. He also seems to have lost a bit of weight, judging from his gaunt cheekbones. Is it possible he's been worrying about me? I wonder what I look like to him. My fringe needs trimming. My prison uniform of navy blue baggy tracksuit and top doesn't do me any favours. And I'm aware I smell a bit. The showers have been out of action for a while and I am still waiting for my delivery of deodorant. Still, at least there isn't the same level of violence in this prison as there'd been in the one when I was younger.

'Thank you for seeing me,' he says.

The atmosphere between us is horribly stiff. Formal. Yet what did I expect?

'Is Jasper all right?' I blurt out.

'Absolutely fine.'

My heart lightens in relief.

'He misses you, of course, but he's cheered up Gladys no end. I take him with me to see her. She sends her love too.'

'Really?'

'Yes, really.'

'Freddie said you had something important to say.'

He shifts from side to side. I can tell something isn't right.

'Please,' I say. 'Just tell me.'

'I've been keeping the cottage clean for you in your absence,' he says. 'Gladys asked me to. She doesn't want to let it out to any other tenants while you're in here, in case you want to go back.'

'How can I return to a place where everyone will talk about me?' I ask.

'You'd be surprised how quickly people forget. She says she can't wait to have you back again.'

'Does she forgive me?'

'I haven't asked her that. But she talks about you all the time, fretting about how you're doing.'

'Please give her my love back and tell her that I'm all right.'

'She wanted to visit but she's not very mobile at all now.'

This doesn't sound good. 'I'll write to her.'

'She'd like that.'

There's another silence. I am too scared to break it. Then Steve speaks.

'The thing is . . . that when I did some cleaning in your old room, I found something.'

My heart quickens. Drugs that Freddie might have hidden? Please, no. Surely I'd have found them when I tidied up. Besides, he'd always sworn he was clean.

Steve holds out my old art notebook that I'd been unable to leave behind when we left London. It was full of my sketches.

'These are amazing, Sarah. I didn't know you did life drawing.'

I feel the colour rising in my cheeks as I glance at a self-portrait, sketched from my reflection in a mirror. 'It was part of my old life. It feels silly now, but I was trying to decide whether Freddie and I should leave Tom or not. Drawing someone naked lays them bare. It can help you get to the bones of a person. I was just attempting to get to mine. But then I discovered I wasn't interested in life drawing any more when we came down to Cornwall.'

'Why not?'

I struggle to explain. 'I didn't like the person I'd become. I'd broken the law yet again. It was a relief to turn to pottery instead.'

He nods. 'I get that. I had a change of life too.'

'You did?'

'I was a lawyer.' He sounds uneasy. Whenever I'd asked Steve about his past, he'd said something vague about doing a boring office job and that he'd left the 'proper career' to his brother.

'I know we said we wouldn't discuss our parts, but I wish you could have shared this with me.'

He looks at me with such love and shame and regret that I want to cry. 'I feel the same about you not sharing with me, despite what we promised. But the truth is that I was embarrassed about quitting. Derek made a go out of it and, though I'm proud of him, I regret messing it up.'

'Messing it up?' I repeat.

Steve looks at me steadily. 'It's why I wanted to see you. To share my secret with you just as you shared yours.'

'Go on,' I say.

He sighs. 'I was representing a woman who had been accused of neglecting her toddler. The neighbour claimed that she heard constant shouting and yelling next door. The thing is that there wasn't any hard evidence. This neighbour was known as a busybody. The people on the other side said they didn't hear anything. Then . . .'

He stops in his tracks.

'Go on,' I say.

'Then the child "fell" into a hot bath and got third-degree burns. The mother said she always put in cold to begin with but had "forgotten" on that occasion. She was so distraught. I believed her. So did the jury. She was acquitted and allowed to keep her child.'

I sense something awful is coming.

'A year later,' he says slowly, 'she was in court again. This time for manslaughter.'

'What happened?' I whisper.

'She hit her son on the head with a saucepan for no apparent reason. Said she'd just snapped, but she was high on drugs at the time.'

'That's terrible.' I take in Steve's haunted face. 'But it wasn't your fault.'

'Yes. It was. I'd been so certain that she was innocent. I wouldn't have taken on her case if I hadn't thought so. I was sure my client was a victim of discrimination.'

'But you weren't the jury. It wasn't up to you to decide if she was a fit parent or not. And even if you hadn't taken her on, another lawyer would have done.'

'I know. That's what Derek said. But I couldn't cope with the responsibility any more. I couldn't handle the fact that a child had died. It also made me question my ability to judge other people's characters.'

I go silent.

'After that, I gave up and did odd jobs. I began to drink too much. My wife left me. I wasn't the man she'd thought, apparently. If it hadn't been for Derek, helping me to come back to Cornwall, pull myself together and give up the booze, I don't know what I would have done.'

So that's what he meant when he'd said the marriage ending was 'his fault'.

'I'm sorry.'

'You and he are the only ones who know,' he says, 'apart from the rest of the village.' He makes a wry grimace. 'But they're good enough not to talk about it. And if you don't mind, I'd rather you did the same when you get back.'

'*If* I come back,' I say.

'Please. Don't give up on me. But most of all, don't give up on yourself. We'll be waiting for you, Jasper and I. Just like your beautiful little granddaughter. Mattie needs you, Sarah. We all do.'

But I am still troubled. 'You said just now that your terrible experience made you question your ability to judge other people's characters.'

He nods.

'I have to ask you, Steve. Does that include mine?'

He hesitates. It's only a few seconds, but it's enough. 'I did have some doubts when it all came out about Freddie. But they went away almost immediately. What you did was different. You loved your child.'

Maybe too much.

I'm so choked I can't speak.

'Everything will be all right in the end,' he says. 'By the way, you've had a postcard from someone called Zac.'

I'd asked Steve to check my mail. I wanted him to know I had nothing to hide any more.

'Zac was an old art school friend,' I said.

'He'd like you to call him. Do you want to write down the number?'

Making calls from prison isn't private. There's a half-open booth on one of the corridors of each wing. And there's always a queue. Everyone listens in.

I'm conscious of this as I ring.

'How did you get my address?' I asked.

His voice still had that smoker's raspiness. 'I tracked you down from the details in the paper. I've been trying to get in touch for years.'

'I know. Please don't. We're history.'

'But we're not. You see . . . there's something I never told you. It's about Emily.'

My chest tightens. 'What?'

'That night . . . it wasn't all your fault. Emily kept pestering me for pills. I was high myself. So I gave her a couple.'

'Was that before or after she found my bag?'

'Before.'

'But it was my batch that was contaminated.'

'Maybe it was my supply. Or maybe we had them from the same source. I had a reaction myself but not as bad as hers.'

'You didn't tell anyone?'

'I'm sorry, Sarah. I was scared. But the thing is . . . I'm just as much to blame as you.'

67

Two Years Later

'Granny, show me how to build a sandcastle again! Mine keeps falling down.'

I'd do anything when my granddaughter smiles at me like that, with her gappy grin and long, glossy black plaits that she flicks over her shoulder as she speaks. I remember doing that myself when I first met Tom.

We are sitting on the beach in Shell Cove. Mattie, me, Steve, Tom, Hilary and Flick. We're having a picnic with hummus, pitta bread and homemade nut roast. No alcohol. None of us drink it, for our own different reasons.

To an outsider we might look like an ordinary family. The funny thing is that I don't feel uncomfortable with Hilary here. I should do. But my second time in prison has made me more accepting of other people. Besides, she seems like quite a nice woman, and I can tell she's much better for Tom than I ever was.

I've been out for a year now. At first, I was scared about coming back to the village. But Gladys decided to sell her cottage and asked if I was interested in buying, so I used the rest of my money from the sale of the London house that I'd been too nervous to touch. It's good to put down roots. I feel at home here, and I like to think of it as a bolt hole for my granddaughter in years to come. I've even made a pottery sign by the front door in my trademark marine blue with the name GLADYS'S COTTAGE painted on it.

'I'll always think of it like that,' I tell Gladys. 'It's thanks to you that I found the first place where I've really felt at home.'

She'd given me a big lavender-soap-smelling hug. 'I can't think of anyone else who I'd want to live there,' she whispered. 'And always remember something: no one is perfect. We just try our best.'

A few people, it is true, have given me a wide berth. And some had mixed feelings. 'I was cross with you when I first found out what your boy had done,' said Blockie. 'I helped you because I thought your husband had hurt you. But then the wife pointed out that I'd willingly break all the rules in the book if it would bring back our boy.'

'I'm sorry,' I whispered, grasping the hand he held out to me.

Steve stayed over at my place for the first week and then suggested I might like some time on my own. 'Actually,' I said, 'would you mind hanging on a bit longer?'

'I thought you'd never ask!'

He hasn't left.

Meanwhile, I visit Freddie every week. He's doing an OU course. I'd told him about Mrs Moheim's visit. He wrote the family a letter of apology. There was no reply. Despite what my visitor had said about trying to see all sides, there are some crimes for which there can be no forgiveness.

On one occasion, I found myself queuing up to visit Freddie at the same time as my by-then ex-husband. 'I didn't know you were coming,' I said, embarrassed.

'It's my first time,' Tom replied. 'I'm pretty nervous, to

be honest.' He twisted his fingers awkwardly. 'But he's our son. I have to.'

'What does Hilary think?' I couldn't help asking.

'She understands how important Freddie is to me. She says that maybe I needed his absence and then the shock of the trial to realize that.'

He flushed as he spoke.

'It sounds like you've found the right woman.'

'Yes,' he said. 'I have, even though it's come at a considerable cost to both of us.'

That was so like Tom! Always talking in figures and quantities.

'I'm glad you've found some happiness too,' he went on.

'Thank you.'

'So, do you plan to get married now the divorce is through?'

'No. Neither of us feel we need it. We're strong enough as we are. What about you?'

'Next month, actually. Both Hilary and I want to formalize our relationship.'

I wait for a twinge but it doesn't come.

'I heard from Olivia,' I said. 'You probably know that she's married to a Frenchman now.'

'Actually, I didn't.'

'Didn't Hugo mention it?'

Tom tightened his mouth in the way he used to do when he didn't like something or someone. 'I don't see him any more.'

'Why not?'

'I had a falling-out with him.'

'Why?'

Tom shifted from side to side. He was clearly uneasy. 'After you left, I had a lot of time to think about what had happened to Chapman. I told Hilary about it. She suggested I went to see Hugo and tell him that I never wanted to see him again.'

'And you did?'

'Yes. I don't know why I didn't before. Perhaps it was the old scared child inside.'

'You seem to be more in touch with your feelings now, I have to say.'

'That is Hilary's influence.'

Of course, I'm pleased, but at the same time I can't help recalling that when he'd been married to me, he'd considered emotion to be a 'weak indulgence'.

'I also visited Chapman's widow. But she told me to leave.'

I sucked in my breath. 'That must have been hard.'

'It was. But also understandable.'

'I'm proud of you for doing that.'

'Thank you. So was Hilary.'

It was time for me to step aside. He and Hilary were a 'we' just as Steve and I were. Yet Tom and I would always be bound by our son and granddaughter.

Of course, I see Mattie as much as I can. She and Flick are still living with Flick's parents. They seem decent people. I cannot help wondering what they think of me. I also feel a little jealous that my granddaughter knows them better than she knows me.

'My daughter is lucky to have six grandparents,' says Flick as we walk in the park near their home.

She's working for some clever tech firm now. It's one

of those modern jobs that I couldn't even describe, let alone understand. I genuinely like Flick. And if it hadn't been for her courage, my son might have got life.

'It's important for Mattie to know her roots,' she adds.

I feel the same. It's why Marigold and I see each other regularly.

I've told her about Emily's death now, and my part in it, as well as Zac's. 'It doesn't take away my guilt,' I say, 'but it helps to know I wasn't entirely responsible.'

'I get that,' she said, squeezing my hand. 'I felt terrible about your mother too.'

One day, Tom rings out of the blue. 'We're having an open evening for our Wednesday group,' he says. 'It's to show people what we do. Hilary is coming along. She suggested you might like to be there as well.'

It was an eye-opener in more ways than one. Many of the boys had written about their experiences of abuse as children and these stories were on the wall. But what really brought a lump to my throat was the number of them who came up to me and Hilary, telling us how much Tom had helped them.

'He made me realize how important it was to stand up and not to blame ourselves,' one said.

'Incredible isn't it?' said Hilary.

This woman, with the sensible shoes and short, no-nonsense haircut, is never going to be my best friend. She had an affair with my husband, after all. But it's good to know that she is a stable figure in his life – as well as in my son's and granddaughter's.

Mattie is our fresh start. She is the child who has brought us all together. We have to help her adjust to gaining a father and then losing him to prison. And we need to give them space when he is released so they have a chance to be a family.

Our granddaughter has also brought out a relaxed side to Tom. My ex-husband is, I think now, as he gets down on all fours and plays 'animals' with her, better at being a granddad than he ever was at being a father.

Steve has proved to be a brilliant step-grandfather of sorts. He makes up funny poems for Mattie. Her favourite is about a frog who lives in a bog.

Isn't life strange, the way it turns out?

'Freddie and I are going to live together when he comes out,' confides Flick, as we go for a walk along the beach. Mattie is running alongside us, scouring the sand for shells.

'It might work,' she adds, 'and it might not. But we won't know till we try, will we?'

Then Flick gives me a warm hug. 'Don't worry. Even if Freddie and I don't stick together, I'd never stop you seeing Mattie. You're her flesh and blood. Nothing can take that away. And besides, she's artistic. Like you. Can't wait to get her hands on that wheel of yours.'

My pottery helps to keep me sane. Round and round goes the clay. Round and round goes my mind. Coil pots with each stage of my life, stacked one on top of the other.

Daphne from the WI has suggested I give a talk about being in prison. I'll say this for her: she doesn't give up.

'I don't think it would go down well,' I said.

'You might be surprised,' she answered. 'There we all go, but for the grace of God and all that. I'll schedule you for next month, shall I?'

I get the feeling that there's more to Daphne than meets the eye. Like all of us.

'Granny,' calls out Mattie, cutting into my thoughts. 'Look at this one! It's purple on the inside.'

'It's called a mussel,' I explain.

'I'll show Daddy when we visit. He'll like that, won't he?'

'Yes,' I say, bending down and scooping her up in my arms before gently putting her down. I do this at every opportunity. I have so much time to make up for. Then my lovely little granddaughter – who seems to do a growth spurt every time I see her – puts her left hand in mine and the right in her mother's.

The three of us walk back up the beach towards the others and whatever lies ahead. 'I love it when you smile like that, Granny,' says Mattie.

I didn't even know I was. Perhaps that's because my smile is no longer an expression that I plaster onto my face to hide my fears. Instead, it's a natural reaction to being truly happy. No more pretence now. No more lies.

Of course, I will never forget the Moheim family. And nor, I know, will Freddie. I wonder, as I often do, what my granddaughter will think of us when she knows the truth. Will she be ashamed or – even worse – not want anything to do with us? Or will she forgive our crimes, just as I have learned to forgive my mother for my strange childhood and my father for leaving.

As for my own regrets, the jury is still out on that one.

Would I do it all again? Would I try to save my boy from the consequences of his actions?

Yes.

No.

Maybe.

I always used to think that a mother's job was to protect her child.

But here's the real truth. At least, the way I see it.

When it comes to a mother's love – that boundless, almost undefinable, primal, umbilical-cord-wrenching bond that cannot be broken – there are no rules.

Yet there's something else I've learned too. At the end of the day, we are all responsible for our own actions. A child has to make – and learn from – his or her mistakes in order to be a responsible adult. That's why we can't protect our children for ever. A parent's job is to let them go while being there as a steady hand if they need us.

Easier said than done.

'Can I steal your grandmother away now?' asks Steve. He's got a surfboard under each arm.

Mattie frowns. 'Stealing is bad.'

'I didn't mean it like that,' Steve says quickly. 'I meant, I just want to borrow her.'

'Only if you give her back,' says my granddaughter solemnly.

'Of course I will. We want to show you something. Don't we, Sarah?'

'Yes,' I say, bending down to give Mattie a kiss. 'We've been practising. Well, I have.'

I run down to the water. *You can do this*, I tell myself.

The waves are perfect. Not scarily high. But big enough to catch.

Like this one. It's rolling towards me. Gathering speed. For a minute, all my old fears come back, tightening my throat.

It's almost here now. I get ready with my board just as Steve has taught me. I wait for the wave. It still scares me, but I know what to do. Most important of all, I have the confidence.

'Go, Granny, go!'

Here it comes!

And I fly.

Acknowledgements

Where do I start?

My wonderful agent Kate Hordern from KHLA, who introduced me to Penguin and whose kind, thoughtful advice has been such a rock.

My Viking Penguin editor, the extraordinarily talented Katy Loftus, who has a magical eye for instantly understanding my plot and characters while helping me bring them to life.

Her brilliant assistant Vikki, who suggested that Olivia should come out from the wings and take a more central role. Thank you! I had such fun with Sarah's new best friend.

The efficient, kind, always-on-the-ball Jane Gentle – the sort of publicist that every author dreams of.

The amazingly tech-savvy Ellie Hudson, who has painstakingly helped me with social media.

The ever-sunny Olivia Mead, who is so good at events whether virtual or physical.

Sam Fanaken and the entire Sales team, who have always got amazing slots for my novels.

The astounding Foreign Rights team, who have sold my books to over thirty-two countries.

David Grogan for the beautiful cover design.

The DeadGood and the Pageturners teams at Penguin, who always support my novels online.

Natalie Wall who managed my book through production with such efficiency.

My eagle-eyed copyeditor, Trevor Horwood, who helps to remind me that Wednesday doesn't come after Thursday. Mistakes like this are easier to make than you might think. (Congrats to Trevor and Bev, by the way!)

Many thanks to my proofreaders, Sally Sargeant and Sarah Barlow.

My film and TV agent, Italia Gandolfo, who possesses amazing tenacity and a fantastic network of contacts.

Retired judge Richard Gibbs, who never seems to mind when I email a 'Could this happen?' court scenario.

The Law Society, for putting me in touch with solicitor Richard Atkinson from Tuckers Solicitors, and to Richard himself for generously giving legal guidance on court procedure and crimes. (Any mistakes are mine. I have also taken the liberty of using a certain amount of artistic licence.)

Thanks to Kim Macdonald for her help with naming one of the characters. The runner-up prize goes to her father-in-law, Robin.

The legendary Betty Schwartz, who gave me faith in the early days of my career.

Harry Anderson, the gifted potter from The Town Mill Pottery in Lyme Regis in Dorset, who talked to me about his work. Any mistakes are mine!

The Institute and Faculty of Actuaries Research (again, any mistakes are mine).

The Prime Writers, a group of wonderful published forty-plus writers, who have become my friends. Thank goodness for those Zoom meetings during the first lockdown.

The Freelance Media Group, Bev Davies and The University Women's Club.

My loyal readers, many of whom have also become friends.

All you fabulous bloggers who work so hard. I really am grateful.

Everyone who sells books. Where would we be without you?

My audiobook reader, Sian Brooke.

Best friends everywhere – always remembering mine.

Crystal Williams and Steve Leather, who kindly bid for their names to be used in aid of the Clic Sargent appeal.

And of course, my family, especially my husband and children.

Because at the end of the day, it's love that counts.

A Good Daughter

JANE CORRY

He just wanted a decent book to read ...

Not too much to ask, is it? It was in 1935 when Allen Lane, Managing Director of Bodley Head Publishers, stood on a platform at Exeter railway station looking for something good to read on his journey back to London. His choice was limited to popular magazines and poor-quality paperbacks – the same choice faced every day by the vast majority of readers, few of whom could afford hardbacks. Lane's disappointment and subsequent anger at the range of books generally available led him to found a company – and change the world.

'We believed in the existence in this country of a vast reading public for intelligent books at a low price, and staked everything on it'
Sir Allen Lane, 1902–1970, founder of Penguin Books

The quality paperback had arrived – and not just in bookshops. Lane was adamant that his Penguins should appear in chain stores and tobacconists, and should cost no more than a packet of cigarettes.

Reading habits (and cigarette prices) have changed since 1935, but Penguin still believes in publishing the best books for everybody to enjoy. We still believe that good design costs no more than bad design, and we still believe that quality books published passionately and responsibly make the world a better place.

So wherever you see the little bird – whether it's on a piece of prize-winning literary fiction or a celebrity autobiography, political tour de force or historical masterpiece, a serial-killer thriller, reference book, world classic or a piece of pure escapism – you can bet that it represents the very best that the genre has to offer.

Whatever you like to read – trust Penguin.

read more
www.penguin.co.uk